11/10

Also by Michelle Huneven

Jamesland

Round Rock

Blame

Blame

MICHELLE HUNEVEN

Sarah Crichton Books

Farrar, Straus and Giroux

New York

Sarah Crichton Books
Farrar, Straus and Giroux
18 West 18th Street, New York 10011

Library of Congress Cataloging-in-Publication Data
Huneven, Michelle, 1953–
    Blame / by Michelle Huneven. — 1st ed.
        p.   cm.
    ISBN: 978-0-374-11430-5 (alk. paper)
    1. Drunk driving—Fiction.   2. Traffic accidents—Fiction.   3. Psychological
fiction.   I. Title.

PS3558.U4662B55 2009
813'.54—dc22

                                                              2008054299

Designed by Jonathan D. Lippincott

www.fsgbooks.com

1   3   5   7   9   10   8   6   4   2

For Jim Potter

PART ONE

July 1980

The first thing Millicent Hawthorne did after scheduling her surgery was to enroll her daughter Joey in a summer typing class at the local high school. Joey was twelve and had never set foot in a public school, but she'd refused to go to camp that year, and Millicent wanted her occupied.

First-level typing was at the end of a long corridor in a double-sized classroom where hulking blue typewriters with blank keys sat on each desk. A wall of windows overlooked a courtyard of blooming roses.

Although she would not make a single friend among them, Joey was intrigued by her fellow typists, especially the girls with their defiantly short skirts, long, straight hair, and expert makeup. How could they be so easy with one another? They tried to draw Joey into their huddles at the break, then left her alone, for which she was grateful.

Joey was instantly good at typing, surprising herself. She assumed she'd be bored by its lack of content. Typing, she found, was like playing the piano, minus the tones. A-S-D-F-J-K-L-Sem caught in her head like an arcane chant, a secret alphabet. Class got out at eleven fifty-five, and Marlene, the Hawthornes' housekeeper, would be waiting out front in her red VW station wagon. Together, they drove back to the house, where Marlene made crustless ham and butter sandwiches, one of the few things Joey would eat at that time.

The first week Joey was in typing class, her mother had a radical mastectomy. The doctors, claiming success, sent her home. When Joey went in to say hello, Millicent, an athletic six foot one, now seemed like a small, folded-up packet of herself, with eyes so sunken, Joey saw the contours of her skull. Millicent reached out a hand, and Joey, taking it, experienced the curious sensation of having her legs turn into water. The home nurse said she'd fainted, but Joey insisted that she never lost consciousness.

It soon became obvious that something more than pain was impeding Millicent's recovery. She went back into the hospital, and the doctors found a system-wide fungus and a new, invasive form of cancer in her spine.

Because Joey had collapsed after her mother's first surgery, she was not allowed to visit, at least not until Millicent had recovered somewhat. Joey had no doubt this would come to pass, because nobody told her otherwise and because one night her father asked her to help him pick out a gift for her mother's birthday four months away. They decided on an add-a-diamond necklace from the Gump's catalog, clearly a gift for someone with many birthdays to come.

During her fifth, penultimate week of typing, Joey walked out of the old brick high school to find not Marlene, but her tall, dazzling uncle Brice leaning against his Studebaker pickup.

Hi, beautiful, he said. Marlene was running an errand, he explained; Joey's father and grandmother were at the hospital. And I, he said, am at your service.

The family had drifted so rapidly into extremity that their long-held rules—no public schools, no discussing problems—had given way like spiderwebs. Thrilled as she was to have her renegade uncle fetch her from school like a common babysitter, Joey knew slippage when she saw it.

Brice was her mother's kid brother. He was twenty-eight and had already burned through his inheritance, more than a million dollars. Joey's father, in rare good humor on the subject, said that it was breathtaking and almost admirable how Brice, in an attempt to recoup the initial heart-stopping losses, had managed to obtain and lose trust money he wasn't even due to receive until he was thirty-five.

Brice was six foot four, with dark gold hair, overly tanned skin, and a nose he referred to as "the big old hook." Joey loved him thoroughly and irrationally and planned to marry him the moment she turned twenty-one and came into her own trust fund. (She'd heard there were states in the Deep South where uncle and niece might wed.) Joey dreamed of restoring Brice to the lifestyle and financial bracket where he rightfully belonged, although she also imagined dispatching her money with the same profligacy with which he'd already flown through his, if only for the sheer, exhilarating *blur* of it.

Clutching her flat typing manual against her chest, too smitten to speak, Joey climbed into the tobacco-scented cab of the rare Studebaker and Brice drove them to the Bellwood Hotel for lunch.

•

Joey's parents' best friends, Cal and Peggy Sharp, owned the Bellwood. Cal had inherited it from his father, and did what he could to keep it running in a town where the Sheraton, Hilton, and Doubletree had cornered the convention trade. Cal shut down two floors, rented residential suites to wealthy widows, booked offbeat conventions (rare books dealers, grandfather clock collectors), and housed two private clubs: the Downtown Club, where membership could be purchased, and the more exclusive, invitation only, Mojave Club.

Joey's father, Frank Hawthorne, was on the board of the Mojave Club, and the Hawthornes used the Bellwood as their second residence. Whenever Millicent called in the painters at home—she did that *a lot*—the Hawthornes moved en masse to the Bellwood's penthouse. And until their large, architecturally significant but deeply flawed glass-and-concrete foothill home had air-conditioning installed, the family sought refuge in those refrigerated rooms during heat waves. Frank and Millicent Hawthorne were both famous for their tempers; each time one or the other stormed out of the house, Joey and her two brothers knew where to find them.

The July day Brice drove Joey to the Bellwood, it was a hundred degrees out, dry and bright and as still as glass.

Brice was not a member of the Mojave Club. He never could've managed dues, even if he'd finagled an invitation. But with Joey trotting alongside, he headed straight into the Mojave dining room with its filigreed columns and mahogany wainscoting. The tables were padded and double clothed, the sterling polished, the water glasses heavy. Huffy, the Mojave's maître d', glided toward them on the diagonal in an attempt to steer Brice toward a middle table, but Brice sailed past to claim a coveted window booth.

Since returning from his four-year international spending spree last January, Brice had worked for Cal Sharp, who also owned the Lyster apartments on Avalon Street, where Brice was the resident manager and renovator. The Lyster had seen better days, and Brice's job was to reverse its course. Joey's father referred to the four-story faux château as "the ever-listing Lyster." Hello there, Brice, he'd greet his brother-in-law. How's life at the ever-listing Lyster?

The waiter brought Brice a beer in a V-shaped pilsner glass and Joey a Coke in a brandy snifter, her preferred glassware of the moment. She was just beginning to wonder what she and Brice would say to each other when she heard her name.

Joey, my girl. Cal Sharp stood over her, tall and important in his silvery suit and matching hair. His wide hand cradled the back of her head. His cologne was sharp, citric; and his other hand, resting on the tablecloth, was perfectly manicured, the nails pink and so smooth. You just missed March and Stan. They were here for breakfast, he said quietly, his grip tightening on her scalp. They'll sure be sorry they missed you.

March was Joey's age, but Stan, two years older, had been her great companion growing up, until he became a tennis star last year. At the Mojave Spring Fling he and Joey had ditched March and climbed up the fire escape to sit, swinging their legs off the side. There, Stan explained that if they were seen together so much at the club, people would think they were boyfriend and girlfriend. And while they would always be friends, he wanted a different kind of girl for a girlfriend, a pretty girl with long blond hair who was also an excellent tennis player.

You doing all right there, sweetheart? Cal murmured, leaning down. Everything okay?

His large male face so close to hers made it impossible to speak. Cal Sharp had never taken such notice of her before. And his eyes were growing red around their rims.

We're all praying for your mom, he said quietly. You know that, we're praying as hard as we can.

Oh. Her mom. That's right.

Most remarkably yet, Cal kissed her forehead. Then he kept his hand on the back of her head and talked to Brice about awnings for the Lyster's south-facing windows.

The waiter brought Brice a small club steak with french fries and Joey a crustless ham and butter sandwich. Joey hadn't been to the Bellwood since rejecting lettuce some days back, and seeing the thin green line dividing the pink meat and the white bread, she slid into what her mother called a fit. Joey never agreed with this term. Wasn't a fit some kind of muscle-flapping thrashing about? Whereas, when faced with the insurmountable, she simply froze for anywhere from a minute to an hour. There was no predicting it. Most episodes were brief, brought on by a food or something mean one of her brothers said. Her mother, who was often the only person to notice, was always enraged by what she felt was Joey's willfulness. But Joey really could do nothing other than wait for the so-called fit to pass, as she did now, with Cal Sharp's large hand cupping her head while he and Brice debated whether to buy striped or solid canvas. Cal, noting her untouched plate, tousled her hair. Forgive me, he said. I'll let you two eat.

Not hungry, baby? Brice said when they were alone. Want some steak?

Joey shook her head. Brice ate a couple of fries and glanced at his watch. I have to make a phone call. I'll be right back.

Alone, Joey pushed her sandwich aside and stole two of Brice's fries. The waiter removed the sandwich and, with a wink, set down a thick glass cup of pineapple sherbet, cold and perfect, tasting like snow.

Soon the waiter took Brice's steak away and returned it wrapped in foil in the shape of a swan. Joey took the swan, signed the check, and went looking for her uncle. He wasn't in any of the phone booths. She told the concierge, If Uncle Brice is looking for me, I'm in the ladies' snooker room.

The women in the Mojave Club used the ladies' book-lined snooker room for meetings. The snooker table was gone, replaced by big, comfortable chairs that pitched you back so far it was hard to get out of them. A large volume devoted to Michelangelo sculptures sat on the coffee table. Joey took this up, intending to continue her ongoing study of male anatomy.

Today, however, she paused at the Pietà, one of the few women in the whole book. Mary wore nunlike robes with beautiful folds and had Jesus' skinny dead body draped across her lap. People always referred to Joey's mother as "statuesque," but here was an actual statue, and it had nothing in common with Millicent Hawthorne. Mary seemed so delicate and calm, completely unlike Millicent, who always looked angry, although she always denied it.

Millicent had never fussed over Joey. She was an impatient mother who brushed Joey's fine hair roughly and tied her shoes and sashes with quick, harsh tugs. The two spent little time together; they never cuddled or confided in each other. Joey, in fact, made it a point to stay out of her mother's way so as not to annoy or inadvertently antagonize her. Yet despite the mutually cultivated wide, empty spaces between them, Joey was connected to her mother as if by a fine silver wire. If her father spoke angrily to Millicent, Joey burst into tears. If her brothers back-talked, Joey bristled in her mother's defense—she would not have been at all surprised to learn that she experienced her mother's feelings more keenly than her mother did. That day when Millicent came home from the hospital and Joey took her hand, Joey had inhaled both the dry, sickly-sweet must of sickness and her mother's terror, and it was more than she could bear.

Joey wandered again past the phone booths and over to the elevators. She pressed the button and considered going up to the roof to stick her feet in the pool, but when the elevator doors opened, out stepped Uncle Brice. Oh! There you are, he said jauntily. What shall we do now? How about a movie?

She wanted to go home, change out of her stupid school clothes. But going to the movies and sitting next to Brice in the dark was irresistible.

The Sound of Music was playing at the Big Oaks Revival House. Brice bought a tub of buttered popcorn, half a pound of Raisinets, and a box of ice-cream bonbons. During the previews he nosed the big old hook through Joey's hair until it rested against her ear. I'll be right back, he whispered, and stacked all the food on her lap.

Joey couldn't concentrate. She was embarrassed by the clumsy way that Julie Andrews ran, and by the fake way the nuns broke into song. She kept turning to see if Brice was coming back. There were only three other people in the theater, two men and an older woman who was eating noisily. Then cool moisture oozed from the box of ice-cream bonbons and some of it went on her skirt. Setting everything down on the sticky floor, Joey left for the ladies' room.

Nobody was in the lobby or at the candy counter. She ran upstairs to the lounge and sponged her skirt with a paper towel. She did not want to see the rest of the movie, but there was nothing to do in the lobby, so she returned to her seat and practiced typing on her knees— transcribing the movie as fast as she could.

•

The ticket takers and countermen were back at their stations, and still Brice had not come. She studied the movie posters in the lobby until people arrived for the second matinee, and she kept studying them as they stood in line and bought their snacks. When the lobby was empty again, she decided to call both hospitals in town to see if Brice was in an emergency room. Since she had no money with her and was too shy to ask for any, she decided to walk back across town to the Bellwood, where Huffy would let her use the phone, if he wasn't too angry about the steak-filled swan she'd left in the ladies' snooker room.

Joey set off down Green Street in the dusty, late afternoon heat. She'd gone about five blocks when the Studebaker pulled up alongside her. Patsy, Brice's girlfriend, smiled in the passenger seat. Hey there, she said.

The truck's door swung open. Patsy had long yellow-blond hair and long, tanned legs and a wide, happy smile that revealed all her perfect, straight teeth. She taught history at a local college, though Joey's father said she didn't look like any history professor he ever had.

Patsy kissed the side of Joey's head. Hi, kitten, she said. How was the movie? Ridiculous drivel? Yeah.

Show her what we got for her, said Brice, and Patsy handed Joey a tiny black velvet box.

Inside was a necklace—a small oval glass pendant on a thin gold chain, with matching oval earrings. All three ovals contained the same picture: the black silhouette of a palm tree and grass shack set against an orange sunset—exactly the South Sea paradise where, Joey imagined, Brice used to live.

Here, Patsy said. I'll fasten it. Her long nails grazed Joey's neck.

Look, Patsy said, and parted Joey's blouse at the neck so Brice could see the pendant. You're prettier every day, Patsy said. Isn't she, Brice?

Brice said, I've been in love with Joey since the day she was born.

Were they drunk? Both held bottles of beer between their knees.

Darn, Brice. Her ears *aren't* pierced. Well, that's easy enough. Patsy threw an arm around Joey's shoulder. We'll exchange these for the un-pierced kind.

Or I could get my ears pierced, Joey said. She'd asked to have them done this summer, but her mother said pierced ears were primitive and low-class.

Patsy squeezed her shoulder. They were driving east now, away from the Bellwood, school, home, everyplace Joey knew. Aren't we going to my house? she asked.

I have to stop in at work, said Brice.

He pulled up before the four-story white building, with its skinny turrets and pointy roof. Ah, said Joey, the ever-listing Lyster.

Brice and Patsy burst out laughing. We know whose daughter she is, Brice said.

•

You girls go on up, said Brice, I'll be there in a minute.

Brice's apartment on the fourth floor had high ceilings, dark polished floors, and almost no furniture, just a few old rugs and some large pillows covered in strange, coarsely woven fabrics.

He's so damn Zen, your uncle, Patsy said, and drew Joey into the kitchen, where there was a table and actual chairs. Sit, she said, Let's see what's to drink.

Joey still held the black velvet box. She opened it and looked at the earrings. Mother promised I could get my ears pierced this summer, she said.

Oh, baby. Patsy touched Joey's cheek. So sorry your mom's so sick.

Yeah, Joey said. And now I'll never get my ears pierced.

Oh, you will. You just walk into any jeweler's, they have a gun, and *bang!* it's done, said Patsy. I'd pierce them myself right now if Brice had a needle.

Maybe he does, said Joey. I bet he has a needle somewhere.

Patsy gave her a long, compassionate look. Well, let's just see.

In Brice's bedroom, Patsy rummaged in his dresser drawers, taking out several brown bottles whose labels she read intently. Is this what I think it is? she said, looking at a small gray packet. Eureka! she cried. A sewing kit!

•

Back in the kitchen, Patsy pulled an Olympia from the refrigerator. There's no Coke, she said, but here. She poured beer into a tumbler. This will help you relax.

Will it hurt a lot? Joey asked.

Just for a second, like getting a shot. Maybe a little worse. Patsy shook half a dozen triangular orange pills from one bottle onto the white enamel tabletop, then a whole rain of tiny yellow pills from the second bottle. Oh, aren't these so teeny and sweet? she said, and, putting her finger on a yellow pill, dragged it from the pile. Using a paring knife, she cut it into two crumblike pieces. Here, she said, giving Joey the smaller piece. This'll take the edge off any pain.

Patsy swept all the pills into her hand and dumped them into a side pocket of her purse, then took the bottles away and returned with rubbing alcohol, cotton, and a bar of soap. Just pretend it's a tetanus shot, she said.

I don't mind shots, Joey said.

Patsy wrapped two ice cubes in a dish towel for Joey to numb her ear. Turning on a gas burner, Patsy held a needle in its flame until the needle glowed red-orange. She swabbed first the needle, then Joey's ear with alcohol. My roommates and I did this in college, she said, and snuggled the bar of Ivory behind Joey's earlobe. Ready?

Pasty jabbed the needle through the lobe and into the soap. Joey heard a sound like rustling paper, followed by a sudden rushing in her head. Patsy pulled the soap away, and Joey's eyes flooded with tears. Her body temperature shot up. Her entire skin was suddenly stretched tight. And then came the pain. Her ear stung as if a bee with a thick stinger was stinging it without end.

Now come on, I gotta get this in, Patsy said. The earring post was thicker than the needle, a thicker stinger yet. Joey tried to pull away, she couldn't help herself, but Patsy held her by the ear. Just give me a minute here, said Patsy.

Ow ow OW, Joey said. Patsy wiggled the earring, her warm, sour breath coming in short, ragged bursts, her eyes wild and, to Joey, terrifying.

Stay still, Jesus Christ, she said sharply, yanking Joey by the ear.

Joey whimpered, and Patsy let go. Okay, okay, she said, try the ice cubes.

They looked at each other, both panting. Joey applied the ice. Cold water ran down her arm.

I'll be fast, Patsy said, and again, terrible stinging and wiggling until Patsy suddenly withdrew. One down, one to go, she said. Let's take a break.

They moved into the living room. Joey was suddenly, deliciously relaxed. She curled up on a cushion and drifted in a glow the same dull yellow as the half pill she'd swallowed. Patsy went to the kitchen and brought back two Olympias. Better shore up for side two, she said, handing Joey a full bottle, then settling down on a cushion beside her. Now you do something for me, okay? she said, stroking Joey's arm. Tell me about Brice's other girlfriends.

Joey tried to think. He used to go with Joan Vashon, she said.

That was before, Patsy said. I mean now.

I thought *you* were his girlfriend.

Oh, I am. Patsy laughed. Such as it goes. I was just wondering about my compatriots in the cause.

I don't know any of the others, Joey said.

But there *are* others.

You just said . . .

Oh, I don't know that for sure, said Patsy.

Well, I don't know any others, Joey said.

It could be he likes boys, said Patsy.

Oh, that Brice, Joey said, sounding on purpose like her father. He likes everybody!

Patsy's face froze; then she laughed loudly. That he does, she said. A true omnivore. Preys on everything equally. Okay, sweetness. Patsy tugged on her own ear. Ready for side two? She drained her beer and struggled to her feet. Oops! Gotta pee.

While Patsy was in the bathroom, Joey went to the kitchen table and dug into the side pocket of Patsy's purse until she found another tiny yellow pill. She glanced around for the knife to cut it in two, heard the toilet flush, then stuck the whole thing in her mouth and washed it down with beer.

This time, Patsy said, she'd push the post in right behind the needle, and the second earring did go through with only one long rush of burning pain.

Joey ran to the bathroom mirror. One earring was noticeably higher in the lobe. Behind her, Patsy said, Not bad. Just cock your head to one side, nobody will ever notice.

•

Brice had to wake them up. Patsy, holding her hands over her eyes, demanded that he take them to the Bellwood for dinner. Brice said it was the Trestle in La Canada or nothing. Move it, he said.

Joey stumbled down the stairs after them, her feet as heavy and un-manageable as bricks. In the truck, she fell back asleep between them, surfacing when Brice shook her. They were in the steak-house parking lot. Did you get her drunk, Pats? he said. Jesus.

They sat in a red leather booth. Brice ordered, and large, squat tum-blers of amber whiskey arrived, along with a clear pink Shirley Temple for Joey.

Patsy opened the oversized red menu. I myself am partial to a big ole piece of meat, she said. Aren't I, Brice?

Are you? said Brice.

I like to take a nice wobbly filet and put the whole thing in my mouth . . .

Patsy, Brice said sternly. Cut it out.

She turned to Joey. Uh-oh, she said. We better watch out. Can't make him mad. Or, god knows, he'll go make one of his phone calls.

Joey gazed down at her hands in her lap. Patsy leaned in closer. You ever notice he's never in any phone booth? she said. Ever wonder where he goes when he makes one of his calls? Hard to believe men's rooms are so entertaining.

Keep it up, Patsy, said Brice, and I will leave.

But he winked at Joey, indicating that he and she would hightail it out together. Joey was willing to leave right then and there, and hoped that Brice was calling the waiter over to ask for the check. Another round, my friend, he said.

In the long silence, Joey dozed again. Waking briefly, she spotted a beet slice leaking its pink ink onto white salad dressing; she couldn't get anywhere near such a thing, so sank back into sleep. Next an oval steel platter appeared, with a slab of charred meat, a foil-wrapped po-tato, and adorable fluted paper cups of chives and sour cream. Joey ate some potato, but chewing was an effort. Neither Brice nor Patsy was eating either. They sat, closer now, drinking.

Patsy saw Joey looking at her. Hi, gorgeous, she said thickly. You are jus' so gorgeous. She snuggled against Brice. I need another drink, baby.

Even Joey knew another drink was not what was called for—and didn't Brice see that in addition to the glasses they held, there were al-ready whole new drinks on the table? But Brice raised a hand for the

waiter, and another round arrived. Joey now had three undrunk Shirley
Temples. She fished out the cherries, ate them, and—although she knew
better, knew her mother would never have tolerated such a thing—lay
down on the booth and slept.

•

When Joey woke up next, Patsy was grabbing onto her arm so hard it
hurt. Ow! Joey cried. Quit it.

Let go of her, Pats, said Brice, who was outside and trying to pull
Patsy out as well through the driver's side door. Patsy held on to the
steering wheel with her other hand, the one that wasn't gouging Joey's
upper arm. No, no, no. Patsy was sobbing. No, Brice. I don't want to go
home.

Joey saw then that they were parked in the driveway of Patsy's little
white bungalow up in Altadena. Joey had been there once before, with
her parents, for Brice's last birthday.

C'mon, Pats, Brice said, softer now. He reached in and, one by one,
uncurled Patsy's fingers from the steering wheel. Just when he got all
five fingers free, she reclasped it. This happened two, three, more times,
until Brice finally managed to give a good yank at the exact moment all
of Patsy's fingers were free. Patsy grabbed onto Joey and pulled her out
of the truck as well, and Joey's back hit the running board as she slid
down to the ground.

Brice shoved Patsy toward the dark bushes behind them, then
grabbed Joey by her torso as if she were a baby, lifted her up, and swung
her back into the truck. Joey knew he didn't mean to hurt her, though
his fingers dug into her, and she knocked her funny bone against the
steering wheel. Ow, ow, Joey cried, and slithered across the bench seat
away from him just as Brice slammed the door. Rubbing her elbow,
which hurt like crazy, she sat up and watched Brice catch Patsy and
hold her in his arms until she stopped trying to get away. He lifted one
hand off her back and made a motion to Joey that she understood: lock
the truck's door. The button going down sounded like a gunshot.

Brice managed to get Patsy around the front of the truck and up into
the house. Lights came on. Joey could see into the living-room window, the white bookshelves, and the big brown wing of an open grand
piano. The house was set far back from the street, the front yard was

a dark lawn with tall shade trees that seemed like a beautiful park. Joey herself lived with her family six miles out of town on five acres of scrubby chaparral and crumbling granite boulders in a huge, mostly glass house designed by an architect named Halsop, whose neck Joey's father perpetually yearned to wring. Joey yearned to live in a plain wooden home with a bow window, just like Patsy's, in a neighborhood with big trees and straight streets you could roller-skate on, and next-door neighbor kids to play with.

Waiting for Brice to come out, Joey was suddenly, acutely thirsty. She'd get out and go look for a spigot, but if he caught her, Brice might get angry again. So she stretched out on the seat and when she woke up next, the truck was moving, with Brice at the wheel.

Where are we? she asked.

Well, look who's awake.

She saw then that they were driving down Lake Avenue, the city lights shimmering below.

What pills was she on? said Brice. Do you have any idea?

No, Joey said.

You doing okay?

Yes.

You know what? Brice looked down at her. You're a real good girl.

She assumed that he'd cut west soon to take her home, but he drove through downtown Pasadena to the Bellwood instead. I have to talk to Cal Sharp. Then I'll call someone, he said, and find out what in the hell I'm supposed to do with you.

•

The Bellwood lobby was deserted except for the new night concierge with the snotty English accent. While Brice went to look for Cal, Joey drank out of the drinking fountain by the ladies' room until her temples throbbed. Using the repeating pinecone pattern on the carpet, she played listless, makeshift hopscotch down a side hall until she came to an unattended housekeeping cart by the service elevators. She helped herself to a foil-wrapped chocolate and one small shampoo. A key sat in the service elevator controls, and just to see what would happen, Joey turned it. The doors opened, so she got in and rode all the way up to the roof. The elevator let her off behind the wet bar by the pool house.

On the other side of the roof, the penthouse was dark. In between, the large rectangular pool glowed, lit by one lamp in the deep end as by a single suffusing intelligence. Chaise lounges, in neat double rows, were covered with sheeting. Joey walked over to the edge of the roof, a tar-papered hump planted with a wrought iron fence. The three-quarter moon looked like a partially dissolved butter mint. The mountains were black. Directly below was the Bellwood's parking lot, where Brice's pickup and the hotel's airport van were parked side by side. As Joey watched, another van, white with a dark orange stripe, turned into the lot and stopped with no regard for the parking lines. Two men hopped out and threw open the back doors. An ambulance.

The attendants pulled out a gurney and raised it up like an ironing board to full height. Strapped on the gurney was Joey's mother, her face alone visible. How could Joey be so sure? The chestnut hair. The pale, broad forehead. The familiar quickening of fear.

A man—unmistakably Cal Sharp—walked out from the shadow of the hotel and stood by the gurney as the attendants unloaded tall chrome stands the height of saplings, and squat green tanks of oxygen.

As Joey watched, Cal Sharp touched her mother's face. He leaned down and kissed her on the lips, and put his cheek beside hers, and cupped her face with his hand. He kissed her again and stroked her brow, and kissed her again and again, all over her face. He stopped, turned his head as if to hear a whispered secret. Then he stepped back, the attendants moved in, and—Joey really couldn't see this because of the foyer roof—everyone must have gone into the hotel.

The service elevator's door had closed, so she ran across the roof, past the pool and the draped chaises, to the customer elevator by the pent-house. She pressed the button. Waiting, she half expected the doors to open and her mother to appear with full entourage. But wouldn't lights be on in the penthouse suite, the door unlocked, the rooms aired and air-conditioned, with fresh flowers and the usual cellophane-wrapped fresh fruit basket awaiting her mother's arrival?

The elevator took a long time to come, and was empty. On its descent, it stopped at four of the six floors, although nobody waited at any of them. In the lobby Joey ran to the desk. The British concierge was writing something in a ledger. Hey, she said. What room is my mom in?

The man looked up slowly. I'm sorry? he said.

My mother's here! I saw her with Mr. Sharp.

He began writing again. Mr. Sharp has gone home for the night. Your *uncle* is in the Mojave bar.

But, she said.

The man would not look up.

Brice was at the end of the bar. Mother's here, she said. I saw her come.

Brice raised his dull, bloodshot eyes to hers. Your mother's not here, honey, he said. She's in the hospital. She's very sick, you know. Very sick. This time, sweetheart, she's not going to make it. Tears spilled down his cheeks.

No, Brice. Joey tugged his arm. Really, I saw her arrive.

He pulled her to him. His body felt taut and hard and made her think of the canvas cots at summer camp. His chest shook against her. Embarrassed, she waited for him to stop.

Uncle Brice, she said. Mom arrived in an ambulance, and Mr. Sharp met her at the back door. They came into the hotel. I saw.

He touched her cheek. Come on, kitten, he said. I'm taking you to Mother's.

•

Grandmother Court was out on the porch when they arrived, her hair as white as the roses flanking the door. She grasped Joey's shoulders and searched her face. Go on in, dear, she said kindly. There's a cookie for you in the kitchen.

Joey walked into the quiet carpeted hall, then through the dining room to the kitchen, where the light was bright and two store-bought oatmeal cookies sat on a plate on the table. The clock said eleven-forty. Joey could hear the adults talking in muffled tones. The white cat with black spots arched her back against the sliding glass door. Joey opened the door, and the cat swept past her knees. Joey stepped out onto the back deck, where the voices were fainter. The lawn rolled down the slope into a dark ring of trees. She pulled on the necklace around her neck. She pulled until the fine chain cut into the skin, and kept pulling until it broke free. She hurled it out into the yard. Lit by the yellow bug light, it flew through the air, a kinked golden arabesque.

•

Joey did not attend the last seven days of typing class. She never did learn to type her numbers. She stayed at her grandmother's house through the weekend. Her mother died early Monday morning. The funeral would be Friday, at 2:00 p.m. at St. Thomas's Episcopal Church. Her aunt from New York flew in, followed by her aunt from San Francisco. Her brothers were called home from camp, and the whole family was in constant movement between the Hawthornes' glass house in the hills and the Bellwood Hotel.

Thursday night, Joey went up to the Bellwood pool with March Sharp. With their bare feet in the water, she told March that she had seen her mother come to the Bellwood in an ambulance. Your dad was there, and he kissed her all over her face, Joey said.

March kicked her legs slowly; her shins rose to the surface of the water, then submerged. My father is buying me a new horse, she said. An Arabian.

At the memorial service, Joey sat with her brothers and father in the front row. She stood when the minister said please stand and sat when he said please be seated. She read aloud the unison readings and the necessary responses. She rode to the gravesite and stood by as the coffin was lowered into the ground. Her grandmother had given her a linen handkerchief edged in delphinium blue tatting, but Joey did not use it. She did not cry at the funeral or at any time afterward, as she knew for a fact that Millicent Hawthorne was not really dead, but alive and free from them all in some as-yet-undisclosed suite in the Bellwood Hotel.

PART TWO

1

May 1981

Patsy MacLemoore came to on a concrete shelf in a cell in the basement of the Altadena sheriff's department. Her hair had woken her up. It stank. She sat up, pushed it over her shoulder, and closed her eyes until the nausea subsided.

She had said she would rather die than come back here. She'd said that both times she'd been here before.

The little jail had no windows. Fluorescent tubes quivered night and day. A fan clattered, off-kilter. The cinder-block walls were a high-gloss beige, the enamel so thick prisoners wrote in it with their fingernails, the obscenities inked in by grime. Each of the three connected cells contained a seatless stainless-steel toilet and a tiny, one-faucet sink.

Her head seemed to be in a clamp, and she was desperately thirsty. Lurching to the undersized sink, she drank from it sideways, cheek anchored against the greasy spout. The dribble was tepid and tasted of mold. In the next cell over, June's haughty face loomed. Did she fuckin' *live* here? Every time Patsy'd been in, she was too. June's top lip was like two paisleys touching—pandering lips, if ever there were any. What'd you do this time, Professor? said the lips.

Patsy let her mouth fill, the in-head sound a metallic gargle. Swallowing, she pulled back. Don't know, she said. D'n'D. De-dicking some cretin. No idea.

Not what I heard, June said. And lookit your face.

Patsy resumed drinking, but her fingers went right to a ridge of scab crystallizing along her cheekbone, down to her jaw. No wonder her head hurt.

Returning to the shelf, she noted the itchy rasp of the prison gown. Lead blue, unrippable, it was made of 45 percent stainless steel, according to the label. She was naked beneath, not even panties.

I hear you're in deep shit, Professor. Impossibly, June's bangs were set in a pink foam curler. How do you get curlers in jail? June had a real mirror too, not the stainless-steel square provided before you face the judge, but a small, plastic-framed mirror propped up on her sink. And a hair dryer. A zippered sack of makeup spilled open on her sleeping shelf. Like she lived here.

Patsy's own home, 729 Pomelo Street, was just six blocks away. Walking distance. Hell: crawling distance, if only they'd let you—ten minutes of sidewalk, then left on Pomelo, with its shingled cabins, thick-armed oaks, mountain views. So close, if only she could get there.

Hey, Professor, wanna borrow my brush? A turquoise paddle with mashed black plastic bristles slid through the bars, but Patsy knew better than to reach for it, lest the brush be retracted again and again, as many times as she'd fall for the ruse, only to be offered at a price, as if she kept a twenty rolled up in her privates for such expenditures. Naw, Juney, thanks anyway. Patsy gathered her long, damp, sharply sour hair—the mats as large and thick as trout—and wound it into a loose knot. But this proved too much tug on her scalp, and she shook it free, three painful shocks, each a silvery flash behind her eyes.

She couldn't be in too deep shit, she thought, if she was still in this small-town dump. When'd I come in, Juney?

You were here when I come. Snoring in your own mess. Stinking up the place. We made 'em spray you down. What'd you do to make 'em so mad?

Who knows? said Patsy. Maybe I used too many big words, or lectured 'em on the progressive era. Hell, Juney, I have no idea. Oh, but we'll find out.

O'Mallon was at the cage door. Hiya, Bitsy, Patsy said, using the jailhouse joke about a supposedly small part of him.

He opened the door, beckoned with a curt tilt of his head.

Lemons for breakfast? Patsy asked, though she couldn't say for sure what time of day it was down here where the sun never shone. Standing, she realized she was still quite drunk. Well, they needn't know that. She straightened her spine, causing more quick bright flashes of pain, and set off at a stately pace. O'Mallon, blocking her, produced cuffs.

Uh-oh. Daddy's mad.

He drew her hands behind her back, clasped them in chrome, shoved. God*damn*, Bitsy. See ya, Juney, over her shoulder.

O'Mallon steered her by the upper arm down the floor-waxed hall to what Patsy thought of as the conversation room, another drab and battered place with a stoic oak table, plastic schoolroom chairs, and street-level windows with chicken wire in the mottled glass. Benny, the lawyer who had represented her in other drunk-driving episodes, sat inside the door. Did I call you? Patsy asked, for she had summoned him on more than one previous occasion with no memory of doing so. She grazed his shoulder with her hip. We have to stop meeting like this, she said.

Benny ignored her—her own counsel!

Lieutenant Peterson sat across the table. Also, Ricky Barrett, who had just last year been a continuing education student in her twentieth-century cultural history course. Those continuing ed credits had paid off; he was Detective Barrett now, working out of Monterey Park, as she'd learned during her last incarceration.

Everyone's mouth was a down-turned crescent. She was not invited to sit.

To what do I owe such a . . . summit? she said. Such a meeting of the minds? None but the county's best and brightest?

Shut up, Patsy. That was the world-weary Peterson. White-haired and monotoned. Just shut the fuck up.

But then nobody else said anything.

Really, you guys. What's up? Why the faces? I can't remember a thing.

Try, suggested Peterson.

Patsy pulled out a chair, sat, and tried. Monday morning survey, America 1865 to the present. Office hours. Personnel committee dinner at Anne Davis's house, blankness setting in around the soup course, not her fault, the wine so cheap and bad. What time is it, anyway?

Noon.

Day?

Wednesday.

Shit. When'd I come in?

Last night.

So she'd missed the 9:00 a.m. survey that morning. They'd finished Reconstruction on Monday and were to start the Gilded Age today. I lost Tuesday, she said.

Across from her, Ricky Barrett snapped the elastic band on an accordion file, a battered and cloudy-brown thing, the corners worn to white. Patsy couldn't help but read the word felt-tipped on its side. HOMICIDE.

The taste of wet metal filled her mouth, and fear hit. She thought perhaps she'd misread, and looked again. HOMICIDE. Yes, but it was an old file, probably used for something else now—used for whatever county sheriff detectives detect: stray dogs, rabid skunks, backyard keggers gone rowdy.

Something like this was bound to happen, Patsy. Now Benny was speaking, darling, patient Benny. We'll-get-you-off-this-time Benny who, in fact, never had. She should probably fire him, should've done so two cases ago and saved herself some big fines. But he had the clumsy charm, if also the legal facility, of a Labrador retriever, and she hadn't wanted to hurt his feelings. The way you were going, he was saying now, you had plenty of warning. There's what, three priors? A suspended license?

Is that it? she said. Was I driving again? *Moi?* Sans license?

The men gazed at the nicked and thinning oak veneer as if they were poring over a war map, as if, again, she were not in the room.

Okay, what'd I do? Or do I have to beg? Benny? What, are we going to play twenty questions? Or can we behave like adults here? She was almost shouting, then caught herself. But really, they were so grim-lipped and obtuse. What is it? I really *don't* remember. Did I kill someone?

Peterson's mouth did something—a wince, or a smile suppressed.

Understanding flooded her. Oh, you guys! You *guys*. You're just trying to scare me. Damn! You really had me going there!

Then Ricky Barrett, the hopelessly unerudite plodder whose childish, big-shouldered handwriting she recalled from ill-argued essays, reached into his battered file and extracted a sheet of paper. Using his usual word-by-word, finger-pointing method, he began reading aloud. *Jane Robin Parnham, female Caucasian, aged thirty-four, massive contusions to ribs and right arm, cause of death, crushed pulmonary cavity, suffocation. Jessica Elizabeth Parnham, female Caucasian, aged twelve, contusions to rib cage, shoulder, spleen, and kidneys crushed, cause of death, extensive internal bleeding.*

The words flew at her like bats, but before she made any sense of them, and before everything else that was to follow—arraignment, indictment, preliminary hearing, sentencing—and even as guilt stood poised to swallow her in a towering black wave, she took one swift,

light-washed sweep through her Pomelo Street home: the red Formica
kitchen table and gleaming toaster in the breakfast nook, a blue vase
stuffed with homegrown daisies on the baby grand, the front yard's
white-limbed sycamore and deep grass, all of it simmering, soaking in
the thick yellow sunlight of late afternoon.

That life, she thought, that beautiful life is over.

2

Patsy's mother came down from Bakersfield, posted bail, and drove her to Pomelo Street. Patsy went immediately into the shower, then slid into her bed, under the covers, turned her back to the door, and refused to open her eyes or say why she'd left the water running or what she wanted to eat.

For a week she did not speak or look at anybody. She barely ate, and waited until her mother was asleep or on the phone to use the bathroom. Once, when they met each other in the hall, Patsy brushed past as if they were strangers. All the liquor had been cleared out from all of her hiding places—her father's handiwork. He knew the drill firsthand.

Patsy lay in the dim, pleated shadows beneath the sheet, perfectly still, because to move hand or shoulder was to stir up the new facts of her life, which arrived anyway, in waves, to their own inexorable rhythm. Arc of steering wheel, booming car hood, a terrible tumult in the dark. The rasp of soft ridges, like corduroy. And with them, a horror without bounds.

•

They were Jehovah's Witnesses, mother and daughter. They'd been walking down her driveway, having left two tabloids rolled in the handle of the screen door. Patsy hadn't been going fast. Her car, a 1963 Mercedes sedan so dark green it looked black, weighed forty-eight hundred pounds, according to the registration. Two and a half tons! The girl died at the scene, the mother some hours later in intensive care.

Patsy pictured them again and again, as if they were borne on a conveyor belt from some charred storehouse of memory: young and older, two ink-blue skirts and sodden, moonlit blouses, sensible shoes, hair thick and rippled over the ground, faces pressed into deep black grass.

•

She had taken her car out before the accident only once that she remembered, when she and Brice Court were breaking up. Although he had
disappointed her constantly, she could not bear the thought of not seeing him or talking to him. When he would not answer her phone calls
one night, she took the keys from the tiny drawer in the antique coffee
grinder and drove to the Lyster. She'd gazed up at his lit rooms, their
high plastered ceilings, the curt edge of a mantel, a shifting shadow
most likely cast by him. He was alive, and she knew where to find him.
She drove home weeping but satisfied and returned the keys to their
musty box.

•

Her father came down for the weekend to speak to her, *do something* with
her. This was bound to happen, Pats, he said. After a certain point, our
disease takes us only to hospitals, jails, or morgues. C'mon, let's go to a
meeting.

Then Wes, the chair of her department. God help us, Patsy, this
could happen to anyone. Your students are taking a collection for your
legal fees . . . And her best friend at Hallen, Sarah. I hate that this has
happened, Pats, I can only imagine how you feel. Now, Patsy, please
talk to me, look, a pot of tea . . . And her brother, Burt. Shouldn't we
turn on the French Open? More people filed in, wraiths from her former
life, their voices buzzing across the divide from the everyday world, a
place she now knew as cheaply constructed, brazenly false.

The foot of the bed sank, and a certain voice opened her eyes: Brice
himself, who now looked as spurious as the others. Poor husk and
wastrel, his big-nosed, well-bred looks were never so useless.

I have something for you, Pats, he said in a luring tone she never
could resist. She hoisted herself on an elbow to see, in the cup of his
palm, two jewel-red capsules. And here's water to wash 'em down.

He held the back of her neck as she drank. What? What'd you say?
Leave the others. I know you have more.

Brice laughed. Not on your life, baby girl, he said. Not on your life.

Her life. A rathole.

At least Brice, that chronic charmer, understood what she wanted:
to feel neither better nor worse, but nothing at all. He held her hand,

not minding that she did not clasp his in return, no doubt preferring it. As she watched, shadows gathered around him like a dirty cloud, cloaking his shoulders, chest, neck, and chin until only the big hook nose floated in the darkness.

•

She awoke to hear her mother snoring in the other bedroom. She rose and peed and felt her way down the hall. In the kitchen, she opened the utility drawer, located the black-handled shears. Slipping a thick rubber band from around the kitchen faucet, she gathered up her tangled hair. The scissors, dull as chopsticks, sometimes only pinched and jammed. Her arms grew tired, the handles bore into her thumb.

In the morning, her mother, emptying coffee grounds, would spot the snarled, flaxen, thirty-inch-long ponytail in with the butter wrapper and junk mail.

•

At the arraignment, Patsy had agreed to an early preliminary hearing in ten days' time. Now, with the date looming, Benny appeared bedside in his budget suit, suggesting, then urging delay—Let's continue it, he said. He seemed tired, gentler, though distant.

No, she said into the pillow, why put it off?

Because prison is hideous, Patsy. Because you don't want to go there before you need to or stay any longer than you have to.

Let's get it over with, she said.

Then Benny's mood improved. The district attorney was in a bargaining mood, thanks to a hampering technicality: Patsy had killed in her own driveway and not on a public roadway, and intoxication was only a factor on public streets. Thus they could trade murder/manslaughter for criminal negligence. Though for two bodies, he could not get her less than four years—she'd serve two and some with good behavior. How did that sound, two and some?

Two and some, five hundred and some. All the same to her.

•

For the first hour, she sat in the wood-paneled courtroom between her mother and her brother Burt. She held their hands as if they alone tethered her to safety. Then Burt left to make some calls.

She had been here before, or in an identical courtroom, where the cherry veneer walls were alternately smooth and perforated and the overhead lights looked like giant ice-cube trays. Five or six such rooms filled this floor alone, with many more above and below. The judge may or may not have been the same balding older white man who had revoked her license and fined her a thousand dollars the last time.

In the front of the room, beyond a waist-high partition, a small industry functioned with no particular urgency; bailiff, court recorder, clerk, and district attorney stayed put as defense lawyers and defendants came and went, their assorted felonies processed one after another. Assault. Armed robbery. Burglary. Nobody was in a hurry. Nobody raised a voice in anger, annoyance, or regret. Another assault. Battery. All but the judge spoke with their backs to the room, so much of what was said was inaudible to those on the long wooden pewlike benches who waited for their cases to be called.

The bailiff, a big black man dressed all in khaki, followed the proceedings with an alert interest that seemed intelligent to Patsy, as if he, of all the people there, registered everything. Several times, after perusing a paper, he left by a side door, only to reappear minutes later with a prisoner in shackles and faded orange pajamas. Whenever that door opened, Patsy craned to see where they'd come from. A stairwell, an iron banister, ascending concrete steps.

A woman slid into Burt's seat, a trim, handsome Latina in a tan leather skirt, a fringed tan sweater, tan high-heeled boots. She touched Patsy's arm. Do you know how I could find out who's representing my son? she asked. She did not look old enough to have an adult son. I called Legal Aid. They couldn't say.

I'm sorry, said Patsy. I have no idea.

Nobody does. She lifted her chin to indicate the lawyers, judge, bailiff. Nobody here knows anything.

A man who'd attempted to rob a small grocery store was given a suspended sentence. A trial date was delayed for a shaved-headed gang member held on three hundred and sixty thousand dollars bond. Led back through the door, the kid blew a kiss, no hands, just kiss and puff. Patsy followed the kiss to an ancient grandmother. After this, another general shuffling ensued. The judge scratched an eyebrow as he turned pages, and the court recorder ate a few quick spoonfuls of yogurt.

The woman in tan leaned in close. They're so nonchalant here, she said, pronouncing it with a soft *ch*, like *shhhhh*. And they're dealing with people's lives. Their *lives*, she said.

Yet the calmness of the court was a comfort to Patsy. The routine, the barely audible proceedings. She drifted until she became aware of two women on the other side of the aisle. They searched her out before sitting down, agreed with each other that she was their object. The accusation and loathing in their faces seemed like the first unadjusted expressions Patsy had encountered since the accident, and part of her was relieved, finally, to see such naked dislike, and part of her rose up against it too, some tiny, undefeated shred of self. The judge, glancing at some papers, said her name. Benny looked back at the courtroom door, and his eyes flickered.

Entering was Ricky Barrett, her former student, and with him a man she would have recognized anywhere, he looked so stunned by sorrow. Like her, he'd been led to this impersonal shuffle of ritual and governance. He slid into the bench behind the two women. They reached back for his hands.

Patsy faced the front of the court again and let him look at her.

Her name was called again. She went forward and took an oath. I do, she said, holding up her hand.

The district attorney was a young and pretty woman. Pale, freckled, possibly Irish, her face was framed in frizzy red curls, and she was solemn to the point of coldness. Do you understand these charges against you? she asked Patsy. Have you had an opportunity to discuss these charges and any defense you would have to them with your attorney?

The words were certainly rote. Patsy needed only to ignore the surges of confusion that rose in response to them. Yes, she said, nodding. Yes.

It is my understanding, the D.A. went on, that you wish to plead guilty to two counts of criminal negligence resulting in loss of life. The maximum sentence on those counts would be twenty-five years. But today your attorney and myself have agreed that upon entering your plea, you will receive the following sentence: four years in the state prison. Is that what you want to do?

Again, a rising intimation of complexity, of weeds tangled underwater, a sensation too vague to address when a simple answer was expedient, and expedience was her goal. Yes, Patsy said.

And then came the waivers—Benny had rehearsed her—when she relinquished rights, one after another. The right to a preliminary hearing, to a trial by jury or by court. The right to confront and examine the witnesses against her, the right to present her own defense . . . the right not to testify against herself. They flew off like crows flapping off a tree limb, black rags in a wind. Do you understand and give up these rights? The young woman's seriousness seemed at once stagy and dire.

After the waivers came the consequences: Patsy would go to prison and afterward be released on parole; any and each violation of parole would result in another year of prison. And she would pay a restitution fine—two hundred dollars. She stifled a yelp at the paltriness, the *joke*, of the amount.

Have you been advised of all these consequences of your plea? the D.A. asked Patsy.

Patsy saw that the bailiff was looking at her, attentive, interested, like the best of students. Yes, she said.

Are you pleading freely and voluntarily because you did in fact commit the crime and violate the state penal code by driving negligently and causing the fatal injuries of Jane Robin Parnham and Jessica Parnham?

Yes, Patsy said, looking back at the bailiff.

Are you pleading guilty because you are indeed guilty?

She stood before the court and touched the dark tumult, the awful thumps and booms, bodies on the ground, a wheeling of stars; with such images came the inevitable, engulfing nausea of knowing it could never be undone.

Yes, Patsy said, the word spanning a sea of uneasy feeling and linking death to blame like a stitch closing the lips of a wound so that healing could begin. Thus could the case, whatever its remaining mysteries, be at least officially closed. *Yes*, spoken aloud, seemed the least and only thing she could do for the enraged women and shipwrecked man sitting on the other side of the room. She said yes, and cleared her throat and realized from the court recorder's expectant pause and the continuing gaze of the judge that she might not have spoken at all. Yes, she said, this time loud enough, she hoped, that the man and women felt a loosening, some small uplift, an easing.

The judge set the sentencing twenty days hence and her bond at three hundred and sixty thousand dollars, same as that gangbanger's.

Benny and Burt, who had reappeared, shouldered her out of the courtroom, her mother right behind. At the women's row, she twisted toward them. I would like . . . , she said to Benny, who grasped her arm above her elbow. Burt, I want to . . . But neither man paused, and Burt wrapped an arm around her waist as if she were stumbling. Even so, as she passed the man, Patsy looked directly at him. Darkness met darkness, though in his gaze she also saw bright, glinting splinters of grief.

3

Twenty days, neither in prison nor free. What do I do? she asked Benny.

You take care of business, he said. And behave. You keep out of trouble. For god's sake.

With her mother's help, Patsy cleared out her office at school. Another day they visited the bank, changed the names on her home deed lest a civil suit be filed, and found an agency to manage the leasing of her house, the mortgage payments, and taxes in her absence. (She'd said, Oh, give them the house, give them everything, but her father had made the down payment, so Pomelo Street was really not hers to relinquish.) She rented a storage unit. She packed her woolens with blocks of cedar, rolled her yard-sale china and glassware in newspapers whose words would be at least two years old when next read. Her home grew ever more sparse.

One night, as her mother snored, Patsy walked down the hill six blocks to the Sav-On directly across the street from the Altadena sheriff's station. The man in the liquor section did not know her, and he wordlessly sold her two liters of Jim Beam, lightweight plastic bottles with handles and, because she still had money, a same size bottle of vodka. The bag was heavier than she had anticipated, so she carried it like a real sack of groceries, in that usual practical hug, six uphill blocks to Pomelo Street. A sheriff's black-and-white passed her going the opposite way; she expected it to turn around and slide up beside her, but this did not happen. Her hair, she realized. She did not look like herself.

She stashed two bottles under the camellia bush against the shed, took the other to her bedroom. She rinsed out her mother's teacup and filled it to the brim. Bourbon, she noted, was remarkably tea-colored. The first mouthful, as big and sweet and hot as gasoline, caused tears to spring from her eyes.

•

Of course she was found out, sooner than she thought possible, the first thing the next morning, with less than a quarter of one bottle gone, a waste, and of course all hell broke loose, a lecture from everybody, and Benny so angry he grabbed her shoulders and shook until she looked him in the eyes. Listen to me, you ungrateful monster. I busted my fuckin' balls for that plea, but it's not written in stone. Screw up now, you'll get ten to fifteen, easy. Or all twenty-five. And fuck all, you'd deserve it. But what do I care? I'm outta here. I'm through.

But he wasn't really. Somebody talked him back. Patsy thought, not for the first time, that he was probably a little in love with her.

She had round-the-clock sitters after that: mother, father, her friend Sarah, a burly Russian housekeeper allegedly hired to clean the place for prospective tenants, though that wouldn't normally involve spending the night, would it?

Only once more, again on her mother's watch, did she slip out late one night to the geriatric Wagon Wheel on Lake Avenue. Just two, Jim, she told the bartender.

I heard about everything, Patsy, he said. And I shouldn't do this. But okay, two. Any fuss after that, I'm calling the sheriff.

He poured her one big one, generous as god, then another, then said, It's time. Ah, Jim, she said, but he reached for the phone, so she left on her own accord and was home in time to answer when her mother called out. In the kitchen, Mom, she said. Just drinking a glass of water. Which was true.

•

The morning of the sentencing, she was dressing when she looked out her window and saw, on top of the wooden fence, a squirrel holding an orange. His rusty tail was fluffed and curled over his back to rest between his ears. He grasped the orange the way a child holds a large ball, and efficiently spat peelings aside until the top half of the fruit was all luminous white pulp. Slowing, he ate calmly, sank his face into the meat, his small hands rotating the sphere in quick, tiny adjustments. His cheeks shimmered with movement; he regarded her with a shiny black challenging eye. Abruptly he tossed the half orange to the grass, where it tipped toward her, a hollow bowl. The squirrel scurried along the fence top and down the other side. Patsy fastened her skirt.

•

The man and the two women were also at the sentencing, today seated several rows apart.

Hers was the third case called, after a robbery and a domestic assault. The district attorney—appearing older, more severe, yet even lovelier in a charcoal gabardine suit—announced that the probation report had been filed. She corroborated no previous felony convictions and attested to Patsy MacLemoore's reliability as a citizen and college professor. Thus she recommended that the plea, as agreed upon by herself and opposing counsel, should be accepted by the court.

However, Your Honor, she continued with her relentless, dire calmness, family members of the victims have expressed the desire to file victim impact statements prior to sentencing.

Benny had warned Patsy about this; the mother, he said, was in a swivet about the plea. Indeed, the older woman rose and worked her way out of the long, narrow bench and up to the front, where she faced the court in a mint green dress and paste pearls the size of filberts. She held a gray cardboard folder and opened it to reveal two color photographs, and she held them up as if sharing a storybook with the court. Both pictures revealed the cool, mottled blue background of department store portraiture, and even from a distance were heartless in their detail. A plump dark-haired woman on the left, a young girl with lighter braids on the right, the two in matching red Christmas sweaters. Jane and Jessica, the woman said, and shook the pictures and began to cry. My daughter and granddaughter, she added, her voice breaking. They never hurt anyone, not even accidentally.

Patsy's mother, skinny and tanned, tightened her grip on Patsy's wrist.

My Jane and Jessica, the grandmother continued, and waved the photographs at Patsy. I know that you were drunk. I know the truth.

She turned to the judge. How can she kill two people and get only four years in prison? Four years—*less!*—when my girls are dead forever? She sobbed in deep, painful gasps before them until the other, younger woman came up and led her away.

Anyone else, Counselor? asked the judge.

The man came forward. Mark Parnham, he said to the recorder, and waited as she typed it in. He wore a suit, pressed well enough—it was his posture that gave him a crumpled, staved-in look. In front of the court he seemed to fight his way up from some deep private place and into the room. He blinked and searched her out. I've driven drunk, he said. More than once.

He reached over and put a finger down on the corner of the bailiff's desk and leaned over it, a pivot. He frowned. I guess the law has worked out the sentences and stuff. It's not for me to say how much time anybody should spend in prison. I have to trust the court on that.

His shoulders sank, and he winced, perhaps trying not to cry. Above his nose, his forehead creased in two deep lines. A victim impact statement, he said. Hard to know the impact, it's still so new. I'll try. He spoke to the two women. For me, it's like two bright lights have gone out and the world is just a much darker place. And it's probably going to stay like that. He waited—they all did—to see if he had more to say.

Surely, Patsy thought, he would mention the boy now doomed to a motherless life.

Thank you, Mark Parnham said to the judge, and walked back to his seat.

Nobody else came forward, so the judge sentenced her to four years in the state penitentiary and asked if she cared to address the court.

She made her own way to the front. On the benches before her sat the other cases waiting their turns in family clusters, all indifferent to her own proceedings. She and Mark Parnham looked at each other directly, steadily. They might have been alone in an empty field.

I'm sorry, she said. I'm sorry for the pain I've caused the family. I hear there's a young son, and I—

Her words seemed so trite and inadequate, but none others came to mind.

I didn't intend to hurt anybody. I don't really even remember what happened. But I'm sorry with all my heart, and if I could, if there was any way—

She stopped herself. As for prison . . . She lifted one hand helplessly. It can't be worse than what it's like now.

She wanted to say more, something honest and comforting, but nothing came to her. Okay, she said, and looked to Benny.

The judge spoke rapidly, conclusively, too quickly for her to catch. She waited for his final word, his turning to a new page, the gap between cases, so she could feel the clasp of her family's arms, press her face against each of theirs. And someone did touch her: the tall, barrel-gutted bailiff had come up beside her and grasped her upper arm.

I must demand any personal property on your person, he said.

She had been told to expect this, and last night had removed watch and rings and necklace, the gold hoops from her ears. Today she'd dressed in a basic old teaching skirt and white cotton blouse, a wool cardigan. Clothes she'd be comforted to see again when she was settled in prison.

Her family stood up behind the partition, her mother trying to hurry them forward, her father's face dark and curiously wrinkled. Was he weeping?

What? she said to the bailiff.

Your pin.

It seemed she must also hand over the bobby pin holding the hair off her face. Too long for bangs, too short to tuck behind her ears, this hair fell forward and curtained her eyes.

He gave her a minute to kiss her family one by one, Mom, Dad, Burt; then she again felt his touch on her arm.

Turn around and put your hands behind your back. He spoke with the same tender firmness he might have used elsewhere, in private. With the clasp of handcuffs came a warmth and pressure from his hands. A light touch on her lower back—a gentlemanly nudge.

Dad, she whispered, pausing, wanting to touch her father's face.

Come along now, said the bailiff, and decisively led her by the arm past the recorder and the witness stand. The door the prisoners passed through swung wide at his push and slammed shut behind them.

Down they went, on concrete steps. Flight by flight, the bailiff's large hand remained on her arm, not cruelly—in fact, almost companionably—all the way to the basement, where they pushed through thick metal doors into a corridor and passed through other doors and corridors to a central lockup where half a dozen women crouched on a concrete floor still moist from a recent hosing. Patsy waited against the wall alongside two silent prostitutes for an hour or so. A single steel toilet sat in the middle of the room. Clogged, it overflowed with each use.

Her name was called. Eventually she and the prostitutes were led to a loading area. The sheriff's bus took them the three blocks to the jail. There, she was asked to strip, then sprayed with some pressurized corrosive delouser, allowed a tepid shower, and issued the usual scratchy poly-steel gown. She rode an elevator half a dozen stories up to a cell occupied by a Korean-speaking bar girl with a nasty head cold. For two days she sat or lay on the upper concrete bunk, listened to her cellmate cough and spit, and searched for patterns in the bubbles of the poured concrete ceiling. Then the state prison's bus arrived and took her east.

•

Surely, county jail had prepared her for prison. She expected no amenity, civility, or consideration from the guards. She expected grime and hopelessness, and how the refrigerated hours slowed to a standstill. She knew how to pull in deep. But who could go deep enough for the bus ride to prison, a two-hour coed excursion. From the moment of boarding, the male prisoners said everything imaginable to the women, about their faces and bodies, their wrinkled, stinking genitals and not-so-secret passion for rape. Patsy found the guards' noninterference as shocking and hateful as anything the men said. No, more so.

She was twenty-nine years old; her dissertation had been accepted six months earlier, almost to the day.

They rode east for more than an hour; then the driver left the freeway and drove through the backside of a warehouse district, the factory yards full of rusted and leaking metal drums, heaps of pipes and rods, and unidentifiable pieces of steel. The bus bumped over train tracks, passed pockets of houses with tiny yards, people sitting on porches, dogs standing in the streets. They came to what looked like a vast, ugly elementary school in dark pink stucco. Flower beds spilled crabgrass, and what might have been lawns were expanses of packed dirt and low, trash-snagging weeds. A few dark, tenacious, struggling juniper bushes hugged the buildings; otherwise the yards were bare. The bus swung around the back, stopping for a long time by a high steel fence. On the bus, the men went from fractious to frenzied, ready to rampage the place and its female population, if that were only possible. A gate opened; the bus pulled in and idled in the sun on an asphalt field. After some minutes a guard in the back of the bus stood and herded the women off. They filed out, clutching small totes, trash bags, grocery sacks. Patsy had her gym bag. They moved slowly in their clanking shackles while the men whistled and catcalled and banged the windows with the flats of their hands.

Once off the bus, the women funneled through solid steel doors into an entryway. Once they were all inside, a set of iron gates opened with much buzzing and creaking, and they were ushered into a longer passageway where three guards frisked them, patted them down, and took their bags. Gone were Patsy's books and asthma inhalers. The next gate opened, they funneled through, and the gate shut behind them. The whine of the hinges, the clangs of closure were terrible, loud, unnecessarily theatrical.

The guards told them to open their mouths and shake their heads. The waxed floors and empty hallways and wide stairs divided by steel pipe handrails resembled nothing so much as an abandoned school, one so battered and harshly lit, so completely devoid of any nicety, the effect could only be intentional. The women shuffled finally into a large, open room where more guards were stationed all around, their legs apart, their right hands poised over their guns. Along a counter on the far end, six women waited like bank tellers. Registration, somebody said. It takes hours.

No talking, said a guard. That means no talking.

Even though the new prisoners were silent, the noise of the place was intense, layered, insane: the banging and clanging of steel, the slamming of doors, the incessant pinging of vehicles in reverse, the voices of women nearby and far off, yelling and shrieking, their words bouncing off the floors and walls, echoing, pouring in through open transoms. And from underneath their feet came a constant mechanical throb, as if some enormous engine rumbled in the basement. Outside, it had been ninety degrees, but in this room the temperature was no more than fifty-five. The guards wore jackets.

Patsy waited in a long line for fingerprinting, then stood at a taped line on the floor for a photograph. A male guard took her into a smaller area, where she and three other women were instructed to take off their street clothes, squat with knees pointed out, and cough. Still naked, she was led to the showers. She'd done this before, but always under female supervision. She had two minutes under cool water.

The guard gave her a towel. What happens next? Patsy asked him.

You want to know what happens next? Hey, this one wants to know what happens next, he called to another guard. Imagine that. Well, I'll tell you what happens next, young lady. Anything I want to happen happens next.

I'm just worried about my asthma inhaler.

You should have worried about that before you did what you did, he said, and, taking her towel, led her, still naked, down a long hallway. This one's worried we won't take good care of her, he said to a female CO coming up the hall. The woman gave Patsy a quick, worried look and hurried on. The guard unlocked a small cell-sized room with only a narrow concrete shelf in it and motioned her in. Here, madam, he said. Here is what happens next.

Patsy sat naked until finally someone unlocked the door and handed her a set of thin orange pajamas and a sheaf of forms, a pen. No, she could not use the bathroom, not yet. She filled out form after form—name, permanent address, next of kin, health history, drug allergies. She finished and tried lying on the bench, but it was too cold. Time passed, an hour or more, and a woman corrections officer opened the door and took the forms. No, she couldn't use the bathroom. Just a few more minutes, the woman said.

More time passed, and another woman wordlessly handed Patsy a stack of clothes and bedding and led her to a dormitory crammed with bunk beds. Patsy had to squeeze in sideways to get to her assigned place. The bunk bed itself was undersized, as if imported from a children's camp or hospital, the frame bolted to the floor, the springs loose and twangy, the mattress less than two inches thick. Patsy had the top bunk. She unfolded a green army blanket raveled at the edges, coarse white untearable sheets reeking of chlorine bleach, a crackling plastic mattress pad. She was assigned a banged-up metal lockbox at the foot of the lower bunk.

Patsy filled her lockbox with her new possessions: another pair of the prison pajamas, two pairs of used blue jeans, two T-shirts, white cotton panties, a gray sweatshirt, canvas slip-ons, and a plastic bag of toiletries—toothbrush, toothpaste, deodorant.

Do you think we'll get our own stuff back? she asked a young woman watching her from the neighboring bunk.

Don't aks me, I don't know jack.

4

Patsy had imagined prison to be like life in the convents she'd heard about in Catholic school, places where novices were made to scrub perfectly clean floors in silence. But no work, no activities took place in Receiving, or RC, as it was called, where women were evaluated for disposition elsewhere. RC lasted sixty or more days. Patsy had one half-hour meeting with a counselor. She also compiled her visitors' list, then signed and sent visitors' questionnaires to everyone on her list, one morning's chore.

Prisoners sat around the open dorm or in the television room. They did each other's hair and nails and passed around three-year-old women's magazines. Some tried to clean around their beds, several compulsively, polishing the floors with hoarded napkins, Kotex, any rag they could scrounge.

Now, girls, the COs said. Now, girls. Time for bed, girls. Count! Attagirls. Keep to the right, girls. No talking, girls. Keep those voices down, girls.

The dorm held forty-two women. Some spoke only at the top of their lungs and did so day and night, even very late at night and at dawn, day after day. They talked without ceasing, to themselves, to anybody who would listen, to nobody at all. They argued, picked fights, sang the same snatch of song over and over again. For hours at a stretch, a short, fat woman named Doris sang, *It's a small world after all / It's a small small small small world.* Others vocalized nonsense, like parrots. Patsy marveled: Didn't these women ever crave silence?

No, they labored constantly and mightily against silence.

Patsy hadn't been in RC for a week when a woman tapped her shoulder on their way to the dining room, in the hall where the sour odor of rancid food adhered like resin to the block walls. The woman was in her late twenties, tall and muscular. Who you? she said. You pretty.

A caress down Patsy's arm ended in a grabbed wrist. Then the woman was flush against her in what seemed to be an embrace—the woman's face was close, as if for a kiss—except that she'd twisted Patsy's arm up behind her back.

Oh no, Patsy said. Please. Please, let go. She had to speak right into the woman's lips with their awful curved smile. The woman's eyes looked over her shoulder, as if bored.

Patsy had no idea what the woman wanted, except to work her arm like a lever and make her emit small high cries at will. Please let go, Patsy said. The lever administered more pain. And again. Patsy lifted her foot and pulled her leg up as high as she could. She had been drilled in self-defense in childhood by Burt. The three N's, he said, never forget: neck, nuts, and knees. At such close range Patsy couldn't get enough swing for the knee, so she stomped as hard as she could—given her flimsy canvas slip-ons—on the arch of the woman's foot. A loud baying right in her ear, and the next moment the woman was off her and there was only shouting. My lord, my fucking jesus fucking white-ass bitch.

Patsy stood there, disoriented; she hadn't expected the stomp to work. Then again she'd never before stomped on anyone's arch as hard as she could. Terrified of official discipline and of the other women—who flowed on into the dining room around them like water around boulders—Patsy fled to her bunk and waited for a guard to loom, for six or ten women to encircle her bed, however retribution would come. For the next twenty hours she stayed on her bunk until a CO ordered her into the yard for exercise.

Looking around the dirt yard, Patsy couldn't identify her attacker. She walked close to the fence and avoided looking anyone in the eye. A plump older woman came up alongside her and said in a low voice, You had to do what you did, it was the right thing. Nobody will bother you now.

And mostly, nobody did.

•

In RC, there were no cubicles for privacy, no chance to be alone. No letters were allowed in, no packages, no visitors, no contact with the outside. No books. No street clothes. No commissary goods. Patsy took three-minute tepid showers every third day. She sat on the toilet in full view of male guards, some of whom watched with obvious interest, one of whom always put his hand on his crotch. She learned to close her eyes for privacy. When allowed, she went outside, walked in slow circles for twenty minutes, talked to some women, avoided others. Mostly she walked with Ruth, a tall and quiet mother of two boys. Her husband was the manager at a fluid technology plant. Patsy had no idea why Ruth was in prison, but heard women call her firefly. Why do they call you that, Ruth?

Somebody must have read my file, and blabbed it 'round.

Why, what does it say?

Says I set a fire.

Where? Not your house?

No, said Ruth. Up a canyon.

A firebug. Patsy wanted to know more, but Ruth wouldn't talk about it.

Word got out on her too. *Professor* followed her to RC. And *Teach.* And her being a drunk was clearly in the public domain. Small World Doris tried to sell her a little jar of clear hooch, some jailhouse concoction closer to kerosene than vodka. Patsy's eyes watered from the fumes and yearning.

Trade me sumthun, Doris kept saying, but Patsy had nothing.

Don't you got no coffee powder? No canny bar?

Annie tried to lure her to AA meetings—Annie, who confided she'd been a banquet waitress until she cut up her boyfriend's face and kited a couple thousand dollars of his checks. I was sober for six years, she told Patsy, then had a slip. In two weeks I was freebasing. *Me,* who'd never even tried cocaine.

C'mon, Patsy, Annie said. You might as well get sober inside, cuz it's a hassle to drink here, and AA helps with parole. And meetings are good here.

Maybe someday, Patsy said, thinking of the little jar, those fumes.

Also recruiting for AA was the plump older woman, Gloria, whom the women called Granny, who was in her late fifties, ginger-haired, stout, and tough. Gloria had already been sober for twenty-four years, but she'd stopped her lithium and, in a manic episode, had stolen a hundred thousand from her business partner and set out across the country, giving cash away to strangers. Gloria was the closest thing to a den mother in RC. Her daughter was a cop and had connections. Gloria had privileges other women didn't—a job in the kitchen, and visitors. Anytime you want to come to a meeting, Patsy, she said.

Patsy tried sitting in the television room, but there were too many women talking and yelling and she couldn't hear the program. She spent most of her days on her small, ache-inducing bed.

She missed going outside at will. Walking down streets, and driving. Beautiful mobility. She missed the phone, the miracle of talking to a person whenever she wanted. She yearned for her own home and for the very friends she'd ignored when they came to console her after the accident. She even missed those weeks, the awful stretch of guilt and self-revulsion. From here, those emotions seemed more pure and true than any she'd have in this stultifying dorm. In RC she did not brood—or even think—about the deaths she'd caused. If and when her victims crossed her mind, they seemed only remotely and incidentally connected to her present circumstances. When she'd declared in court that nothing could be as bad as how she already felt, she'd been hopelessly, laughably, presumptuously wrong. It was all she could do to keep hold of herself and do what she was told. RC finessed guilt and sorrow with its filth and demented noise, the pervasive smell of rancid food, the arbitrary ever-shifting rules—walk on this side of the hall, no *that* side of the hall—and the absurdist, make-up-the-rules-as-you-go-along games, such as how to get a sanitary napkin from the CO who had a case of them right there, beside her, in plain sight.

I need half a dozen, please, said Patsy. Six.

I'm out, said the guard.

But . . . Patsy could see in the cardboard box the soft, squarish corners of pads stacked like so many tiny mattresses. I really need at least one, she whispered. It's kind of an emergency.

I just don't know what to tell you, said the guard.

So Patsy bled onto her socks, wearing and washing them in rotation.

•

She lost thirty pounds in her first month at RC. She had started out going to the dining room with the others, taking a tray and accepting the gravied meats, long-cooked vegetables, and powdered eggs, but it all had the same rankness, and she stopped being able to put any of it into her mouth. After she kicked the woman, she refused to go near the dining room. Patsy was five feet eleven inches tall, and in forty days she was down to a hundred and ten pounds.

One morning, she could not get warm. Her teeth chattered. She huddled under a blanket. Some women said, Look, she's turning blue. Someone went for Gloria, who had four or five women sit on the beds around Patsy, putting themselves between her and any CO. You're starving, Gloria told her. That's what's wrong with you.

Patsy shrugged.

I can get you some sugar water, for a start. Or you'll go into convulsions.

So what.

Yeah, but then they'll put you in the infirmary, said Gloria. And trust me, you don't want to go there. You're shackled to the bed in a room full of lunatics. You pee and crap on yourself. They don't care. Nobody looks in on you.

I don't care, said Patsy.

Gloria looked up and down the dormitory and at the backs of the women sitting on the nearby beds. Well, you're going to have to find something to care about, Patsy, she said. Or you're going to die in here.

I know, Patsy said, and began to cry, not because she might die, but because, to her shame, she couldn't go through with it, she wanted to live.

Gloria stood close and made an occasional humming noise and didn't touch her, because in prison there was no such thing as touching for consolation or mere warmth, not here, not even between people who understood such gestures, who could differentiate between pure and clouded intentions.

When Patsy calmed down, Gloria gave her a paper cup of sugar water and, when that stayed down, said, Would you eat some crackers for me?

Patsy managed two saltines. An hour later, two more.

How 'bout this, Gloria said that evening. Would you take a job if I could arrange it?

What kind of job?

In the kitchen, with me.

Maybe. Patsy said this not because she wanted to work, but because she couldn't spurn any kindness under these circumstances.

In the kitchen, Patsy found hot water. She would wash her arms, her armpits, her face. Hot, scalding water proved a saving grace. And in the storeroom she located a crate of saltines and, with Gloria keeping watch, stole a handful every morning, although the theft, if detected, could have cost her additional prison time. She ate other things that could be washed under the hottest water: an apple, a banana. She didn't gain much weight, but she survived her last three weeks in RC, at the end of which another bus took her and nineteen other women north.

5

The mother and daughter she'd killed found Patsy again at Bertrin, a men's prison off Interstate 5, where one wing had been allocated for a women's minimum-to-medium security unit.

Bertrin did not look like any kind of school. It looked like a prison. Billowing tangles of razor wire topped twenty-foot hurricane fences. Men with rifles could be seen in the two towers. Nearby stockyards infused the air with the cloying, almost sweet stink of manure.

Patsy, being a low—level two—security risk, was housed in an open dorm; had she been more violent, she would have been assigned to a cell. This time she and fifteen other women were to live in one large room divided up into cell-sized areas by thigh-high cinder-block partitions. Each partition contained a bunk bed and two lockboxes chained to the wall, two shelflike desks. Her bunkmate, Rhoda, a morose, quiet woman in her late forties, had already claimed the upper mattress.

Some of the women had knitted or crocheted or quilted blankets and bedspreads, and useless yellow curtains flanked the windows. Rhoda had a small nightstand with drawers, provenance unknown, that Patsy had to squeeze past every time she left and returned to her bunk. Their neighbor had a wobbly chair. Treasures.

A large plate-glass expanse separated the dorm from a guard station and dayroom, an open space with eight widely spaced round concrete tables and benches bolted to the floor. This dayroom served two dorms, with a bank of toilets and showers, also behind plate glass, between them. There was a kitchen they could use across the way, as well as a separate TV room with pink fiberglass bucket chairs and a small seminar-style classroom for groups and meetings. The telephone, a modified pay machine sunk into a stainless-steel counter, was in an alcove behind the guard station.

Twice a day, after breakfast and before dinner, the women lined up in front of their dorms for count. Count lasted from ten minutes to an hour, if someone wasn't speaking up or the COs had something to say.

The guard station/dayroom cluster, with its dorms and amenities, was called a cottage, a term Patsy took to be intentionally ironic, as nothing could less resemble the small, scenic dwelling the word implied. (She later learned that women prisoners were once housed in real cottages, with the idea that a safe, attractive home could rehabilitate. The term had since devolved to mean the number of women such a cottage once accommodated: thirty-two.)

Patsy knew roughly half of her cottage mates from RC. Ruth was in her dorm; Annie and Gloria were in the adjacent one.

Her gym bag was restored to her, so she could wear her own sweater and underwear. A package from her mother arrived with more clothes and books, a saucepan.

Patsy signed up one day to use the telephone, called her mother the next. Mom, Mom, you there? she yelled over a steady buzz of static. Can you hear me? How's Dad?

Mommy Mommy can ooo hear me? The echo, in sarcastic baby talk, came from a large, ferocious-looking woman from her dorm named Joyce, who waited to make a call.

Are you okay, hon? Her mother's voice wobbled in and out. Can I send you any . . . you heard that Burt is apply—

This call is from the California Correctional Institution for Women . . .

I need books, Mom. Paperbacks only. And clothes, but remember to leave the prices on . . . The cord was short. Patsy had to cozy up against a small, sagging stainless-steel shelf. What did you say about Burt? Mom?

Burdy burdy burdy, sang the voice behind her.

Yes, but what books, Patsy? Can you speak up?

This call is from the California Correctional Institution for Women . . .

Any kind. Novels. Biographies.

Okay, hon . . . see what I . . . The cadence of closure already sounded in her mother's voice. Your father's going to be so upset he missed . . .

But what about Burt? Did he get the transfer?

This call is from the California Correctional Institution for Women . . .

We'll see you soon, sweetheart . . .

Mommy mommy mom-eeeeee. Joyce lumbered up to the phone.

•

At Bertrin, there were no drugs or alcohol, for the simple reason, Glo-ria said, that the guards were searched when they came on shift. The staff in general seemed less sadistic than their RC counterparts, more like weary civil servants, their games less practiced and cruel. Still, Patsy did what she could to stay below their radar.

She never went to the dining room, for it exuded the exact same sour odor as RC's. She relied on the commissary, which was like a badly stocked convenience store. On her allotted forty dollars a month, she bought off-brand raisin bran, tuna fish, and ramen noodles. She boiled the ramen at odd hours in the kitchen, taking the cheap aluminum saucepan back to her locker after each use.

Patsy wrote letters and read books on her bunk. Big, nineteenth-century American novels: Wharton, Howells, Twain. She'd always heard there was time in prison. Time to read, to write, to make yourself into a lawyer. Nobody mentioned that the time was filled with the am-bient sounds of women raging, gates clanging, an ever-crackling public-address system.

Lights-out was marginally dimmer here than at RC, so sleep was deeper, once Patsy got there. Now, as she closed her eyes, the plump thirty-four-year-old woman and her adolescent girl rose to mind as if emerging from some dark lake, drenched and inscrutable, their faces in shadow. Patsy could not have recognized them on the street, yet here they presented themselves night after night, bringing a wave of guilt so black and suffocating, Patsy never believed it would pass.

•

When the guard led her parents into the loud, filthy visiting hall, Patsy blamed her mother's pallor on the gauntlet of metal detectors and frisks and the two-hour wait to see her. Both parents seemed forlorn, old, and fragile, but her mother looked ill, her skin pale, her belly oddly swollen. Patsy wept throughout their visit. Mom, don't come again, Patsy told her. We'll talk on the phone, we'll write. Send Dad and Burt. Don't go through this again.

We'll see how it goes, honey, she said.

Her father and Burt alternated after that. Her friend Sarah made the tedious four-hour drive from Pasadena once. Otherwise, Brice was her most regular visitor, showing up every month or so. Patsy first wondered at this constancy, so missing when they were lovers, then came to rely on it. He always caused a stir in the visiting room. Some women were convinced he was a movie star or Paul Newman's brother. A somebody.

Patsy, and all the others, lived for letters, proof they weren't forgotten.

I went down to Altadena last week and met with your new tenants, wrote Burt. *He's postdoc at Caltech—microbiology—and she's an economist looking for work.*

Your father prays for you every night, her mother wrote. *I hear him in the kitchen talking to his Higher Power.*

Sarah wrote, *I miss you, I worry about you, please let me know what I can do, what I can send you to read.*

•

Gloria and Annie half hoisted her between them. Flattered that they bothered, she went along.

Nine women sat in a circle in the classroom behind the guard station. Gloria and Annie, of course, and Ruth too, who wasn't a drunk but applied the program to her pyromania—*I am powerless over setting fires.*

Yvonne told of having her kids taken away and shooting up her pimp with bad heroin. Barbi described waiting tables drunk, spilling soup and drinks on customers. Gail's mother got her drunk the first time when she was six. All the women sang the glories of AA, of God, of not having to drink.

Patsy recoiled at the loser litanies and simplistic religiosity. She might have a genetic propensity for alcoholism, but she'd always stayed on track, accumulating degrees and honors and publications in spite of a concomitant taste for liquor, pharmaceuticals, and rich boy wastrels. She'd been valedictorian *and* Party Hardiest in high school, the first in her family to matriculate into a University of California grad school *and* a California correctional institution. She, at least, had range.

Not for me, Patsy told Gloria afterward. Besides, I'm not sure I want to give up alcohol for the rest of my life.

How 'bout one day at a time?

That's sophistry, said Patsy. Everybody knows it means forever.

They do? Gloria shrugged. So drink till you're done. Then, if you feel like a meeting, they're around. Oh, look, here's Ruth with coffee.

After the big show Gloria and Annie had made of dragging her to an AA meeting, she thought, they might have fought a little harder to make her stay.

•

Benny came to see her. This is a surprise, Patsy said.

I told you I was coming.

I mean the sport shirt. I've never seen you outside a suit. She pointed to the wall of vending machines. You buying?

They sat at one of the long metal picnic tables, chips and sodas between them. So, Benito, whassup? she said.

In fact, someone would like to visit you, Benny said. Someone not on your list. Mark Parnham?

Fear squeezed her veins shut.

Name ring a bell?

Don't be sadistic. What does he want?

To talk to you. Get to know you a little. You up for it?

Oh god. What could I say to him? But I should see him, if he wants that.

You don't have to. Or there can be a mediator.

I'll see him. But alone.

You'll have to put him on your list first.

And send him the questionnaire, thought Patsy. That would take at least a month to process. What does he want? she asked. Did he say?

To meet you. Talk. But it's up to you, Patsy.

How can I refuse him?

•

I have a new boyfriend, wrote Sarah. *Do you remember Henry Croft, in anthropology? We started talking at a party at Kelley's and haven't stopped since.*

I got that transfer, wrote Burt. *Bonnie and I both think life will be better for the kids once we get 'em off TV and onto ponies.*

Your father went out to get a haircut and came home with a used Vespa, her mother wrote. *I'm fit to be tied.*

•

Don't tell Larena you offed a couple JWs, said Gloria.

She one?

All day every day. Armageddon's comin', baby.

Larena lived in Gloria's dorm. She was twenty-two years old and in for cashing a bad check—here in minimum-to-medium, some women gabbed freely about their crimes in group. Patsy found Larena painting her nails in bed. Hey, Larena, can I ask you some things about Jehovah's Witnesses?

You want me to witness you? Course I will. Larena put down the tiny nailbrush, drew a newsprint magazine, *The Watchtower*, from under her pillow, and handed it to Patsy. On the cover, Jesus in robes looked askance at a big modern church. This will get you started, Larena said.

Patsy rolled the little tabloid into a tube. So what do you guys believe?

Larena blew on her orchid fingertips. Well, personally speaking, I've found that God is Jehovah, and my life is all about serving Him. His Kingdom is coming, and I'm just doing everything Jesus tells me till then.

Oh, so you believe in Jesus.

Well, sure. But we know Jesus isn't God. Only God is God. Jesus is King and God's son, but he's a human, same as us, only perfect. And he died on a torture stake and not a cross. That cross business come from pagan times and was just added to make pagans believe.

You sound like a Unitarian, said Patsy.

A what?

Never mind.

You know, Teach . . . Larena gazed at the floor beside her bed, where missing linoleum revealed ridges of crusty black mastic. This idn't the real world. The real world is yet to come. And it will be paradise. We'll all live in big ole mansions on wide bullyvards. So hurry up, Teach, time's running out on you.

When is this paradise supposed to come?

Nobody knows. They used to say dates, but that was a mistake. But there be plenty a warning. The earth'll crack open, the sky'll rain blood, the rivers, they'll boil up outta their banks. The walls of this ugly ole prison'll crumble down like Jericho. It'll be the big cleansing of the earth, just like Noah's time, only the angels'll come with their flaming swords to sort out the wheat from the chuff.

Her voice had risen almost into song.

But what about forgiveness? said Patsy. Where do you stand on that?

Oh, you gotta forgive. You gotta put shit behind you, or it eat you alive.

Yeah, but what about angels slashing everybody. Won't they forgive?

God give everybody all the time in the world to come to Him.

Ahh.

Larena handed her an *Awake!* and more *Watchtowers*.

Patsy scanned the little tabloids at her desk, searching for some hint about the sad man who had seemed so fair-minded in the courtroom. She had assumed such generosity was religious. She found an article about "community," but it only explained that JWs deplored churches and clergy—everyone taught god's word. Another article said god was angry at the world, the illustration a bearded white man in the clouds, clutching thunderbolts.

Patsy had harbored some religious sentiment as a child—she once dreamed that Jesus liked her in particular. But twelve years of Catholic education had eroded such feeling, and the two summers during high school when she worked in the parish office finished it off. The priests! Each had his own carton of milk in the refrigerator—whole milk, skim, half-and-half, liquid Coffee-mate—and each kept obsessive track of fluid levels, convinced the others were helping themselves. So many accusations, lost tempers, and hard feelings over dairy products! Later on, her training as a historian further demystified the Church and made Patsy immune, even hostile, to institutionalized faith. In every intro-level and survey class she taught, Patsy used the historical Jesus to demonstrate the rigor of historical scholarship. If we examine Jesus' life as historians and we look into *all* contemporaneous sources, she'd say in lectures, we are able to establish exactly three facts. Jesus was born, he ate some meals with people, and he died—possibly by crucifixion.

She'd wait for the murmur of discomfort, the hiss of disbelief, the secular titters, then add—And *that's it.*

•

In the hot, rank afternoon, the air heavy with stockyard fumes, Patsy left off reading and sank into a sticky near-sleep, where once again she dreamed of taking the big, sweeping left turn to home, only to see in the old Mercedes' headlights the two in their white blouses and dark skirts, the mother's mouth round in surprise. Then the booms and thumps, a spray of stars, a veering off, leaves brushing metal, a small white hand sliding off a dark fender.

Jesus fucking Christ. Patsy kicked her legs to wake up, opened her eyes, took more breaths, then turned on her side. In the heat and ricocheting noise, she sought another route to sleep and this time wandered past mansion after mansion under towering elms along broad, deserted streets.

6

Unlike her mother, who would not accept the extravagantly surcharged collect calls when her father wasn't there, eternally broke Brice never once turned down the prison operator. Would you do me a favor? Patsy asked him. Would you find out about Mark Parnham?

What about him?

General stuff. He wants to see me, and I want a sense of him first. Don't talk to him or anything. But if you could check him out somehow, find out if he's as nice as he seems.

●

Long, loud, too-bright clanging days passed. The deputy warden offered her a job teaching high school history and English geared to the high school equivalency test. She met nine students three times a week for two-hour sessions. Half her students, including Larena, read at or under fourth-grade level. Twenty-seven cents an hour was deposited in her commissary account.

Lying on her bunk in sticky October heat, what Gloria said drifted back to her, about drinking till you were done. *Done.* Could *she* ever be done with alcohol? All that fun! Collapsing into a chair with a good stiff drink. Starting to make dinner by pouring herself a glass of red wine—was there a better moment in the day? If a drink was large enough and strong enough, the very first sip relaxed her, filled her with well-being. Could she ever be done with such fast, effective relief?

Her father's sobriety had been such an effort, such an event, the great life-changing hinge in the whole family history. *Before*, all was shouting, late-night smashings, and creepy-wet bourbon-scented bedtime kisses. *After* was the incessant low talking and intermittent laughter of men in the house at night, the phone always ringing with calls from sponsors, sponsees, strangers trying not to drink, a whole household industry of sobriety. And meetings, meetings for everyone, for her dad, her mom, even meetings for Burt and her. How she hated those church classrooms with the small chairs, the too-kindly adult, the other children weirdly eager to describe their parents' cruelty and misbehavior.

Sobriety was her father's greatest accomplishment. How pathetic!

But *drinking till you're done*—the phrase implied a natural cessation, no force or rupture. How appealing to think she might one day have had enough, and walk away into the rest of her life without craving or a thundering sense of loss. The idea offered release, and the mental clarity of a thin, clean pane of glass.

Possibly, she was already done. Hard to be sure. At Bertrin no little jars appeared, no tempting, cloudy tinctures distilled from rotting cornflakes.

Afternoons, before final count, she'd see women in the meeting room, their chairs in a ragged circle. They were laughing in there.

•

Brice was escorted into the visiting hall. A few low whistles greeted him, and he waved jauntily to the whistlers. Stop it, Patsy whispered as he reached her. She dreaded calling attention to herself, even by proxy. I'm not kidding, she hissed. Nobody's supposed to talk to other visitors. You'll get us all thrown out.

Hi there, Brice, he said, overriding her. So nice of you to drive four hours just to tell me the poop on Mr. P. that you so thoughtfully unearthed.

So nice, she said. I mean it. It's just . . . She gave a wild glance around the room, then smiled at his face. You look good, great—that's a terrific haircut. You're a marvelous human. Now, tell me everything.

Do you really like the cut? You don't think it's a little froufrou in back?

And the sides. And front, especially the front.

Brice grinned and touched his tarnished blond hair.

They sat down at one end of a concrete picnic table. Another couple sat on the opposite end, hands clutched across the table.

She and Brice did not clasp hands. Your guy lives in West Altadena, near the arroyo, he said. I looked him up in the phone book. A little ranch house, I cruised it—don't worry, nobody was home. One of those fifties stucco jobs tarted up with wood siding. Fruit trees in the front lawn. Kid's toys lying around. Guy could use a gardener, and arborist.

Did you see him? Or the kid?

Nobody was home. But—Brice paused dramatically—the house next door was for sale, and I disturbed the occupant. Said I was on the verge of an offer, but since I was moving because of bad neighbors, I didn't want to repeat the problem. She was young, her husband was at the Jet Propulsion Lab but had been transferred to Cape Canaveral. At first she talked to me through the screen door, but I got her out on the stoop. She told me right away about your guy and what happened. His son is her son's best friend, and she'd had both father and son over for dinner a lot since the accident. They'd become close, she said, and that hadn't been the case when the man's wife was alive. Not that the wife wasn't nice, but— Do you want to hear this, Patsy? Brice stopped, checked Patsy's face.

Every word, Patsy said, though she was already weirdly cold.

I guess Mrs. P. was extremely shy. She'd bring this neighbor lady bags of fruit from her trees, but leave them on the porch without knocking. The only time she ever went inside the neighbor's house was right after she became a Jehovah's Witness. To convert her.

I can't believe you found all this out, whispered Patsy.

And that's just for starters, said Brice, turning to look at a woman at the next table over who was humming at him.

Hah, baby, whispered the humming woman. Hah, handsome.

Brice, Patsy hissed. What else?

He turned back. Let's see. Yeah, well, I asked the neighbor lady, Isn't the husband a JW too? And she was like, Oh no, god no, not even close. He hated that his wife got all caught up with that.

He's not a Jehovah's Witness?

Defiantly not. Distrusts them. After the accident, a dozen Witnesses got to the hospital before he did. Some janitor there had put the word out. At first your guy was really touched, you know, that her church group had rallied, but soon it was obvious that they'd only come to talk him out of authorizing a transfusion. They don't believe in transfusions.

I can't believe she told you all this, said Patsy.

Oh, she was a talker, said Brice. Of course he did authorize a transfusion.

Of course, said Patsy. Boy. You hit the gold mine.

Yeah, though I also had to hear about the guy on the other side who parks his RV right by her bedroom window, and the witch across the street . . .

I owe you, said Patsy.

Teach? *Teach!* One of the women a few tables away whispered sharply. He's on a show, ain't he, Teach?

Patsy turned further away from the woman.

C'mon, Patsy, called another woman, sotto voce. Just say what show.

She can't say, Brice stage-whispered to the second woman.

He's on a show! I knew it, I tole you, the woman crowed.

Don't, please, Patsy murmured to Brice. I have to live with them.

•

As she courted sleep at night, Patsy drifted now to West Altadena, to the little orchard with the thick grass that the man was too grief-stricken or overwhelmed to mow. Or perhaps the woman had always mowed it, steering a push mower around slim-trunked trees laden with plums and nectarines, the daughter raking up behind. She imagined them in long skirts and long-sleeved blouses, working with the patience of former centuries, gathering fruit into wooden buckets or galvanized pails, fruit for pies and cobblers and preserves in clear glass jars, fruits parceled into bags and distributed through the neighborhood. And then, the orchard was untended, the fruit swelling and softening and falling into the thick grass, where it burst and rotted and was eaten by ants.

•

You win, Patsy whispered to Gloria as they began to say their names around the room. Annie, alcoholic. Rondene, ack-aholic.

Patsy, she said at her turn.

Good to see you, whispered Gloria.

The dad wants to meet with me, Patsy said. I have to do something.

The next afternoon, they asked Patsy to lead the meeting.

In for a dime, in for a dollar, Patsy said, and recounted her life of heedless careening, only to fill the room with laughter. I went to classes drunk. I lectured undergraduates about my sex life. I lectured bartenders on military history. I peed in my office wastebasket, then held office hours. Drunk, I'd sleep with anyone in my path—boys, girls, husbands, wives, students, teachers. That's what I'm told. There's much I don't remember. I used to call people to find out if I had fun the night before or caused another disaster.

And this kid, Ernest Cruikshank. Funny I remember his name. His chippy little girlfriend was bawling in my office: Your own student. How could you?

I had no idea what I'd done. I told her not to worry—as far as I knew, it never happened. Even my old boyfriend Brice yelled at me once for feeding his little niece booze and piercing her ears. The girl was fine, but his mom—the girl's grandmother—yelled at him for subjecting her to lowlife like me.

A woman named Nel whispered to Patsy at the break that she too had hit someone with her car in a blackout, in her case, a policeman waving her through an intersection. She'd broken his leg, and a rib that nicked his lung. He was still alive, healed up in fact, and there in court to see her sentenced, the dickhead. Nel got five years, would be out in three, her lawyer clearly not as skilled as Benny.

The next morning, Patsy woke up, sick with shame. In telling her stories, she'd heard them for the first time herself. The ease with which she'd dispensed cruelties! She'd never considered herself thoughtless or immoral. Fun, a little hell-bent, maybe, impulsive, but always amusing. And basically a good person. Now, seeing the miles driven drunk, the pranks, the commitments ignored, the marriages violated, and her obliviousness throughout, she seemed despicable.

Was there ever coming back from such actions? Or does a person round some bend and the path back is lost for good?

And she still hadn't sent Mark Parnham the questionnaire. The simplest request by her main victim, and she'd put it off.

Gloria told her to write a list of people she'd hurt when drunk, then write letters to them all. *Sorry I got your boyfriend/husband/kids drunk . . .* , she wrote. *Sorry I had sex with . . . Sorry I borrowed your camel coat and those Italian books and lost them. Sorry I smashed your garage door, sorry too about the crape myrtle. Sorry I fed you pills and alcohol and pierced your ears.*

Dear Benny,

I want to make amends for my ingratitude and all the ostensibly clever but actually very rude things I said as you were really in there, trying to save my life.

Not all the letters were sent, only those that wouldn't reopen wounds or injure afresh. It never occurred to her that people would write back.

We're so proud of you, darling.

I appreciate your forthrightness. But I forgave you years ago.

I was not surprised, her former best friend Hannah wrote,

to hear you were in prison. Sooner or later somebody was going to have the good sense to lock you up—though I'm sure you've already found some married guard to schtup, or someone else's girlfriend, someone too weak or kind to deflect your freight-train come-ons. Patsy, you say you're sorry and want to make amends to me? You want to know how to do that? Cross me off your list! Never contact me again! That's the only true amend you could ever make to me.

Sincerely, H.

And this:

Dear Patsy,

I got your letter. I hope you are all right. I'm fine but I don't like school this year. I have boring teachers except for English.

I am on a big reading binge lately, are you? The best thing I read lately is The Alexandria Quartet which is actually 4 books in 1 box. Uncle Brice gave it to me for my birthday. (I just turned 14!)

About what you said in your letter. Don't feel bad about the beer and stuff. You didn't see me, but I stole a pill from your purse and took the whole thing. That's why I was so sleepy that night. Don't worry about piercing my ears, either. I really wanted them pierced. Anyway, the second my grandmother saw me wearing earrings she made me take them out. My ears grew right back.

Yours Truly, Joey Hawthorne

·

Still going to meetings, Pats?

As always, her father was too interested, too hopeful.

Don't, she said. She hated the flaring of hope in his eyes. Then she hated the fear that replaced it.

I go, she said.

Thatagirl.

What else is there to do? Patsy studied the other families in the visiting room and thought about her list of those she had harmed, one of whom was her father. In college, she'd stolen three hundred and fifty dollars from him. He'd overpaid her tuition one quarter and the bursar sent her the refund check. If she'd told him about it at the time, he probably would have told her to keep the money. But she cashed the check and spent it recklessly, pointedly, paying for drinks and meals until all of it was gone.

Women were in Bertrin for stealing less. Larena got two years for paying rent with a two-hundred-dollar check drawn on a closed account—granted, not her first offense. And fifty-nine-year-old Rondene pulled two years for cashing a $137 welfare check nicked from a neighbor's mailbox—though Rondene's case was different. She didn't even need the money. I jus loves to steal! *Loves* it! she told Patsy. I cain't wait to get outta this place and steal some more!

She couldn't pay her father back, not now. She'd write him a check one day when she was out.

Guess what, Dad? she said, and again, his face ignited with hope.

I might go to fire camp in February, she said. I have to run a ten-minute mile and be able to do ten men's push-ups and chin-ups. But it's safer and easier time, and outdoors. This older woman I know, Gloria, qualified, so I don't see why I won't.

Oh, Patsy, he said, his eyes filled with tears.

•

MacLemoore!

She woke to darkness dropping away, a black wing swooping past.

What's that?

No tenting, you know that.

Oh, CO Hefferton, the night witch. Patsy rubbed her face to wake up and determined that Rhoda overhead had kicked aside her blanket so it curtained the lower bunk—and looked like tenting, what women did here for privacy, sex.

Do it again, I'll write you up.

Rhoda kicked off her blanket the next night too—hot flashes, she said—but another CO was on and didn't care or notice. Sensitized, Patsy soon woke up on cue when the blankets fell, gloried briefly in the fleeting darkness and seclusion, then yanked the blankets to the floor. A write-up could cost her a chance at fire camp.

Eventually the two women swapped bunks. Patsy liked it up high, where the acoustic tiles blurred into chalky landscapes, and something about the altitude recalled the dorms at St. Catherine's, her high school, and lolling around with the boarders there, eating cookies by the sackful, smoking cigarettes leaning out of windows. Prison, she thought again, was not unrelated to milder institutions. Those small-town rich girls, like her dorm mates at Bertrin, had also mocked her intelligence.

Not until she got to Berkeley had she found kindred minds, male and female. She'd met her first Jews too, who were city-bred, cultured, political, as exotic to her as royalty. She'd vowed to marry a Jewish intellectual. How they'd talked and argued, mostly about books. And how everybody drank. Closing bars. Straggling up Telegraph, University, in the fog-socked dawn.

Even then some said, We can't keep up with you, Patsy.

The story of her life: nobody could keep up.

She'd always balanced her excesses with hard work. She held it together, or thought she had, until she applied for jobs. Neither of the two tenure-track positions she'd been asked to apply for had come through. Pomona had courted her so assiduously, she'd gone apartment hunting while interviewing. But the offer never arrived. She had no idea what happened until last April, a few weeks before the accident, when she'd run into one of the search committee members at a conference in Irvine. He admitted that during her candidating, she'd been a little too . . . *hilarious* with a waiter. You know, on the social night, he said. When they take you out and get you drunk to see what you'll do? No, no, you weren't inappropriate, not exactly, but maybe not so appropriate either, not for an interview. Later, if you were already on board, nobody would've taken issue . . .

Something similar must have happened at ASU, since the faculty chair there said that her lecture on Jim Crow was the most incisive she'd ever heard. Patsy's third choice, UMass, had passed on her as well, but that was expected, she wasn't really nineteenth century, as they'd specified and eventually hired. She ended up at her fourth choice, the small, second-rate trade school turned liberal arts college in Pasadena, where the department was so pleased to get her, they knocked a class off her schedule.

Good old pedestrian Hallen College. Her department chair, Wes, said they would take her back when she came out. They had no clause forbidding felons. A couple profs in criminology had done hard time, he said, and that had only added grit and weight to their teaching. Of course Wes had heard the legal version, that she'd swung into her driveway too fast at dusk, the hard-to-see time, and accidentally killed two people, a tragedy that could happen to anyone.

•

I'm having a hard time with the note, she told Benny.

Just send him the damn questionnaire, he said. It's been months already.

I should write something. Or it comes across as too cold.

You know, Patsy, you don't have to see him.

It's the least I can do. Even if he just wants to yell at me.

He won't yell, said Benny. He just wants to talk about what happened. And I think he's concerned about you. That's the impression I get.

He's concerned about me?

Well, Jesus, Patsy, who isn't?

•

What if she and Mark Parnham met and fell in love? What if they already were, a little? She imagined them collapsing into each other's arms, blindly burrowing into each other's bodies, love neutralizing grief, extinguishing guilt. Could they make a life from that?

Even she would have to say, Impossible.

•

Please know that I've stopped drinking and am active in a program to help me maintain my sobriety so that I will never drive drunk again.

That could only be cold comfort to him.

I grieve for them. I hope to lead my life in a way that somehow pays homage to their lives.

Me me me. Too much about me. She crumpled the paper, lobbed it into the brown sack she used for trash, her aim improving.

The mother and daughter hovered right where her peripheral vision ended. So what should I say? she asked them. And while we're at it, what does he want?

The two stirred, shifted, gave nothing away.

After Christmas came good news, and she wrote:

Benny A. says that you wish to meet with me, and if that's still true, in about a month I'll be transferred to an honor work camp near Malibu. It's much closer to you and will be a much easier place to visit than where I am now. I hope to see you there.

Sincerely, Patsy MacLemoore

7

Handcuffed and shackled (feet and waist) for the ride south, Patsy sat in the front of the van with the driver. Two male convicts, likewise cuffed and shackled, and a male guard occupied bench seats in the back. Patsy expected her spirits to lift after passing through Bertrin's gates, but there was nothing gladdening in the heavy stink of the stockyards and the dirt-brown low hills. The men muttered among themselves behind her. Their chains clinked softly. The scenery did not change. The sun shone through her window, and she dozed in its warmth.

She opened her eyes when the van slowed. They were leaving the freeway in Bakersfield. Big treat, the driver announced, and pulled into the drive-through lane at a Wendy's—unbelievably, the same Wendy's she'd frequented in high school. The same plate-glass windows and blue vinyl booths, the usual truckers and roughnecks who'd hissed and made kissing noises at her and her girlfriends. Three miles due east, a flat, easy bike ride away, her parents were no doubt home in their house on the fairway, on Clubhouse Drive.

The driver bought them cheeseburgers, french fries, and chocolate shakes. Biting into the hot, crisped meat brought tears to her eyes. Melted cheese and mayonnaise oozed onto her knuckles. She got lost in the saltiness, the juice, the warm, moist layered thickness of the burger pressed against her face. They all ate without speaking, rummaging in their french fry bags and gulping like dogs.

Less than an hour later, salty saliva flooded her mouth. Oh no, she said, Officer? They were on the interstate, between exits, so she looked frantically for a litterbag or receptacle. Finding nothing suitable, she tucked her knees to one side and vomited onto the van's floor, her retching loud and helpless, like a strange and desperate form of sobbing. This made one of the men behind her gag too.

Oh Jesus shit, the other convict said. Shit shit. You stinking sons of bitches. If you can't hold your burgers, don't eat 'em.

Hell, the sick man said. It was as good coming up as it was going down.

Bile stung high in her throat, behind her nose. Her eyes watered. She was weeping, it seemed, and no longer fit for regular food. The driver got off at Frazer Park and had them clean up in a gas station parking lot, the job hampered by handcuffs and shackles and the van's interior carpet. She scooped up her mess with paper towels and, shuffling and clanking alongside the guard, carried the clump to the Dumpster behind the station. On the other side of the Dumpster was a berm of filthy snow and acres of high desert scrubland before the scraggly town of Frazer Park. She stood for a moment taking in the cold air, the sweep of pewter-colored mountains. She imagined slipping off into the scrub, then up a canyon, evading pursuers, sleeping curled around a campfire on the dirt.

The guard grunted, and as Patsy turned to go back to the van, a teenage girl came out of the restroom and registered the shackles with a visible start. No doubt curious to see who wore such things, the girl looked directly into Patsy's face. Patsy met the gaze with frank coldness—eight months in prison had made her fluent in intimidation. The girl averted her eyes and scuttled.

I must remember that for students, thought Patsy.

•

They reached the camp in the green hills north of Malibu in the late afternoon, when the light was pale and fuzzing up with marine moisture. Two guards met them at the entrance and performed a cursory search of the van before activating the gate. Then they zigzagged up the side of a grassy hill to a parking pad beside a Spanish-style building. Two female COs met them. The driver came around and let Patsy out of the van. He removed her handcuffs and shackles. These're Bertrin's, he said, as if she'd try to claim them.

Patsy was taken to an office, where she filled out forms. In a smaller room, she was given a swift strip search by a red-haired female CO, then handed a bundle of used jeans, T-shirts and flannel shirts, the usual toiletries, and bedding. Next stop was across the courtyard at the clinic, where an older prisoner rubbed Neosporin into her raw wrists and ankles. You ready to work? the prisoner said. Cuz here, honey, they put you to work.

The redheaded CO, Sweeney, took her into an equipment room and had her try on leather firefighting boots, knee-high and laced up, until she found a comfortable pair. You'll need them starting tomorrow, she said, and carried the selected pair as she led Patsy to her barracks. They passed three women crouched in a vegetable garden, and through the windows of the first barracks Patsy saw someone sweeping. Otherwise the place appeared deserted. On the other side of the high hurricane fence was a eucalyptus forest, tall dark trees standing deep in their own shed bark.

The camp's layout and rustic charm seemed familiar; the public area looked like a California mission with its courtyard, fountain, and fruit trees. The barracks were stacked like stairs on the hillside and looked down through pine trees to the mirroring sea.

In the third barracks Patsy was shown to a row of iron cots with lockboxes chained to their legs. Lumpy, hand-knotted rag rugs sat next to two of the beds. Desks were built into the walls.

Toilets are there, Sweeney pointed. Patsy stuck her head in to see two stalls, with doors. Only six of you here at present, Sweeney said. They're out on the bus till five. It's four now, so you might want to shower before they get back, or you'll never get in. Dinner at five-thirty. Any questions?

When was this place built? Patsy asked.

In the Depression, said Sweeney. By the California Conservation Corps.

Camp Ohwanakee in the Sierras, her own Catholic summer camp, had been another CCC project, more alpine, but with a similar layout. The familiarity was disconcerting, in the way places merged in dreams: I was at camp, only it was also a prison . . .

Patsy was making up her bed when a woman appeared in the doorway. I'm Lima, she said. Is there anything you need?

No, thanks.

I'm grounded with a sprained wrist—she held up a wrapped arm. Black prongs of gang graffiti poked out of the Ace bandage. Can I come in?

I need to shower now, Patsy said. She knew nothing about this Lima and had no interest in her.

I could come back.

That's okay.

Do you have a cigarette?

Don't smoke.

You got coffee?

A woman's voice from outside: Leave her be, Acevedo.

Ramen?

Acevedo! said the voice.

Patsy opened her lockbox and started placing her possessions inside. When she had finished, Lima was gone. The door hung open. Wind soughed through the trees.

•

First wake-up was 4:45 a.m., followed by a general scrabbling in the darkness. Someone said, If you want breakfast before hike, come on.

You want eggs, tell Gloria, another roommate said.

Gloria!

And there she was at the food window, with a pencil.

The camp has its own laying hens, she told Patsy, but when I got here, all the cook set out was a tub of scrambled dry. A waste of fresh eggs. You better have three if you want to make it through PT.

Patsy's eggs came, scrambled soft, impossibly yellow, fluffy, and rich.

PT—physical training—was a daily hike, two to three hours long. Patsy and four other new inmates were last in the line. Today's route was "the Burn," six miles into the mountains behind the camp and back. The women moved fast, and Patsy trotted along, kept up as best she could. Sun, ocean, and green hills pulsed in rhythm with her heartbeat. Some of the women sang, but she barely heard them over her own hoarse breath.

You people mean business, she said to a CO bringing up the rear.

You'll feel it tonight, but you'll get used to it.

Somebody farted, to general laughter.

Wait'll the downhill, an inmate called back. They fart like horses.

But this trail was all uphill. Only at the very end did they swerve into a gulch and half run, half slide a mile down to camp, and Patsy forgot to listen.

Lunch was a tuna sandwich, a mealy apple. Patsy got up from the table, and her thighs were sore to the touch. Her face was tight and pink, as if scalded. She'd have to ask her mom to send sunscreen. But she was lucky, no work detail today. It was Sunday, visiting day. She slept straight through till dinner.

Monday's hike, "Eternity," was not as steep as the Burn, but three miles and an hour longer, ridge after ridge, the ocean a steady aluminum shimmer below. They came back and, without showering, loaded onto the two camp buses—con buggies, they were called. This is a little on-the-job training, a CO said. Patsy's bus went miles inland to a public campground where two ten-woman crews cleared firebreaks using Pulaskis—a heavy hybrid ax, maul, and hoe—which proved very versatile; they hacked through root systems, chopped down saplings, and, when swung at a precise angle, sliced like scalpels through the most matted duff to hard, mineral dirt.

After a twenty-minute break for lunch (peanut butter and jelly sandwiches, milk gulped from small cartons like first graders) the women worked, with water breaks, till four, when the bus took them back.

They don't call it work camp for nothin', Patsy's roommate, Antonia, said.

Patsy went to bed before lockdown. The front windows of the barracks were many-paned, like a classroom. She looked out through the pine trees, over wrinkled green hills, all the way down to the sea, a smear of fading light.

Five a.m. came many hours too soon.

•

At Bertrin, Patsy had been in with petty, unmalicious felons—drug users, wallet-filching prostitutes, check kiters—but in Malibu she lived with killers, assaulters, armed robbers, anyone who'd done good time and had fewer than two years left to serve. Every other woman, it seemed, had stabbed or shot or poisoned some man, although Antonia confided that she was in for killing her mom.

Your *mother*?

A doozy, huh? said Antonia. I was thirteen.

She'd come to Malibu from the California Youth Authority a year ago. The mix is better here, she told Patsy, not like the CYA, where it's all gangs and the guards have at the girls and you gotta put out to get anything. Here, it's all weedin' to freedom. I could've got out at twenty-one if I'd shown remorse, but the situation was more complicated than that.

•

Lookouts. Communication. Escape routes. Safety zones. Those were the LCES, the *laces* of fire crew safety.

Patsy was studying on her bunk before lights-out when Lima walked in and lifted her T-shirt. A flat pint of bourbon gleamed brown in her waistband.

A huge part of Patsy sprang to attention with longing and terror. Get out of here, she said, then heard Lima shooed away, bed to bed, like a raccoon in a campground.

Gloria had mentioned that someone was throwing booze over the fence.

Weighing the brown gleam against a clear mind, Patsy couldn't sleep. *Someday, maybe, but not now.* Drinking would undo what small part of herself she'd managed to gather up in prison. Plus, she had her fire-safety exam in the morning. And Mark Parnham was coming on Sunday.

8

He was smaller than Patsy remembered. He had a short, clipped mustache on a long, narrow face, a loose chin. His proportions were odd—too long a head, or too-short limbs, Patsy couldn't pin it. He was reserved, conventional, a chamber of commerce sort; that was a red Tournament of Roses badge on his ivory Windbreaker.

They sat at a picnic table under a large pergola in the visiting yard. Thank you for letting me come, he said, surveying the lawn where families picnicked and the track surrounding it where others walked. How is it here?

Better than where I was, she said. I like being outside all day.

You fought any fires?

Fall is fire season, she said. For now, we've been clearing hillsides, shoring up trails, cleaning up campgrounds. She resisted showing him her hands, blistered despite gloves. And you? she asked. What do you do?

Civil engineer, he said. I just now started back. I don't know if you heard, but I took nine months off to be with my son.

She shook her head. Brice's informant had not relayed this.

After the accident, he said, I went back to work and my mother-in-law watched Martin. But I called him all the time, went by at lunch, made a general pest of myself, till my pastor suggested I take a leave to be with him. Best advice I've ever gotten. That, and to join a grief group.

I joined a group too, Patsy said, thinking that groups were like nets strung around the world to catch people as they raced off the cliffs. Only a few were bagged, embraced, set to right.

One of the reasons I wanted to see you, Mark said quietly, is I'm having a hard time picturing what happened.

He wanted to know how a car going five or ten miles an hour could kill two people. And after they were hit, were they conscious at all? Had they suffered? That's what haunted him, what he couldn't bear the thought of—their suffering. The leader of his grief group encouraged him to contact Patsy. Perhaps she could help him, perhaps she saw something.

I have only the faintest idea what happened, said Patsy. I remember they were wearing white blouses and dark blue skirts.

No, he said. Jessie was in jeans and a puffy jacket that she called her sleeping-bag coat. And Jane had on a pink pantsuit. I know. I brought those clothes home from the hospital.

I'm sorry, Patsy said. But my driveway is uphill and you have to accelerate to get up it, and probably that's what happened. I probably hit the gas. It was a very heavy, big old Mercedes.

I see, he said.

Maybe we should walk, she said, pointing to the track around the picnic area. Come, let's walk.

The afternoon in early April was chilly in the shade, warming up in the sun. The long grass on the hills rippled in the breeze like a pelt.

I'm sorry I don't remember, she said.

I didn't come just for that, he said. I also just wanted to see you and talk like this. Face-to-face. It's a relief.

You know, she said, her voice rising. If there was a way to undo it, for it never to have happened . . .

I know, he said. I know you never meant—

I swear, given the choice, I would trade places in a—

Oh, he said. You don't have to say—

I would. I would change places. Seriously. It's so wrong the way things are, with me being alive while they . . . Patsy saw that her blurted apologies were distasteful to him. I'm sorry, she said. I wish there was something I could do. And once I get out, I will, I'll do whatever I can.

Gloria, arm in arm with her long-haired daughter, strolled past them. Gloria raised an eyebrow at Patsy in a way both challenging and comic.

I heard the homeowner's insurance came through, Patsy said in the same nervous pitch. And I'm glad. But I want to do more for you, and your son.

I didn't come for anything like that, he said. The tones of impatience and anger in his voice relieved her and seemed more natural than his unrelenting kindness. He *should* despise her, and find her mea culpas wearisome.

They walked in silence in the rotation of residents and guests. Fast white clouds cast intermittent shadows over them. Seagulls wheeled and cried.

I was at Sears with Martin when it happened, Mark Parnham said. We got home, and a squad car was parked in front of our house. I knew right away the news was bad. The detective said they had you in custody, and that you'd been extremely upset. So I thought you had seen what happened.

Patsy was gratified to learn her response to the accident. Nobody had mentioned it before. I'm sorry, she said. I don't remember any of that.

But you see that I had to ask, he said. The detective was a student of yours. He said you were a great teacher.

Ricky's a good guy, she said, although she'd never thought that before.

They both got lost for a moment, watching their steps where the dirt track had eroded.

With blackouts, said Patsy, you never remember what went on. Before he got sober, my father would tear apart the house at night, and the next morning he'd say, Hey—what happened to the living room?

They passed a Latino family, two girls holding their mother's hand, a third following with her hand hitched to her mother's back pocket.

I've been to any number of prisons for my job, Mark said suddenly. I did some work on climate control systems for the new women's prison going in up north. Hard to see much good coming from such places. This is better, here.

You'd think they could come up with something, said Patsy. So we could come out more educated, or at least less crazy, than we were going in.

In the Old Testament, Mark said, they had cities of refuge, where people who accidentally killed someone could go live without fear of retribution.

Like a wildlife relocation program, she said.

He smiled, a first.

She said, I read in the *Pasadena Star* that your wife taught piano.

I don't know where they got that, he said. She was a singer. We met in chorus at City College. She had the clearest, sweetest soprano voice. We sang at church together until Martin was born.

A Jehovah's Witness church? she asked, knowing otherwise.

We were Lutherans. Jane only got into that other stuff later.

And you didn't?

She wanted me to. Not my cup of tea.

Darkness seeped into his face. She touched his arm. Did you bring pictures?

•

She has a twinkle, Patsy said, pointing to the girl on ice skates, her hands in a fur muff, a matching white fur collar. Her dark eyes reflecting stars of light. Behind her head, the extended leg of a passing skater.

I took her to skating Saturday mornings, he said. In that old ballroom behind the civic auditorium. Here's Jane maybe five years ago.

A brunette in crisp office wear: blazer, butterfly pin, buttoned-up blouse, eyebrows tweezed to a thin line. Dark brown eyes in which the person had not quite surfaced. Shy, Patsy thought before blackness started lapping in her vision and the taste of metal flooded her mouth. As calmly as she could, she handed the wallet back and leaned down to get her head below her heart.

She excused herself, went to the bathroom, rinsed her face. When she returned, Mark had bought Coca-Colas. They drank and watched the fog gathering down at the ocean for its slow roll uphill. Patsy was exhausted, like a cried-out child, but she felt impelled to talk. I want you to know I'm not just someone who had a little too much to drink and drove badly, she said. I had a long history of doing that, and I didn't care enough to stop. You need to know the truth if you're serious about knowing me.

I do want to know. His eyes reddened quickly, still easily inflamed. His big knuckled hands rubbed each other.

My driver's license had been suspended. My father had my keys. But I kept another set in my kitchen. I'd taken the car out once before, that

I remember. I was supposed to be going to meetings. I was lying to everybody about all of it.

Yes, he said. But you're not anymore.

.

May I come again?

His ivory windbreaker was zipped; it crackled softly in the wind.

We're in each other's lives now, he said. We can't change what happened, but we can help each other from here on out.

Earlier in her life, she thought, Mark Parnham's sincerity would have made her suspicious or embarrassed her. Now she wanted to give him something in return. She said, I think I remember your daughter's long, curly hair.

You're thinking of the photos you saw in court, he said gently. She and her mom got pixie cuts when they became Witnesses. Her hair was short.

.

You guys sure talked for a long time, Antonia said.

They were in the barracks, which were swallowed in fog.

Only two hours.

You seemed into it.

He's a nice guy. An engineer. Sings in a church. And barbershop quartets. But you didn't see me almost pass out. He was showing me pictures of his wife and kid. I thought I could handle it, but god . . .

That would kill me, said Antonia.

Yeah, it was almost as sickening as when I first found out. That horrible hot-cold hollow feeling, like I'm now doomed to darkness for eternity, like I've done the worst thing and it can't ever be undone. Know what I mean?

No. But you should say those things, exactly like that, to the parole board, Antonia said. They'd fuckin' love it. They'd parole you tomorrow. They fuckin' feed on remorse. If they heard what you said to me, they'd fling open the gates and give you a fuckin' hundred bucks and send you outta here in a limousine.

Patsy scratched at a peeling blister on her palm. Parole boards didn't pertain to her case. She could be out in sixteen months, unless she blew it.

Will you see him again? Antonia asked.

He says we have a relationship, even though it started out badly. Patsy gave a short bark. Really, about as badly as possible. He says we have the power to make it a good relationship. Whatever that means.

Maybe you'll marry him, said Antonia. Wouldn't that be funny.

Oh god no, Patsy said. Never.

Stranger things have happened, said Antonia. Janella married her rapist.

Patsy had imagined falling into Mark's arms with an urgency that burned through everything, but that was before they met. In person he'd been too sad and real for anything like that. She said, He's not my type. Too bland and boring. I'd never marry anyone who sang in a barbershop quartet.

•

Spring rains saturated the soil, and rather than hoeing and chopping the thick green clumps of weeds along firebreaks, the women found it easier to pull them out by hand. Each clump came out with its roots bundled in heavy mud. The idea of flinging these clods occurred simultaneously. Twenty women swung plants full circle, like lanyards, then let go. The clods flew unbelievably far. The women lobbed them over power lines and were amazed when they cleared with room to spare. Up and over went the clods, then down they came like raffish green-tailed comets plummeting to earth. Simultaneously, as if a new signal were given, the women chose targets, and the air filled with long-haired clods flying horizontally and the weighty, wet slaps of earth hitting flesh. No real malice fueled this fray, and they avoided hitting the CO, who stood there saying, Ladies, now, ladies, now, ladies, please, while shielding her eyes to see the best hits. In a moment of distraction Patsy took a cold clod on the ear—she'd dig out dirt for days—and in the shocked, ringing moments that followed, as the blue sky spun, she heard one beautiful, clear note sung in a woman's sweet voice—one high, spiraling wire of sound, on and on and on, with no break or pause for breath.

9

Patsy was number three Pulaski, Antonia number two. It was filthy, hard work, and during downtimes, they longed for more of it.

Only ten of them were sent out on a dry electric day in October, when Santa Ana winds were kicking up. A small wildland fire not far from Malibou Lake threatened a neighborhood of expensive new homes. They saw the fire crest the top of a hill—a ragged V-shaped line of orange flame frilled with black smoke that billowed up into a plump, dirty pink cloud.

They drove to a new street, where the burning hill was on one side of them, the new homes on the other. As always, the driver turned the buggy around lest they needed to escape.

The county engines were already there, as were the Malibu volunteer trucks, the hand crew of a local private contractor, and a Forest Service vehicle. Men conferred in a huddle. The private crew was getting out drip torches, presumably to burn out the scrub up to the fire. Patsy's crew waited in the buggy, but no orders were forthcoming.

What we have here, their crew boss Mary said, is a genuine clusterfuck. Then she walked over to join them.

They probably can't decide who's IC, said another woman.

Incident commander being the one who called the shots.

The land around them was low-growing coastal scrub, with small, bushy oaks, a few sycamores and toyons. On the same side of the road as the fire, slim wooden survey stakes with orange plastic ribbons marked out the lots of a future development.

That little fucker's fast, Antonia muttered. They should burn it out now.

Up on the hill, the fire's orange, smoke-frilled V had widened almost into a straight line. The smell of smoke filled the cab. But even if nobody did anything, the road itself would stop most of the fire.

Mary stuck her head into the buggy with the order. Out, everyone, she called. We're going to hold this road. Out! Hold the road! Hold the road!

Women shouldered their gear toward the door of the small bus and began leaping down onto the asphalt. Look now, Antonia told Patsy as they were jostled forward, pushed from the women behind. Patsy hunched down to see out of a window. The fire was fully horizontal now, and the flames suddenly much taller, a wall, and sliding down the slope like water.

Then Mary started screaming. RTO! RTO! Reverse the order. Back in the buggy. Now. *Now.* Everyone!

Inside the buggy, they scrambled backward to make room again. Antonia shoved Patsy into the woman behind her as those from outside crammed themselves and their gear in. Fucker's jumping the road! someone yelled.

Embers swarmed and hit the windows like fat, radiant insects. Really, the flames were unbelievably close, a towering mass of shiny red fire that billowed and rippled like wind-whipped silk and bellied out at them as the buggy finally started moving. Then came a blast of dry, hot heat and a loud snapping and crackling, as from a huge campfire. A strange green light filled the vehicle. Softball-sized balls of white flame flew off a blazing tree like an explosion of phosphorus.

The next moment, they were in the clear, under blue sky. The buggy stopped, and the women leaped out. But it was too soon, too close, a mistake, and the instant Patsy landed, before she got her bearings, there was a *whoosh!* and the fire's back wind sucked her off balance, the air so hot and dry and smoky her eyes and nose instantaneously streamed liquid and her lungs filled up.

She staggered and collided with two men hauling a hose. All around, people were cursing and throwing up. Patsy stuck her nose under her shirt.

This is when we die, she thought with unnatural calm, here are the superheated fumes that melt lungs. She was curiously unafraid and very interested. Death by fire, she'd heard, was not like drowning or asthma. With fused lungs, there was no convulsive struggle and not much pain. You could think to the end. She found Antonia, grabbed her, and held on.

The wind was already easing off. Formation! Mary yelled as the smoke cleared, and the new world revealed itself—a blackened ground, consumed to the dirt, the trees now charred, leafless snags, some still burning at their crowns.

Where the fire had jumped the road, dozens of spots burned—many as small as a single sagebrush, a few the size of big, vigorous bonfires. The hose crew went first with water, and the convicts followed, hacking apart the fuel, smothering flare-ups, chasing scampering flames. They were a little delirious.

Oh no you don't.

Take that, you little pizzle sucker.

Soon they were covered in white ash. In fifteen minutes the spot fires were out and the con crew was ordered to go flank the fire. Same old same old, grunt work well away from any non-con crews. They rode up behind the hill and dug line, sweating in their Nomex, their packs chafing. Their tools arced in unison, sliced through the dry duff, four swings every ten feet. They worked their way to the top of the hill and saw, below, that the new houses were safe. The head of the fire, now burning scrubland off to the south, was only a puff of smoke.

•

Mark Parnham visited Patsy again in November, when the season was over and she was back to weeding campgrounds, shoring up trails. He brought photographs of his son, a round-faced, round-eyed seven-year-old with his father's small features, his mother's dark hair. Mark said, Here, he sent you this.

She unfolded a crayon drawing of a spidery yellow sun above a grove of black trees whose branches balanced red and orange scribbles of fire. A stick figure aimed a hose that spewed blue dots at the burning trees. Across the bottom of the page, in ungainly crayoned letters: *To Patsy from Martin.*

•

She was in the shower when a CO stuck her head in the door. MacLemoore? Director wants you.

She turned off the water. Coming.

You can finish. Take your time.

She had never met with such courtesy in prison. *Take your time*—it was the first latitude granted. She turned the water back on. When she stepped out in her towel, CO Kessler, the homely one also called Pig Eyes, waited by the door.

I didn't know you were still here, or I would've hurried.

No problem.

The guard's eyes were indeed close together, reminding Patsy not of a pig but a flounder. Hard to imagine how Kessler coped here among the merciless.

Patsy dressed and walked with Kessler in the winter twilight down to administration. Kessler opened a door for her, followed her into the director's office. The director was a former fire chief who had lectured them in training. Patsy? he said. He wore an ironed, clean khaki uniform. Please, sit down.

She sat in an oak captain's chair across from him. A Christmas wreath festooned with toyon berries hung on the wall behind his head. Perhaps he would ask her to teach English or history, as the warden at Bertrin had.

I'm afraid I have some very bad news for you, Patsy.

She saw Burt shot. Her father collapsed on the golf course. Another stranger dead, and she had caused it. The director, she saw, awaited her signal to go on. What? she said.

I'm sorry to tell you, Patsy. Your mother passed away this morning.

She wanted the words to spool back into his mouth. She turned sideways, glanced around the office with its stucco walls, hung certificates, holiday berries. Kessler's small, ugly eyes had reddened.

I'm sorry, the director said again. Of course you may attend the funeral.

•

At Our Holy Redeemer, Father Paul eulogized her mother. She wished that Father Gaspar or the monsignor was doing the service instead, not that she respected either of them after the dairy wars—Father Gaspar used liquid Coffee-mate, the monsignor skim milk—but because Father Paul wore his guitar. Her mother probably wouldn't have cared who preached; her devotion to the Church had been elsewhere. She'd worked with the nuns at the Samantha Home for Girls and hadn't attended mass for months on end.

Patsy's father sat beside her, tears sliding down his cheeks. She knew she should clasp his hand, but she could not. She could not. Burt, on her other side, wore dark aviator glasses. Bonnie and the kids filled the rest of the pew.

Now Father Paul was singing in his reedy tenor. The Lord is my shepherd. Beside him, an elaborate, three-quarters-sized crèche crowded the altar space, the Holy Family, animals, and kings all absorbed in another story. Everything—the singing priest, the plaster figures, the full church—seemed to exist behind a yellow membrane, an inch-thick sheet of Plexiglas. Patsy jiggled her foot, jammed her hands under her knees.

Burt had picked her up at nine in the morning. We were counting on Mom to last out your sentence, he told her. We figured you had enough on your plate.

Didn't it occur to anybody that I might want to say goodbye? Or make amends? What were you thinking?

Burt had clammed up at her tone. They barely spoke all the way down the hill. Then there was an accident on Pacific Coast Highway and an hour's delay. In Bakersfield they had to drive directly to the church.

And how badly people behaved out in the free world. They stood and talked right in the entrance to the sanctuary while other people were trying to get inside. They blocked the aisle, called out to each other. They shuffled into pews in no particular order, squeezing past people, making others squeeze past them. They shoved. In prison, you'd get cited.

The service ended, and she filed out with the family. Brice saluted her from a few rows back, they made motions to meet outside. In a rear pew sat a man in a black suit who looked like Mark Parnham, only smaller, milder, even more nondescript. As she came closer, he stood.

I have to see someone, she told Burt, and went over.

I'm so sorry, he said, about your mother.

Oh my god. She reached out her hand, and he clasped it. To Burt she mouthed, A minute.

You came all the way up here? she said.

Not so far. Ninety minutes.

Where's Martin?

At his grandmother's.

And he's okay?

Terrific, thanks. He looked at her frankly, with an interest and tenderness that made her straighten up.

It's weird how good it is to see you, she said.

This seemed like the sort of thing we could do for each other, he said.

Patsy turned her back to the mourners so nobody would approach them.

I saw your mom in court, he said. Both times. She held your hand.

She was sick then, Patsy said. But nobody told me.

So it was a shock.

I suspected something when she didn't come to Malibu. But yes, a shock.

Burt came up alongside her. Oh hello, he said, and shook Mark's hand. Dad wants you, Pats, he whispered.

I'm leaving now, said Mark Parnham.

You don't have to, said Patsy. You can . . .

I just wanted to tell you how sorry I am. And I'm thinking of you. He left through a side door.

Outside, Brice handed her a letter.

Dear Patsy,

Brice told me about your mother. I am very sorry. I never met your mom, but knowing you I would guess that she was friendly and very smart, not to mention beautiful. As you know, my mother died over two years ago, so I can guess how you feel. I'm sure you miss your mom as much as I miss mine. Maybe wherever they are they will meet and become good friends.

Your friend, Joey H.

•

Benny came in March with good news: You'll be out June first.

Two months earlier than expected. This brought a jolt of happiness. Are you kidding? She grabbed his arm. Are you sure? How'd you swing it?

I just kept talking to people, asking what could be done. You got points for good work, and Parnham wrote a letter.

You're kidding! Did you ask him to?

He got in touch with Ricky Barrett and me. Asked what, if anything, he could do. Ricky did some looking into it. And your brother Burt. I guess there's a whole law enforcement network.

Those guys, said Patsy, and you, Benny. You've all been so much nicer to me than I deserve.

•

Burt came to talk to her about her plans. Patsy examined her brother's friendly, handsome face. Why didn't the women go all noisy over him as they did for Brice? When Brice came to Malibu, a whole new set of women insisted he was a game-show host or on some soap opera. Burt, she thought, was better-looking, his thick graying hair in curls, his eyes always lit with warmth and humor. Burt, unlike Brice, truly loved women, too many in fact. But Patsy's fellow prisoners sooner rallied to Brice's aloofness and indifference. She'd been that way too. Show her a man who didn't love her and she'd do her damnedest to change his mind.

Burt grinned. Can you believe it? You're getting the hell out. When can you get your house back?

The lease runs till next February. I'll have to rent a place.

You'll need a job. That's the stipulation.

I could get on a fire crew for the summer.

Won't the college have something?

They don't have summer school. But I could probably teach ESL at Pasadena City College like I did before. That would work. And I could live at the Lyster. It's only five or six blocks away.

Brice's place? Is that a good idea?

Oh god, she said. Don't worry about *that*. The scales have fallen from my eyes! He's been a good friend, but that's it! I'd rent my own apartment.

I was hoping you'd come near to us. Dad was thinking a halfway house—

Is he out of his mind? Another institution? Why don't I just stay here?

Maybe your friend Sarah knows a place.

Maybe.

•

Two weeks later, this postcard came:

Dear Patsy,

*   There's a 2 bedroom on 2, north-facing (cool), high ceilings, claw tub, mountain view. Could be ready June 1. Shall I furnish? If so, what's your budget (so I can overrun it ASAP)?*

*   Brice*

PART THREE

Did you hear the one about the two women cellies released on the same day after twenty-five years? They stood outside the gate and talked for an hour.

1 0

June 1983

Patsy had imagined the moment of her release as a big gust of wind lifting her up and over the hurricane fence and toppling her into a new life. In fact, when Sweeney drove her down to the gate, nobody was waiting. The sky above was a pure, clear blue, but at their feet, a fog-bank stretched to the horizon, its surface white and dimpled like a mattress or a frozen, wind-chopped ocean. It was easy to imagine that the world below was gone.

Patsy unloaded her gym bag from the camp pickup.

I'll wait with you, Sweeney said.

They stood outside the gate. Big plans for the day? asked Sweeney.

A bath, said Patsy. And settling in.

Yes, take it easy, that's best, Sweeney said.

At the familiar whine and gasp of hydraulic brakes, they stepped aside. The gate swung open and the camp bus rumbled through, a woman's face in each window, some startled, others jeering to see Patsy there unclaimed.

Never mind, Sweeney said. The fog slowed 'em up. Oh. Listen.

A distant mechanical grind unbraided itself from the bus's rumble, wove in and out of the folds of the hills, coming closer. They listened until a gold and white Blazer nosed into view, Burt at the wheel. Burt alone.

So her father had not come. He'd asked to, and Patsy suggested he visit later in the week. She wanted to slip back into life without fanfare or reunions. But now, she realized, she would've liked to see her father.

Burt, only Burt, in his BLUE BLUE GRASS OF HOME T-shirt, his curls uncombed, his face unshaven, grabbed hold and pulled her off the ground.

•

Patsy had twenty-four hours to contact her parole officer. Let's get it out of the way, she said.

The address was a drab modern building by Pasadena City Hall.

He won't be nice, Burt said in the elevator. Not at first.

Jeffrey Goldstone was a short, bald, middle-aged man in a wide-sleeved flowered sport shirt. Stacks of papers and books listed around him. A blue curtain sagged off its track. Lacing his hands behind his head, he leaned back and delivered his spiel into the air above her head. Patsy was to phone him every day for thirty days, see him twice a month. She could not leave the county without his permission or go more than fifty miles away for longer than forty-eight hours without first informing him of her whereabouts. She was not to contact anybody she knew from prison for a year. His tone was weary and condescending; he spoke with a breathless rapidity that preempted interruption. He could and would come into her apartment and search it without a warrant at any moment. Morning, noon, or night. A home visit, he called it. So you remember, he said, when I go knock-knock, you open up.

He handed her a pocket-sized directory of local AA meetings and a stack of stiff white forms to be signed at each one she attended. Let's start with ninety meetings in ninety days, he said. And monthly urine tests.

Wow, I don't know if—she said, concerned about logistics.

I could make that weekly testing, he said.

It's just that I don't have a car and—

We provide rides. He circled some numbers in the back of a handbook and passed it over. This also lists clinics, counseling centers, employment opportunities, he said. I advise you to use our resources freely. The more you do for yourself, the more impressed we'll be. Five years could shrink to three. Any questions? Then I'll talk to you tomorrow, and don't be surprised when I stop by. Remember, when I go knock-knock, you—

She hoped a nod would suffice, but Goldstone pointed at her face. You—

Open the door, she whispered.

•

Next stop was her storage unit. They took an elevator to the fifth floor, walked down a dim, narrow hall. Prison was all people and almost no stuff, and this place was the opposite. Patsy greeted her sofa, embedded upright in a wall of boxes, all of it so efficiently arranged, there was enough room left to lie down. Why couldn't she stay here, in this muffled, ill-lit room?

She pulled two boxes labeled in her mother's confident felt-tip scrawl: SUMMER BASICS and SHOES, PURSES ETC. These for now, she said.

I've got the truck.

Brice already furnished the place, she said. Who knows what I'll need.

•

She'd forgotten—or had she ever noticed—how much the Lyster was a cartoon of a French chateau, with turrets and a pointy steep-hipped roof. Behind the facade sat a plain brick six-floor apartment building, although with tall Parisian-style windows and decorative shutters.

Number 2C had several such windows facing north. The plastered walls were a soft, floury white, the dark old oak floors distressed but waxed to a sheen. Brice had decorated with salvage from the defunct Bellwood: a moss-colored sofa and bobbin-legged mahogany side table. The white wrought iron table in her new breakfast nook, Patsy had last seen on the Bellwood's sunporch.

We've been at it for weeks, said Gilles, a beautiful teenager whose presence among them was unexplained. Sanding, priming, painting, he said with a faintly British crispness of speech. Junking, going to the swapper. Brice found these in a dumpster behind the Pasadena Playhouse, had them recut.

He petted a sage green velvet curtain that puddled on the shining floor.

Nice, she said. And everything's so clean.

Brice made me take a toothbrush to the baseboards to get out the old wax.

I didn't make you, said Brice.

He did, Gilles said. He cracked the whip.

The boy's skin was milky and blushing, with taupe-colored freckles

to match his taupe-colored hair. His dark, plump lips were so prominent, so rosy and beautiful, Patsy could hardly bear to look at them.

Oh god, a fireplace, she said. On the black marble mantel Brice had
clustered six white teacups of differing patterns, each as delicate as an
eggshell. Picking one up, she saw shadows of her fingers through the
porcelain and a hairlike rust-colored crack. Years had passed since she'd
held anything so fine.

So? said Brice. What do you think?

Lovely, perfect, she said, wanting all of them, even Burt, to leave, yet
afraid that they would. What would roar into the silence once she was
alone?

Then they left. Burt and Brice went down for the boxes, and the boy,
Gilles-rhymes-with-peel, said he would make tea. She wandered into
the bedroom, opened the closet, where a dozen wooden hangers swayed.
In the bathroom, thick white towels hung beside a ledge of Bellwood
toiletries: French soap, tiny toothpaste, the same little giveaway sewing
kit she'd used to pierce Joey Hawthorne's ears.

Her father had lobbied for El Puente de las Amigas instead; a halfway
house, he argued, would see her through the sudden drop of structure,
postprison. He was afraid she'd take up booze—and Brice—again. Her
We're just friends, Dad had sounded tinny even to her. But he needn't
have worried, not if her hunch about the beautiful teenager proved true.

In the living room, she gazed out at the rooftop KASORGIAN CARPET
sign on its rusty struts, and beyond that, a gray opacity where mountains should sit.

Is it everything that you wanted? The boy, Gilles, came up beside her.

Oh! I thought you left.

I'm making tea here, he said. In your kitchen. Have you seen it yet?
Come.

The walls were paved with subway tiles. On the small apartment
stove, a teakettle sputtered water into the flames.

This was such a dirt pit, you wouldn't believe. Gilles poured a little
hot water into a Brown Betty teapot and swished it around. Mrs. Kron-
berg lived here forty-eight years and got so blind she couldn't see how
filthy it was. We used Easy Off on the tiles, then bleach. Brice said clean
was your number one requirement.

Gilles paused to spoon leaf tea into the pot, poured in more water.
What kind of teenager knows how to make a proper pot of tea?

And look, he said, you're stocked up too. He opened an overhead cupboard to reveal Medaglia D'Oro coffee, red boxes of Finn Crisp crackers, ripening avocados. Her old staples. Brice had remembered them, and she had not. In the fridge, a sharp cheddar and half-and-half for her coffee.

And these I made this morning. Gilles pulled aluminum foil up to reveal a plate of stacked tea sandwiches. Jam and butter on the white bread, he said. Cream cheese and watercress on the wheat. Want one?

I'll wait for— She'd forgotten the names of her brother and former lover. Too many subway tiles, groceries, and this eager-to-please, garrulous boy.

Oh dear, he said. Are you all right? Here, sit down. He guided her backward into the breakfast nook and pulled out a chair. Do you want a tissue?

No, no. Through the glass tabletop her hands writhed in her lap.

I can't imagine what today is like for you, said Gilles. I hope the apartment is everything you dreamed of. I wanted to tart it up, you know, with pillows and paintings, and I brought over my big old teddy bear for you. I thought he might cheer you up, like a pet, but Brice is so strict.

He is, she murmured, thinking she might have liked the bear.

Gilles set the table: cups, small plates, mismatched linen napkins, the sandwiches. As the shock of his beauty subsided, she saw typically lax teenage grooming—sloppy shave, straggly hair in his eyes. Sixteen, she decided.

You're so nice to go to all this trouble, she said.

It's practice for my future catering company. Gilles's Meals.

Yes. Perfect. Are you French?

My father was. And I lived in France for two years. But I'm from right here. Pasadena.

You live in the building? Patsy asked.

Until Brice gets grouchy; then I go to Mother's till he asks me back.

A small shock of certainty, a pause in the blood. Of course.

Brice might've said something to prepare her—even if disclosures of a personal nature didn't come easily to him.

Oh—and Brice said to tell you I'm in AA.

You? she said.

Two years without one sip.

How old are you, anyway?

Twenty next week.

You must have started young, she said.

Twelve, he said. But I had talent.

Apparently, Patsy said. I'm two years sober too.

I know. Gilles carried the teapot in its flowered cozy to the table. Brice blew your anonymity. I could take you to meetings, he added. I've found all the good ones. I go every morning, early.

How early?

Six-thirty. I like to get it out of the way, first thing.

I've been getting up at five.

Shall I come get you, then? Tomorrow? Ten after six?

Yes. Patsy gave a laugh of relief. I was wondering how I was going to do ninety meetings in ninety days, she said.

That's what I'm doing! Ninety in ninety. Every time I finish, my sponsor says, Oh, you're doing so well, you've come such a long way, why mess with a good thing? Let's do another ninety in ninety.

Yeah, my parole—

Patsy? Patsy? Oh, there you are, Burt said, and walked straight up to the sandwiches. Those look good.

A phone began to ring.

Is that here? Patsy asked, bewildered.

Gilles pointed to the living room, where a boxy white rotary phone pealed on a side table. Burt tossed her the receiver on its coiled cord. Hello? she said.

It's me, Brice. I wanted to make sure it worked.

You thought of everything, she said.

•

The four gathered at the glass table to drink the tea and eat the little sandwiches. Brice asked after the old girls who'd pestered him at Bertrin and Malibu. So much for my brief and happy life as a movie star, he said.

The tea tasted like some delicious toasted wood, and she loved the sandwiches, the cream cheese with its fattiness and tang, the sweet berry jam and cold shards of butter. Even after she felt vaguely ill, Patsy kept eating and drank so many cups of tea, her fingers buzzed and she felt feverish and chilled at the same time. Gilles was gathering dishes, and Patsy couldn't track what anyone was saying. She wanted to go into the bedroom and put a pillow over her head.

Brice stood. I'm sure you want to unpack, he said. We're right upstairs if you need anything. Our number is by the phone.

Burt saw them out; then he too had to go. He was due at work. I hate leaving you alone, he said. The kids said I should kidnap you.

You heard Mr. Knock-Knock. I can't leave the county.

That douche bag, said Burt. God, what a putz.

Patsy kissed her brother's bristled cheek and closed the door.

Alone! Roaming room to room, she opened and shut cupboards, eyed the telephone, then ran a deep tub foamed with bath oil. Her breasts and knees and toes made pink protrusions in the bubbles. There you are, she greeted them, prison having allowed no time or place for self-inspection. Her legs were the skinniest she'd ever seen them, and muscular from firefighting. She added hot water with her toes, until the heat made her heart race. She got out of the tub and grabbed a towel all too quickly; the air burst into prisms, and she had to sit on the toilet, bent over her knees until the whirling bars of color subsided. Traffic rumbled outside, a bass note to the city's hum, and above that, she heard a faint ringing, so high-pitched, steady, and beautiful it could only be silence.

Wrapped in the towel, she stretched out on the Bellwood-issue sleigh bed with its plain white hotel linens and down pillows. She wished that Brice had told her about the boy ahead of time instead of parading him in front of Burt like that. Not that she was so surprised. In all the months she and Brice ran around together, they spent very few nights with each other. Two, actually. Two nights.

When you get right down to it, sexual indifference isn't that mysterious.

During their breakup three years ago, Brice had said, *Thailand has ruined me.* At the time, she'd taken it to mean that he was drawn only to tiny, slim women and that she was too big, too clumsy, too blond and American to suit.

In renting an apartment at the Lyster, Patsy had neither expected nor wanted to resurrect their romance. But she'd had other ideas—silly ones, she saw now—about soldiering on as devoted, mutually single friends, both unfit for love.

The only thing to do, she saw, was to proceed as planned, stay here until she could move home to Pomelo Street, and keep to her own resolves.

She had resolved to be good, whatever that meant. Her soul, that scrap of energy, was in tatters, no doubt beyond repair. Her only hope was to make herself useful to others, try to balance wrong with right.

Her stomach was still queasy from the sandwiches.

Eating lightly would be good. Possibly some fasting.

And she would let her hair grow long again.

·

A loud jangle woke her and, thinking she was still at fire camp, Patsy stumbled to her feet before recognizing the phone. It's Gilles, said the young voice, so then she thought it was already morning and she was late to the meeting, but the room was bright, and baking in late afternoon heat. The fog had cleared and the mountains sprawled beyond her windows.

Brice says dinner is at seven. Hors d'oeuvres at six-thirty.

What time is it now?

Almost six. Will you come?

She wasn't at all hungry, but company appealed to her.

·

Having encountered no reproach earlier in the day and having had their dinner invitation accepted, Brice and Gilles were relaxed and talkative. Taking turns, they told her how they'd met. The first time was back in February, said Brice, in the produce section of El Rancho. I saw this shopping cart filled with loose vegetables. No bags, just red peppers, zucchini, eggplant, tomatoes—so beautiful. I thought the produce manager was clearing the displays, then I see this guy dump in an armload of red onions.

Actually, said Gilles, it was a stupid way to shop—it took hours to check out. And meanwhile this creature was staring at me. So rude. I said to him, I see you're looking at my feet. And he said, No, no, I'm looking at your vegetables. I had to tell him it was a line from a book. You know it, Patsy—what Seymour Glass says to the girl in the elevator before he blows his brains out?

"'A Perfect Day for Bananafish,'" said Patsy.

Right! I had to explain it to the illiterate one, here. And he said,

Well, I really hope you're not going to do that. The darling. I said, No, I'm making ratatouille for Mother's library luncheon. Then we both got all shy and left.

And that could've been it, said Brice.

Except then, my sponsor said I had to get a job. You know, get off the couch, be a worker among workers. My sponsor—he's also my uncle—owns all this property, and he said I could help fix up apartments, painting and stuff, and sent me to the Lyster. And who's my new boss but Mr. Never Read Salinger—

I read *Catcher in the Rye*, said Brice. I never went on a jag.

And we were all, It's you! It's you!

And we haven't been apart since, said Brice.

That's not true, my love, said Gilles. You kick me out on a regular basis.

I need to sleep. And work, for god's sake.

At this point Patsy checked Brice for his old resistance. His long legs were extended, one arm was flung over a chair, fondness crinkled his eyes. She waited a beat, then another, for him to look elsewhere, to withdraw those limbs. She knew his rhythms, or thought she did. But the brightness lingered in his eyes, his arms and legs did not retract, he remained open, amused—Brice, her old tormentor, complicit in love!

He soon rose and grilled thick steaks on a hibachi out on the fire escape. Gilles sliced and dressed tomatoes. They ate in the dining room with all the windows open, two fans buzzing. In the long June evening, the sun hung in the sky as if it had forgotten what to do.

The fork twisted out of her hands after a few mouthfuls. I'm sorry, she said. I'm not used to such rich meat.

Don't worry about it, said Brice.

We want you to be happy on your first day home, said Gilles. Are you?

It doesn't feel real yet.

What can we do for you? Gilles was up and taking her plate. Oh, I know. Let's go for a drive. I have the Bweek—Mother's car.

French for Buick, Brice said.

They clambered down the stairs to the parking lot and a large late-model cream-colored sedan. I'll sit in the back, said Gilles, and Patsy, you sit up front. Better yet, you and I will ride in the back. Brice will be the driver. Like it's a limousine. Brice doesn't mind, do you, sweet pea?

Where to? said Brice.

I'd like to see my house, said Patsy.

They drove north into Altadena. In the dusk the mountains were a dark gray-violet. Patsy peered out from the backseat like a child, at the cupped and rolling greens of the golf course, then the rustic, broken-up neighborhood across Lake Avenue. There was the park, with its wisteria bowers and green softball diamond. Another turn, and they were on Pomelo Street. The air with the late sideways rays of sun was swollen with drifts of spores and motes sifting down.

Slow, slow, Patsy said. Okay, here, pull over for a sec.

Her house was set back from the street, its clapboard tea-towel white, as were the trunks of the twin sycamores, whose last crumpled brown leaves were being forced off by furry new green ones. How close the mountains were! And the driveway, that driveway—it was two concrete tracks, buckled and cracked, with weeds in between. The oleander hedge alongside it was overgrown and abloom, the white blossoms like wadded tissues among the dark leaves.

In the Bweek's slippery beige backseat, Patsy felt as if she were in one of those dreams where you can't quite get home, you're almost there, but something's off, somebody else—two tenants or three bears—lives there now.

Okay, she said. Before anybody sees us.

Driver! Gilles rapped the side window. Drive on.

Brice turned up the radio, a Vivaldi season. Spring, Patsy thought. They drove south to the freeway, then west. The sun had set, and the world before them was in silhouette, as if cut from black construction paper and pasted against the orange sky. Patsy opened the window, put her face in the air. Her hair blew into her eyes and mouth. Not quite shoulder length, it had been trimmed in exchange for a two-ounce bottle of Taster's Choice by a woman who'd learned cosmetology at the Sybil Brand Correctional Institute. Patsy gathered the flying strands in one hand. Her hair would be long again soon, and Patsy imagined it streaming behind her, a thick rope unraveling, a banner unfurled.

1 1

Before sunrise, Gilles drummed softly on her door. They climbed again into the Bweek and drove in morning fog on Colorado Boulevard, the main street, deserted and colorless except for stoplights. You could see them for blocks, synchronized—green, yellow, then red.

Such a big old boat, said Patsy. Doesn't your mom need it?

She has her Bug. This is the town car.

Nice of her to lend it.

Mother's a brick, said Gilles, considering what I've put her through.

And what have you put her through?

Let's see. When I turned fourteen, I ran away from Hotchkiss to live with this artist in New York. If you and I get to be good friends, I'll tell you his name, he's very famous. Mother didn't approve, so I couldn't let her find me. I didn't tell her where I was for two years.

She must have been out of her mind.

Oh, completely. But I called her all the time—from pay phones and weird places she couldn't trace. I missed her too, but if she could've, she would've kidnapped me and had him arrested. Then I moved in with this writer—he's famous too, more even than the painter—and he lived in Paris half the year. I was sixteen by then, so I made a deal, that if Mom sent me my passport and promised not to call the vice squad, she could visit.

Did she?

Yeah, a couple times.

But she got you home somehow. Because here you are.

That's not why. I just got too hairy and smelly and lost all my sex appeal. Then I got sober, and that was the last straw. So I was sent back.

Was that okay with you?

I was a basket case! I cried for a month, poor Mother didn't know what to do. I hung out on the sofa watching TV and eating and got all pudgy and truly ugly. Then Auntie, that's my uncle Cal, who I told you about, who's also my sponsor—I call him Auntie—he told me I had to get out of myself and be a worker among workers, and the instant I took his direction, there was Brice of the big, beautiful schnoz.

And how long ago was that?

Like three months. Gilles glanced at her, his hair straggling in his eyes. Brice didn't tell you about us, did he? Before you came?

He did not.

He was supposed to. He promised he would. But you weren't surprised, were you?

A little, yes.

But you knew he was queer. He said you knew.

No.

According to him, you used to say—Gilles lowered and flattened his voice to a monotone—Brice, you're gay. Brice, you're gay. In bed.

I did? I sure don't remember. I must have been drunk, she said. There are a lot of things I don't remember. I was a big blackout drinker.

Me too! cried Gilles, as if this were yet another remarkable affinity they shared. I was a big blackout drinker too!

•

At the First Presbyterian Church, Gilles parked around back, where men and a few women clustered in a courtyard.

Hello, ladies, Gilles said to a group of men.

Gilles, they answered, and stared at her.

This is Patsy. My neighbor.

Hi, Patsy, they said, lifting Styrofoam cups. Welcome.

To two men smoking by the planter: Hi, girls.

Oh hi, Gilles.

This is Patsy.

Patsy, they repeated, relishing the flat *a*. Welcome.

Gilles led her to a large community hall where a man in the doorway shook their hands. Welcome, he said. I'm Vaughn, the greeter.

Nice to greet you, said Gilles. Greet Patsy. She's new to this meeting.

Greetings, Patsy. Welcome.

They took seats close to the door because farther in, Gilles said, the cigarette smoke was lethal. At meeting time, since they were right by the entrance, they greeted everyone all over again.

After the opening readings and announcements, the secretary gave Patsy a little plastic disk, like a poker chip, pale blue with gold printing on it. WELCOME on one side. KEEP COMING BACK on the other.

Here's Auntie now, Gilles whispered, clasping the hand of a tall man with clipped snow-white hair. Auntie, here's Patsy.

The uncle gave her a friendly, interested smile. He seemed familiar and was, for an older man, exceedingly handsome, like an old movie star—Katharine Hepburn's elegant father or the retired gunslinger turned sheriff in some spaghetti western. Patsy, he said, taking her hand. Cal Sharp. So glad you're here. We need you to even things out a bit.

He meant the male/female ratio, as there were forty or fifty men and at most a dozen women.

As Cal Sharp made his way up to the front of the room, he squeezed shoulders and shook hands like a senator.

A man talked for fifteen minutes about how he drank his way through the army and two marriages and got sober "with a nudge from the judge." The group's secretary reminded him to choose a topic for general discussion and gave him a sheet to choose from. He picked "Getting Through the Day." Maybe half the people who spoke said that this meeting was what got them through the day. Gilles's uncle was called on—he hadn't raised his hand. He said, Try as I might, I can't get God to speak to me face-to-face. I have to come in here, where God speaks to me through all of you, and I almost always hear exactly what I need to get me through the day.

·

After the meeting, Gilles took her to Barkers Broiler, where she used to come for breakfast at two or three in the morning after a night of drinking. In daylight, the coffee shop was dingier than she remembered. The floors smelled of pine cleaner, and the Formica tabletops were gritty in their seams. People from the meeting clustered at other tables. Vaughn the greeter. Gilles's uncle.

Gilles ordered pancakes with ice cream; she had dry toast and tea.

I sort of assumed it was a gay meeting, she said.

Gettin' a little that way, said Gilles.

But your uncle's not.

Auntie? Father of five?

Is it possible I've met him before?

Well, he owns the Lyster. Were you ever at the Bellwood Hotel?

Brice took me to the Mojave Club for dinner there once.

The Bellwood was Auntie's too, till it sold. The Mojave relocated, you know, to the Altadena Country Club. Anytime you want to go, Mother's a member. And Auntie too, of course. Oh, hello, Derek.

A big-bellied man from the meeting came up to their booth. He had a long, skimpy ponytail, and on his chest a brass Maltese cross hung on a chain that might have come off a hanging lamp. Gilles, he said. The guys and I want to know one thing. How come *you* get to sit with the prettiest girl?

Gilles said, Oh, Derek, you have it all wrong. The correct question is, how come she gets to sit with the prettiest boy?

Derek turned to her. Sorry, ma'am, I just want to say hello, and welcome.

Patsy muttered hello and waited for Derek and his swag chain to leave.

Don't mind poor old Derek, said Gilles after. He means well. And you are the prettiest girl in the room.

She did not consider herself pretty. Too fair, too pink, too easily flushed and mottled. The square MacLemoore jaw was better suited to Burt's manly face. But god, or genes, had made her tall and blond, a cultural signifier for prey.

Looking into Gilles's mischief-lit eyes, she said, And you are the prettiest boy.

•

Her father brought a gift: her mother's copy of *Lives of the Saints*. I thought you might like it, he said.

Briefly Patsy clasped the thick, well-thumbed paperback to her chest, then set it on a side table. Her mother had consulted it every morning over coffee.

I worry that you're depressed, her father said.

Well, of course I'm depressed.

Have you thought of getting any help?

I've only been out of prison three days, she said.

I'm happy to pay, he said. If you want to see someone.

Thanks, she said. That's very nice.

You're only saying that to get me off your back.

How else can I get you off my back?

They were sitting side by side on the couch and looking at the mountains. He crossed his skinny, stiff legs. So. What have you been doing with yourself?

I told you, she said. Going to meetings with Gilles. Looking over my textbooks. Making lesson plans. I start teaching ESL on Tuesday.

Have you seen friends? Had anyone over?

Brice and Gilles. And Jeffrey Goldstone's coming over any minute— my parole officer, she added before he could ask.

How could her father, newly widowed, appreciate the novelty of empty rooms, avocados mashed on Finn Crisp, the deep pleasure of sleeping alone in true darkness and silence?

I only have a couple more days where I don't have to be anywhere, she said. I'm enjoying that.

You're not isolating, are you?

You're here, aren't you? And you aren't looking so ebullient yourself.

No, not so ebullient.

What's happened to Eugenia?

Eugenia was a fifty-year-old woman who had shown up at her mother's funeral and hovered ever since. Nobody knew her—she'd come to the service expressly to introduce herself. Then she began arriving at his door with roast chicken, beef stew, pork chops. Ballet and symphony tickets. She had two teenagers at home; what were they doing when she was feeding Mr. MacLemoore night after night? None of this disturbed the man himself, who found her interest in him natural, her methods pragmatic.

Genie's around, he said. We may go to Australia.

You should.

You won't mind if I leave the country?

I'd leave it if I could, but I can't leave fucking L.A. County.

Pain flickered in his eyes. Tell you what, he said. Let's go to Bullock's and buy you a new dress.

So I can take the world by storm?

That was his line. If only she'd fix her hair and put on a new dress, why, she could take the world by storm.

They compromised. He took her to the bookstore and bought her hardbacks, a luxury after prison. She chose *Webster's Third New International*—who knew when she'd excavate her her two-volume *OED* from the storage unit—and the new biography of Jane Addams, whom she had once disdained for being good.

12

Pasadena City College was seven blocks to the east, an easy, flat walk. She had taught ESL here after her first year at Hallen. This time, her two sections met at nine and at eleven, five days a week, with sixty students between them. She had native speakers of fourteen languages, including Tagalog, Spanish, Farsi, Vietnamese, Italian (from Eritrea), Korean, Armenian, and a Bantu dialect of Swahili. The first day, she had them write essays in class on "Where I Came From." Writing in a second language, she'd found, unlocked inhibitions.

My parents not want me, wrote a Chinese woman, *and I am given to good strangers.*

My spouse has a nail in his buttock by a crude bomb of the guerrillas, wrote a Salvadoran woman. *My brother's wife is taken from her house by soldiers. We find her in a campo without the eyes and the tongue.*

Our boat was entered by Phuket, Thailand, and my brothers took to another boat. I do not know where they are today, wrote a Vietnamese pharmacist who worked in Pasadena as a motel janitor.

They were hungry for English as the key to new life. Patsy taught them doggedly—tenses, sentence structure, idioms, prepositions. She'd be mid-explanation, chalk in hand, when her mind slid into gray fuzz and dread poured through her body. She stood silent and helpless, but they did not rustle or try to set her right. Sometimes they murmured in sympathy, but mostly they waited till she collected herself. Many of them, she was certain, also moved in and out of the present, claimed at moments by random blankness and fear.

Walking home, Patsy prowled through thrift stores. She had not returned to her storage unit, preferring to furnish her new life piece by piece. A tablecloth from the forties with red roses and blue larkspur

spikes, a red blown-glass vase, a crewelwork pillow with pinecones and
red berries: blots of color accumulated in her sparse new home.

•

Brice showed up at her door with a heavy but beautiful old Electrolux
vacuum cleaner, its canister tapered like a bomb, the name in stylized
nickel italics. I found it on the street, he said. I thought I'd strip it for
parts, but it works perfectly well. Look at that beautiful lettering. Even
the casters are good. You need a vacuum, right?

Yes. Thank you, she said as he shouldered the thing inside.

She hadn't been alone with him since coming back. He stood by the
sofa, smoothed the nap on the shaved mohair, as if approving his own
taste.

So, she said. Gilles is adorable.

He did not appear to hear her—an old trick of his, to pretend a person had not spoken. Patsy would not be put off.

You might have told me. I don't blame you, he's adorable. But it was
a shock.

Brice walked over to the windows, made the curtain hang straighter,
gazed out at the mountains. I do like having him around, he said. It
sounds trite, but he's always so happy to see me. I like telling someone
about my day. I never thought I'd be anything but antsy as hell around
another person.

All good, she said. I'm happy for you. Still, I wish you'd said something.

Hey, it's me, Brice. I didn't know how to bring it up.

•

I was beginning to wonder if you were ever going to call, said Sarah.

I had to get my land legs. Settle in a bit.

I'll forgive you, if you come to dinner this Saturday. You have to see
the house and meet Henry.

Yes, but I can't do crowds yet.

The three of us, then, said Sarah. I'll pick you up.

Sarah was as plump and tanned as ever. Eternally dieting, but never
giving up ice cream or wine, she never lost weight. Patsy had always
liked the physical fact of her, her love of the sun and food.

Isn't this nice, Sarah said, looking around Patsy's apartment.
Where'd you get that? She pointed to the sofa.

Brice found it.

And how are things with Brice?

He's good. He has a boyfriend.

A boyfriend? No! she said, ready to commiserate. Well, you always
said!

I did? I don't remember.

You wondered why he wasn't more enthusiastic. Are you okay with it?

Why wouldn't I be?

Sarah shot her an exasperated look.

They drove west to an area near the Rose Bowl where, at the turn of
the century, wealthy midwestern industrialists built enormous family
homes on one-acre lots along curving treelined streets. Together the
houses formed a kind of architectural beauty pageant, the Swiss chateau,
the Craftsman, the Mission revival, the shingled Cape Cod, not one matching its neighbor. The long, graceful gray limbs of bayberry trees over-
hung the streets, filtered the sun through bright green leaves. The
pea-sized berries, crushed by tires, mentholated the air and made the
whole neighborhood smell like a cough-suppressant rub.

Sarah turned down the driveway of a Spanish-style home and paused
so Patsy could admire the dark wood beams, the deep-set windows, the
freshly painted turquoise trim. Henry's a genius with real estate, Sarah
said.

Beautiful, Patsy said, who'd been thinking that the huge house
must have been Henry's idea. Before he came along, Sarah had lived in
what they'd called the view unit, a one-bedroom apartment overlooking
the 210 Freeway.

It needs a ton of work, Sarah went on. We couldn't have afforded it
otherwise. But I do have to warn you. There's a ballroom.

A ballroom? Patsy said.

For giving balls, said Sarah. As in Jane Austen.

Wow. That's rather a lot to live up to, isn't it?

I also have to admit—Sarah lowered her voice—with so much space,
I have this urge to populate the place. Fill up the rooms.

They entered through the back door and a porch the size of Patsy's living room. Behind her, Sarah said, Oh, you look fantastic, Patsy. So skinny.

•

The ballroom was actually three large rooms separated by tall doors that folded back against the walls to form one grand, waltzable space.

So this is what Sarah had acquired, Patsy thought. While I hacked weeds.

In the backyard, Henry Croft was washing out a plastic bucket at a spigot. Tall, lean, sandy-haired, he had thin lips and small, pale eyes, and a warm smile that made him handsome.

Patsy remembered those thin lips from a faculty soiree at Anne Davis's house. She'd gone to the porch with a tall glass of bourbon to drink the way she liked to drink, in big, hot gulps, and to pet the Davises' basset hound. Henry had followed her, and, the dog between them, they'd kissed over the broad, spotted back. But nothing more kindled. She'd found his kisses, and him, dull. Who could have guessed he was a real estate genius with a ballroom in his future?

So glad you're here, said Henry, smiling. We've been on hold, waiting for you. I don't think Sarah will settle in until the house has your approval.

It's true, Sarah cried. I tell Henry, you're the one who knows so much about houses and architecture. I was perfectly happy in the view unit.

Patsy said, It's far better than anything I imagined. So grand!

Henry was tiling an upstairs bathroom and had a friend helping. Better get back to it, he said.

Patsy noted an appealing self-possession she hadn't detected that night on the Davises' porch.

Isn't Henry nice? Sarah said when they were alone in the kitchen. He is the nicest man I've ever met. So much nicer than I am. When you were away, he'd nag me. You have to go see Patsy. He grew up in a religious home. He's rejected all the rubbish but kept the essentials. You know, being kind, feeding the poor, visiting the prisoner. You can't believe how much money he sends to charity. He can't pass a panhandler without forking out. He says this house is going to bankrupt us, but if we do go broke, it'll be because he gives to every beggar who sticks out a hand.

Sarah made tea, put a casserole in the oven, talked. The brilliant new nineteenth-century person, she said, had a shy, stuttering wife. Also, the new building was ready. I hope you like where they put you, Sarah said. I lobbied to have you down from me.

Patsy shrugged. Anywhere's fine.

I guess you had to develop a pretty thick skin where you were, said Sarah.

Or something.

You do seem so quiet, Patsy.

Patsy was not intentionally quiet. They hadn't found a subject yet. Their old standbys, departmental gossip and men, were not serving them. Why Brice wouldn't spend the night or when exactly Sarah's long-distance lover Dan took up with someone else had been yearlong conversations. Patsy had no man to talk about now and, with Henry, Sarah's whole life had fallen into place with a resounding thunk, all tendrils of dissatisfaction shorn clean off.

•

They were four for dinner after all. The smell of moussaka baking had drifted upstairs, and Henry had invited his tiling friend to dinner.

Sarah said, Gosh, Patsy, is that okay?

To force a retraction of the invitation was ruder than Patsy cared to be.

Sarah sent Henry down to the basement for a bottle of wine. It's lamb, she said. Some earthy red. Or retsina, if we have any.

Henry turned to Patsy. I told Sarah that maybe we shouldn't drink tonight out of solidarity with you—

And I said *bullshit*! Sarah rang out, then added, I told him you'd be fine.

Yes, fine, Patsy said, at once touched by Henry's willingness to forgo what was clearly a ritual pleasure for them, and alarmed by Sarah's ferocity.

And Ian drinks too, Sarah added in a softer voice.

It's fine, it really is, Patsy said, and hoped it would be.

Ian was a compact, sharply handsome man—half Japanese, as Sarah had informed Patsy—who spoke with a Southern accent.

Virginia? said Patsy.

No'th Carolina, he said.

Ian's an amazing painter, Sarah said. We have one of his paintings, but it's still up in a show at the David Devine gallery.

Patsy, certain Ian had been filled in on her past in the same excited whisper she'd been told of his half-Japaneseness, said little. They ate in the dining room, with its oak paneling and curly wrought iron chandelier. She monitored the wine levels in their glasses, marveled at how slowly Henry and Ian drank. Sarah went at hers with more gusto. Patsy checked herself for craving or a sense of deprivation. If anything, abstinence gave her an edge and seemed a superior state of being. Poor Sarah, still in alcohol's thrall.

The phone rang, for Ian. Girl trouble, Sarah whispered when he left to take the call. He returned shortly, embarrassed and grim. Minutes later, the phone rang again, and this time they heard him speak harshly.

I won't answer next time, Sarah murmured as he returned, and it rang right then. For eight long peals they looked at their plates, the glistening salad, the ruined layers of casserole. All three wineglasses emptied swiftly.

•

After dinner Patsy followed Sarah upstairs. Henry is strictly forbidden to come in here, Sarah said, opening a door and waving grandly at a bed covered with bridal magazines, rental company price lists, swatches of cloth and ribbon.

Should I give you a shower? Patsy asked. Wasn't that what best friends—and putative bridesmaids—did? Not that Sarah had asked her to be part of the wedding yet.

Oh no, that's the last thing you need to worry about. Now, everybody says I should get a dress right away and not leave it to the last minute. So far, I've bought two—I'll take one back. But I need your opinion.

Okay, Patsy said.

Dress number one. Sarah pulled a billow of smoky pink chiffon from the closet; it settled into a strapless gown. You have to wear it with a crinoline, Sarah said with authority and, reaching back into the closet, produced a stiff, waist-high freestanding silk petticoat.

One thousand smackeroos, Sarah said.

Dress number two was an oyster-gray silk suit—cropped jacket and bell skirt. This was only four hundred, she said. Only! Listen to me. Shall I try them on?

Absolutely, said Patsy, standing by the door. Sarah stripped to her panties, climbed into the crinoline, pulled the swirling dress over her head. Muttering about girdles and strapless bras, she presented her back for buttoning.

Patsy wiped her hands on her jeans, addressed the many cloth-covered nubs.

Maybe a little much, Sarah said. What do you think?

Sarah's tumbling chestnut curls, the pale, trembling expanse of her uplifted bosom, were beautiful. But the yards of floating, wafting chiffon were a little girl's daydream on a stout thirty-four-year-old woman.

Meeting Patsy's eyes in the mirror, Sarah said, You seem a little down, Patsy. Is something wrong? You don't really like it, do you?

Let's see the other one, said Patsy.

13

She'd called a number in Knock-Knock's service directory, and here she was, on a rickety glassed-in sunporch at the Pasadena Mental Health Center with a woman around her mother's age. Unlike her mother, who'd been a slapdash dresser and eschewer of makeup, this Eileen Silver was a former beauty settling graciously into manicured middle age. Her nails were painted pale pink, her dark, syrup-colored hair curled into a squared, sprayed coif. Her beige snub-toed flats matched a linen suit—surely, Patsy thought, this person was far too conventional to be *her* therapist.

Patsy, Mrs. Silver said, her voice deep and calm. What can I do for you?

Well, everybody says I'm depressed. My friends, my father, everybody.

Are you depressed?

I don't know. I'm trying to adjust, get back into the flow of things.

You say "get back into the flow of things." How were you out of the flow?

Patsy studied the smooth, well-tended face. Hadn't Silver seen a file, received some dossier on State of California letterhead? Or maybe she wanted to hear how Patsy would explain herself.

My mother died six months ago. And I just got out of prison.

Silver took a moment before answering. Those are both major adjustments, Patsy, she said. Grief. And coming out of prison. The grief, I imagine, makes settling in all the more difficult.

Yes, Patsy said. I'm not feeling very social. And I'm not drinking anymore. So now everybody wants me to come to parties and dinners and hang out while they're drinking away. They're kind and sweet, but I can't do it.

It's too much for you.

Way too much! And not at all how I want to go about my life now.

How do you want to go about it?

Patsy mimed lifting a large bowl off her lap. I want to surface slowly. I want to fade back into life.

You want to take your time.

And not call attention to myself.

Can you tell that to your friends? That you need time to adjust?

I do, over and over. Give me time. I'm not quite up to it yet. Then they say I'm depressed, and isolating. But I'm not isolating. I see people every day at AA meetings, the college. I eat a meal with my neighbors every night. And even that's too much.

You're overwhelmed.

I'm overwhelmed.

Of course you are. What you're going through is like what a soldier goes through coming home. Moving from a highly structured, stressful environment to a much looser place where messy, unpredictable everyday life has been rolling along as usual. Plus, you're grieving a major loss. Silver shook her head slowly in sympathy. How long have you been out of jail?

Irritation flashed. I wasn't in jail, said Patsy. I was in prison. There's a difference. I'm surprised that you of all people don't know that.

I don't know it, said Silver, unruffled. Will you explain it to me?

Patsy frowned at the flat white sky outside. If Silver was taking referrals from parole agencies, shouldn't she be well versed in the criminal justice system?

Jail is short-term, said Patsy with singsong impatience. Like before you've been arraigned or if you've got a month or two to serve. You can't spend more than a year in jail.

So jail is the county facility.

Right, and I was in state prison.

Thank you for clarifying that, said Silver with a brief smile. I imagine you have to do that a lot.

Not really, said Patsy. Nobody mentions prison to me. The word hasn't passed my father's lips. My friends don't exactly bring it up either. Except for Gilles, the kid I go to meetings with. He wants to know everything about it.

And you appreciate that?

Actually, I do. Yes. I really do.

Silver gazed at her quietly. You know, Patsy, you and I can talk about anything you want. That's what I'm here for.

I know, Patsy said, re-irritated. She had been to therapists before, and they always started in on this you-and-I business—you and I are going to have a real time of it here, as if it were an actual relationship and not a hired ear.

Still, Silver had fielded her snappishness well, even seemed strangely pleased by it. That quick smile, the flash of amusement in her eyes.

•

Binx and Caroline, two tall, strong-looking women who sat together at the morning AA meeting, turned out to be Gilles's particular friends. After giving Patsy a few days to settle in, they reclaimed their places in the booth at Barkers. Binx had broad shoulders and a short cap of mink brown hair. Caroline was taller, freckled and mannish, her curly hair hennaed red. They'd both competed in two Olympics.

Really? What events?

Hurdles and quaaludes, said Binx.

Hammer and vodka, said Caroline. And mannies too.

German quaaludes, explained Binx.

Patsy said, I thought athletes were supposed to be so healthy.

Wherever did you get that idea?

Caroline ran the meeting on Thursday mornings and wanted Patsy to speak. Heat flooded Patsy's face. She'd spoken at many meetings in prison and fire camp, but this was a big meeting, and attendees walked out into the world at large. Not yet, she said. It's too much.

It's so people can get to know you, said Caroline.

I wouldn't know what to tell them, Patsy said. She didn't want to lie or sandbag, but she also wasn't sure she wanted fifty strangers to know she'd been imprisoned. She turned to Gilles.

Never refuse an AA request, he said. That's what Auntie says.

But how much should I tell?

Everything—but in a general way.

Do you tell everything?

Oh, you know me. As my Cuban nanny said, *Gilles no tiene pelo en la lengua.* I have no hair on my tongue. It all comes out, *sin filtración*. And Auntie always says, You're as sick as your secrets. I mean, I never go into the finer details of bum sex, but you know . . .

Patsy told a fifteen-minute version of her story. Then Caroline handed her the list of topics for discussion and she picked one at random: serenity. But anyone arriving late that day would've thought the topic was incarceration, because everyone who talked told about being imprisoned, even some of the best-dressed management types. Even Gilles's elegant uncle, who talked about being locked up for drunkenness and conduct unbecoming an officer.

After that morning, people were friendlier to her. She was asked to speak at other meetings. Men came up to her at the breaks. Hey, did you hear I found a job? they said. Did you hear I moved? Yeah, to a new apartment on Los Robles.

Why do they tell me these things? she asked Gilles.

They want to talk to you, he said. They have to talk about something.

At Barkers, she listened to Caroline, Binx, and Gilles deconstruct the meeting. They laughed at Sean the caterer, who hired two barely clean heroin addicts and was stunned when they vanished with his van, which surfaced, gutted, in Bell Gardens. They made much of Rajid, the Iranian hairdresser who paid for his girlfriend's breast augmentation.

It would've been easy to jump in with the quips. Gives a whole new meaning to tit for tat. She'd had a sharp tongue before. But she'd made a pledge to herself: no harmful speech. She was making a clean beginning here. Keeping her big mouth shut. Her new reticence pleased her, except when she felt like a prig.

She found she could make demands of herself and meet them, a novelty. A meeting a day. Read something of a spiritual nature each morning. Keep a journal. Pray, even if her higher power was To Whom It May Concern.

Not drinking, she discovered, may have muted her sociability, even made her shy, but it was a great aid to self-control. To bridling the instincts.

•

Binx nodded toward a booth in the back, where Gilles's uncle presided over a group of men. I have it bad for him, she said.

You and every other female in AA, said Caroline.

And every widow and divorcée in La Cañada Flintridge, said Gilles. Not to mention San Marino, Arcadia, and Pasadena.

Who are you talking about? asked Patsy. Not Cal. Cal? Really? Oh, but Binx, he's way too old. He's old enough to be your dad.

And then some, said Binx. But who cares? Have you noticed his eyes?

Patsy had. Unusually dark blue and lively. And kind.

I am powerless over those ink blue eyes, said Binx.

I thought you liked his smile, said Caroline.

Oh god, his smile, said Binx. She turned to Gilles. Is he still dating that helmet-head from South Pas?

He never dated her, said Gilles. They're old friends from the club.

Who is he dating, then?

I'm not sure he's dating yet, said Gilles. It's only been four months since Aunt Peg died. Why don't you go over and talk to him? He'd like it, I'm sure.

I can't go alone, Binx said. Caroline?

I have to go to work, said Caroline.

Patsy? Will you come with me?

Sorry, she said. I'm happy here.

She did not want to start up with the boy-crazy stuff.

I'm not up to it, she said. Sorry.

That's okay, said Binx. I know how it is. My uncle was in one of those country club minimum-security places for six months, and it took him two years to surface after he got out.

Well, that's hopeful, said Patsy, who was happy to hear that he'd surfaced at all.

·

I go to AA meetings, and afterward four of us go out for coffee. Gilles and these two women. They gossip about everybody at the meeting. But I can't.

Yes, life has gone on without you. It must be difficult to jump back in.

No, that's not it. I didn't know these people before. But AA isn't my social scene. It's more like, I don't know, my church.

People have friends at church.

I'm not against friends, just gossiping. It feels to me like fouling the nest.

You think they're fouling the nest?

They can do what they want. I'm not judging them. But I don't want to bad-mouth people. Or know their personal stuff or go to another table to flirt with some guy. That's not how I want to be.

How do you want to be?

I knew you would ask me that. I'm learning your approach. You play dumb and toss things back at me. How do I want to be? I want to keep a respectful distance with people so I don't wreck things with 'em. Not to sound all saccharine, but being a good person interests me. A person who doesn't talk about other people's shortcomings to get a little lift. I'd like to do some actual good in the world, since I haven't been very good up till now.

In what way haven't you been good?

Oh, come on. I killed two people. You knew that.

Silver paused and lifted her chin. Okay, she said in her low, calm voice. Let's go back and look at that. Do you want to tell me what happened?

In the air conditioner's hum was a soft, rhythmic cycle of clicks and whirs: the sound of time passing at the sliding scale rate of ten dollars an hour.

Sure. Okay, Patsy said, pushing her hair behind her ears and allowing a tone of prison-bred defiance to dull her voice. A little over two years ago I took my car out when my license was revoked. I was in a blackout and probably forgot I wasn't supposed to drive . . .

Silver was attentive, as if a stone had been lobbed into a well and she was waiting to hear it land. When Patsy was done and the stone had landed, Silver leaned forward and in her deep, unperturbed, unhurried voice said, This has been a great tragedy for everyone, Patsy. Two people lost their lives, and now you have to carry that burden for the rest of yours.

And that's what I'm trying to figure out, Patsy said with feeling. How to carry that burden and make up for it in some way.

Make up for it?

I don't know. More balance it. Balance it with something.

And prison?

What about prison?

Wasn't that your punishment?

Yes, yes.

So you have been punished.

Yes.

And that didn't balance it for you?

Oh, officially, I suppose. In the most acute sense. The official debt-to-society sense. And it really is punishment. Especially for anyone like you or me raised in middle-class privilege. So filthy and loud and ugly. But you don't deal with why you're there, except maybe with the state shrink who's a different person every month. Basically, you sit around. Or in fire camp, you hoe weeds. Nobody cares about how you're going to cope with what you've done. It's like you said, I have to live with what I did for the rest of my life. I've given it a lot of thought. The most I can do, I think, is to add something good to the world, though I'm not sure what. I'm still stuck on the basics.

The basics?

You know, Patsy said. How to be less selfish and not give in to my craven instincts all the time.

What do you mean by instincts?

You know . . . I mean, do you want a list?

Sure.

Drinking. Doing nothing. Sex. Eating all the time. Napping. Gossiping. Or spending whole days staring out the window.

Are these instincts or impulses?

When Patsy didn't answer right away, Silver went on. I ask because I think of instincts as internal indicators that I rely on. I consult my instincts, for instance, about people and decisions. The things you listed—drinking, sex, and napping all day—those to me are impulses. Am I making sense?

Yes. You're saying it's not my instincts, but my impulses I should control.

Control, yes, we like to control our worst impulses. But there are ways to consider our impulses that aren't so antagonistic to them. I've found that impulses also serve as signals. Silver spoke easily and reasonably, her voice a wide, soft path through the woods. If I have an impulse to sleep all day, she said, I know that something's off. Or if I'm overeating . . .

I know, I know, said Patsy. Like if I feel like drinking, I've got to go to a meeting, call my sponsor, get back on track.

Is that what you do?

Yes, except not call my sponsor. She's still inside—in prison. I know, I should get another one. I haven't gotten around to it yet. I have my eye out. There's this completely lovely older guy at my morning meeting I'll maybe ask. Though it should be a woman. But I haven't met that many women in AA yet. I need to go to some different meetings. See? So much to do to get up and running. That's why I can't start gossiping or flirting with guys. I don't want the distraction. I can't get involved with anybody right now.

Okay, said Silver. We have to stop.

Silver's face was set and closed. Did I say something wrong? Patsy asked.

Our time is up, Silver said firmly. We have to stop.

Patsy stared at her for a moment, grabbed her purse, and fled.

14

All week a thread of uneasiness wove through her days and led back to
Silver's sudden and shocking coldness, the abrupt way she ended their
session. *We have to stop.* What had Patsy said to make Silver so cold? Had
she been glib, or bragged, or somehow insulted the woman?

She went to meet with Knock-Knock and imagined the PO's belea-
guered, seen-it-all voice. It's not working out with the therapist, Patsy.
Or, You know, Patsy, you can't steamroll a therapist. Or maybe Goldstone would wordlessly hand her a slip of paper with the name of another therapist.

In fact, the PO was in a light and distracted mood and hardly
glanced at her meeting card. Sounds like you're holding steady. Good.
Keep on the way you're keeping on, he said. See you in two weeks.

•

Her favorite thrift store, the Sunflower Shop, sold moth-nibbled cashmere twin sets and odd bits of old china, the life effluvia of the old Presbyterian ladies who ran it. Patsy bought a linen shift for a dollar, pumps
in ice blue dupioni silk for seventy-five cents. Two boxes of Wedgwood
Drabware china cost six dollars. The shapes were made from the same
blanks as the company's fine china, but, intended for the servants' use,
the glaze was the neutral gray-brown of cooked oatmeal. To Patsy, the
Drabware was plain and vaguely punitive, but Brice collected the stuff.
Otherwise, she wouldn't have known about it. She lugged the boxes
home in two trips. Brice shouted with pleasure. Oh my god! My god!
Where did you find this? Look at this platter! And this coffeepot!

No, he couldn't pay her back or give her anything.

This was how she wanted to be. Generous, surprising people with pleasure. Her own happiness from this transaction carried her for an evening, until a twinge called her back to the lingering worry. That's right, Silver. Our time is up. We have to stop.

•

She was surprised to hear Ian Sasaki's raspy Southern drawl over the telephone. Of course she remembered him, she said, recalling his compact leanness, the shock of thick black hair, his handsome, angular face. Yes, she'd like to see a movie. Neither mentioned the girlfriend who'd called during the dinner at Sarah and Henry's.

They met at the Esquire Theater east of the city college and watched an understated movie about a Texas oil executive trying to take over a small Scottish town. After, Ian took Patsy's elbow and steered her into the soft blue summer night. They walked along Colorado Boulevard, past the college and shut shops. He was two inches shorter than she was, intense and self-contained, and comfortable—too comfortable—with silence.

Can you tell me what kind of work you make? she asked.

I used to make these large abstract polymer sculptures, he said. I had some good years, bought a house in Altadena.

His house, they figured out, was three blocks from hers, two north and one to the west. A knight's move.

Despite all his success in polymer, he continued, or because of it, he'd decided to return to painting. He was making work about aquatic life. Fish.

Fish! she exclaimed. How funny.

Not realistic fish, he said. But they're not exactly abstract either. I just hope they're not cartoons.

He walked in silence for half a block. They may well be cartoons, he said.

Silence for another block. Patsy said, I suppose Sarah told you about me.

She said you teach together. You've been gone for a couple of years.

She told you where.

Yes, Ian said.

So no need for shocking disclosures.

No need. He brushed lightly against her then, and again some min-

utes later. Then at intervals, each brush causing a pleasurable distur-
bance to her system. At Avalon Street she said, You've walked me home.

Swiftly he kissed her cheek, a whiff of turpentine, a flash of chrome-
colored light behind her eyes. He walked away.

In bed that night, she recalled the brush of Ian's arm and touched
her own to revive the thrill of those collisions again and again, until she
played it out. Then her thoughts rolled to dread and tomorrow, after
work, Silver.

•

I got the feeling you were mad at me last week.

What gave you that impression?

You said, We have to stop. Like I said something to offend you.

Normally I say we have to stop when the time is up. As I recall, I
was ending the session because our fifty minutes were up. But let's go
back. Can you remember what we were talking about?

I said I didn't want to gossip. And how I didn't want a social life.
That I wanted to be a better person.

She'd also said that she didn't want to get involved with anybody,
but she didn't want to remind Silver of that, because as soon as they
were done talking about this, Patsy wanted to tell her about Ian.

Well, chances are good that whatever it was will come up again, Silver said. So let's watch for it, and next time we'll discuss it as it happens.

Patsy was impressed by Silver's calm intelligence and heartened by
the implied promise of the therapy continuing.

So I guess I should tell you that I met someone.

Ahh. Someone in particular?

A man, Patsy said. We met weeks ago but went to a movie last
night.

Did you enjoy that?

Yes, but I don't want to start thinking about him him him. I can't
be distracted by a man right now. But it's been such a long time since I
had any affection—let alone sex—it's hard to resist. Not that there was
any sex. But I can see where things are heading.

So maybe you want to take it slow. Not jump into anything.

Honestly, it already feels full speed ahead. Walking next to him and
bumping into him—I got these big, full-body emotional rushes.

And that means?

You know. Chemistry.

Yes, but that doesn't mean you don't have a choice.

What—to see him again or not?

Silver gave her a wry look. I meant, you don't have to rush into any-thing or lose yourself if you choose not to. You can take things at your own pace.

So you think it's okay for me to go ahead and get involved with him?

Is it okay with you?

I don't know! I don't even know this guy.

So get to know him a little before you decide anything.

How do you get to know someone when every time he brushes up against you, it's a tidal wave of lust?

Silver smiled her small, sly smile. Now, doesn't this seem like the perfect opportunity to figure that out?

•

In her dream, she ran down hallways with yellow lines and no doors, no end. She awoke, panting, before sunrise in her cool gray room, and rose, looked out her window. The world was colorless and still. It was Sunday, she would go to a noon meeting with Gilles. She made tea, lit a candle, pulled her books from a drawer. Today's saint was Saint Vincent de Paul, parts of the entry underlined in her mother's hand. _A mother mourned her imprisoned son. Vincent put on his chains and took his place at the oar, and gave him to his mother . . ._

Oh, Mom, she said.

The sky was a whiter gray. Still, no sun had risen. There was a knock on her door—not Gilles's quick gallop of fingers, but a sharp, peremp-tory rap. Patsy tied her kimono securely at the waist. Who is it? she said.

Jeffrey Goldstone.

He was going hiking, he said, and had thought to pay her a call en route. He stood in the living room in his orange Sheriff's Department T-shirt, khaki shorts, and glowing white sport shoes.

Do I take you on a tour?

I'll have a look around, if you don't mind.

And if I did?

She trailed him into the kitchen, past the breakfast nook, where *The Big Book of Alcoholics Anonymous* and *Lives of the Saints* were open by her lit candle. Jeffrey Goldstone took notes, sketched, moved on through the living room to her bedrooms, Patsy right behind him. The rooms suddenly seemed sparse to her, underfurnished.

A little messy, she said about her unmade bed, yesterday's cotton dress on the bedroom chair, underpants she'd stepped out of on the floor.

No fugitive cowered in the closet. No needles were shoved under the bed. Yet her heart raced as if he were on the verge of such a discovery. What if she was doing something wrong and didn't know?

In her breakfast nook, he touched the alabaster wall sconce. For my own curiosity, he said, can I ask what rent you pay?

Two hundred.

Not bad.

Her hands shook as she closed the door behind him.

•

Walking home from another movie, this one about a woman whistle-blower who gave up job and love to tell the truth, Patsy again asked Ian questions, gentle ones, such as females are tutored to ask, to indicate an interest. Did he like teaching? Who were his students? He seemed to find even such mild queries invasive. I do it for money, he said. College students.

So she scuffed alongside him in silence. After some blocks, he took her hand, effectively discouraging any further attempts at conversation. He'd be appalled, she thought, to know how intense her desire was. She herself was ashamed to feel so much with so little encouragement.

Ian stopped, pointed to a metal ammunition box in the window of a surplus store. Great verdigris on that, he said.

A wood-burning stove at the fireplace store drew his next comment. That would be good in my house, he said.

Emboldened, she pointed out a small oil painting in the Sunflower Thrift Shop window, a bouquet of lilies. Not bad, he said, but it's so sun-damaged, you'd end up repainting the whole thing.

At the Lyster's front steps, his swift kiss to the corner of her mouth left her with the afterimage of a bleached-out lily.

•

After the next movie, he did not hold her hand or kiss her.

I'm a history professor, with a Ph.D. I can't believe I'm talking this way, Patsy told Silver. Like I'm in junior high. He loves me, he loves me not.

Do you love him?

I only meant *love* rhetorically, she said. I hardly know him. He hardly talks. He's laconic, mum's the word. You'd laugh to see us, a couple of mutes trundling along Colorado, bumping into each other accidentally on purpose.

How *do* you feel about him?

I don't know. Drawn in. He's so beautifully made, small and so intense.

And you like that?

I don't know. I guess so, she said, thinking how even the most incipient forms of sex—brushing his shoulder, holding his hand, receiving his good-night peck—were momentous.

Gilles, her other confidant, said, They say drinking stalls you out, and when you sober up, you're the same age emotionally as you were when you started drinking.

Which for her meant thirteen. Yes. That's exactly how old she felt.

Saturday we're going to an opening in Santa Monica, she told Gilles.

An opening! That means he's showing you off.

Patsy wore the ivory shift dress and the blue silk-covered shoes. Ian said, Wow, when she opened the door, and blinked as if she were bright. She should've changed then, because at the opening, among the artists and students in their dark, severe clothes, she was the only person in pastels, and the shiny silk shoes revealed themselves for what they were, prosaic bridesmaid pumps devoid of style or irony.

Ian pushed her through the crowd, his hand at the small of her back. They couldn't see the art for the crowd. Many people spoke to Ian, but he was brief, even curt in reply. He grabbed a glass of wine and pulled her outside again, where a sharp-featured woman in a dress with many zippers kissed him and talked intensely about the art school where they both taught. Unintroduced, Patsy stood to one side, ablaze in ivory and baby blue, the dress too scant in the cool ocean air and her sweater locked in the car. A few cups of rotgut Chablis, she thought, would start to set things right.

Ready to go? Ian said. I sure am.

He knew how to get a small private upstairs room in a Little Tokyo restaurant, where once again the dress proved problematic, this time for sitting on the floor. She tucked her legs sideways, tugged constantly at the hem.

Ian held a lengthy, low-voiced consultation in Japanese with the waiter.

I didn't know you spoke Japanese, she said.

I was asking if they had any whale.

Whale? she said. Who would ever eat whale?

You would. It's the most delicious sushi of all.

Never, she said. Sushi had come into fashion while she was in prison; she'd had it only once before, at the home of a Japanese colleague, and a lot of rice—and sake—was involved.

A glass platter of halibut sashimi was set before them, the garnish a cucumber slivered to look like a chrysanthemum. In her mouth, the cool, translucent flesh repulsed her. Sorry, she said. I'm been living on sawdust, more or less. I'm only now getting used to real cheese again, and avocado.

He ordered miso soup for her, and a bowl of bright green steamed spinach, tea. He drank sake from a wooden box. The opening had stirred him up. He talked with contempt about a gallery owner who'd asked to see his paintings, and an artist who was a fake but was having enormous success.

Patsy pulled on her hem, listened. She apparently had missed an entire undercurrent of jockeying, hypocrisy, and insult at the opening. Ian laughed a little and said in his Southern drawl, And then there was you—

Me? What about me?

They were beside themselves, he said. I thought I was going to have to run interference on everyone gawking at your legs.

Sorry, she whispered, tugging on the dress.

Hey, don't you apologize. Ian traced her ankle with his finger.

At the Lyster's medieval wooden door, he wrapped his arms snugly around her and kissed her. His lips were firm, and he tasted, distantly and sourly, of alcohol.

Shall I come up? he asked.

Oh! Not tonight, she said, startled.

I can't come up? he murmured, kissing her again.

She'd prepared herself for the usual peck and run, not this. She didn't like him very much at the moment, after so much self-pity and ill will toward others, not to mention whales.

Ian, she said. We have to stop.

•

In the lobby, Gilles was reading a newspaper in one of those pitched-back hotel chairs. What are you doing down here? she said. Waiting up for me?

Oh, hello Patsy, he said, peering through his bangs. Is that what you wore?

I know, I know.

You look like you're going to a Nazarene wedding. Where did you get those shoes? Ohmigod. Take them off right now.

Stop, Gilles. I can't handle it. I am not cool. I never will be cool.

I grew up at openings, he said. I could've sent you off in style.

I hate men anyway, she said. Heterosexual men, I mean. What is their problem? They strut and posture and eat whale and don't talk, except to rant. Then all of a sudden you're supposed to make out with them?

Exactly, said Gilles. Shoes, please.

She stepped out of them, and Gilles left by the front door, the pumps dangling from his fingers. Patsy heard them hit the Dumpster. Boom, and boom.

15

Ian had two dogs, a black Lab-shepherd mix and a little orange terrier. His dark-shingled, one-bedroom cabin stank of turpentine. A high platform bed took up most of the living room. Like a monument, she thought, or a pyre.

He painted in the bedroom, he said, and motioned her to follow.

The windows were covered in foil, all the light was fluorescent. An easel, a metal stool, a filthy cart holding crumpled paint tubes were the only furnishings. Ian had used one whole wall to wipe his brushes on; the smears of color radiated outward like an explosion. Groups of canvases leaned, face-backward, against the opposite wall.

To see a house put to such irregular use! Not until he began turning the paintings around did there seem any reason for it. Then, fat tunas shone like battered silver bins, a school of anchovies flashed like dinner knives. A big, stupid-looking brown grouper drifted in pale green light outside his dark hole of a cave in a reef. The paint was a thick, luminous impasto. All the water, even the deepest blue-black depths, swelled with volume and light.

If we ever live together, Patsy thought, my house could be for sleeping, eating, our civilized life. She said, Do you put something in the paint to build it up like that?

Nah, he said. It's solid mistakes.

They're so strong yet childlike, she said, thinking that some were silly too.

He looked with brightened interest at his own work. What else?

Patsy talked off the top of her head. Playful. Dark. Existential.

Yes, yes. Pleased, he waited for her to say still more.

Fumes scorched the back of her throat. It's like you're painting the mind, she said.

Exactly, he said, yes, exactly. He looked at her with animation and grasped her wrist.

Patsy thought, We could sell both our houses and buy one in Sarah and Henry's neighborhood, and make *our* ballroom into a giant studio. Desecrate the whole thing, top to bottom, with paint.

He led her to the living room and backed her onto the high bed. Pleasure sluiced through her chest and limbs in warm, fast currents. Alerted by their gasps and cries, the terrier stood by the bed and barked, and wouldn't stop.

Afterward, they sat out on his back patio. He brought her a wineglass of berry juice, and pistachios in a black clay bowl. The old Lab mix curled at their feet. They ate the nuts, dropping the cupped shells into a rusty coffee can. The terrier snuffled under the oak trees. Patsy drifted, twitching with residual pleasure as her body settled. Shells clattered into the can. And then a shift, as if a sheet of glass slid down, a window shut.

Hey, she said.

He didn't answer. Perhaps he didn't hear. Oh, but he must have.

Hot shame spread through her, and she remembered the nakedness and noises and frantic arrangings, the long, sweet looks. Now he wanted her gone. She stood. I need a ride, she said.

He stood as well. No problem.

They drove in silence. Pulling up in front of the Lyster, he waited until she'd opened her door to speak. You know, Patsy, that this has nothing to do with you.

I don't know that, she said, and closed the door.

•

Who did it have to do with, did you ask? said Silver.

No.

Why not?

He can't handle direct questions. He finds them prying.

Are your questions prying?

To him.

And so you . . .

I don't ask them.

They'd been too ardent, or she had. Whenever she thought of their lovemaking—her noises and tenderness—shame washed over her.

She didn't need a lover, anyway. Not now. *Persevere in your good resolutions*, said *Lives of the Saints. It is not enough to begin well; you must so continue to the end.*

But he called and asked her to a movie. They went back to sitting in the dark and intermittent, chaste hand-holding, as if nothing more had ever passed between them. A whiff of solvents from his clothes made her ache. When they reached the Lyster, he'd hug her briskly and leave. No more kisses. Once, he came up to see the apartment. She made twig tea. He soon handed her his mug. I hope you're okay with things like this, he said.

My shrink thinks I should go slow too.

Slow, yes, he said. But slow still implies a destination.

Slow to wherever, she said, shrugging to match his indifference. Alone, she still recalled his intense, affectionate lovemaking and imagined revolving in and out of each other's houses, Pomelo to Oleander Street—this could happen yet, she believed, if she didn't scare him off.

•

The Mojave Club now shared the grounds and services of the Altadena Country Club, another old-fashioned privately run institution with its own dwindling membership. The adjacent golf course had long since gone public.

Gilles insisted they have dinner on the terrace to celebrate Brice's new job. After working as a freelance producer on local commercials, Brice had been hired by the production company. They'd called that morning, and he'd already pre-spent a week's salary on an expensive pair of sunglasses that he continued to wear long after the sun slid behind a dense screen of eucalyptus trees. They ordered cheeseburgers and Cokes. Brice, Patsy noted, had adapted his drinking to Gilles's habits, as he once had adapted to hers. Their talk was punctuated by the pock of the tennis balls, the screams and splashes of children in the pool below.

God, look at those mountains, said Brice, who was always happiest when he had a real job, a fact he never remembered. Don't you love it here, Patsy?

She smiled, but no, she didn't. When the Mojave Club was at the grand old Bellwood, she'd been impressed and intimidated, but this small, local, members-only private club with its anti-intellectual, pro-business Eisenhower parochialism was the culture that grew her. The world she fled for Berkeley. Around them, families were joined by fathers still in business suits from downtown offices and banks. She had her eye on the young father at a nearby table. With a plump two-year-old daughter on his knee, he ordered a second and a third double vodka rocks. His wife and children would leave, she knew, and hours later he would follow, perhaps to pass out on the sofa or dismantle the living room.

Well, well, well. To what do we owe this honor?

Why, Auntie, said Gilles.

Cal Sharp smiled down on them. Of course he would be here too. A club man, even yet. His Mojavian drinking adventures were AA legend— Round for the house, round for the house! One year, he'd told the meeting, his bar tab amounted to the median home price in Pasadena. Luckily, he'd owned the bar.

Brice, he said. Patsy. And shook their hands.

He ruffled Gilles's hair, and Gilles's eyes went soft with pleasure.

Sit down, join us, Auntie.

Now, Patsy, I've been meaning to ask you a question. Do you ride?

Me? Horses?

Sit down, Auntie, said Gilles. Don't loom.

Yes, please, sit. Patsy touched the empty chair beside her. I used to ride, she said. The usual horse-crazy adolescent girl thing. Not so much recently.

Cal had horses that needed riding. His kids weren't around, he couldn't exercise the whole stable. Could she help him out, ride with him on Saturday?

Sure, she said, knowing that it wasn't about helping him out. Cal looked for ways to encourage people, the ones who were new to sobriety or having a rough time. A kind comment. A free meal. A job he happened to know about. A horseback ride.

•

Patsy wondered how many other women had given Cinder a turn. A small, thin-legged bay mare, she had a pretty little canter and a nasty temper. She's gone a bit spooky on us, said Cal. Watch out, she'll shy at a stinkbug.

Cal rode a buckskin quarter horse gelding named Pliny. My sons call him Plywood, he said. They'd started on a private bridle path that wended past the estates in Cal's Flintridge neighborhood—his sprawling brick Tudor-style home on two acres was comparatively modest—then on up by the Jet Propulsion Laboratory, where they turned onto a public trail that led into the Arroyo Seco. Cal's long-eared speckled spaniels boiled around the horses's hooves. The day was hot, but the narrow canyon was shady, with the coolness of damp stone.

A year ago, when the wild buckwheat was drying to a dark iron red and the toyons were beading with green berries, she'd been digging fire lines on hills like these.

Cal took the lead in his fine-weave Panama hat and chambray shirt. He sat tall yet relaxed. Patsy had had enough riding instruction to know that such poise came from years of conscious practice, and she recalled Miss Becky's bored barks: *Heels down, tummy in, shoulders back!* The muscles she'd built in fire camp did not serve her now. Within minutes her efforts at fine horsemanship exhausted her.

As Cal predicted, a dragonfly, its wings a coppery blur, provoked Cinder to a sickening sudden sideways veer. Ho now, Patsy said, and yanked the mare's black mane. You cut that out. But a shadow set her off next, then a breeze, the wing flap of a blue jay. She always veered left, so Patsy knee-gripped and shifted right and got the hang of it soon enough.

Well done, said Cal when he saw.

She understood why men in the morning meeting flocked to Cal, why he sponsored so many of them, why they trailed him to Barkers and sat in attendance. He was so elegant, and easy in his own skin.

They came to a wide access road, and Cal waited for her to come alongside. You're deep in thought, he said.

I was thinking about how you sponsor so many men.

Too many.

Really?

Some days, absolutely.

Really? But I'd like to do that someday—help people the way you do.

What's stopping you now?

Oh, right, she said, thinking of her scant two years of prison sobriety, her parole.

Cal held Pliny close. You have a lot to offer, Patsy, he said. Especially to other intelligent, educated alcoholics. They're some of the toughest cases. The mechanism for recovery is so simple, it eludes them. You could do a lot of good.

Someday, maybe.

No time like the present, said Cal. Get yourself a passel of sponsees and you'll forget you ever had any problems of your own.

I'm not as evolved as you are, she said. Not so good-natured. Or patient.

All a great deception, said Cal.

You can't fake how you are, she said. I really admire you.

And I really admire you, he said.

She gave a little snort. Right.

Think about it, Patsy, Cal said, and steered the buckskin closer yet. You spent two years in terrible circumstances, really the worst, but here you are, working, sharing your experience, strength, and hope at meetings. It's an inspiration to all of us, but especially to Gilles, who was having a terrible time before you came along.

Brice made the difference, she said.

Brice made some, said Cal. But now that Gilles is bringing you to the morning meetings, his own attendance is more consistent. And he's happier for it. But my real point, Patsy, is that nobody would've thought twice if you'd transitioned through a halfway house or holed up with your family. Instead, you took a job, found your meetings, and jumped right back into life.

Cal's generosity was like an open, sunlit field, and for a moment she saw herself as he did, as someone on a sure path.

Pliny's proximity to Cinder was forcing the little bay into an erratic, nervous prance. Patsy pulled back on her reins. She needed Cal to move on.

They rode up the access road along a trickle of a stream, through a beech glade. Cinder stumbled at a passing goldfinch, the friendly bark of an Airedale. They came to a small waterfall and wide, shallow pool. Dismounting, they tied the horses to a shrubby oak and sat on flat gray granite boulders while the dogs stood up to their bellies in the water and scratched at submerged rocks.

You know who's a superb rider? she said. Binx.

Is she one of the lady athletes?

The high jumper. She'd love it up here.

A Valkyrie, said Cal.

That's a little gruesome, said Patsy. Valkyries haul the dead off bat-
tlefields.

Both those gals look like they could do some serious hauling.

I think Binx is beautiful, she said.

She's the one with curly hair?

No.

On the ride back, Cal said he was going to grill steaks.

I can't stay, said Patsy, who was going to a movie later with Ian.

They unsaddled at the barn. Patsy went up to the house to use the
bathroom off the service porch. Coming out, she saw movement in the
kitchen. Thinking Cal had come inside, she went to join him, and found
Brice's niece, Joey Hawthorne, pouring herself a glass of pink punch.

Hey you, said Patsy.

Patsy! Oh my god! What are you doing here?

I went riding with Cal.

Joey put down the jug and embraced her. Oh, it's so good to see you.
You went riding? she said. Cal didn't put you on Cinder, did he? God,
she's a goon.

Not too bad, said Patsy. I liked her, actually. So what are you doing
here?

I'm here for the summer, she said. Escaping the evil stepmother.

Brice told me your dad remarried.

Yeah, the hideous housekeeper. But oh! Joey cried. What about
Brice! It's just like you said, Patsy—he really does like boys.

Is that what I said?

Yeah, that time you pierced my ears. I never forgot. It could be that
he likes boys, you said.

I guess I said that a lot, Patsy said. Have you met Gilles?

Like when I was born. His mom and mine were friends.

Through the kitchen window, Patsy saw Cal lugging a saddle to the
tack room. I better go help him, she said.

What's going on with you two, anyway? said Joey.

Cal? We went for a ride up the arroyo.

Anything else? Joey grew still and intent.

What? Oh, come on, Joey. And besides, I have a boyfriend, Patsy
added, fully aware that Ian would never accept the designation.

Okay, then, said Joey.

Patsy was amused by Joey's sternness. What do you care?

March doesn't want a new person around. Riding her mom's horse and stuff.

I know, said Patsy. My dad's already seeing someone—this woman who crashed my mom's funeral.

God, doesn't that make you want to claw her face off? said Joey.

Oh, if she hadn't snagged him, someone else probably would've. He was so lost. Didn't know where the sheets were kept, or the toilet paper. But mostly, Patsy added, I'm grateful I don't have to take care of him.

Yeah, but he should take care of you. He's your dad.

I can take care of myself, said Patsy. Through the window she saw Cal brush his jeans, look up at the house.

I should go finish up down there, she said.

Yeah, and tell Cal he should put Cinder down. Chicken her out. Before she puts someone in the hospital. Joey tossed her head, and something glinted.

Hey, said Patsy. Stepping forward, she pushed back a dark blond hank of hair. There, in Joey's earlobe, a small gold hoop.

I had them done again. Joey showed off both ears. Even-steven this time.

•

You did what? said Binx. Riding with Cal? When?

I told him to ask you next. I said you were a great rider.

I've been on a horse twice in my life.

Anyway, I put in a good word for you.

Did he ask you out again?

It was nothing like that, said Patsy. His dead wife's horse needs exercise.

But he asked you. He singled you out.

Yeah, like he singles out all newcomers—to be of service.

You're hardly a newcomer, said Binx, with two-plus years of sobriety.

Yeah, but I am fresh from the pokey.

16

Patsy, with Gilles behind her, pushed through the turnstile in Prebles' Market and spotted in the checkout line the long face, high forehead, and soft chin that could only be Mark Parnham. Beside him stood a miniature, darker version of himself. Before Mark saw her, Patsy dashed deep into the store, pulling Gilles with her. That's him, the father and husband of the people—the people I, you know, *hit*, Patsy whispered. His son too. They look regular. So normal. They didn't look so unhappy. Do you think they looked unhappy?

I didn't see them, said Gilles. Let me go back and look.

No! she said, seizing his arm again.

She had told Mark Parnham that she would get in touch with him when she got out of prison, but so far, she'd only sent a change-of-address card. To bump into him like this was embarrassing—and, given the boy, even harmful.

You should've said hi, said Gilles. Now you have to call him.

I do? said Patsy.

As soon as we get home, he said.

Why? she said.

You can't be hiding from people in grocery stores.

I can't?

Back at the Lyster, Gilles got out of the elevator on her floor. Let's get it over with, he said.

Mark Parnham was kind. Of course you could've come up and talked to us. I'd like you to meet Martin. I've been wondering how you're doing. How are you?

Okay, said Patsy. I'm glad to be out.

We're doing well over here too, Mark said, and thanked her for calling. Next time, say hi.

There, Gilles said. That took care of that.

At the morning meeting, she talked about Mark Parnham, how willing he'd been to forgive her yet how hard it was to see him, when mostly, she just wanted to forget what had thrown them together. Afterward, a woman came up, a regular at the meeting who was a reporter for the *Times*. She wanted to interview Patsy and Mark together. I see it as a feature on forgiveness, she said, with sidebars on the legal and mental health issues. It could inspire a lot of people.

Patsy said, Let me call him first and see what he says.

The article ran two weeks later. Patsy was afraid she came across as wordy and overintellectual. Gilles said no, smart.

. . . The two are calm and respectful with each other. When asked if they are friends, they both start to answer at the same time; then each gestures for the other to go first.

"The term friends makes it sound as if we chat on the phone and have lunch," says MacLemoore. "And we don't. We're something else—if you want to be technical, we're forgiver and forgiven. Which is its own powerful bond."

Parnham nods as she speaks, and then it's his turn to answer the question. Does he consider them friends?

"Yes," he says. "I think we are."

For days, people who saw the article phoned, wrote notes, and came up to Patsy at meetings. She was asked to speak at *six* other AA meetings. Cal Sharp said, It's a beautiful story, Patsy. Of her ESL students, only Nadia, the Italian-speaking Eritrean woman, mentioned it. I am so impress with your candor, she said.

•

Mother has asked to meet you, said Gilles.

He drove Patsy to the house on a Saturday evening. Father died of a headache, he said. Brain aneurysm. I was eight. Mother's been through a lot. But she's a lovely bird.

Audrey Sanger was tall and impeccable in white slacks and a crisp ironed blue shirt. Glossy brown hair in a smooth chin-length bob. Pearls at home.

At last, she said, an East Coast flatness to her speech. I've heard about you, read about you—for weeks it's been nothing but Patsy this, Patsy that. Stepping closer yet, Audrey kissed her cheek.

Like Gilles, Patsy thought: loving.

Audrey led them to a garden room off the kitchen. She and Patsy sat on a small sofa while Gilles paced in front of them. Beyond the French doors grew a ficus tree with a trunk so wide a person could live in it.

I hear you've been riding with my brother. He says you know your way around a horse.

A couple times, and only trail riding. Not dressage or anything.

He's a dirty old man, Gilles put in. He's got his hairy eyeball on Pats.

Don't even say that, Gilles, Patsy said. You're trying to embarrass me.

Yes, go away, Gilles. Make a beverage and let us talk. Audrey batted at him, her fingers freighted with gold rings, one large ruby. Tea or coffee, Patsy?

She likes tea, Mother.

Gilles went into the kitchen, and Audrey leaned in. I'm so glad he's found Brice. What I've gone through, chasing that child all over the globe. I hear you used to go with him?

Patsy didn't follow her at first. Oh, Brice, she said. I tried.

Yes, well, haven't we all tried that sort of thing at one time or another. There's something off, you can't put your finger on it, it's . . .

Mother, don't whisper, Gilles called from the kitchen. And let Patsy say something once in a while.

Audrey kept her voice low. I never had to wonder about Gilles, though. He arrived as is. When every other boy at his nursery school was mad about trains, Gilles was organizing my lipsticks by shade.

Gilles coughed in the kitchen.

Audrey sat back and raised her voice. But god. When he ran away from Hotchkiss—oh! Then—Paris! That took years off my life.

I couldn't tell you where I was. Gilles appeared with a tray holding teacups and spoons, sugar, milk. Mother had to come around, he said to Patsy. She wasn't always so open-minded.

I came around, yes. But you should've seen him when I got to Paris. He was supposed to meet me at Roissy, but I had to take a cab to his apartment.

I was nervous, said Gilles.

Nervous! He was so drunk, he was like one of those characters stuck in glue, couldn't pull himself up off the ground. And the apartment's all Louis Quatorze, gilt this, gilt that, boiserie for miles, John and Messieurs Hangers-On sprawled on petit point sofas like lizards, all of them smoking, drinking champagne. I wanted to arrest the whole crew.

Now, Mother, Patsy's heard my story, you needn't give it warmed over and slanted. Nobody was pouring wine down my throat. John hardly drank. I was thoroughly, genetically alcoholic.

True, true, said Audrey. All the men in this family! My father—and you know my big brother, Cal. He was the worst. He'd come into this house—he and my husband were great friends, you know, that's how Fred and I met, through Cal, they were in law school together at Boalt Hall. Anyway, Cal would come in and—see those big ice tea tumblers over there?—he'd take one and fill it with gin. No ice, no soda. It looked like tap water, only heavy and clear. Ten, twelve ounces. I would say, Cal dear, at least let me get you a little juice.

A little juice! cried Gilles, delighted. Like that would help!

Of course we all drank like fish back then. We didn't know alcoholic from tipsy. Even so, Cal distinguished himself. It was the heyday of the Mojave, dances every Saturday, and you'd see him curled up in the lobby, right on the carpet, snoring away. Or sleeping at the bar. Marjorie—his first wife—got to where she couldn't take it anymore. I don't blame her.

Audrey paused because Gilles was having a coughing fit.

I don't like the sound of that, she said when he stopped.

I know. I cannot shake this stupid cold, he said. It's not even like I'm congested—it's a reflex, a dry tickle, so annoying.

Go call Edie Rose right now, said Audrey.

The pediatrician?

Yes, but she'll give you a prescription over the phone.

Gilles went into the kitchen.

Her number's right there in my phone book, Audrey called, and turned back to Patsy. Where was I?

Patsy said, I didn't know Cal was married before.

Oh yes, first to Marjorie. She was a Gillette, you know, razors. Very beautiful, smart, a wonderful mother. They had two kids, Andrew and Roberta, and she had two more with her second marriage. Nobody blamed her for leaving Cal. But it shocked the hell out of him. Shocked him sober. But too late. She'd already found someone else.

I had no idea, said Patsy. I thought the one who passed away . . .

Peggy? That's a whole nother story. Cal met her downtown. She was demonstrating for civil rights on the steps of the courthouse, and the police were trying to arrest her. She was also very beautiful, blond, and so smart, like you, but I'd have to say plump. This was the early sixties, when people were marching, having rallies. Here she was, failing to disperse, and here comes Cal, fresh from court. He looked like Gilles back then, just a superbly handsome man. He sees what's going on and starts in on the cop. Don't you dare talk to her like that! Don't you dare lay a finger on her!

And then he followed them to the police station, bailed her out! He was smitten, gone, like he'd fallen into a hole. Her father ran a print shop in San Pedro. She didn't even know enough to be dazzled by Cal and what kind of life he was offering her. She refused to marry him till he was a registered Democrat.

She sounds kind of great, said Patsy.

Peggy? I loved her. Everybody did. You couldn't not. But Cal must have had some kind of unconscious radar, because she was more like him than you'd think. Just a terrible alcoholic. Here he'd given up drinking, and who does he go and find for himself? He got her into AA, but it never took, and the rest of her life she was in and out of treatment; she had hepatitis and chronic liver problems, and still she couldn't stop. She got cirrhosis at forty-four, liver cancer at fifty, was dead at fifty-one.

Gilles carried in the teapot in a cozy. Now, Mother, he said. You must give Patsy a chance to talk.

•

Cal asked Patsy to ride on another Saturday, but she was throwing an end-of-term barbecue—already!—for her students and had to get ready. The party was to be in the small backyard area behind the Lyster where Brice had put in new sod, nursed an old rose garden into blooming, and set two salvaged picnic tables on the grass.

Patsy had hired Gilles's Meals to cater, and in the last few days Gilles had made tubs of potato salad and a pasta salad with tortellini, pesto, and sun-dried tomatoes. (Sun-dried tomatoes had come to California while she was in prison, and Patsy found their salty, oily intensity alarming, but Gilles assured her they'd be a hit.) That morning, he barbecued chicken and made a mauve-colored fruit punch whose secret ingredient was black tea.

Patsy's Urdu speaker was the first to arrive; she brought Patsy a small, heavy lump wrapped in tissue: a pot metal statue of the elephant god, Ganesh.

Our god of new endeavors, she said. May he bring you success.

The Vietnamese pharmacist showed up with a box of See's chocolates. Patsy had told the students to bring whatever beer or wine they wanted, and a couple of six-packs and a jug of inexpensive rosé appeared. She was amazed, not for the first time, by how little alcohol other people drank.

All her favorite students and a few surprises came, maybe thirty people in all. Gilles, terrified of running out of food at his first paid gig, had made enough for eighty, and Patsy had bought a sheet cake for fifty. People ate at the tables and on blankets spread on the lawn. Patsy walked around making sure everyone had enough to eat and someone to talk to. After the cake was cut and served, one of the Korean women clapped her hands and proposed a toast.

Patsy tells us many times the best place to learn new language is between the sheets, she said. But I say best place is class, with Patsy for professor.

Punch cups and beer cans were raised and clacked, and afterward people began trickling out. Patsy talked for a long time to Nadia, the Eritrean, and joked amiably about the Dodgers' losing streak with the Nigerian rake, who had come despite her refusal to change his B minus to an A.

Nadia touched her shoulder. Your father? she whispered.

Cal Sharp was talking to Brice by the punch bowl. Then Cal saw her, and light slid over his face.

Landlord, Patsy said, getting to her feet. Excuse me.

Hey, Cal, she said. You're our first party crasher.

Had to make sure you weren't wrecking the place.

Ah, but the night is young, she said, even as she waved to four more departing students. I hope you're hungry.

I am, he said. I've been hearing about some tortellini goulash all week.

Patsy handed him a paper plate and gazed at the Lyster's silly green shutters. Of course: Cal was here for Gilles, and for the maiden flight of Gilles's Meals. And she had thought, for a moment, that he'd come for her.

1 7

Gilles, at his bossiest, had insisted on dressing her. Mother has a million gowns she never wears. She says come over and find something.

This was for Sarah's wedding. She'd be seated with Ian, Sarah told her, but he couldn't pick her up. As best man, he had to be with Henry.

So she was not a bridesmaid after all.

Then again, all summer she had seen Sarah only a handful of times. For coffee. A few walks around the Rose Bowl. At the shower.

Patsy browsed through plastic-sheathed dresses in Audrey's walk-in closet. This, Patsy said, pulling out a white silk shift brush-painted with pink peonies.

Too much white. Mustn't upstage the bride, said Gilles. S'rude.

Of a stretchy, multicolored Missoni skirt and structured silver jacket, he said, Too hospital benefit.

Patsy was three inches taller than Audrey, and larger all around, but with flats, she could pull off a backless bronze silk dress with beadwork at the neck.

She curled her hair, then piled the curls atop her head. Long wisps escaped, framed her face.

Gilles drove her to the house. Now, stand up straight, he said. Shoulders back. Chin up. *Formidable!*

She arrived moments before the ceremony began and was directed into the backyard, where white chairs were arranged in a semicircle. Torches had been lit, and small white lights glittered in the trees. Patsy sat to one side, toward the rear. A quartet played Mozart, crisply. On this warm, smoggy summer night, in a sea of tailored linen, only one other woman, a teenager, had gone backless. And one small woman with choppy black hair wore what looked like a dark green slip with crude red beads and a large cross on her chest.

Patsy? Annette Keller, the ancient German professor, swathed in purple gauze, squinted down at her. How elegant you look, dear.

Patsy clasped her hand, though she hardly knew the old woman.

Judith Farmingham, twentieth-century American lit, lifted her chin in greeting. Filing into the next row, Melanie, the department secretary, didn't—or wouldn't—catch Patsy's eye.

Patsy had worried about seeing her colleagues again, so much so, Silver had been stern with her. *You're there to show up for and support the bride*, she said. *It doesn't matter what anybody else does or says.*

A tall, unsmiling Henry Croft and his two groomsmen took their places at the front. Hair spilled over Ian's forehead; his bow tie was crooked. Patsy was sorry she hadn't found him beforehand, smoothed and straightened him.

The music changed to a march. A little girl strewed rose petals down the aisle, ignoring her mother's loud hiss to *slow down*. Sarah's sister came next, followed by none other than Lorianne Gull, biology.

Skinny, dull Lorianne was Sarah's bridesmaid? She'd been at the shower, but this honor wasn't mentioned, not to Patsy. To see Lorianne hunched in pink satin, wringing her bouquet, was so astonishing, Patsy couldn't stop looking, even as everybody stood for the bride. So Lorianne was who Sarah chose when Patsy was away. And continued to choose, even though Patsy was back.

Patsy surreptitiously checked to see if anyone was registering her humiliation. Of course not. All eyes were on the bride.

Then everyone sat down.

Someone, Patsy saw, had steered Sarah to beauty. The final dress was white, a simple A-line, crepe de chine. Tiny rosebuds had been woven in her hair.

A friend of Henry's, ordained by a mail-order church for the occasion, instructed the couple to exchange vows. They complied so quietly, Patsy caught only *To care for, encourage, and amuse.*

•

Ian found her as people milled for cocktails. I know nobody here, he whispered, touching her elbow, her lower back.

But then he was called away for more photographs.

Patsy slipped into a downstairs bathroom and, from there, into the library, where she sat on Sarah's old Herculon couch and skimmed an article in the *New York Review of Books* about Winston Churchill's rise to power. The key to Churchill's character, the author wrote, was his unassailable faith in himself.

•

For supper, the ballroom was lit with hundreds of tapers and not a single electric bulb. The light was soft, flickering and lively. Faces were ruddy and burnished, the crystal and silver glinted modestly. Plates of food looked like Flemish still lifes. Patsy did not begrudge Sarah Henry Croft, but the grand enchantment of this house was impossible not to envy.

They'd been seated with her Hallen friends. Well, don't you look smashing, said Wes, the history chair. You've been doing something right, said Anne Davis, Renaissance, who then colored deeply.

Her colleagues talked mostly among themselves after that. Patsy was quiet, being with Ian and not drinking. Drinking, she would've barged into conversations, told stories, insisted on the spotlight. But it was good to be more self-contained. The food kept them busy, then coffee and dessert.

Ian had spotted the black-haired fine-boned woman in the little slip; then he couldn't stop staring. The black cross on that bony chest did look anything but religious. Patsy held her shoulders back, her chin up. Nobody need know her insides were turning into tar.

The bride and groom made their rounds. You look fantastic, said Sarah.

Who's the woman in her underwear? Patsy said.

Helene? Oh, that's Ian's old girlfriend. We had to invite her, Henry knew her first. Poor Ian was so worried about seeing her. I told him to take you, and Helene would rue the—

The bandleader called Sarah and Henry up for the toasts. Sarah's father took the mike. Champagne glasses were filled. Patsy watched as strings of tiny bubbles formed and wobbled to the surface of her glass. She imagined the faint fizzy abrasion in her throat, the headachey high.

I gotta get out of here, she said to Ian.

But Ian had to give his toast, which he did so quietly nobody heard it. She poured her champagne into his glass. Then he had to dance with the bride. After that, as soon as they could, they fled.

At the Lyster's door, with a quick upward glance, he asked to follow her upstairs.

She was more careful this time. She made no noise and kept her eyes closed. They wouldn't exceed themselves as they had before—at least she wouldn't. In an hour, when Ian slid his legs out of bed, she watched him dress and leave and she didn't say a word.

·

He was back at her door, in his spattered work clothes, a few nights later. I'll go, he said, if it's not okay.

It's fine, come in, she said, keeping her voice dull to mask her triumph.

He smelled like a wet painting. She made them cups of twig tea, but by the time it brewed, they were in bed. Afterward, he fell asleep. Patsy remained wide awake as his smooth, compact body breathed and twitched on top of the sheets. She kept watch lest he up and disappear.

Then he woke up and disappeared.

Something of a pattern emerged. He often came Thursdays after his evening class and Saturdays after ten at night. But he showed up on enough random nights that she was always wondering if he would come, always waiting for him. One Thursday, knowing better, she asked if he was coming on Saturday. He didn't know, he said, and didn't show up. Thus, she learned not to ask.

·

Who answers the door? said Silver.

I know I know. But by then I've been good so long—like I've been with a strict chaperone all week. So when he shows up, it's like I got what I wanted by being so strict with myself.

How are you strict?

You know. Going to meetings. Meditating. Reading, getting ready to teach. Not calling him ten times a day—or ever.

Out of curiosity, and don't think too hard—how old is the part of you that needs a chaperone?

Oh, I don't know. Twelve.

And what was going on in your life when you were twelve?

Twelve? she thought. Books cascading from shelves. The sofa's squat legs thrusting skyward, dust bunnies festooned on black webbing.

That's the year my dad got sober, she said. The last year of his drinking.

What was that like?

Toward the end, he tore the house apart, god, two or three times a week. He'd go on the rampage—that's what we called it. We got so we could tell by how he slammed the car door and burst into the house: Uh-oh, he's on the rampage, we'd say. He'd destroy the place, starting with the bookshelves. Then he'd turn the furniture over, yank down the curtains. My mom constantly had the plasterer and painters in to fix where the curtain rods came out. She'd say, If I could only get the darn kids to stop swinging from the drapes.

She covered for him.

Oh, completely.

And what would you do when your father was on the rampage?

Go to my room.

Where was your mother?

In her room.

And your brother?

His room.

What would you do in your room?

I'd sort of crouch near my door and listen. I got so I could tell what he was doing. That's the armchair. There goes the sofa. Oh god, the china cabinet.

And what would've happened if you went out there?

It's funny you ask. Because I did. I hadn't heard him come home and was on my way to the kitchen, and there he was, his arms around an armchair like he was wrestling with it, like he had it in a hold and wanted to flip it. But each time he made his move, it would scoot away, with him sprawled out behind. Then he'd crawl up and try again. The look on his face—he was concentrating so hard. When he saw me, he stood up, all meek and embarrassed.

What did you do?

I was like, Uh, don't mind me, I'm getting a drink of water. And he motioned, like, Go on, go ahead, but I went back to my room. He left, I think.

You never talked about it?

Why? He wouldn't have remembered. He'd wake up the next day and ask why the house was in such a shambles.

Let's say you had a chaperone. What would this chaperone have done?

Watched out for me, I guess.

Like a parent?

Like a parent should've done, yes. That's right.

So someone watches out for you all week, Silver went on. Making sure your work gets done, you stay sober, keep up your spiritual practice. Then Ian shows up, and where's the chaperone? Who's watching out for Patsy then?

Patsy wanted to get up, move around the room. The chaperone, she said, is making sure I'm not being too needy. Or bugging him.

What about him bugging you? What about him showing up without calling and leaving when he feels like it? Who's watching out for Patsy then?

I know I shouldn't put up with it. But I'm hooked. And I hate it. But at least it's not drinking, or drugs.

But it was like that, of course. All the time waiting for him.

•

She read a book, a cultural history of World War II, until the sun set, the sky darkened, and she could barely see the print. The phone rang. Are you sitting in the dark waiting for your painter man? said Gilles.

Not really.

Liar. Do you have any onions? he said. Can I come get one?

The moment Gilles walked in, someone knocked at her door. And exactly what she never wanted to happen, happened.

Oh hello. Are you the famous Ian? Gilles said.

I just stopped by, Ian said. I can't stay.

Let me get Gilles his onion, said Patsy.

From the kitchen she heard Gilles chatter. For my cold. An old wives' cure from France. You slice the onion, sprinkle it with sugar, let it sit overnight. You drink the juice that comes out. Completely vile, but your cold is gone.

I think I'd rather keep the cold, Ian said.

This one's lasted months, said Gilles. I'd drink motor oil if it would help.

Heads up! Patsy called, tossing the onion. Gilles caught it handily.

Thanks, Patsy. Lovely to meet you, Ian, he said, I've heard so much.

The door shut. *What* was that! said Ian.

For a moment she saw Gilles the way Ian did, silly and extreme.

That's Gilles, she said. He lives—

God, he's like a poster boy for pedo—

He's my best friend, she cut in.

Maybe I should leave, said Ian.

But he didn't.

18

Auntie has invited us all for dinner. You, me, and Brice, and Mother's coming too.

Patsy put on her white peasant blouse with the crochet work and her red crinkled skirt—skirts were required in the Mojave's formal dining room. She was surprised, then, when instead of heading north into Altadena, Brice turned the Bweek onto the freeway heading west. Where are we going? she asked.

Cal's house—didn't I say? cried Gilles. And it will be terrible! Poor Auntie can't cook, and his housekeeper is worse.

Maybe we should eat something on the way, said Brice. We could have the London broil appetizer at the Trestle, and tortilla soup.

Oh let's, said Gilles.

But well before the restaurant Brice drove into the neighborhood of deep yards and vast homes, where oaks had been left growing in the middle of the streets like tiny, one-tree islands. Gilles said, You've been to Auntie's, right?

To the barn a couple times, she said. The kitchen once.

Oh my god, said Gilles. He and Brice exchanged a glance.

Why, is it terrible? she said.

Very Sister Parish, said Brice. All chintz and American folk art.

Aunt Peggy was the opposite of Brice, said Gilles. Tastewise.

They parked behind a station wagon cluttered with bumper stickers. QUESTION AUTHORITY. TOM BRADLEY IN '82, BEDTIME FOR BONZO. Audrey drew up behind them in her gold Volkswagen Bug.

Cal was out on the patio at the barbecue. In shirtsleeves, he waved the tongs as greeting, then, thinking better of it, came forward and kissed Audrey on the cheek. Before I forget, Audrey, he said, I found a canyon oak for you on the other side of the barn. I set out the shovel and a can.

He shook hands with Gilles and Brice, and took Patsy's hand too, then brought it to his lips.

Oh, she said.

So glad you could come. Help yourself to drinks in the kitchen. This mesquite is not cooperating.

Gilles, holding tightly to her arm, steered Patsy into the living room. Everything has a skirt, he hissed, and it was true. Chairs, sofas, tables. Even the stereo speakers were sheathed in linen toile.

And look at this. Gilles pulled her to an end table and, lifting the chintz skirt, revealed a crumpled tissue and one flip-flop, well chewed by a dog.

They were there the last time I was here, he said, and the time before that. Since Aunt Peg died. Poor Auntie, he is so out of control.

Brice plopped down on the striped chintz sofa. Show Patsy the magazine, he said.

Yes, look. Gilles lifted a thick *House & Garden* from a stack and opened it to a bookmark. After a moment Patsy saw this very room, the colors in the photographs darker, more orange. A vase of huge white mums exploded on the very coffee table now supporting Brice's Top-Siders.

Look, it's March, whispered Gilles, and pointed to a little girl with long, heavy brown hair and strong dark eyebrows, standing by a speckled puppy.

I thought Peggy was some big, easygoing populist, said Patsy.

Yeah, but she had to do something to draw Auntie home from the club.

Even once he was sober?

Auntie loves people, said Gilles. He likes meetings, clubs, parties. Where two or more are gathered . . .

By then Gilles had steered Patsy into the formal dining room, with its cool gray walls and floor-to-ceiling glass case of Victorian-era dolls.

Don't look too long. They have real hair, you'll get nightmares, Gilles said.

Only the TV room signaled recent human use: books splayed open, newspapers strewn about, someone's sweatshirt bunched in a corner of the sofa.

In the kitchen, Gilles introduced Patsy to Vilma, the housekeeper, who was cleavering a head of iceberg. This salad, with bottled dressings, she allowed Patsy to set on the buffet, next to a plate of baked potatoes and two loaves of oily, store-bought garlic bread.

Come eat, Cal called, setting down a platter of meat. Here, take a plate, Patsy. Rare or rarer? He forked a bleeding porterhouse onto her plate, then went to call the others.

Too shy to start, Patsy examined the buffet with pretended interest and was joined by a short, plump teenage girl who eyed the food with frank disdain. Patsy recognized the dark curly hair and prominent dark eyebrows.

Hello—you must be March. I'm Patsy, she said, and received the same disdain awarded the food.

Would you like to split this steak with me? It's far too much for—

I don't eat meat.

Patsy! Joey Hawthorne called shrilly, coming into the kitchen. I didn't know you were here. A jostling hug ensued.

That hug, the falsetto surprise—Patsy knew she'd been discussed.

The buffet area was crowded. Patsy stood to one side, now waiting to serve herself. On the patio, Cal was seating people. Patsy, you're here between Audrey and me, he called, slapping the back of a chair.

By the time Patsy filled her plate, March was in the chair Cal slapped, and the only place left was down at the other end, with Cal's boys and Brice.

They were good-looking boys. The older one, Spencer, had wild black curls and was home from Stanford for the summer—his was the car with the bumper stickers. Stan, the tennis star, was trimmer, in a limp white polo shirt; he had his father's intense blue eyes. Both boys were petting the heads of two speckled spaniels and slipping them strips of fat cut from their steaks. One wet, quivering nose pushed under Patsy's elbow to rest on her lap.

Just push him away, said Spencer. The beggar. They both are.

She picked at her food and sneaked most of her steak to the dogs—one, then the other, trying to be fair. The men talked around her. Spencer, it seemed, was in the Stanford band and was going back up north to practice before classes started.

You guys actually practice? said Brice.

Hey! Our halftime formations are very intricate, said Spencer. You think it's easy to do Richard Nixon's nose? A traffic bollard?

A traffic bollard? said Patsy.

You know, those things that look like orange trash barrels.

How does anyone know what it is?

That's what's so funny about it, said Spencer. And I'm not kidding, Brice, he went on. Regular bands have it much easier. They just march from formation to formation. We assemble out of chaos.

You never march?

We'd rather die than march.

What did you say? March's clear, aggrieved voice rang down the table. Are you guys talking about me?

In the sudden hush, Spencer spoke quietly. We were just talking about marching, he said. As in marching bands.

March opened her mouth to say something more, but Gilles called out, Marching bands! I love marching bands. The uniforms! Those weird tall thingies the drum majors wear, like muffs on their heads!

March's lips lifted off her teeth. That's stupid, Gilles.

Cal said something into March's ear.

I don't care, Dad, she said loudly. He makes me puke.

On the way home, Patsy said, That March is a piece of work.

Her? said Gilles. She was bit by a dog when she was three, and she's been mean ever since.

•

August was nearly over. Gilles let Patsy practice parallel parking in the Bweek. When she was ready, they drove to the Glendale Department of Motor Vehicles. She took the written and the driving test and passed easily. There never was anything wrong with her sober abilities. Her father gave her three thousand dollars to buy a used car. Brice found a '62 Volvo for her, but she chose an orange Datsun station wagon, boxy, lightweight, and peppy. Gilles named it Kaki, French for "persimmon."

•

Labor Day weekend, Patsy's father and Burt came to see her. Bonnie and their kids were supposed to come too, but the night before, Bonnie had seen Burt kissing the babysitter in the front hall and all hell had broken loose.

It's not like I've even slept with her, said Burt. Of all the things Bonnie could go ballistic over, this is the silliest. Then again, isn't it a cosmic rule that when you finally get caught, it's for the one thing you didn't do?

Not in my experience, said Patsy.

Her father wasn't in good shape either. After six weeks in Australia he was disillusioned with Eugenia. She took forever getting ready in the morning, he said. Even in the outback, we'd be lucky to be out of our room by noon. Then she'd step out into that wind, and *like that!* a morning's work for naught.

That's funny, said Patsy.

Your mother was up and at 'em first thing.

.

My family's falling apart, Patsy told Silver. My father's a mess and Burt's ridiculous. My two stalwart standbys, she said. Both of 'em deconstructing.

And you?

Me? I'm fine.

So maybe it's your time to be their—what did you call it?

Stalwart standby. Yeah.

Now that you're thriving, on the up-and-up, maybe they feel that they can relax their guard and address some of their own problems.

I'm thriving? said Patsy. Really?

Aren't you?

Oh god, no. I mean, what about Ian?

What about him?

I'm so obsessed with him. That's not very up-and-up.

But Patsy, we—all of us—have our mortal struggles.

A mortal struggle? Really? Such generosity coming from a woman with a tight, molded coif and thick gold wedding band floored Patsy. Wasn't her attachment to Ian better described as a weakness or folly?

To find love is the great human undertaking, Silver said, and it's always complicated by our compulsions and unconscious patterns, to say nothing of issues of trust and control.

Yes, but I know Ian won't come through, said Patsy. And I still can't give him up.

Suppose for a moment that you do give him up, said Silver. What would letting go of Ian look like to you?

God, Patsy said. That's easy. Leaving the damn house for a change. Moving into the world. Fresh air. An end to waiting, waiting, waiting.

•

Classes at Hallen started up after Labor Day. Coming from her first lecture to her new office, Patsy felt *back* in a way she hadn't before. Her colleagues seemed friendlier, more themselves than they'd been at Sarah's wedding. They spoke to her in the halls and stopped by her office to complain about the new building—windows that didn't open, air-conditioning that wouldn't turn off. Only Melanie, the department secretary, was chilly—but she'd once filed a complaint about Patsy's xeroxing demands, only to be rebuked herself by the dean.

Patsy had considered Hallen beneath her abilities, a trade school with liberal arts pretensions, but now she was grateful to be taken back, grateful even for the heavy course load, with two large lecture courses and one upper division seminar to teach.

At the end of her first week she lugged a briefcase full of textbooks into her apartment and found Brice, who had let himself in, sitting on her sofa.

I didn't want to miss you, he said. I took Gilles to Huntington Hospital this morning. Audrey's there, and he's asking for you.

Let's go. Patsy set her briefcase inside the door.

They climbed into Brice's old truck, with its dusty, hot metal smell. He's okay, isn't he?

We'll see, said Brice. He got all wheezy, and then he couldn't breathe. Scared the hell out of me.

When they pulled under the hospital's porte cochere, Brice said, Room two nineteen. I'm going to get flowers.

Gilles sat in bed, an oxygen tube taped under his nose. The rosiness had leached from his face, and his beautiful lips had chapped and cracked.

Look here, sister-boy, Patsy said. What's this all about?

There you are, said Gilles. Now I'm fine. Where's Brice?

He went to the florist's.

Good. He's terrible in hospitals. Glowers and paces. I made him go get you, to get him out of here. And Mother's as bad. I sent her to buy pajamas. Sit here. And pardon my pinafore. He plucked at a hospital gown with its pattern of little green medallions.

Patsy sat on the bed. So tell me, she said.

I had an asthma attack. Poor Brice didn't know what to do. My inhaler was empty, so he drove me down here.

You should've called me. I have inhalers. So why are they keeping you?

My lungs need to clear.

In all her own childhood asthma emergency-room visits, Patsy had been sent right home. But then her mother wasn't on any hospital board either.

Pajamas and a deck of cards arrived with Audrey. The three played hearts, the women sitting on the bed on either side of Gilles until Brice arrived with masses of unusual greenish blue hydrangeas. Cal followed, bringing *The Big Book of Alcoholics Anonymous* and chocolates. Gilles passed around the chocolates and said, I want Brice to myself for a while. Auntie, you drive Patsy home. Mother, don't forget to eat.

Patsy walked out with the brother and sister. In the wood-paneled elevator, Audrey murmured to Cal, Sorry to drag you back here.

It was good, he said. We had old home week at the nurses' station.

They separated in the parking lot, Audrey going alone to her Bug. In the cool mercury-vapor lamplight Patsy glanced at Cal's fine, handsome face. He was so calm and urbane, it was easy to forget that his wife just died.

In the front seat of his Lincoln, she turned to him. You know, Cal, I've never asked about your wife, and I'm sorry. You must miss her a lot.

I do, he said. But she was ill for a very long time—over seven years. So there's some relief. Or is that a terrible thing to say?

No, not at all, you're right. There's relief. For her especially, I hope. Audrey's told me how smart and what fun she was.

I'm sorry you missed her, said Cal. You two would've hit it off.

And you—Patsy felt woefully inadequate talking like this; she was only truly conversant, it seemed, about her own unhappiness—are you okay?

I keep going forward, he said. Right foot, left foot. One day at a time. Having the kids helps. I have to show up for them, keep it together.

How are they doing?

The boys soldier on. They don't talk much, but they sometimes mention their mom. The other day they were laughing about the things Peg hated—which basically came down to Ronald Reagan, Ronald Reagan, Ronald Reagan. But March isn't there yet. She's much more volatile.

That's the age.

You're telling me, said Cal.

He insisted on walking Patsy to the front door of the Lyster. As they approached, the door opened and out came Jeffrey Goldstone. Well, well, well, said Cal. I know this reprobate.

To Patsy's horror, the two men hugged, slapped each other's backs. Here on business? Cal asked.

I was, Knock-Knock said and, with a wave, gave Patsy the floor.

He's my P.O., she muttered.

Great, great! said Cal. You lucked out—both of you.

In an act of gallantry that stunned Patsy, Cal came upstairs with them.

After Goldstone's cursory peek into bedroom and fridge, he and Cal stood and chatted—gossiped, really—in the living room. Both were on the board of a halfway house, and it seemed that they were going to discuss each resident. Patsy recognized names from the morning meeting. Vaughn. Derek of the ghastly neckwear. Otto, a de-licensed anesthesiologist.

You're sponsoring Derek Mabury? Well, as they say, some are sicker than others.

Oh, he's doing great, said Cal. Took a chip for six months clean Thursday.

Goldstein, in his big sneakers, rocked back and forth, deferring to Cal. Well, who'd a thought . . .

Tonight was Thursday, a possible Ian night, but he rarely showed before ten. Then, suddenly, it was nine-thirty. Patsy put a hand on each man's arm. You guys want water or anything?

They turned in tandem, as if surprised to see her there.

No, I better get on, said Goldstein. Leave you two to your evening.
I'll walk out with you, said Cal.

Alone, Patsy poured herself a glass of cold water and took it into the
living room. In a minute she'd turn on the table lamp and read until Ian
came, if he came. But first she wanted to relive Cal's chivalry and seeing
Knock-Knock so dimmed and defanged in Cal's dazzling presence.

The thought of Ian, too, paled in comparison. After Cal's easy ele-
gance, Ian seemed skittish and irritable, a smaller, secretive soul fueled
by some deep underlying pain—pain that he refashioned into luminous
paintings of fish.

But Cal had transformed himself. And he himself was luminous.

If she ever had a husband, Patsy thought, she'd want one a lot more
like Cal, only younger by twenty or thirty years.

It was already after ten. If Ian didn't show up tonight, that'd be all
right.

But he did show up, and that was all right too.

19

The note on her door read *G back in Huntington.*

What's going on in here? she said, walking into the hospital room.

I need someone who can hold it together, he said. Take care of business for me. Brice is a mess, Mother is a mess. Auntie is way too busy. Dr. Truescorff is a real person, but also busy. So it's you, Patsy.

It's me, she said. It's me for what?

I probably have that kind of pneumonia that only queers get, he said.

Well, I'm at your service, she said, trying to remember what she'd heard. Gays and Haitians got it. You could get it from dentists, mosquito bites. A colleague at Hallen told Patsy he'd stopped going to the gym because of sweat left on the exercise equipment.

I need some reality here, Gilles said, his voice rising. Auntie says to turn to my higher power, but I'm not very fond of my higher power right now.

I'm not so fond of your higher power either, Patsy said, and leaned down to embrace him. He clung to her with such tenacity her own terror ignited. He was such a small human, really, with thin little bones, and he sobbed into her neck like an eight-year-old. His lungs mewed and rustled like static on the radio. The more he wept, the more congested he became. Fear somersaulted through her—she'd also heard that bodily fluids, spit, and even tears could carry the disease. If that was true, it was already too late, her neck was drenched. She didn't care, she thought, though in spite of herself, her heart galloped with the dread of infection. She stroked his head—his hair was not very clean—and held him until he began to wriggle free. He dried his eyes and blew his nose. There, he said. Enough of that.

Her own life had taught her that the surges of terror, the sense of drowning in a cold black wave, were temporary. Sooner or later a person crawled back onto solid ground. Gilles, she said. We'll get you through, whatever it is.

Maybe not, Patsy, that's the thing. So don't get all cheerleader on me.

Okay, she said.

You weren't a cheerleader, were you?

No.

Mother was.

•

A trim, big-eyed woman in a white coat came into the room. Truesy, this is Patsy, said Gilles. Patsy's my best friend and our man on the ground. Tell her everything.

Dr. Truescorff, the woman said, and shook Patsy's hand with a brisk maternal air. She turned to Gilles, and the brightness on their faces receded.

I have it, don't I, he said in a low voice.

She took his hand. The results came back positive.

Patsy's own heart began whapping like a helicopter; terror swept through her, hollowing her out. She stood there waiting for Gilles to ask questions, for the doctor's reassurances, the list of treatment options. But moments passed, and the doctor and Gilles continued to look into each other's eyes with such frankness and intensity that even Patsy was drawn in. Doctor, patient, and witness together bypassed all that could be said to look squarely at the way things were.

A familiar terror began to bloom, and Patsy had to turn away. She slipped unnoticed into the hall.

•

Gilles lived at Audrey's after that. Patsy picked him up for the morning meetings, and Brice took him out for lunch. Most afternoons Patsy found him in Audrey's living room on a chaise. Oh, his highness on his chaise, she'd say.

No, Patsy. It's properly called a fainting couch.

That fall was hot and smoggy. They watched reruns of sitcoms— *I Love Lucy, The Andy Griffith Show*—in the air-conditioning and ate coconut Popsicles. Caroline or Binx would drop by later, and Patsy would go home or stay and help Audrey with dinner. Evenings, Cal stopped by en route from work. Brice was in and out. He'd quit his job to freelance again and was fixing up another apartment at the Lyster. When Gilles's other friends were there, Brice always found an excuse to leave. Patsy thought him selfish.

Brice is all right, said Gilles. He's doing the best he can. I mean, poor guy finally sticks a foot out of the closet and this happens.

Some nights, if Gilles was up to it, they went to the club for dinner. Then Audrey was asked not to bring him anymore.

Cal's kids have been talking too much, Audrey told Patsy. Telling their friends, who tell their parents, who panic.

Audrey resigned, and Cal followed.

Patsy found the Lyster dull without Gilles upstairs. No more barbecues on the fire escape. No more chatty dinners. Only Ian, on Thursdays and the rare Saturday. Once, he invited her back to his house. He wanted her to talk about his art again, and then they went to bed.

Her time with Ian came to seem a small excess, shameful, but her own, like secret cigarettes or hoarding Heath bars. Only rarely, in bed, with pleasure racing through her, did Patsy think she was in love and predict a shared future.

One night she came home from Audrey's to find a painting leaning against her door—the luminous grouper and his cave. Ian had worked on it for months. She brushed at small smudges, saw that the paint was gouged.

I'd started to scrape it down to paint over it, Ian said when she called to thank him. Then I remembered that you liked it, so I thought I'd give it to you and start from scratch on something else.

Thank you, she said. I guess.

•

Gilles had a series of lung infections, a long bout with hives, and other reactions to medication. He was always nauseous, and lost a shocking amount of weight in October. He had to go to the hospital the day after Halloween for a week. His friends took turns sitting with him, making sure he was never alone. Brice bought him a wide cashmere throw, six-ply, hand-knit, a deep, saturated brownish purple that obviously cost hundreds of dollars. Gilles immediately took to calling it the old rag. I'm chilly, he'd say. Where is that old rag? Or, When I die, I want to be wrapped in the old rag and buried under the fig tree. Or, You're so good to me, Patsy, I'm thinking of leaving you a life interest in the old rag.

That's a nice shawl, Binx said when she saw it.

This? It's some old rag.

Some afternoons Patsy sat grading papers or going through her lectures while he dozed. He was quiet for long stretches, sometimes thinking so hard that his brow furrowed, his chapped lips moved, his fingers pinched the throw.

It's like sitting next to a beehive, Patsy told him.

You know, Patsy, he said after one long stretch of thought. At least now I don't have to take that stupid GED test.

Another time he said, Catering is really hard. I had fun cooking for your party. But I'm glad I didn't actually have to *do* Gilles's Meals. It's way too much work, and for not nearly enough pay.

•

By Thanksgiving, Gilles was too sick to leave the house and Cal began bringing an AA meeting to him on Thursday nights. Rajid, Derek, Caroline, and Binx came, and Patsy too, although then she had to race home so as not to miss Ian. Once, when a meeting ran late, Ian had come and gone.

I can leave a key out for you, she told him.

That's okay, he said.

I'll put one under the runner, on the far side from my door.

He said, That's okay, Patsy, don't worry about it.

She put the key there and told him. The next Thursday, she stayed after the meeting to clean up, and when she got home, he wasn't there. Yes, he said later, he had stopped by. No, he hadn't looked for the key.

I don't want to start with that, he said.

It's like he's committing adultery and feeling guilty, she said to Sarah.

I'm sorry, Sarah said. I kind of knew it wouldn't go well. I should never have given him your number.

So why did you?

I thought you two could have fun. I mean, you're both single, and neither one of you is in any position to start something serious.

What makes you say that?

Well, god, Patsy. Ian's fresh out of a twelve-year relationship and you're getting reacclimated. That's all. You're not even in your own home yet.

And for that, I don't get to have a real relationship with a decent person?

That's not what I'm saying. You didn't have to go out with Ian. Nobody made you. You can stop seeing him anytime you want.

Maybe I envy Sarah, Patsy told Silver. She's got the husband, the ballroom. And then she says I can't have it, like I'm not entitled.

•

I wish you had wine, Ian said. He had shown up late. His painting clothes were now reeking on the floor by her bed.

I don't have any wine, Patsy said. I don't drink wine.

I know, I know.

So why bring it up?

Shhh, shhh, he whispered, tapping the sheets with his fingers, his eyes closed. This is so nice, right now. Can't we enjoy it?

Not without wine, apparently, she said. Plus, I figure I have a minute before you shut down completely, and there are some things I want to say.

Ian closed his eyes, pretended to sleep, willing her to silence. She hadn't planned any announcement, but now that she'd started, she was curious to see what she might say.

It's not going to get any better between us, is it? she said.

Better in what way? he said. This is pretty nice.

You know. Doing other stuff. Talking on the phone. Going out—

I can't, Patsy. I can't do that right now.

Why not? We did it for a while.

Look, he said. What's the point? Neither one of us is in any position to get serious, settle down with someone.

Says who? Sarah? I don't think either of you should speak for me.

He slung an arm over her. You should have everything you want, Patsy. Dates, phone conversations. But I can't give them to you. I'm not the one.

He kissed her then with such warmth and affection, she felt flung airward, woozy, as if she'd inhaled gas.

Oh god, she said, and breathed several times. Ian moved to kiss her again. She turned her face away, fury rising in her chest. What are you doing? she said. You're being too weird.

Something like shame crossed his face, the briefest crumpling.

You know what? she said. I think you better leave now.

In an instant he swung out of bed and started gathering his clothes.

I mean for good, she said, and stood.

She went into the bathroom and closed the door. In the mirror, her hair was snarled. A feral glitter lit up her eyes.

Showering, she thought she heard doors closing. She leaned against the old rectangular tiles, which were still cool in all the water and steam.

It had to be done, but she hadn't meant to do it tonight.

He was gone when she got out.

Never mind. Never mind, she whispered to the upsurge of regrets, regrets gathering like beggar children.

She pulled off the sheets, scrubbed at the small oval of sperm that had seeped into the mattress pad. She stuffed the sheets into the laundry basket, took clean, crisp ones from the linen closet, and opened them with a great flapping over the bed. A vanquishing.

But she could not sleep.

At the morning AA meeting, Patsy raised her hand to share. Why is it, she said, when you actually do the right thing for once, it doesn't feel good? In fact, it feels so awful you think you're going to die?

The question was rhetorical, and no cross talk was allowed; she did not expect an answer, except maybe of the indirect variety, when people countered with stories of similar experiences. Today, nobody addressed Patsy's question, even obliquely. They all had their own crises and complaints. Child custody battles. Chronic insomnia. Letters from the IRS.

Cal Sharp came up beside her as she left the meeting hall. He was dressed for some boardroom in a graphite gray suit, white shirt, silver and black striped tie. His face had been steamed, shaved, and slapped to a high polish.

You feel like you're going to die, Patsy—he leaned in so close she inhaled his green-smelling cologne—because some part of you *is* dying. Some entrenched old tyrant of the soul, and sweetheart, she's not going easy.

20

Patsy spent Christmas at Burt's, and when she got back, a hospital bed had replaced the fainting couch in Audrey's living room. In the late afternoons she'd find Gilles napping there, sometimes with Brice reading beside him. Patsy read too, for her lectures.

She looked up once to see Gilles watching her. You know what, Patsy? he said. When I lived in Paris on rue Jacob, I used to walk to the Luxembourg Gardens at this time of day. All those green chairs clustered around statues would be filled with middle-aged women reading novels. The chestnut trees, that Parisian sky. That's the main reason I ever wanted a sex change, to guarantee my happiness in middle age. I'm sorry I'll never be one of those ladies. But at least I didn't have to have surgery. Brice! he said sharply.

What'd I do?

Gilles pushed him. You're on the old rag, he said.

The cashmere was freed. Really, Patsy, you shouldn't look at me like that. Don't feel bad for me. I've had a wonderful life.

Patsy couldn't read through the tears trembling in her eyes.

She's upset I called her middle-aged, Gilles stage-whispered to Brice.

•

Cal arrived at dusk and laid a fire. His kids were away at school again, and he could stay to eat. Patsy and Audrey set out a small roast and green beans. They ate on trays, with Gilles presiding from his bed like a young, ailing king. Cal and Audrey were in chintz chairs by the fire, while Patsy sat on the brick hearth itself, close to Cal's knee. He wore old charcoal corduroys, a sweater the same marine blue of his eyes. Through French doors, Patsy saw shapely trees and high hedges illuminated as if by moonlight, though in fact Audrey'd had them lit.

Cal was flying up to San Jose the next day for meetings with the re-development agency. The family land company had holdings there.

Is San Jose going to put in an Aswān dam too? asked Gilles. That was what he called the monumental, doorless regional mall recently constructed near Pasadena's City Hall.

Something akin, said Cal. But anything will improve downtown San Jose. It's literally a big dirt pit right now.

Gilles said, Another thing I'm glad I won't live to see.

Patsy washed dishes with Audrey while Brice and Cal got Gilles to bed. Tired from sadness, she pulled on her camel hair coat, kissed Audrey.

She met Cal in the hallway. Are you leaving? he said.

She stepped aside, against closet doors, so he could pass. He touched her shoulder, and because solace seemed natural, she moved into his arms. He was tall and broad, and made her feel childishly small, a feat. Far too shy to embrace him fully, she held her hands over his shoulder blades, poised as if to subdue any rustle of wings. How soft his sweater was on her cheek. He murmured into her hair, Patsy, Patsy. Then, god almighty. He kissed the side of her head. Cupped against his shoulder, she began to worry that she was the one prolonging, and dropped her arms. He murmured something she didn't hear and let her go.

In the dim hall light, his fine face shone with suffering and kindness. Her departure was clumsy, a bumpering off a wall, a goodbye called too loudly.

Stars spattered the cold black sky. Patsy drove home in confusion. In the calm gray shadows of her bedroom, confusion churned into hope.

•

I'm not positive, but I might start seeing someone new, she told Silver. And I know what you're thinking: she no sooner gets out of one mess than she's into another. But this isn't like that. It's not sui generis. I've known Cal the whole time I've been back, I see him every day, he didn't pop out of nowhere. The man I was thinking of asking to be my sponsor. Who takes me riding.

Whose daughter was unkind to you.

Patsy gave a short laugh. Her worst fears may be coming true.

She sensed something before you did, said Silver. Her father's interest.

I thought he just wanted me to ride his dead wife's horse. Though I'm not positive he really is interested in something more.

Are you interested in something more?

With him? God, I hardly dare think of it. I mean, sure, but so is every woman in AA, every matron in La Cañada Flintridge and Pasadena. He's immensely attractive, and charismatic. He could have his pick.

And he picked you.

Oh, but I'm not sure yet. I have no idea what he sees in me. What would he want with a cultural historian fresh out of prison?

What would you want with him?

Oh, but he's beautiful. And unbelievably kind.

She left out rich, lest she sound crass.

•

Cal was out of town all week. Patsy would see him again on Thursday evening, at the meeting he brought to Gilles. She went about her routines with a fullness of heart and elegiac calm. Her morning candle, her spiritual reading, the hours still dark and clear. Teaching. Audrey's.

Gilles eyed her with suspicion. The Grouper is back, isn't he?

He meant Ian. No, Gilles, she said.

She did seem calm, even to herself. Calm and stately.

And if she were mistaken, or if Cal thought better of it himself, what would be lost but a vaguely imagined future involving a house in Flintridge, stepkids, horses, and dogs that were not hers. To relinquish such a big life—even before she had it—was in itself a relief. Her own future was so much smaller and simpler: move home to Pomelo Street in March, Hallen ad infinitum.

A committee meeting Thursday afternoon made her late. The AA meeting had started without her. The announcements and book passages that were read aloud were finished, and Vaughn was talking about his job. Only two table lamps were on in Audrey's living room, and there was a lively, snapping fire. Cal glanced up as she came in, and she knew then, or thought she did. She sat behind Gilles's bed, almost in darkness. Derek, Caroline, and Binx shared; they were going around the room. Rajid talked about his girlfriend drinking too much. Cal spoke of his trip north, and how he'd run into an old business associate at an AA meeting there. The last time I saw him, we killed two bottles of Scotch and possibly the bartender, he said.

Gilles reported feeling stronger; his T cells were up, his appetite was back. I may be faced with the prospect of living, he said.

When it was her turn, Patsy said, I'm very happy to be here tonight.

The circle was formed, the prayer spoken, thy kingdom come, thy will be done. She gathered the coffee mugs, took them into the kitchen, and waited.

·

I was struck, Cal told her, by how beautifully tall you were. How you looked so dazed and amazed to be free in the world again.

He said, You were so shy and intelligent, so well-spoken. I wanted to carry you off and listen to you talk all day.

·

She saw him every night. They went to Monty's Steakhouse and the Trestle. She introduced him to Pie 'N Burger.

He wanted to buy her a horse of her own. If she wanted one. And if she didn't like the Flintridge house, he had two others she could choose from. He could dislodge the tenants. Or buy her a new house altogether.

All this, even before they were lovers.

He had to go to a board meeting in Switzerland in July. How did that sound—a week in the Alps next summer?

·

Well, it turns out that he does like me.

You didn't know that?

No, I mean, he likes me seriously.

Silver was quiet.

I guess he did have love in mind. He admitted to daydreaming about me.

Silver sat, her lips pursed.

Aren't you going to say anything?

No, said Silver.

Why not? Patsy said.

I don't have anything to say.

Her coldness frightened Patsy. Oh, I'm sure you're thinking a lot of things, she said. I can feel the thoughts seething in that head of yours.

And what are those thoughts?

You're thinking, Oh, god, here we go again. She's like a teenager. Some guy looks twice at her, and off she goes like a firecracker. But at least this isn't like it was with Ian, where I was a goner from the get-go. This is much calmer, no beeline to the bedroom. I don't feel like I'm being swept away.

Is that good?

Didn't you say it's better not to hit the hay first thing?

Ideally, there's *some* erotic charge.

Who said there isn't? I'm saying we're not being impulsive.

When Silver didn't answer, Patsy said, You're awfully hard to please.

But Silver was only taking her time. When she spoke, her voice was quiet and low, in the way Patsy loved. All possibility bloomed in that voice.

The reason I suggest going slow, Silver said, is not to delay sex for the sake of delaying sex. It's so you don't burden a new, fragile acquaintanceship with all the expectations and emotions sex stirs up. Going slow allows you to stay current with yourself, and with each other, so you can face your emotions as they arise and not in one undifferentiated swirl. So you know what you feel and what you need each step of the way.

That's what I'm trying to do. Move at a manageable pace. Though I do think, deep down, all this taking it slow stuff is a myth. I know that once I kiss a guy, I'm going to sleep with him, and if that goes okay, I'll move in with him. Unless he bails out on me first, this means that eventually I'll have to break up with him because I never liked him *that* much in the first place. You'd think that knowing all this would keep me from kissing anybody ever again, at least anybody I didn't completely adore. But you know what I mean.

Not really, said Silver. I think you're saying you've already kissed this man.

Well, yes.

And then, you're planning to break up with him.

Not necessarily. I'm trying to say that getting involved isn't as incremental as you suggest. Once juices get stirred up, it's specious to pretend that some step-by-step decision-making process is in motion. It's more like two people agree to leap off a cliff.

I disagree, Silver said quietly. What you describe is a proscription, a set pattern, not intimacy. It is possible for people to remain conscious as they get to know each other. That way, commitment comes from affection *and* self-knowledge.

Self-knowledge is overrated, at least for us alcoholics, said Patsy. There's even a saying in AA: *Self-knowledge avails us nothing!* I *know* that once I fall in love, I'm as blindered and impelled as a racehorse. I only hope that the next guy is kinder than the last.

But isn't there a higher, truer self, a self that's free of addiction and obsession, that knows what's best for you? said Silver. And isn't that why you come here? To find and nourish that authentic, unenslaved self?

No, Patsy said with wonder. Not at all. That never even occurred to me.

So tell me, Patsy, why do you come here?

Guilt, she said. How to live with guilt.

•

Cal did seem to be taking his sweet time.

He seemed oddly satisfied with a few minutes of kissing on her sofa.

She'd thought Silver would be pleased with their—or rather, Cal's— pace. But no. Now she had Patsy worried: there should be some erotic charge.

He kissed her in the parking lot of the Trestle, but only for minutes. One night he didn't even come up to her apartment after dinner for some tea. Stan was home, he said, and he wanted to see him.

She and Cal rode up the arroyo on Saturdays. She packed lunches, which they ate at the waterfall. On a warm day in February he took her down a new trail into a small, sunny meadow. The grass was green and moist. They unrolled the wool army blanket he carried, Patsy got out the food, but she had no sooner poured water than Cal began kissing her. He nudged her down, rolled on top.

Why, Cal, she said, and his hand cupped between her legs.

She was game, sure, and interested—but caught off guard.

She hardly had time to think; it was thrilling, or would be, if she weren't so self-conscious about being in an open field a few yards off a public trail. Someone might see, she murmured as he unfastened her jeans.

Just take off one leg, he said, and had to repeat it twice before Patsy understood. One *pant* leg, he meant.

As ordered, she peeled her jeans off one leg, and that indeed made her available to him. How did he know this pant leg trick? It seemed so expert and clandestine. And how surprising to discover that yes, he was sexually proficient; that had come to seem almost too much to ask. Yes, quite proficient, so much so, she was already coming—that was quick, yet lovely too, out here in the sun and smashed grass, Cal gasping beside her. What a relief that he had some gallop left in him, not to mention naughty expertise.

Well. She couldn't wait to tell Silver.

•

Of course Cal would go for you, and who can blame him? You're very attractive. You two make quite the pair.

Audrey and Patsy were separating irises in the backyard. It was the wrong time of year, Audrey said, but it needed to be done.

You're like a good mix of Marjorie, his first wife, and Peggy, she said. Marjorie was sensible and strong, and Peggy so smart, but also fragile and self-destructive. It always amazed me that Peg had three children, with all her illnesses. She had help, of course, a whole cadre of nannies. She never had to do housework—you won't either. And like you, Peg loved to laugh. She loved her pills too. Half the time she ran on Valium and vodka.

How did Cal put up with that?

Cal has beautiful detachment, you'll see. And the truth is, Peg had no talent for reality. You seem to have a much better handle on that than she ever did. But what I'm wondering is—have you and Cal talked about children?

Yes, Patsy said. I don't want any and Cal can't have them.

He did that after March. Well—I'm not supposed to tell anyone, but you should know—when March was two, Peggy came up pregnant again, and they made a deal. Peggy would take care of the immediate problem if Cal took care of it on a more permanent basis. So you'd better be sure what *you* want.

I'm sure, Patsy said.

You'd be missing out, Audrey said, dropping her voice. Even with all this, she said, and nodded toward her house, I wouldn't want to miss any of it. How could you pass up the chance to have your Gilles?

Oh, Audrey. Even if I wanted kids, I don't deserve them, Patsy said. And don't argue with me. It's not something I can explain.

You deserve kids as much as anybody, and you might change your mind.

I won't, said Patsy.

If Audrey had pushed her, Patsy would've said she'd chosen a career over having children, but really, the accident had complicated her desire for children. How dare she have a child when she'd killed someone else's? She saw a time in the future when people would say, You know, she never had any children of her own, and that gave her a small shot of satisfaction, to imagine the sacrifice made and acknowledged.

After digging up the thick, soil-encrusted rhizomes, the women broke them apart, the interior root a startling creamy white.

Well, I'll be blunt, Audrey said. I can only say these things before you marry, never afterward. I find May-December pairings unseemly. Men with women their children's age, and women wanting daddies and money. To me, marriage is between equals who can build a life together. I'd want equality, parity. And I'm too selfish. I could never take on someone else's family. I'm willing to think that you two have your own reasons. But I have to put this on the table.

Audrey, I want to spend what time I can with Cal. What time there is.

Time? Time you have. Thirty-five, forty years. Longer than you've been alive! Cal may seem old to you, but he's not even sixty-five! Look at our father. At ninety-two he knows the balance in all his accounts— it's the great-grandkids' names he can't keep straight. Cal's here for the long haul. You have to be sure he's what you want. You're at such different stages in life. You're really coming into your own—why hide your light under a rosebush in Flintridge?

Actually, Patsy said, the age difference works in my favor. Men my age are so competitive. They don't want an equal, let alone anyone smarter. At Berkeley, guys said I was too opinionated. Or take Brice— he'd say, go easy on the polysyllables, Pats, they make a guy feel dumb. Cal's beyond all that. He wants me to have my career. And he's not fusty at all. Brice is far fustier than Cal.

Amen, sister, cried Gilles from inside the house.

Somebody woke up, Audrey said.

Also, I don't know another straight man who's as relaxed around gays.

Cal doesn't care about that. Audrey motioned Patsy farther into the iris bed so Gilles couldn't hear. But my life is no place for a thirty-two-year-old. Golf, library luncheons, hospital benefits. The geriatric card leagues loom. That's our gang, Cal's and mine. The time may come when you want *more* . . .

I can't imagine what *more* might be, said Patsy. Cal is simply the best man I've ever met. He's never been anything but affectionate—and steady. Shows up when he says he will. No on-again, off-again crazy-making stuff.

But those are mere fundamentals. Why would you get near a man that doesn't show up or makes you crazy?

Patsy pried a thick corm from the dirt. Still, I have yet to see anything I can't tolerate.

You will, you will. And it will probably be what you most admire now. His goodness might eventually grate on you. You might want him to pay less attention to the wounded birds of the world and a little more to you. His children wish that.

But he and I are on the same page there. Part of sobriety is helping others.

Cal does like to help people, Audrey said with dryness. But you don't strike me as someone who needs it.

Me? Are you kidding?

What do I know? Audrey said, stabbing the ground with her trowel. You're determined, and you've been very patient. I would hate myself if I didn't speak up and you were unhappy down the line. But that's it. I've had my say. And don't think you can't come complaining to me, because you can. I'll never say I told you so. No marriage is perfect, and you'll need an outlet.

Expect it, Patsy said, and, ducking under the brim of Audrey's hat, kissed her soft, pale cheek.

21

I had my beautiful years, Gilles said. I would look around, Patsy, and nobody had eyelashes as thick, or such lips. Only babies had skin like mine. I used to look at my arms and think, How come I was so lovely—me, of all people? But then these disgusting wiry hairs popped out on my legs and I thickened up all over. So repulsive. Mother told me I would look like Auntie. Terrifying.

But he's great-looking.

In that gross, thick-necked bull elk kind of way. You know, he was a beautiful boy too. Have mother show you pictures. I don't know how the pervs missed him. Maybe they didn't.

Gilles slept, and Patsy sat with Audrey in the garden room, where Audrey talked and talked. Talking was her métier. It momentarily eased her anxiety, which was tremendous, and she was good at it. She talked about her childhood in Boston, of Cal and her marriage and all about Gilles. He was such a sweet and beautiful baby, it was all I could do not to put him in dresses.

Patsy kept her apartment at the Lyster for the time being. She gave her tenants another year's lease on the Pomelo Street house. Now, driving through Audrey's neighborhood and Sarah's, she watched for FOR SALE signs and a house she and Cal might want to buy.

Patsy's father came down to meet everyone. He and Cal knew people in common, businessmen in Bakersfield and some AA lions.

Sure this is what you want, Pats? her father said.

It's what I want, she said.

I won't state the obvious. But I do wonder what the rush is.

Gilles, Patsy said. We want him at the wedding, Dad. Gilles is the rush.

•

Cal and Patsy drove up to Montecito on a cold, clear wintry afternoon to have dinner with his older daughter, Roberta, a cardiologist, who lived with her surgeon husband and their two-year-old daughter Minnie in a white stucco-and-glass Modernist hillside home above the Pacific.

Roberta and Patsy were close in age—Patsy was younger by three years. Audrey had put in a good word on Patsy's behalf, so Roberta was inclined to kindness. Together in the kitchen, the two talked about Gilles.

I like Dr. Truescorff, Patsy said. Gilles loves her.

I met her when I was down, said Roberta. She's superb.

The child of beauties, Roberta did nothing but scrub her clear skin and blow-dry her thick brown hair—no makeup, no perm. She was brisk in the way of doctors, athletic and precise, setting the table with an appealing economy of movement, tossing the salad with small, precise rotations.

Gilles also said many good things about you, said Roberta.

I wish March liked me half so well.

Yes, March, Roberta said. Well. I'll see what I can do.

The ocean had a metallic sheen; the islands were dull blue. Patsy had almost this view from the fire camp barracks, still less than a year ago.

Roberta handed her a glass of sparkling water.

•

Cal said, It's time.

March was home for the weekend. And the boys were gone.

Cal had asked March to help him cook; despite her vegetarianism, they made his staple meal, steaks, baked potato, garlic bread, and set the table in the kitchen. Patsy sat across from them. March perched sideways on her chair, poised to bolt. Cal gave Patsy a bright, hopeful look.

How do you like Thacher? Patsy asked, about her boarding school in Ojai.

March gazed off to one side. I have to go to the bathroom, she said, and left.

Cal and Patsy waited, and when she didn't return, Cal went looking for her. Soon Patsy heard their voices. March's rose.

I don't have to.

Just send me back to school, then.

But, Dad, she's a murderer. She killed two people, in case you didn't know.

He took her deeper into the house, out of earshot. Patsy sat at the table for a while, then walked around the kitchen. She didn't know where they'd gone and didn't want it to appear as if she were looking for them, so she walked down to the barn and patted Cinder's humid muzzle and put her cheek against the mare's dusty coat. But Cinder was not an affectionate horse and drew away to nose her feedbox for stray crumbs of rolled corn.

•

Gilles said, She'd hate anybody Auntie chose. She hates everybody, anyway. Ever since that dog.

Audrey said, Do all the right things, and someday, with luck, she'll see that you behaved admirably. That's the best you can hope for.

Cal said, She's probably one of us.

He meant alcoholic. Restless, irritable, and discontent. Only she had not yet discovered the magic potion that would make her at home in the world.

Silver said, Her mother has recently died, and her father, whom she needs very much, is choosing to love someone else instead.

But I would never—

I am telling you what feels true for her. So you can be cognizant of her suffering. Which is enormous, and real.

Patsy began to boom with guilt, that familiar grimy darkness.

Silver's low voice persisted. It doesn't mean you shouldn't get married. Or that she gets to call the shots. But you need to be aware of what she's going through.

All right, Patsy said. But it hasn't even occurred to her she might be gaining a mother. And one who's not strung out on pills and alcohol, someone who can actually pay attention to her and love her.

She has a mother, Patsy, Silver said with discernible curtness. Her mother may be dead, and she may have been a terrible drug addict and alcoholic. But that's her mother. You will never be her mother. You may, in time, be a friend. If you play your cards right and wait her out.

That's what I don't know how to do. No card I play seems right.

She needs room, Patsy. Lots and lots of room.

•

The wedding was set for an April day in Audrey's garden. The day before, as Audrey and Patsy were puzzling out the dinner seating, Brice came into the kitchen. His highness requests your presence, Pats.

Gilles was in his bedroom, whose French doors opened to the brick patio and swimming pool. With hives again from a drug reaction and a large Kaposi's lesion on his neck, he was hiding out from the florists and rental people.

You rang, your honor? she said.

Sit down, Patsy, he said, his voice low. Here, where I can see you. I have an amends to make to you.

I doubt that, Patsy said. You are my angel.

No, listen. And let me talk. He settled a dark, bottomless gaze on her. Way back when Brice and I were fixing up your apartment, Brice talked so much about you, I decided that you and Auntie should get together.

Oh you did, did you? Patsy gave his bedspread a playful tug.

Don't interrupt, he said. Aunt Peggy died, and Mother said Auntie would marry again within the year, 'cause that's what he did after Marjorie. Didn't let the bed get cold. Even before I met you, I decided you were It. In person, you were even better than I thought, so gorgeous and tall. No, let me finish. There was difficulty at the beginning, like the *I Ching* says. I'd talk about you to him, and he wouldn't bite. I'd talk about him to you, and you'd look bored. I told him he should take you out. No go. Then I said you had a bad boyfriend and needed cheering up—that caught his attention. So I hauled us all up to the club when he would be there, and he finally asked you to go riding. I made him come to your student party, and it was my idea to invite you to his house for dinner.

Aha! So absolutely no free will was involved! Patsy said.

Auntie became willing, but nothing was his idea. He was in a fog. I probably could've foisted Rajid on him and he would've gone along with it.

Then I can only be grateful to you, Patsy said, for foisting me instead.

Yes. But, Patsy, I wasn't really thinking what might be best for you. I never thought that it would actually take. I'm afraid I railroaded you into something you might regret, and I feel terrible.

Don't be ridiculous.

No, seriously, Patsy. You don't have to go through with it if you don't want to. Nobody would hold it against you.

Patsy burst out laughing. Now you tell me!

I feel so responsible, said Gilles. Seriously.

Cal and I—we're grown-ups, remember?

I was playing a game, Patsy, like I was in a movie, like *The Parent Trap*.

And it worked! she said. Thank god.

But maybe your painter was better for you. Or someone else would've been. Gilles, agitated, shook his head. Auntie's so straight, Patsy. And so old.

Not that old, Patsy said. Not even sixty-five.

Also, I feel really bad for March.

·

Patsy had a restless night, roaming her bedroom, reconfiguring her history with Cal. She didn't worry about or even credit Gilles's alleged meddling; it was her own meddling that concerned her: How dare she invade the Sharp family circle and cause the girl distress?

Deep in the early morning, Patsy resolved to give Cal up, for March's sake. She would sell her house, quit her job, and move to London or Paris, some true city of refuge, where she wouldn't run into her victims' family in the produce market and teenage girls wouldn't call her a murderer.

She must have slept through the alarm. The sun was up when she awoke. She recalled her decision to cancel the wedding, but not the emotions or logic that fueled it. Cal's call came as she lay on her bed; his kind, lovely voice summoned her back to the crush of last-minute details and ongoing heartbreak. Her wedding day.

·

Forty people came for the ceremony, and all but one stayed for the dinner. Mark Parnham slipped out after the kiss. Her father, reunited with Genie, shared a table with Burt, reunited with Bonnie, and their kids.

All of Cal's children were there, dressed up and kind to Patsy—even March, who allowed and returned a rustling embrace in the receiving line. Roberta, whom March revered, had come down with little Minnie, taken March shopping, bought her a lavender voile dress.

The newlyweds did not go on a honeymoon, because Gilles's condition was so grave. He was down to a hundred and five pounds, always fatigued. He sat in the sun, wrapped in the old rag in a wheelchair on the patio, and spent hours in conversation with Brice. Patsy and Audrey saw them by the pool or fig tree, Brice taking notes on a yellow legal pad.

Cortisone shots had made Gilles's hair thin, and his waxy scalp shone through. Patsy often sat with him.

I want to see the sky and daylight, Mrs., he said. It's dark where I'm going. Or dim, anyway.

So what about it, Gilles? she said one day. What have you learned out of all this?

Gilles's fingers worked through the cashmere. I've learned how kind people are, he said, and how generous. So generous. I'm glad I found that out.

•

Gilles died at home in June, wrapped in the old rag, in his bed, when Audrey left the room, as if he'd been waiting for two minutes of privacy to complete his life. Audrey said she knew as soon as she headed into the hall with the hospice nurse. There was a weird curl to the air down by his room, she said, and such stillness.

Gilles had planned his own funeral, the menu, the flowers, the minister, the songs, the singers, who should speak and in what order. That's what he and Brice had been doing together with the legal pad.

Gilles left Patsy his diaries—she was his "literary executor"—and, as promised, the old rag. She offered the cashmere to Brice, who said its dispensation had been much discussed and long ago resolved.

Gilles had started the diaries in Paris, but Patsy first read the last two, written since he'd come home. At first he'd been full of self-pity and despair about his lost glamorous existence. Then came much gushing about Brice—*His nose! Aquiline supreme!*—followed by little until he was diagnosed, when complaint and vituperation gushed from his pen. Patsy was relieved to discover he wasn't so angelic after all. He wrote how his mother bought him the wrong kind of hand cream, then the wrong brand of orange juice, of disposable needles. She was vague, and a crybaby. Brice wasn't around enough, and when he was, he couldn't sit still, he had some kind of attention disorder and generally was incapable of love. Nor did Patsy escape the diarist's bile. She had walked too heavily around him and made an unforgivable sound by dragging the tines of her fork against her teeth. Who knew? The Ox, he called her in many entries. Then Clumper. *Clumper clumped in today and stayed for-fucking-ever. Only in Bakersfield would she ever be society.*

22

Despite offers made in the heat of wooing, Cal didn't want to buy a new house, at least not until March went away to college. So Patsy moved into the Flintridge Tudor. She brought her books, her clothes, one red glass vase, and one painting of a fish. She slept in Peggy Sharp's marriage bed, ate off her wedding china, cooked out of her cookbooks, guided by her annotations. (*Cal likes*, she had written of an orange cake recipe.) Peggy had been Patsy's age when she married Cal, and knowing this, Patsy came to conflate poor never-sober Peggy with her own former, wilder self—both of them, Patsy thought, well rid of.

Patsy visited her stepdaughter's room, browsing for clues to her nature. A shelf of soccer trophies, a nightstand drawer with crinkled tubes of acne cream. Above the headboard of March's twin bed, precisely where a mother kissing her child good night would gaze, hung a small sign in an old-fashioned font:

LIPS THAT TOUCH LIQUOR
SHALL NEVER TOUCH MINE.

So Patsy was not the first mother figure scorned.

Oh no, said Cal. Those two fought to the bitter end.

Deceased, Peggy had ascended in March's estimation. My mother let me boss the housekeeper around/use good towels at the pool. My mother said I didn't have to go out to eat/to the doctor/to summer camp.

Unlike Joey Hawthorne, who hid out at their house, March did come home to her father most weekends. She emptied her suitcase into a snarled heap of clothes and books on the spare twin and either joined her father and Patsy for meals or refused to.

At Cal's urging, Patsy took March shopping for her sixteenth birthday to Bullock's on South Lake Avenue in Pasadena. At five feet two,
March was plump and short-waisted. A floral print shirtdress transformed her into a stout little housewife—an uncanny vision of things to
come. She added crisp white blouses, gabardine slacks, and a tortoiseshell headband, her taste as starched as Patsy's was rumpled. Patsy
wrote checks without a word. She still wore T-shirts and wrinkled In-
dian cotton skirts, though her sandals were better made now, and Cal's
first birthday gift to her, a yellow-gold curb link bracelet, clinked softly
when she moved her arm.

They lugged March's many shopping bags into the elevator and ordered sandwiches in the tearoom, with its panoramic view of the San
Gabriel Mountains. Their older waitress said, Now let me guess. Aunt
and niece?

My stepmom, March answered without sweetness, but with such a
lack of rancor Patsy considered the day a victory.

By breakfast, the birthday clothes had joined the churning snarl on
the bed and March refused to eat with them.

The boys came and went that first summer, polite and good-natured.
Patsy teased them; she knew how, from teaching. She called them "the
hollow-legs," professed shock at how fast they dispatched whole loaves
of wheat-berry bread, jars of peanut butter, strawberry jam.

A handwritten invitation to the Trinity Lutheran Youth Choir's
recital brought Patsy to the back row of a pink stone church in Pasadena.
Mark Parnham caught her eye, mouthed a welcome. The ethereal sound
of young voices made her weep. She wrote a check to the church—there
was a locked wooden box for donations—and slipped out before the
punch and cookies.

In July she flew with Cal to his board meeting in Switzerland. The
other wives, into whose company she was consigned, were older, and
cool to her. Their eyes flickered at her more casual clothes; she was
shouldered out of their shifting groups as they shopped in Gstaad and
visited a cheese factory in Château-d'Oex. One morning, Patsy stayed
in the hotel to read; at lunch Cal let her know that this was unaccept-
able. Mortified—she had thought it impossible to displease him—she
rejoined the group and, over the years, at many such meetings, never
went AWOL again.

Cal took the whole family to the Kauai time-share in August. The large wooden house sat on stilts in the sand. Roberta and Minnie came for a week, along with Audrey, followed by Andrew, the eldest, and his family. March brought Joey Hawthorne, in whom Patsy had an ally. (At least he didn't marry the housekeeper, Joey said within Patsy's earshot.) The boys surfed, the girls walked to the shopping center. Cal and Patsy sat in the sun, read books, visited the local AA.

She had not anticipated so much family life. She tried to do right by them, cooking, offering to do laundry, loading the dishwasher, sweeping the kitchen floor of sand and more sand.

Once school started in the fall, the Tudor was empty again during the week, and Patsy had Cal to herself. I can't get over how calm marriage is, she told Silver at the six-month mark. How adult.

Say more, said Silver.

I'm surprised, Patsy said. There really is a whole subtle world of adult privilege that a single person never accesses. I always suspected it. Marriage is the door, the key to the kingdom. And you get to be like the king and queen living happily ever after—or not so happily, as the case may be.

In this case? How's the queen?

Me? Oh, god, happy. She laughed. You know, Cal actually is so regal. I was watching him work the room at a meeting last night, and he was like FDR visiting Congress: this elegant swan touring a duck yard.

Swans and kings, said Silver. Sounds like a fairy tale.

Don't forget the evil stepmother, said Patsy.

What about the more concrete, down-to-earth areas of the marriage?

You mean sex? How's our sex life? Patsy said, and recalled her husband's assured, proprietary hand on her rib cage, his long, slim almost hairless leg hooking over hers. Proficient was still the word that came to mind. We get along, she said. No worries there.

Patsy was putting on a bit of a show for Silver, to prove that she hadn't rushed into folly and was as happy as she believed herself to be.

She understood by then that Cal was neither as rich nor as influential as she'd assumed. He was employed by the family corporation, true, but he was not a major player there. The houses he'd offered to her early in their courtship were not, strictly speaking, his alone to give.

Cal's great talent and accomplishment was in AA, after all. She couldn't admit this to Silver, could not bear to address the glaring comparison.

I married my father, she did wail to Gloria, who was now over a year out of prison as well, and living in nearby Azusa.

Who doesn't? said Gloria.

For the first year of their marriage Patsy went with Cal to meetings, sat beside him, holding her spine straight—Audrey had been on her for slouching—and ached with pride while waiting for the leader to call on him. Cal never had to raise his hand.

And neither did she now. Husband and wife were asked to speak at meetings all over Southern California, separately and as a team. People called them role models, proof that sober alcoholics could find love and happiness.

The time came, of course, when subjects arose that Patsy couldn't talk about in front of Cal. Nasty bits of her past that haunted. Feelings about his children, or living in right-wing, all-white Flintridge. Things Cal didn't need to hear. Gloria directed her to go to women's meetings and to seek out her own groups.

They were almost two years into their marriage when Derek, of the thin ponytail and terrible necklaces, phoned Cal from County Hospital. He'd tested positive for HIV, his intravenous drug use coming back to haunt him. They rushed over, found him on a gurney in the hall.

And so it began again, Cal bringing meetings, Patsy sitting bedside in the afternoons, picking up Derek's mother at the airport, taking her to buy him pajamas, toothpaste, a hairbrush. After his third hospitalization Derek was too weak to live alone, and his mother could not afford another plane ticket, let alone a hospital bed. Cal said, Let me talk to the kids.

The kids said, Just not upstairs. So Derek moved into the maid's quarters off the kitchen. Patsy, Binx, and Caroline cleaned out his apartment, held a yard sale, dismantled his life. He lived at the Sharps' house for six months, until his death.

After Derek, they brought in a fifty-eight-year-old musician, also from the morning meeting, then a thirty-year-old gay banker. By then the disease was flaring all around them. The man who cut Patsy's hair. Hallen's librarian and the assistant drama professor. Binx's brother. Only Brice evaded the virus, crediting a non-penetrative technique he called the Princeton rub, and then celibacy post-Gilles. Audrey's Episcopal church in Pasadena set up a nonprofit agency to address the emergency. Audrey volunteered full-time, and Patsy spent three afternoons a week setting up clients with medical care and counseling. After three years, she was the only volunteer left from her group; the others had burned out, moved on. Even Audrey had left to become a docent at the Arboretum. The agency's new director would have been glad to replace Patsy with one of his own people. She stayed on for two more years. She had found a way to be good.

PART FOUR

23

Winter 1999

Lewis came in with the fiddle player and her red-haired daughter. He slouched like a cat and laughed with pleasure when greeting Burt.

After dinner, when the players were tuning up, Patsy saw him drinking a nonalcoholic beer. Does that actually taste like beer? she asked, and admitted she'd been too afraid to try one, afraid it would launch an old craving.

I'm sober too, he said. Eleven years. And I never even tasted one of these—he waggled the bottle—until last year. And the strangest thing. I drank one and didn't want another.

He offered her a sip, but she declined. I better not.

Oh, I see you two brains have met, said Burt. No? Well, you should. Professor Fletcher, Professor MacLemoore.

Lewis was comp lit, French and Russian, but not tenured. He taught at three different colleges—a freeway flier. As he and Patsy talked, the red-haired girl, Susannah, ran back to him again and again. Eight years old, she perched briefly on his knees, hung an arm companionably around his neck. He kissed her red curls absently.

The band played away.

> *You ought to see my Cindy, she lives deep in the South*
> *She's so sweet the honeybees swarm around her mouth*

After his divorce four years ago, Burt had moved to Rito, a tiny old town in the orange groves, and married Umparro, the broad-faced mandolin player in his bluegrass band. They held a potluck dinner and band practice every Thursday. Once a month, when her father drove down from Bakersfield, Patsy came up for a night or two. Burt's kids came too, so the family was together.

Cal demurred. He didn't care for bluegrass—he was a Boston Pops man—and liked his own bed or those at the Santa Barbara Biltmore, but not the blow-up mattress Burt offered. Cal was in his seventies. A mattress on the floor, he said, was simply too far down there.

Just as well. Patsy's father and Cal had never struck the right note with each other. Cal called her father a sad sack. Her father found Cal kind but dry. I can't really *get* at anything with him, he said.

Me neither! Patsy said. But so what? What's to get at, anyway?

> *Get along home, Cindy, Cindy; get along home, Cindy, Cindy.*
> *Get along home, Cindy, Cindy; I'll marry you someday.*

The fiddle player was marvelous, and Patsy said so.

You should hear her play Beethoven, said Lewis, turning. You're not Burt's sister who's married to Cal Sharp?

The one and only, she said, and watched him process the age difference.

So you kept your maiden name, he said.

Burt forgets I'm a Sharp. And I publish under MacLemoore. When my thesis was coming out as a book, I couldn't stand that Patsy MacLemoore did all the work and Patsy Sharp would get all the credit.

Fair! Lewis said with an abrupt laugh.

The little redhead ran up again and sat on his lap for a long time.

As he left, Lewis touched Patsy's elbow. I heard your husband speak at a retreat last July. Now, there's a man with a beautiful soul.

The next morning, Lewis phoned Burt's house on the off chance Patsy was still there. He wanted her to speak that night at his AA meeting. A speaker had canceled.

She brought along her father, Burt, and Umparro, who had never heard her story. Afterward they all went out to eat at a Mexican restaurant. That was when she found out the fiddle player was neither Lewis's wife nor lover, but an old friend whose child, the red-haired Susannah, was his goddaughter.

Within the week, Lewis wrote Patsy a charming note in dark gray ink to thank her for speaking.

> *Your story was so moving and powerful. We're all still ringing from it.*

When Patsy heard Hallen was looking for a French-language adjunct for the winter quarter, she phoned Lewis, then talked him up to the language chair, who hired him to teach French 2, a bore. But comp lit asked him to teach the Russian short story as well, which made the hundred-mile commute worthwhile.

Patsy showed him around the Hallen campus, with its Mission Revival architecture, olive, oak, and eucalyptus groves. They split a sandwich at the student union. That weekend she brought him to the faculty picnic—Cal had long since bowed out of those—and they spent the whole two hours talking on Wes Gustafson's sofa.

He'd had one bad novel published—No, seriously, Patsy, it really is an embarrassment—and had started work on something else, about the drunk farm where he'd sobered up and the man who ran it, his first sponsor.

It's part memoir, part biography, he said. Which reminds me. For my research, I'd like to talk to your husband about how he runs his house.

His house? said Patsy.

Don't you have some kind of unofficial halfway facility down there?

No. A few boarders now and then, said Patsy. None if I can help it. It's not a *facility*.

She was already loath to bring him home. Lewis had idolized his former sponsor, the one he was writing about; he'd be just as susceptible to Cal, and Patsy didn't want to share.

●

Patsy had long been looking for a new house—Cal being content in the Tudor—when six years ago, on a meandering trail ride together in the foothills, they'd come across a weedy four-acre spread. Built in the sixties by an industrialist, the eight-bedroom redwood-sided ranch house was modeled—loosely—on the famous home in a TV western. There was also a separate apartment that the selling agent called "the possum trot," a cactus garden, lily pond, wrecked pool, falling-down pool house, and barn. Having languished on the market for years, the place went for a song, with escrow closing on the Sharps' tenth wedding anniversary. All along, they swore they'd ditch the name, but they'd already gotten into the jokey habit of using it. The Ponderosa. The Pondo.

The move had given them both a burst of energy; she painted rooms and furnished under Brice's strict supervision. Cal rebuilt the barn, put in a pipe corral and hay shelter. Antonia, Patsy's former prison chum turned landscaper, restructured the gardens and stocked the lily pond with expensive koi, to the delectation of local raccoons. The canyon contained forty oak trees, plus citrus, loquats, persimmons, black figs, and a variety of purple-skinned avocados with oily, delicious flesh. They harvested in laundry baskets.

Cal's kids and sponsees cycled in and out, especially March. Brice rented the possum trot for two years after the Lyster sold, though *rented* wasn't exactly accurate; some combination of bartered for and squatted in was closer to the truth. Lewis must have heard about the six months Burt lived with them after his divorce, for that in particular was a period of great conviviality. Boarders lounged around the living room as if it were the lobby in some rustic mountain lodge; they built eucalyptus wood fires in the gaping river rock fireplace, read, talked, napped. People took turns churning out dinners—Burt, at loose ends and on stress leave from his job, had cooked often. Someone would ring the rusty iron triangle hung from a porch rafter, and everyone would gather in the dining room, with its exposed log truss and chandeliers of tangled antlers. Cal and Peggy's daily wedding china (place settings for twelve) was often augmented with the picnic Melmac, depending on how many girlfriends, boyfriends, and other drop-ins crowded around the table, with Cal always at the head.

Patsy was spending long days in research libraries by that time, only sometimes showing up at the dinners; even then she might grab a bowl of stew or piece of chicken to eat in her office. She didn't begrudge Cal the company he needed, and he, in turn, didn't begrudge her the time and solitude for her work.

Since Burt's tenancy, things at the Pondo had quieted down. March had married, moved to Sunnyvale with her younger dot-com husband, and given birth to Ava. Brice, after another fling with high-paid commercial production, was house-sitting to get by. Now, only two AA newcomers bunked in the east wing, although Stan was splitting up with his wife and would no doubt move home.

Patsy had never once thought of the Pondo as *a halfway facility*. Her term for all the hubbub and moochers and revolving stepchildren was *upscale crash pad*.

•

The first time Lewis phoned her, he had a pretext, an annoying bit of Hallen red tape about parking on campus. They talked for an hour. She found her own pretext two nights later—would he speak at her Friday meeting?—and this time they stayed on for two hours, she on the sofa in her home office, wrapped in the old rag, he fifty miles away in his bungalow in the orange groves near Rito.

They started meeting for lunch between classes, and later, when they were done teaching, took brisk walks into the hills above Hallen, Patsy's exercise on teaching days. They swapped books, discussed them, adjusted each other's tastes—Really, Tolstoy was in a different league from Turgenev, he said; her attachment to *Fathers and Sons* might not withstand an adult reading.

Didn't he know that Hofstadter, as lucid and elegant a writer as he was, was already old guard; he should try Susman, her favorite.

Patsy had finished her second book, *Raised Up*, a study of Hull House graduates, and was researching her third, a more literary effort, *Situated Women: Gender, Geography, and Possibility in the Novels of Edith Wharton and Willa Cather.*

Lewis had never read Cather. He was a quick study, though: two, three books a week. *Death Comes for the Archbishop*, he said, knocked him out.

A crush. Her friends had all had one or more. Sarah was in agony for months over the new Asian studies professor, and Margaret, a colleague who taught at Pitzer, had fallen for a nineteen-year-old poli-sci student, female. But one didn't act on such feelings. One suffered, deliciously. And took it out on unsuspecting husbands, who were the real beneficiaries. Crushes brightened the days, restructured the weeks, reinvigorated the nights. Gave those droopy old marriages an infusion of starch.

You have a cruh-ush, Sarah sang.

He sounds yummy, said Margaret.

Patsy considered her situation of a different order. She and Lewis were a true match, both chatterers, debaters, always brimming over with yet more to say. Not only were they both sober, their sympathies were unusually alike: each took a panel of AA members to talk to prisoners once a month. Patsy went with Gloria out to Corona. Lewis took a gang from his old drunk farm to the Acton honor farm.

•

Patsy wished Silver were around to talk, and maybe to regulate her a little. But after they'd worked together for fourteen years, Silver had retired and moved to Tucson, Arizona.

It occurred to Patsy that this business with Lewis might be her post-therapy acting out. Now that she wasn't giving a weekly account of her life to someone, it was time for a little regression, and fun.

Waiting for him to finish class and rid himself of lingering students, with their questions about the essay, the midterm, and if they could do extra credit, Patsy sat at her desk with her back to her door and gazed out at Hallen's new red clay track, where hammer throwers, shot-putters, and hurdlers trained. She'd turn at his quick knock and see his thin, jagged face, still lit and amused by some undergraduate's take on the Russians—"The Darling" was just codependent, or "The Nose" was like the dating process.

Let's go, Lewis would say. They'd stride into the hills behind Hallen, through the neighborhoods of big, theatrical homes with walled gardens and old trees. One night they walked as far as Audrey's old house, three miles. Strangers lived there now, but Gilles's gritty ashes moldered under the great ficus tree.

Lewis wore jeans and pressed shirts and big pullover sweaters that hung well on him. He had a slim, lanky body and that easy feline swagger. In fact, all his clothes looked good on him, except perhaps his loafers, which were too pointy and down at the heel; he'd bought them in Italy three years before.

His hair was iron-colored and curly, his hands and arms expressive. He talked with a chronic intensity that Patsy couldn't get enough of, and often he slid his long fingers into his curls and gave his head a good scratch, as if to stimulate fresh thought. She found him wonderfully appealing, handsome, and heartbreaking. What was he doing roaming strange neighborhoods with a married woman?

They waited forty-five minutes in a crowd of students and young families for thin-crusted eggplant and jalapeño pizza at Casa Bianca. They drove into Pasadena to eat boysenberry pie with overlarge scoops of vanilla ice cream at Pie 'N Burger—she would've enjoyed it more if a man she knew from meetings wasn't a few seats down and watching them. She saw how the two of them must look, chattering face-to-face, with Lewis tapping the Formica countertop to make a point and leaning into her, cajoling her to agree.

•

On the days they didn't see each other—that is, most days—they talked on the phone, often for hours, which she hadn't done with a man, ever. They were both good at talking about themselves—lots of practice in AA—and revealed their checkered pasts with good-natured one-upmanship. She'd finished her coursework at twenty-six, before her drinking got too out of hand, whereas he, at twenty-six, had been working in a car parts store, failing to keep current with a mounting cocaine debt, and wouldn't even start his coursework for another year.

He too had woken up from a blackout to find himself in custody—in his case, in the rubber room of a county detox, with no idea how he got there.

That's the thing, said Patsy. I didn't know why I'd been arrested either. They wouldn't tell me. Then a detective started reading the homicide report.

That sounds sadistic.

They were pretty mad at me, said Patsy. And for good reason.

You don't remember anything about the actual accident? said Lewis.

No, she said. I thought I remembered something, but when the husband came to see me in prison, I found out I had it all wrong. I'd imagined long hair, and uniforms, like Salvation Army members.

Patsy tucked the old rag more tightly around her. Actually, when I talked to your meeting, she said, I didn't mention that they were Jehovah's Witnesses. I stopped saying that because once, at a big Hollywood meeting, I said, I swung too fast into my driveway and hit two Jehovah's Witnesses, and the whole room burst out laughing, as if I'd told a joke.

Ouch, he said.

Yeah. Patsy was silent, recalling her dismay when the people kept laughing as she'd tried to set them straight.

We don't have to talk about this, Lewis said.

I don't mind, she said. In fact, it had been a long time since she'd spoken in any detail about the accident or prison; she used to talk to Silver about those things, and there'd been times with Cal, early on in the marriage, when she was haunted and couldn't sleep, but not recently.

I've only been to jail twice, Lewis said, and never for more than a day. But I rank it among the worst experiences I've ever had. How did you get through all those years intact?

Who says I'm through? said Patsy. Or intact?

Yes, but you've obviously moved on.

From prison itself, to some extent maybe. But I think of *them* every day. The mother and daughter. I'm involved, still, with the father and boy. I go to the kid's recitals. I help with his schooling, we give each other birthday presents. They're my other, secret family.

Yes, and look at you. Even with all that, you've been so productive—all your books and teaching and running that big house.

Just two books, so far. And I've been lucky, Lewis, she said. That man whose family I killed happened to be an exceptional human being. He forgave me right away. I'd be nowhere without his generosity. And when I got out of prison and was so sad and lost, Cal took me in and gave me this privileged, stable, secure life. And for the record, *he* runs the Pondo. I have nothing to do with it. You go to him if you want a room or need a month's grace on your phone bill. He's the one who tells the housekeepers to make a vat of soup. He keeps the troops happy. Me, I'd kick 'em all out today, every one, for five minutes of peace and quiet.

•

At night, when Cal was already asleep, they delivered themselves to each other in sentences. How they'd lived before, how they lived now, what happened in between. Lewis was chronically single, he said; his last love was a minister who became too involved with her congregation and had no time for him. Patsy was careful when she spoke of Cal; she never complained that he was growing old or slowing up, or that she'd never had a conversation with him remotely like those she and Lewis now had on a daily basis. She groused mildly about Cal's generic tolerance—You should meet some of the strays he brings home!—and his habit, after thirty-odd years, of attending AA every day. She and Lewis were both down to one or two meetings a week and the monthly panels they took to their respective prisons.

They talked until it was a fight to stay awake. They signed off, and the next night, picked up where they left off.

•

Patsy hoped to keep this conversation going alongside her marriage forever. Not at the same high pitch, of course. The novelty would dim, their fervor would cool, Lewis would probably fall in love with someone at some point, but why couldn't their steady, voluble friendship continue?

As if in preparation, they told the stories of their friends and friendships, discussed the odd and unexpected arrangements people made for happiness.

He had been lovers with Libby, the fiddle player, before her marriage to his sponsor. In fact, there had been a love triangle between Lewis, his sponsor, and Libby. I lost out, Lewis said, and I deserved to.

But he and Libby had ended up very close—family, he said.

•

Sarah's feelings for her Asian studies guy had quieted to workable levels within two years; the two still drew together at school get-togethers, still fluffed up in each other's company, but Sarah's pain and longing had bled off—and this de-escalation was accomplished without a single declaration or kiss. After riding the whole wild arc, Sarah had landed safely within her marriage, her daughters blessedly ignorant. And what had thin-lipped Henry Croft even noticed? He'd replaced their back lawn with grapevines and was learning to make wine.

Margaret's young poli-sci major had proved immature and dull; the infatuation died in six months, the whole of it conducted and concluded with only a few inadvertent hand brushes, the great swells of Margaret's passion having been adroitly redirected to her unsuspecting Sam.

•

Well well well, said Cal. What brought this on?

Accustomed to initiating, he was possibly disconcerted. But he warmed up, and his long, smooth, pale legs nudged hers apart.

He was seventy-six, calm and thorough. He now made a soft, popping noise when he kissed. The same noise her grandfather had made when she was little. An old man's kiss.

His new doctor, a men's health specialist, had said that Cal's testosterone levels were remarkably high. I can tell by the blueness and clarity of his eyes, the doctor told Patsy, and also his mental acuity.

Lewis's eyes were brown.

•

Is there a reason you've never invited me to your house?

Yes, she said. I don't want to see you of all people go gaga over Cal. And you will. He's got that AA charisma, like your old sponsor had. He has groupies by the dozen. I don't want to see you join their ranks.

His laugh was always surprised, as if the world had found yet another way to catch him off guard. I may not be as susceptible as you think, he said.

I'm not taking any chances, she said.

A few weeks later they were in his office, a reconditioned janitor's closet assigned to the rotating adjuncts. Bookshelves lined the long walls, leaving room for a desk and two plain chairs, but Lewis and Patsy were standing, discussing where they should have dinner.

So why is it you've never taken me to the Ponderosa?

I told you. I want to keep you for myself.

How seriously do you mean that?

I mean it, Patsy said, but catching a new seriousness in his tone, she waved her hand. If you really want to, we could go tonight. I think Haydee made carne asada today. But remember—I'm not sharing you with Cal.

And what if I don't want to share you with him? Lewis said in a low voice. In the pitiless fluorescent light, his face was white with fear.

Don't! she said. Stop. Time to change the subject! Ding!

He caught her wrist. This is love, Patsy, he said. In case you didn't know.

•

She had not said what was on the tip of her tongue: I'd never leave Cal for you. She held back because she wanted the moment to last, she wasn't ready for it all to be over just like that.

Oh, she said. Oh god.

Didn't Lewis know that she wasn't a person to act on grand passions or inflict gratuitous pain? That she was still working off a backlog of guilt?

He said, We have to be together, Patsy.

She shook her head. Not like that, she said.

Like what, then? Like I'm your brother or your pet? No!

He caught himself and, bowing his head, gave his scalp a good scratch. He seemed calmer when he looked up. At least think about it, Patsy. Let's not make a decision now. Let's just go get something to eat.

But she couldn't. She was sweating and shaking, and had to get away. What made him think there was a decision?

I can't, she said. I have to go.

It was mid-February, cold and freshly dark. The first stars were pink and overlarge. She was nauseous and elated and furious. If he'd only kept his mouth shut, they could've ridden it out to a lower key and gone on for years.

She hadn't driven far when she thought, Well, why not leave Cal? His kids—well, at least March—still considered their marriage unseemly. Her family probably did too, but they were too guarded and polite to say so. Of course, in AA she and Cal were regarded as royalty. No harm in popping that bubble.

Even Lewis had been incredulous: You're married to Cal Sharp?

Yes, yes she was. And she did love Cal, for his goodness, his generosity to her, his unfettered acceptance. *Oh, he's not so bad, he's a good egg*—how many times had she heard him say that of one wretch or another? He'd say that about Lewis if he'd witnessed their last scene.

And how many lost souls and wounded birds, in the sway of Cal's benignant goodwill, had pulled together a few meager strands of self to prove Cal's assessment correct? Patsy herself had flourished in the great open field of her husband's acceptance. He asked little of her except that she enjoy her life, accept his dry pop of a kiss, and be kind to his children. She might not have intense literary discussions with him or love his children and sponsees as much as she'd intended to; she and Cal might never engage in verbal thrusts and parries, but this had rarely bothered her before. They never conversed in depth, never had. She'd had her girlfriends, her colleagues for that.

She was driving in the neighborhood behind Hallen, up and down the hilly streets, half hoping to see Lewis, slouching and furious, searching for her. She went past the campus again, slowly by the parking lot. His funny little car, a 1969 BMW 2002 with an exhaust problem, was gone.

She couldn't imagine nights without talking to him. He'd ruined her for Cal alone. Cal, who had almost no idea what she did, what concerned her, what occupied her day after day.

The previous week, she'd shown Cal the 1993 film *The Age of Innocence*, thinking the movie could give him at least some idea of what her next book was about. He said only that Madame Olenska reminded him of Audrey. When pressed for reasons why, it was because both had moved to Paris.

And later, in bed: That little girl? Cal said. The one Archer married? She would've been all right no matter what. She would've found someone else.

Otherwise, he'd had little patience for the plot, found Newland Archer's struggles with convention unnecessary, overwrought.

Of course, Cal's own life had become unconventional; he'd gone from urbane clubman of impressive inherited wealth to AA lion with dwindling fortunes and an ex-con wife.

And those fortunes had seriously dwindled.

The extravagant family vacations they'd taken had been paid for with capital, as had his children's educations, everyone's cars, the down payments on his children's homes, his and Patsy's twenty-thousand-dollar Morgan horses. He'd sacrificed the Lyster to stanch a cash-flow crisis. It had taken the shock of losing the Lyster for Patsy to realize Cal was actually profligate. He came from old money, scads of it, but had not mastered the art of preserving it. He would have squandered even more, Audrey told her, if his brothers and nephews hadn't periodically intervened.

Even so, she and Cal were not poor. Not by a long shot. They had the Ponderosa, two six-unit apartment houses in Glendale, Cal's income, and other family trickles, not to mention the very investment funds that, having tanked in '91, were again picking up speed. Patsy was always able to give away as much of her salary as she wanted and had divided it between Burt's kids and Martin Parnham, whose father, as a low-level civil engineer, could never have sent him through Flintridge Prep and Pepperdine without loans.

Cal had been reliably generous to her. He'd never burdened her with money worries, perhaps because he was insufficiently worried himself. What she'd expected of their marriage—security, mutual comfort, the

room and encouragement to do her own work—had been freely provided. Cal may never have been a voluble soul mate, but he had never
given her any grounds to leave or cause him pain.

She could, apparently, cause Lewis pain. But he had forced her hand.
Why did he have to speak out and name their predicament?

Once home at the Ponderosa, Patsy went straight to her office. She
called Gloria, who said, Hoho, I saw this one coming from about a
thousand miles off, ever since you brought Mr. Scruffy Sexy to the meeting some months back.

Love pain, Gloria went on, it's the worst. It's what people with ten,
twenty, fifty years of sobriety drink over. So I'd stick close to the program, hit a meeting a day till you're through this.

So Patsy went to a Thursday night meeting and to her home group
on Friday. She did not share, she listened, gathering bits to arm herself
for whichever loss was to come.

During the day, she shut herself up in her home office and lay on her
couch and let herself imagine life in the orange groves in Lewis's little
house (which she had never seen) and farther flung locales. Lewis went
to Paris and St. Petersburg each year and had been looking for something small to buy—a studio apartment, a maid's room in the tenth arrondissement, or some wrecked dacha on the Volga.

Patsy went to a women's meeting on Saturday morning in a church
near the Rose Bowl. Three newly sober young women in a row waxed
hyperbolic about the glories of Alcoholics Anonymous. Bored and annoyed, Patsy left during the break and drove through Old Town Pasadena,
thinking she'd get a coffee, but couldn't find a parking place.

As was their custom, she went riding with Cal Saturday afternoon, a
slow amble along the foothills and up the arroyo. It was true, she saw,
that they barely spoke. They pointed out birds to each other; junco, redheaded sapsucker, rufous-sided towhee. They murmured to their own
horses, siblings from different years, Zeno and Diotima, sure-footed
bays with intelligent black eyes and pricked, shapely ears.

On Diotima, Patsy dawdled behind Cal through the glens of thin-
trunked beech. His great talents had been in AA, but Cal was no longer
universally adored there either. For years he'd eschewed psychiatry and
even therapy, and had only recently started to come around on antidepressants, which he'd long classed with mood-altering street drugs. If a

man he sponsored had started on Prozac or Effexor, Cal told him to find another sponsor, one more knowledgeable about such things. Patsy periodically hid her own Zoloft in her office.

She'd probably be doing so again, shortly.

Up ahead, Cal pulled Zeno to a halt and pointed. Red-tailed hawk, he said.

•

She phoned Audrey in Paris and spilled the beans. I finally get what you meant about a peer, Patsy said.

Do you have to cut him entirely out of your life? said Audrey. Can't you bring him home, have him be friends with both you and Cal?

Never, she said, already hoarding what they'd had.

And *une petite affaire*? said Audrey. Out of the question?

It wouldn't be *petite*, said Patsy. And I couldn't live with myself.

Well, that's good, for my brother's sake. I don't know about yours.

That night, in bed beside Cal, guilt hit in a toxic black blast, for confiding in Audrey and betraying Cal even that much.

Her fourth meeting in as many days was another women's meeting, this one on Sunday in a side room of a Lutheran church in Altadena. Patsy knew most of the women around the table, and one, Yvette Stevens, raised her hand to start the sharing.

Yvette was tall too, and willowy, and ten years older than Patsy. She wore her pale gray hair in a soft pageboy; her eyes were round and olive black and quick. She was a high-up administrator at the County Art Museum and moved with social ease between cranky artists and the city's billionaires.

Yvette, it seemed, was facing a near replica of Patsy's own dilemma, with a new curator, younger, full of fire, a soul mate if she'd ever met one. Things between them had heated up, Yvette said. And I know where they're heading.

Patsy had met Yvette's husband, a good-natured round-shouldered older man whose chin bumped out of a wide, fleshy neck. Buzz Stevens was not unhandsome, despite that neck, and he was very rich. He managed an exclusive mutual fund and made other people rich too. Patsy and Cal ran into them at the opera, at benefits and museum openings.

If I was drinking, I'd jump in headfirst, Yvette went on. And to hell with everyone else. My kids, his kids, our respective spouses.

Patsy admired Yvette for talking about her situation so openly, as she herself hadn't spoken up once in four meetings.

But after twenty-one years of sobriety, Yvette continued, I might just step around this one. I don't *have* to sacrifice my marriage, home, and kids to my own erotic impulses. I don't even have to kick up a ruckus with my husband. I can choose to behave like an adult. A sober adult. Who knows? Renunciation may bring its own rewards.

Well, okay, Patsy thought, walking back to her car in the church lot, that's that. No privileging my own erotic impulses over my husband's well-being.

No kicking up a ruckus.

So that's that, she thought again, driving home. Could it have been spelled out more clearly? Wasn't that what she'd gone to meeting after meeting to hear? She'd thrown herself upon the program, and her higher power had spoken through the thin, prettily curving lips of elegant Yvette S.

Okay, she muttered, not without relief. If that's the way it is.

She would not be Anna Karenina, or Emma Bovary, or the Lady with the Lapdog.

•

Lewis said not to come by his office, not to call, not to cross his path. Let's not draw it out, he said. I'm an old hand at this. The cleaner, the better.

I think that's right, she said. But if you ever want to be friends . . .

I'll call you, he said. And if you ever change your mind, you call me. But not until.

She couldn't eat. Her concentration evaporated. There was nothing she wanted to do or see. Teaching gave her some relief; she could show up for her students, lecture, answer questions. Then she found a carrel in the second floor of Hallen's library, where on Tuesday and Thursday, in the late afternoon, she could see Lewis leave his building and walk a diagonal path across the commons to the parking lot. She once invoked faculty privilege to evict a student and all his books to claim her vantage point.

Lewis had a large black knapsack and a black leather car coat; he walked aslant, the backpack slung over just one shoulder. Intercepted by a student, he stopped. Patsy saw the sudden freeze of his shoulders and then his head tip back—and even from eighty, a hundred yards away, she knew he was laughing.

Laughing. He could laugh.

She was furious all night, rising from her bed to go to her office, to call him, to browbeat him for his laughter, for being able to laugh.

But he had told her not to call unless she'd changed her mind.

She could hardly bear Cal's presence and felt her lips start to curl at everything he said. When he placed his hand over her rib cage one night, she firmly removed it and left the bed, as if insulted, to sleep in her office. But sleep was no longer her primary nocturnal activity. She thought and kicked, and turned on the light and stared miserably at the line where the ceiling and wall intersected. She attempted to calm herself by counting breaths, losing count, going back to one, again and again. She tried to relax her muscles starting with her toes and heels, the way her yoga teacher ended classes in *shavasana.* Corpse pose. She went tense again in seconds, then rose, sat at her desk, clicked through the World Wide Web, her attention lasting a few sentences into any news story.

Gloria told her to make a gratitude list:

1. This beautiful world
2. Not being in prison
3. Human consciousness
4. The existence of L.F.
5. Diotima

A lot of help that was.

Gloria's next assignment was an inventory, in which Patsy was to write answers to these questions: *What do I want? What am I afraid of? Who am I lying to? How do I want to appear?* She wrote the questions down on a legal pad and threw the pad across the room.

Burt called to invite her up for Easter. No, she said, and lied about having other plans.

She could not bear going back to Burt's living room, where they had met. Her own office at Hallen, the floor where Lewis had stood, the chair he sat on, the bookcase he'd ranged back and forth in front of all bore witness to his absence. Driving past Casa Bianca and seeing the people waiting out front was like glimpsing a bright warm world from which she'd been expelled. There was no place she cared about being; everywhere she was, some essential animating force had been bled from the surroundings.

•

On Palm Sunday she and Cal went to Spencer's home for dinner. Spencer had married his girlfriend from Stanford, Anna, a molecular biologist who'd quit a job at GenTech after their daughter was born. They lived three miles from the Ponderosa in a tidy suburban neighborhood full of affluent young families.

Anna served grilled chicken breasts, rice, and green salad. Afterward they sat around the table drinking mint tea. Three-year-old Lily, who'd been set up with a video in the next room, wandered in in her pajamas.

Go to Ruthie's house, she said.

Oh, but honey, Anna said, lifting Lily onto her lap, it's way past your bedtime. And Ruthie, I'm sure, is already fast asleep.

But Lily was not dissuaded. Ruthie's house, she said. I want to.

Denied again, she began to weep. Anna, smiling gently, stroked her back, murmured into her hair. The sobs grew louder, the breaths more ragged.

Spencer checked out the window to see if there were signs of life at the neighbors' house, but the lights were out.

The crying escalated into chordal wails. Then, screams.

The patience of these young parents amazed Patsy, whose own mother would've tolerated half to one of those extravagant, long, high-pitched whines before sending the child to her room, to cry and rage herself to sleep.

Oh, Lily dear, Patsy said, thinking she might break the spell. Ruthie can't play tonight. But you'll see her tomorrow, I'm sure.

Anna's hand fluttered up off Lily's back, signaling that Patsy needn't bother. The girl was beyond comfort, inconsolable. She roared and kicked the table legs and screamed bloodcurdling screams. Her face grew red and swollen, her eyes were slits, a clump of hair stuck in her mouth.

I'll take her to bed, said Spencer finally.

I'll do it, Anna said, standing. She apologized to Cal and Patsy for leaving them. I'll be back, she whispered over her daughter's sweaty brow.

And for another half an hour, from another part of the house, came sobs and roars and the mother's patient murmurs.

She's overtired, Spencer said.

More tea was poured. Father and son talked about the new Audi convertibles. Patsy monitored the child's impossible, ongoing fury.

A tantrum. Throwing a tantrum over something that wasn't even possible. Wanting what she wanted, when no agency on earth could grant it.

And not even a mother to hold her.

Silver would have at least let her vent. Silver wouldn't have made her write gratitude lists or inventory her motives. Silver would have let her rant and rage with the same amused, motherly detachment Anna employed, albeit for fifty minutes only.

The convulsive sobs. Screams thickened with fury.

Where did such oceans of sorrow reside within a human being?

•

Cal came to bed in flannel pajamas that were a little raggedy but soft like skin. Their room was chilly; they both liked to sleep with a window open for the air and the sound of the stream. Will you do me a favor? she asked. Will you just hold me?

She fit into the curve of his body. He slid one arm under her and pulled her closer, clasped her around, and kissed the bone behind her ear.

At first she could barely stand it. All of her muscles coiled to repel him. He sensed this and began to rub her arm, her shoulder and back.

Consciously, she set about relaxing, one muscle after another, giving them over to him. Cal hummed and cupped her forehead in his wide palm, caressed her face, stroked her neck and down her sternum. He knew, without her telling him, that she didn't want sex. For this intuition she was grateful.

As she relaxed, she began to weep, silently at first, but then she couldn't hide it. Cal tried once to turn her to face him, but when she didn't comply, he desisted. In a low voice he said, Do you want to talk? She shook her head no, and he didn't ask again. Never was she more grateful for his incuriosity, his aversion to probing conversation. Her sobs grew louder and quite painful but were even more painful to suppress. So she wept like the tired child, and Cal held her and sometimes caressed her, reclasped her, and kissed the back of her head again and again until her crying subsided and they both fell asleep.

•

She woke in the daylight. Cal was filling his pockets from the top of his dresser. Keys. Change. Billfold. Money clip. She turned, and through a gap in the curtains could see a slice of mountain ridge in dark shadow, and above that a milky sky. No, this wasn't where she wanted to be. And Cal, now threading his belt and looking at her with some concern, was not the person she wanted to be with. But these thoughts arrived with less force than they had, and with somewhat less urgency. And that was a start.

PART FIVE

24

Spring 2001

March was visiting again, as a family of four.

I wish they'd waited till after my break, Patsy told Cal. I have so much work to do.

Grading. And a seminar on Modernism to prepare.

They're easy, Cal said. You can hole up and nobody'll mind.

They had arrived three days earlier than Patsy expected. She came in from an afternoon ride to find everyone in the kitchen: Ava, three; Beckett, nine months; Forrest, passing apple slices around; and March, on the brink of evicting Bob the boarder from the guest suite.

We always used to stay there before, said March.

Bob stays put, Patsy said, hoping he'd overheard none of this. You can have the possum trot again. Or take all three bedrooms in the east wing.

I don't see why Bob gets the best guest rooms, March said.

We want him by us, in case your dad needs him.

But we're here now. We'll keep an eye on Dad.

Patsy said, I'm not making Bob move each time someone visits.

Just out of curiosity, said March. Where does Roberta stay when she comes down?

The Huntington Sheraton, said Patsy. Ted gets a special rate—two, two-twenty a night.

I hate the trot, said March.

Really? said Forrest. It has those views.

Forrest, she said.

He hauled suitcases and fold-up crib to the east wing, trip after trip. He was fit and lean, a devoted runner, snowboarder, and sailor—a pleasure seeker, said Cal, who had disapproved of the marriage.

I'm sorry, Cal said when Patsy caught him alone. I thought I told you they'd be early. I know I meant to.

It doesn't matter, said Patsy. They're here now. But the beds aren't made up, the rooms aren't aired.

They don't care.

They did care, Patsy thought. Haydee wasn't working today, so March would have to make up the beds herself, unless she helped.

She helped.

That first night, Patsy scrubbed potatoes, put a pork roast in the oven, picked her homegrown lettuce for a salad. They ate in the garden room, Bob the boarder joining them as usual. Cal sat with three-year-old Ava on his lap. Beckett, strapped in his high chair, screeched like a seagull. So sweet of you, Patsy, to cook such a nice dinner, March said. But didn't Patsy remember that the children don't eat pork? Also, potatoes turn into sugar the second you swallow them. You might as well feed kids Snickers bars, March said. Nor was the salad safe. Yes, she knew the lettuce was organic, except that it had been fertilized by stable leavings, and the horses had had antibiotic shots, hadn't they? I try not to expose the children to secondhand antibiotics, March said. Luckily, she had brought tofu dogs and apples, which was all Ava wanted to eat, anyway, and Beckett was satisfied by his mother's breast and certified organic carrot puree from a jar.

Bob the boarder helped Patsy load the dishwasher. I'm not sure, he said, but technically, aren't we talking about *third-* or even *fourth*-hand antibiotics?

•

March installed herself in the kitchen. Forrest set up his computers in the dining room. Five years earlier, he and some college friends had started an Internet company that hooked up twentysomethings with global travel, shopping, and dating; venture capitalists bought them out for a small fortune.

It was high time now for another, larger fortune; Cal had been sending checks for Ava's school and, recently, a tax bill.

Patsy came home from giving her last final with a boxful of blue books and term papers from her twentieth-century U.S. cultural history class. En route to her office, she stumbled over Beckett. He'd shot out from nowhere. They stared at each other with mutual amazement, and he took off. Preparing to crawl, he had an idiosyncratic, leg-dragging scoot that was surprisingly fast. He propelled himself up and down the Ponderosa's long halls with the clumsy swiftness of an alligator. Patsy worried that the boy would fell Cal like a tree.

March was heating a slab of tofurkey and simmering a big pot of soup in the kitchen. Patsy peered into the watery broth, with its bobbing carrots. If it's okay with you, she said, I'll just take a bowl to my office.

But we're eating in ten minutes. And it's important for the kids to have the family all together at mealtime, March said.

After so many false starts—biology major, a short stab at law school, a Realtor's license—March had found her calling. Expert mother.

•

Your new kitchen too! Sarah cried. Couldn't you declare it off-limits?

And cause World War Three? said Patsy. It's only for a couple weeks, and Cal's so happy they're here.

A couple of weeks!

But he did agree to Cambridge, said Patsy.

She'd been invited to give four public lectures in the fall and do research for her next book. Cal had promised to come along, accompany her on a work trip for once, although he was already muttering about the plane ride, his hips, the damp English weather.

After all those hideous board meetings he dragged you to? said Sarah. He owes you *years* in Cambridge.

I don't know, Patsy said.

•

For a time, post-Lewis, Patsy had tried to think about her marriage, but it was like trying to focus on air or the ground as you were walking someplace. She could only do it for seconds at a time, and didn't come up with much. It did seem that, with the latitude Cal gave her, she'd wandered too far afield, lost sight of him. So she'd resolved to stick closer. She planted vegetables and had plans drawn up for a smaller, cozier kitchen, with an attached garden room such as Audrey used to have.

I need more of a home life, she'd told him.

We're here, Cal said. Anytime.

That first person plural irked, and she began the remodel by moving the old six-burner restaurant stove and two refrigerators into the possum trot, making that whole first floor into a kitchen and eating area they'd use during renovation. Afterward, the boarders would have it.

She'd enlisted Brice for design advice, and together they drove all over the county for appliances and knobs and had a lot of fun, until they quarreled over flooring and Brice quit in a huff. That was near the end of the project, fortunately.

She started cooking most days. Cal came and ate with her when summoned; he admired her meals, the new garden room and garden; he'd never, he said, seen chard, artichokes, and peppers planted in among roses.

Some days Patsy came home from Hallen to find he'd already eaten. One of the boarders had offered him pasta or a big salad and he saw no reason to refuse it.

But Cal, I had dinner all planned, she'd say.

He was sure whatever she'd planned could keep till tomorrow.

It was a boarder who left the message on Patsy's cell phone a year ago: Cal has a headache and can't see out one eye. I'm driving him to Huntington.

The stroke was minor, and the slight loss of grip in his right hand had cleared up with a month of physical therapy. But it spooked Cal, and he resigned from his boards, stopped driving at night, and refused to go to Paris to see Audrey that year. He couldn't face the plane ride, he said, or all that walking once they got there.

Patsy cited Cal's health in clearing out the house. We can't take on so much anymore, she told all four boarders, and since the previous July she and Cal had lived alone, despite frequent inquiries. You can ask, she'd say, but we're not doing that anymore.

The crash pad days were over.

She drove Cal to his meetings and sat beside him as she hadn't for more than a decade. Her pride had turned protective, tender, vigilant. He was still revered, if also humored. He told his same old stories—of drinking vanilla extract, of his conduct unbecoming an officer. After forty years of sobriety he could hardly be expected to produce a new drunkalog, but sometimes he forgot key details and punch lines, and Patsy caught the glances exchanged, the tight, tolerant smiles.

She grew tomatoes of all different colors that summer, some the size of small pumpkins. She got Cal out riding most days. She threw him a big seventy-eighth birthday bash in August, barbecued ribs, potato salad. All the kids and grandkids came, and scores of drunks. He announced in bed that morning that he was done horseback riding. His hips. I tallied it up, he said. I've ridden close to seventy thousand miles in my life. And that's enough for any man.

She thought they should read together in the library at night, but Cal was too drowsy after eating to concentrate, and preferred TV with the volume on high. So Patsy slipped off to her office, where she read on her sofa, a near replica of the one Brice had found for her Lyster apartment—shaved mohair, moss green. Who could predict the objects of future nostalgia? A creature hopping in the brush outside or the laughing bark of a coyote might pull her from the page. She'd frown at the red walls, the shelves of books, assay and regret the long hallways and doors between her and Cal. She'd go to check, and despite the earsplitting action on the screen, he'd be dozing, mouth open, remote in hand.

She strove to do well by Cal, and she never gave up hope.

And what was it she still hoped for?

His full attention.

Her old P.O., Knock-Knock né Jeffrey Goldstone, had referred Bob to them in the fall—smart guy, Knock-Knock said—and this time, Patsy relented. A wry, underexercised bachelor, Bob had been a high school English instructor until he was fired for teaching while intoxicated. Patsy thought he'd be fun to talk to, and he was. In exchange for room and board, Bob drove Cal to AA meetings and kept an eye on him when Patsy was at Hallen. Cal reeled him in with charm, and in no time, the younger man was a goner—and an almost-free full-time companion, not that Cal required one. Cal still had an ageless, leathery vigor, still chopped wood and hauled bottles of Arrowhead in from the storeroom. His eyes stayed clear and blue and quick.

But he disliked driving, even in broad daylight. He refused to go to movies at night—I just fall asleep, he said—and he declined Roberta's invitations to spend weekends in Montecito as well as Audrey's for weeks in Paris. Come here, he told them. We have all this room.

Come here, he'd no doubt said to March.

•

The finals for Patsy's twentieth-century cultural history class were the usual mix of passable and lazy, with a few standouts. *And your point is?*

she scribbled in one margin; *Wrong Roosevelt!* in another. She graded the blue books on her office sofa until she fell asleep, then woke up there the next morning in her jeans, wrapped in the old rag. Bob was already in the kitchen, reading the newspaper. Another chronic sofa-sleeper, his face was puffy, his eyes crusty. He looked at Patsy with a brightness she found irritating.

Why couldn't the men in this house boil water, grind beans, pour A through B?

Bob, she said, cool and brisk. Let me show you how to make the coffee.

I know. I just didn't want to make noise, he said.

It's a sound everyone in this house is thrilled to hear, she said, and, flicking the switch of the grinder, let it go perhaps longer than necessary. The coffee would be strong.

I hope I'm not too in the way with the family visiting, Bob said.

You live here, Bob, said Patsy. Try not to let March get to you. They'll be gone soon enough.

Last night she told me to clear a space in the garage for Forrest's boat.

A boat? What boat?

A shrug. I guess he's bringing a boat down.

You didn't do it, I hope?

No. I figure it's not my stuff to move around.

Good, Patsy said. Because give her an inch and our little program director will run you ragged.

She carried a cup of coffee into the bedroom, where Cal was sitting up in bed. She set it on the nightstand beside him.

Why, thank you, darling, he said absently. He was winding his father's beautiful old watch with the silver link band.

Patsy pulled open the curtains to a clear, bright, breezy day. Across the stream, long grass rippled on the canyon wall. Cal, she said, why is Forrest bringing a boat down?

He slid the watch on his wrist, gave it a shake. They're putting their house on the market, and the Realtor wants it out of the way for the open house.

Couldn't they dry-dock it somewhere?

It's that boat he's been building. It's not finished.

Oh, right, Patsy said, remembering. Since his buyout, Forrest had been building a sailboat in the rec room of his Sunnyvale home.

It'll cost a fortune to ship, she said. No, don't tell me. I don't want to know.

At her dresser, she pulled out black jeans and a soft gray T-shirt. They're actually selling? What brought that on?

Don't you think it's time? Cal sipped his coffee, watching her.

Are they thinking of moving down around here?

They'd like to. It depends where Forrest finds work.

That's good. As long as they're not moving in with us.

They may need to for a while, sweetie, Cal said.

She stood there with her folded clothes. Oh, Cal.

But not till after the house sells, he added.

The large, sun-filled master bedroom had two big easy chairs covered in natural linen. Patsy threw herself down in one. I don't want them here, she said. I finally got this place cleared out. I don't want it filling back up.

But this is family, said Cal.

Which is worse, said Patsy. March has already staked out my new kitchen and is ordering Bob around like he's a servant. That's okay for a week or two, but any longer, there's no excuse. Besides, Cal, if you let them come home every time they hit a rough spot, they'll never be independent.

Cal climbed slowly out of bed, sliding his feet right into slippers. Nobody's moving in tomorrow. The house hasn't sold yet. Nothing has been decided.

One thing has. I don't want them moving in with us.

•

Midmorning, Haydee tapped on her office door and asked to clean the room, so Patsy carried her finals—twenty-two down, eighteen to go— to the kitchen table and worked there until three-year-old Ava ran in.

Head off! Head off!

Two parts of a baby doll, torso and head, tumbled over the open blue book. A stiff flange at the top of the doll's neck had to be reinserted into the head's hole—far too stiff a job for any three-year-old fingers.

Here you go, Patsy said, delivering the resurrected doll as March came in with Beckett on her hip.

By the way, Patsy, said March, opening the refrigerator. Spencer and

Anna are coming to dinner tonight. With Lily, of course. I hope that's okay.

Of course, Patsy said, though your dad and I won't be here.

Dad says he will. One-handed, March pulled out a glass bottle of milk.

He must have forgotten. We're going out.

But he wants to see Spence, and Stan's coming too, with his new girlfriend. March, crouching now with Beckett still on her hip, searched in a lower cupboard. Taking out a large saucepan, she swung it up over her head to set it on the counter, but Beckett grabbed her arm, skewing her aim, and the pan hit the counter's edge with a loud crack.

Oh no. Sweetheart, get off me for a sec, March said, prying Beckett's hands off her arm and giving him a little shove. Go on, now. Go find Ava.

Even from the table Patsy could see the long, lighter green chip off the counter's edge, a pale pistachio gash in the smokier celadon.

Oh Patsy, your counter, said March, fingering it.

Patsy did feel a terrible, sickening twinge, as if she'd taken the physical insult.

Don't worry, she said. It was bound to happen sooner or later. Maybe it's good to get it out of the way. Don't feel bad. I knew going in that we'd get dings and stains.

That's why Forrest and I chose granite, March said. Stone is beautiful. But, god, it would last about a minute at our house.

Or less, thought Patsy, who, feeling frail, gathered up her papers to move back to her office.

Off again! Off again! Ava ran up and pushed the beheaded baby doll into Patsy's hip.

Patsy set down her papers and reinserted the neck flange into the head hole. Now don't keep pulling it off.

Beckett pulls it off.

Is there any chance you can ditch your plans tonight? said March. It would be so good if you could both be here.

Any other time, Patsy said. But this is something we've been doing for years.

•

All afternoon, as she worked, the chipped counter drifted to mind, a floating afterimage, long and tapered like a narrow lake on a map or the blade of a knife. It made her queasy and, in a small, ridiculous way, grief-stricken.

She blamed Brice for introducing her to soapstone, then encouraging that extravagance.

Last time March and family visited, Ava had pulled over a full bucket of ammoniated water Haydee was using to wash windows. It saturated the carpet in the guest suite, and they'd had to run electric fans for days to dry it out and banish the smells of ammonia and wet wool. No telling what water damage lingered in the subfloor.

Already March's rooms in the east wing were a mess, clothes and toys strewn everywhere. Motherhood hadn't made March any tidier.

But March's carelessness wasn't nearly as irritating as her ambition. Every time she visited, she convened large family gatherings, cooked her famously bland food, and presided over the table like a precocious grande dame. Patsy herself had no interest in playing the matriarch, but that didn't mean the position was up for grabs.

Cal, she realized, had no idea how difficult these visits were for her. For his sake, Patsy had allowed and endured March's intermittent incursions with apparent good cheer. To be fair, March made an effort toward Patsy as well, and on the face of it, their relationship had improved so much, Cal assumed it was affectionate.

And Patsy was fond of March; she was, if warily. Mostly she was grateful that March interacted with Cal, whatever her motives. Cal talked to his three younger children almost every day and took an obvious, deep pleasure in his grandchildren. If Patsy's own feelings for his offspring were less ardent—Roberta was the only stepchild she adored—she wouldn't interfere. Time was short, after all. Her own father was now in managed care; he had vascular dementia and no longer knew who she was.

•

March was right. Cal had not forgotten about the dinner at Sarah's; he had decided to stay home with his family instead.

I wish you'd told me first, said Patsy.

I should have, he said.

You've always come, she wailed softly. I can't believe you're bailing.

And if you really insist, Patsy, I'll go with you.

But she didn't insist. She never insisted.

Patsy put on a cashmere shift, stretchy and comfortable, and pat-
terned black stockings, knee-high black boots, clothes Audrey made
her buy in Paris the last time they were there. (You dress like a big-
bottomed La Cañada matron, Audrey had said. And you don't even have
a big bottom.) A tortoiseshell clip held her hair in a big loose knot.

You're so dressed up, said Sarah at the door. Where's Cal?

His kids are home, Patsy said, and handed over a bag of greens.
Here. Not organic enough for March.

The party was all couples.

This was an ongoing end-of-term tradition. Patsy and Cal hosted at
the end of the fall term, Sarah did winter, Anne Davis spring.

Cal's all right? Anne asked when they moved into the dining room.

Fine, said Patsy. Only his daughter's down, and the grandkids
trump us.

At least the food was good here. In addition to learning everything
about wine, Henry Croft had become a serious cook. He served a lamb
daube with chunks of bacon, the sauce made with long-simmered
cabernet and black coffee. Laughter rose and subsided into the usual
academic plaint, then rose again as Henry dispensed his wines. Patsy's
lettuce, dressed with lemon and olive oil, was vigorously praised.

Cal should have come. He needed to get out more at night, and not
just to AA meetings. March would've been fine alone with her brothers
and their families.

Afterward they moved into the living room to sit by the fireplace for
coffee and truffles. Georges, who taught European culture, said he'd
been tapped for the comp lit search committee. You should tell that
friend of yours, Patsy, the one who taught here a couple of years ago.
Though he was French and Russian, right? Be better if he was German
and Russian, but he was good, he should apply. Do you have his e-mail?
I've been meaning to ask.

Before Patsy could reply, Sarah rushed in. Oh, you guys missed the
boat on that one. He has bigger fish to fry these days. He's had a bestseller and moved to France.

Patsy knew all this, of course, through Burt. She'd been the one to
tell Sarah.

And Lewis's book hadn't been a bestseller; it had only received many
good reviews. Very good reviews.

Not that we could hire a white male anyway, Georges said. Not with this committee. The chair told us flat out, We want a woman of color, preferably a lesbian, ideally with a not-too-noticeable disability.

The fire snapped, and a ribbon of smoke curled into the room, which was in fact two-thirds of the ballroom. The partition had been in place since right after Sarah and Henry's wedding and, with so many couches and bookshelves shoved up against it, seemed permanent. Patsy glanced idly at the high coved ceiling and clad beams above. She'd been so envious of the ballroom!

Maybe when one of Sarah's daughters married, the dividers would be folded back and the room returned to its former glory.

25

Patsy looked up from a term paper on Friday morning—she'd finished the finals—to see Forrest's crated boat delivered on an airbrushed candy pink flatbed truck such as transported high-end custom race cars. Couldn't Cal at least have hired a mid-priced boat hauler?

Forrest had rearranged the garage.

The truck and trailer left, and the house grew quiet. The family had gone to the zoo. At noon Patsy took a break and went out to cut some lettuce for lunch. It had rained in the night and now the sun was out, so the world glistened and smelled of sage and eucalyptus and clean, wet granite.

Since Christmas, rain had been frequent. The fattened little stream filled the canyon with its boisterous crashing, and all the hedges and shrubs had grown leggy and lush. The lettuce leaves were wide and vivid in their greens and bronzes, also tender and given to inhabitants; she had to examine each head for slugs and the thin, lively worms that hid in the Bibbs.

When the phone rang in the house, Patsy paused. Cal probably had his headphones on and couldn't hear it, and Bob never answered. At the third ring Patsy set down her knife and ran.

Caller ID read Joey Hawthorne. Patsy hesitated, not because she wasn't happy to talk to Joey, but because March was out, and Patsy didn't have time for a greet-and-catch-up session, not with thirty-odd term papers yet to grade.

What the hell, she said, and picked up. Joey Hawthorne!

I hate caller ID, said Joey. How are you, Patsy?

Good, fine. But you missed March. She won't be back till late.

I didn't even know she was down, Joey said. I called to talk to you.

Me? said Patsy. How nice. Where are you, anyway?

Here. West Lost Angeles, Joey said, but just back from Toronto. I flew in this morning. But something came up there that I need to talk to you about. Are you home?

Yes, said Patsy. But I'm deep in grading hell. If it can wait till tomorrow, you can see March and the kids too.

That's okay, said Joey. And I don't think it can wait. Seriously.

Only then did Patsy recall some vague ill will between the two younger women. The last couple of times March was down, Joey hadn't come around.

Okay, then, said Patsy. Come right now and I'll make us a little lunch.

You don't have to do that.

I need to eat, so it's no trouble.

Okay, then, said Joey. I'm leaving right now.

Patsy finished picking lettuce. She had some idea what Joey wanted to talk to her about. Until a year ago, Joey had been living alone in the little house in Altadena her father had left to her, and trying to write a screenplay. Then she rented out the house and moved to New York—for a job or a man, perhaps both, Patsy wasn't sure. But she was back within months, this time settling in West Los Angeles. Brice was in touch with her, and he kept Patsy updated.

At thirty-two, Joey was a Hollywood freelancer—a producer, whatever that meant. She worked long hours when jobs came her way, and Brice said she was good at what she did. But nothing more ever came of it, no studio job, no leg up, no movie that made her reputation. Waiting for the next paying gig, Joey got by on catering jobs and, recently, the rental income from her Altadena house.

Only days ago, Brice told Patsy that Joey's house had been trashed by its tenants and, coincidentally, was about to be seized for back taxes. The entire ten or twelve years she'd owned it, Brice said, Joey never paid the county a cent.

Washing the lettuce in the kitchen sink, Patsy picked out a thin, active worm and tossed it outside into the rose bed.

Joey probably needed money or a place to live, or both.

These young women from wealthy families, Patsy thought, who wobbled on the edge, never quite functioning fully . . . Look at March, with Forrest chronically unemployed, a staggering mortgage, two kids in diapers.

Patsy washed and spun the lettuce dry, and tried to recall what had passed between Joey and March: not an out-and-out rift, but hurt feelings. Joey hadn't come to a baby shower, or hadn't sent a gift or paid due homage to March's reproductive achievements.

Cal wandered in and opened the refrigerator, his way of signaling hunger. Patsy made him a tuna sandwich. You may want to eat it somewhere else, she said. Joey Hawthorne's coming for a tête-à-tête.

Haven't seen hide nor tail of her in ages. How is she?

We'll see. You want some salad with that?

No, *gracias*, said Cal. She still trying to make movies?

She just made one.

Tell her to poke her head in, say hi before she leaves.

Patsy took out some cold salmon and roasted beets—another dud meal in March's opinion—and arranged them on a plate. Outside again, she dried off and set the patio table. On her return to the kitchen she found Joey Hawthorne in the doorway. Cal or Bob must have let her in.

Joey had lost weight and was lashed into a cropped wraparound brown blouse, and cargo pants, with glimpses of enviably smooth midriff in between.

You look like a movie star! Patsy hugged Joey, felt how thin she was.

You're beautiful as ever, Joey said, lifting a hank of Patsy's long hair.

Together they carried out the food and sun tea. A baguette.

Oh, Brice told me about this patio set, Joey said.

The rusty wrought iron table and chairs were French and old. Brice had found them for her at a yard sale. One strand of Patsy's ongoing friendship with him involved Brice finding ingenious ways to spend her money, since he so rarely had any of his own.

Cal thinks they're ramshackle! Patsy said. Here, sit.

Joey frowned at the loud scraping her chair made. She wore her fine hair in a stringy, streaked blunt cut; her glasses were odd trapezoids of a bright, grassy green, kooky and severe at the same time.

Thanks for going to all this trouble, Joey said, rocking her silverware with her hands and bouncing a little as she sat. But Patsy, I have something to tell you, and you'd kill me if I didn't say it right away.

Let's just get started here, Patsy said. Settle in a bit, and then I'm all ears.

Patsy was hungry, with only coffee since waking. If Joey was going to ask for money or a room, surely it could suffer the loading of plates, the tearing of bread. Patsy poured the iced tea. Before anything else, she said, tell me a little bit about how you are, what you're up to.

I've been in Toronto, working on a film, Joey said. That's always fun.

I've heard films are the most fun. Patsy spooned beets onto Joey's plate, a tumble of red, orange, and pink cubes. At least try these, she said. I grew 'em.

I love beets now. Thanks. But Patsy . . . Joey said.

Patsy's mouth was full. Joey did look about to burst. Patsy nodded, waved her fork—Go ahead.

It's just that I heard something in Toronto, said Joey. About you. And I have to warn you, it's big. Not bad—but brace yourself, because it'll be a shock.

Joey's bossiness amused Patsy, who swiftly considered what Joey might find shocking. Some voluble old college boyfriend claiming to still love her? Or maybe Joey ran into Lewis. More likely, somebody told Joey a salacious tale from her drinking days, some outrageousness she wouldn't even remember.

Ready? said Joey.

Let's have it.

The thing is, Patsy—Joey rubbed a drop of water on the rusty table edge and looked up. Her eyes were a beautiful olive green and full of excitement.

You know those people you hit with your car? she said. Those Jehovah's Witnesses? Well, I found out that you didn't kill them. It wasn't you. You weren't driving. I'm not kidding. Someone else was driving your car. And I found out who. A woman I met in Toronto knew all about it.

Toronto? said Patsy.

A man was driving, a guy you'd been drinking with. His name was Bill Hogue. Does that ring a bell? Bill Hogue?

No. Patsy had begun to tremble. Although she had spoken openly about the accident over the years, nobody had ever brought it up to her so bluntly, in such a peremptory way—not even Cal, her sponsor, or therapists. Lewis had been interested, but tactful. Only Gilles was so direct, so long ago. *Those people you hit. Those people you killed.*

You met him at the Hilton, said Joey. In the bar.

What was the name again? Patsy asked. And just how did this come up?

That's the amazing thing, said Joey. In Toronto our company has this liaison to the city, a woman named Lucia Robinson, who gets all our permits and police. She's completely friendly and professional, so great to work with. At the wrap party—god, to think that was just two nights ago—we finally got to talking about something other than work. I mentioned that I had a house in Altadena, California, and she said she'd heard of Altadena, that her ex-husband had been there, and actually, she had a strange question to ask. Her question was, Had I ever heard of a hit-and-run accident involving Jehovah's Witnesses there? I said, No, not exactly, but I did have a friend who'd killed a couple—

Joey! Patsy cried out.

Sorry. Joey cringed in her seat. I don't mean to sound like a jerk.

It's just . . . Patsy sighed, gave up. Go on.

I told her the accident that I knew about was a long time ago, back when I was a girl, and it wasn't exactly a hit-and-run, and that my friend—you—went to jail because of it. And Lucia immediately was like, Oh my god, how long ago, can you tell me her name? Was it Patsy?

She said that?

Even before I told her! And when I said, Yes, Patsy, Patsy Sharp, I thought she was going to keel over. It was like someone hit her in the face.

Joey leaned forward and lowered her voice. I guess her husband— her ex-husband—only ever knew your first name. You guys met at the Hilton bar—do you remember any of this?

No, nothing. I was in a two-day blackout.

Anyway, it seems as though you were too drunk to drive, so her ex drove, and *he* ran over those people. *He* killed them. And he walked! He left the scene of the accident before the cops came. He told this to Lucia the night before they got married, in this big truth-telling session. That was his big confession, that he'd left the scene of an accident. Though he had no idea anyone died. And he said he hit a woman and a boy. I thought it was a girl, right?

Right, Patsy said, and thought, Okay, boy, not the same, wow, false alarm.

But the boy's the only discrepancy, Joey said with authority. And Hogue didn't stick around to get a close look. Maybe the girl was in jeans or something.

Yeah, Patsy said. She was, I think. Her father told me she was. I thought she was wearing a skirt and had long hair, but I was making it up, trying to fill in the blanks. The father said she was wearing jeans and had a pixie cut. So she probably did look like a boy.

Well, see? So this guy Hogue swore he never meant to leave, but— Joey stopped and squinted at Patsy. Were there some bushes along your driveway?

Oleander. A hedge of them.

Well, he'd veered off into that, and then he had to squeeze out of the car and fight his way through branches, and I guess it wasn't so easy. When he finally got through, he came out in this alley—would that be right?

Yes, Patsy whispered. Exactly right.

So he found himself in this alley and started walking. He got to a main drag, which had to be either Fair Oaks or Lake, and took a bus back downtown. Nobody came after him, so in the morning he flew out as planned.

Where to? said Patsy.

Toronto, I guess. I didn't ask. But you can ask Lucia. She wants you to call.

I'd like to talk to *him*, Patsy said.

Yeah, Joey said, except he's dead. He died like six years ago. They were already divorced. He got some rare cancer. So thank god he confessed everything to Lucia, or we never would've learned the truth. We both wanted to call you right away. Lucia couldn't believe you went to prison. She says she'll go to court, do whatever you need to clear your name. Then we thought I should break the news in person because you and I are old friends—

Yes. Patsy scanned Joey's flushed, animated face. That was right.

So here's her card.

God, Joey, Patsy said, and took the ivory card imprinted with LUCIA ROBINSON, MEDIA CONTRACTOR, CITY OF TORONTO, and the city's tiny round seal. Lucia herself presumably had handwritten a home number and *call anytime!* in pen.

Patsy set the card half under the rim of her plate. She was thinking of a long beige room with low mauve couches, tall mauve drapes, and, at one end, a mirrored bar lit so that the bottles gleamed with a clear white light, as if heaven itself shone through them. Bartenders wore crisp white shirts.

I did use to go to the Hilton, she said. It was a good place to drink alone, because so many hotel guests were by themselves and it didn't seem so pathetic.

See? said Joey. So will you call her? I talked to her on the way over. She's expecting to hear from you.

I'll call. In a bit. I need to get a grip first, said Patsy. Look.

Her hand trembled in a frenetic little wave.

Joey took Patsy's hand between her two cool palms. It's so exciting, she said. God, after all this time, the case gets solved. And you're innocent! Innocent!

We'll see. It's a little strange she asked you out of the blue like that.

I know, said Joey. But that was her association to the place. Altadena, Pasadena—she always connected them to her ex-husband's story. She's asked a lot of other people over the years, anyone from Pasadena, Burbank, but nobody'd ever heard of a hit-and-run with Jehovah's Witnesses before.

Patsy stood and walked across the courtyard toward a border of sage and lavender. All the bushes seemed looser, airier, with more space between each leaf. She stifled a sudden hysterical impulse to laugh, then an urge to speak sternly: *This better be for real, Joey Hawthorne.* Because what if Joey had it wrong?

She pulled off a sprig of gray-green lavender, rolled the leaves between her fingers, sniffed. The sharp, soapy astringency momentarily cleared her head.

Joey's story did seem fantastic. Out of nowhere.

I need to be careful here, Patsy thought, taking another sniff of the soft crushed leaves. And yet exultation gathered in her chest. What if?

Something was already leaving, she almost glimpsed it, half birthed, a snarl of black feathers.

She turned to Joey, who was at a pitch. Flushed, eyes bright and brimming, watching her every move. Of course—to be the bearer of such news!

Their plates were barely disturbed. Lunch was a bad idea, said Patsy. You tried to tell me. But you should eat.

I'm way too excited. But I'll clean up.

No, no. Patsy sat back down. I'm sorry I'm not more— I'm a little dazed.

Of course you are. It's a big deal.

Maybe, Patsy said. Actually, I'd really like to hear the whole thing again.

Joey started with the wedding eve confession, the Hilton, the drinking, the oleander hedge. Bill Hogue sold medical equipment, he'd been at a convention: that was the one fact Joey hadn't mentioned the first time around.

I wonder how he knew they were Jehovah's Witnesses, Patsy said.

That's a good question for Lucia.

If I didn't really do it, Patsy thought, then what a relief. But if Joey's story is bogus . . . But why would anybody make it up? Careful, careful.

How 'bout this, Joey said, getting to her feet. I'll help you clean up here, then go and let you process. Make your call. Unless you want me to stay.

Patsy looked up sharply. Joey was smiling, even merry.

No, that's all right. I'm okay.

I'll be in the 'hood. I'm picking up Brice—he's coming to look at my poor wrecked house to see what needs to be done. I'll have my cell.

You didn't tell Brice about this, did you?

No. I thought you should be first.

Yes, perfect. Thanks. Patsy stood and put her arms around Joey, hugged her hard, and kissed her head. Letting go, she smoothed back Joey's fine, streaked hair. In four new piercings, from the top of the ear to the lobe, diamonds flashed orange and ice blue.

●

Alone, Patsy wandered across the property to a stone bench beside the stream, whose juicy roar matched something in her chest. I DIDN'T DO IT! But before she gave way to jubilation, she thought, she should call Lucia Robinson and make sure Joey hadn't glossed over a major contradiction. Although so many details lined up, all but the boy, who was probably the pixie-cut girl. Probably. A fluffy cloud moved off the sun. Rain had scrubbed the rocky hillside; even gravel flashed with specks of light. A dazzling day. She stood and started back to the house.

They were home. She heard Beckett screeching, doors shutting, March calling for Cal. Patsy was too undone, too burst open, to face any of them, so she nonchalantly veered north, to the corral, where Diotima and Mamie the pony stood in mud. Diotima sauntered over and nuzzled Patsy's neck, her black whiskers stiff as wire. Hold on, said Patsy, let me get the bridle.

They took the trail that climbed the mountain in switchbacks, east, then west through sage and buckwheat, all of it lush with tender green new growth and heavy with rainwater. Patsy's jeans soon were soaked through. Diotima's hooves made sucking noises in the muddy low spots.

She never once had imagined another driver or even dreamed of one.

The trail branched, and Patsy considered going up the arroyo behind the Jet Propulsion Laboratory, the first trail she'd taken with Cal. Then she drew Diotima east, away from the deepening privacy of the canyon. She wanted room, and perspective. She thought, This is the last time I'll ride before others know. When the news is still contained.

Clouds were piling up against the mountains, forming a shelf overhead. She could see out from under it, all the way, in fact, to the Palos Verdes hills, the valley between still brilliant with sunlight.

Assuming the news was true. As a historian, she was well acquainted with the vagaries of oral history and stories that changed, teller by teller, like the game of telephone. In her excitement, Joey could have blurred the details, and in fact, Bill Hogue might have hit someone in Alhambra in 1989.

She'd talk to Lucia soon enough. Until then, she'd at least have this lovely aimless ride in innocence. If Joey's tale checked out, a slow saunter up a mountainside would only steady her for the great turn to come.

Too bad the news hadn't arrived before her father's mind left.

Too bad, too, she couldn't tell Lewis.

Nobody was better with surprise. He'd stare, dead still; his eyes would slowly brighten, as if with tears. Moments would pass. Then a fast gulp of air and the gratifying, profane shout. No fucking way!

But she'd kept her word and left him alone for the last two years. And he hadn't called her either.

Patsy nudged Diotima left onto a spur leading to a promontory. Below, the Ponderosa's blue slate shingles overlapped like feathers on a bird. Haydee was beating a rug with a broom behind the breezeway. Given the size and pale madder hue, it could only be the old Bokhara from Cal's office, which probably shouldn't be thwacked so violently, lest its dry wool weft crumble to bits.

A drop plopped on her head. Diotima's pointed ears flickered. They headed back down to the barn.

•

Of course she'd put off calling too long. It was already 7:00 p.m. in Toronto, a Friday night, and Lucia Robinson was not home.

Which left the ragged stack of term papers, untouched since before noon, more than half still unmarked.

She worked for an hour, then went into the kitchen and made herself a plate with the now-well-marinated salad she and Joey hadn't eaten—a few beets, a clump of cold salmon. She put the baguette in the oven, and while it heated, she found Bob and Cal watching the evening news in the dark library. I'm just going to eat something now and keep grading, she said.

You okay? Cal asked. You didn't catch cold out there on Diotima, did you?

I'm just deep in grading hell, she said.

She wouldn't tell Cal her news till she'd spoken to the wife. The lawyer in him shared her mistrust of single sources and thirdhand anecdotes. No sense inviting his cross-examination before she'd had her own questions answered.

Cal came to check on her before he and Bob left for their meeting. Don't stay up all night, he said.

She kept the door to the deck cracked, to hear the rain. After each paper, she looked up and squinted. *What if I didn't do it?* And excitement would surge, a sensation that, in childhood, she'd assumed was happiness.

She worked on the sofa in her office, wrapped in the old rag. Her comments on the papers tended toward glowing. Checking back through the stack, she saw she'd given A's to nine of the last ten papers. *Lovely*, she'd written by one title. Lovely?

2 6

This is Lucia, a woman said. Cool, crisp.

It was Saturday morning, seven o'clock. Ten in Toronto. It's Patsy Sharp, she said. I hope I'm not calling too early.

I was hoping it was you, said Lucia, her voice softening. I've been up for hours. So Joey told you everything.

Yes, and I'm a little stunned, as you might imagine.

I'll bet, Lucia said. I'm in a state over this too, and I'm fairly removed.

I really appreciate your taking it so much to heart.

I always had a feeling there was more to Bill's story, the way he kept bringing it up. Anyhow— A certain crispness returned. How do we do this? Shall I just tell you what I know?

If this is a good time for you, Patsy said, pulling over a yellow legal pad on which she'd jotted questions: Exact dates? Make of car? Died when?

Perfect time. I have a couple hours before my daughter's basketball game. She's twelve. Bill's daughter, Debbie.

I see, said Patsy, and wrote down, *Daughter, 12*.

•

Bill Hogue and Lucia Robinson met in the fall in Chicago in 1987 and were married a year later. The night before the wedding, Bill sat Lucia down. There were things she should know about him beforehand, he said, so they would never surprise her, so no ex-girlfriend could burst into their lives with stories that Lucia hadn't heard from him first. So Lucia would know what bad came with the good.

He spoke of women he'd been unkind to, or slept with when he shouldn't have, and other sexual missteps. He felt badly too about an ac-

cident he'd been in years before, a hit-and-run. He still thought of it
every day.

He'd gone to a sales convention in Pasadena. On his last day there, after the convention ended, he met a tall, funny blonde in the hotel bar, a
wild schoolteacher named Patsy. They had a drink at the hotel, then Patsy
wanted to move. She was bossy in an amusing way and his plane didn't
leave until the next morning, so he went along with her to a bar she knew,
a dark, old-timer's dive on the main drag, and after a round or two there,
she suggested her house. She was weaving as she walked, so he asked for the
keys to her big old Mercedes. She directed him north, toward the mountains, into the town of Altadena. It was getting dark. She told him where
to turn. Her driveway, he said, was unexpectedly steep. He pushed down
on the gas, and at first nothing happened, so he pumped the pedal, and
the heavy sedan sprang. He saw the woman and boy the same instant he
hit them, and there was an explosion too, of what looked like white birds.

Pamphlets and papers went everywhere. One person—he couldn't
see which, as the windshield was mostly papered—rolled over the hood
and pressed against the glass before sliding off. He never understood
what happened next, maybe he hit the gas instead of the brake, but the
car leaped again, and he may have hit one or both another time before
the car swerved into the bushes.

Patsy was yelling and screaming. Outside, the woman crouched by
the boy. Both were moving, and he saw no blood. He intended to help
them, but he could barely open his door. He'd run the car into a thick
hedge and had to squeeze out, and could do that only by climbing up
into the hedge itself.

This is the part that I never understood, Lucia said. Bill said he
climbed through the hedge, then found himself in an alley. Does that
make sense to you?

Yes, whispered Patsy. There was an oleander hedge along that driveway. On the other side of it was an old trolley line that used to run up
to Mount Lowe. The tracks were removed in the thirties, but the old
easement still cuts through several blocks.

·

Bill Hogue, Lucia went on, must have been in shock, because his judg-
ment was clearly impaired. He wasn't one to abandon injured people to

save his own skin. He'd always regretted leaving the scene; he said it was the worst thing he'd ever done.

He walked down the alley, then took regular streets in plain view. Sirens looped nearer, a helicopter stuttered overhead, its beam focused behind him. He didn't try to hide. If the police pulled up, he planned to open the back door and get into the squad car without a word. But no black-and-white materialized, and soon he came to a wide, busy street and a bus stop. Sitting on the bench, he saw that he clutched a pamphlet. *The Watchtower.*

That's how out of it he was. He'd carried the pamphlet the whole time without noticing.

All night long, he waited for the police to knock on his hotel-room door.

In the morning he caught his flight and was home in Chicago by 10:00 a.m.

I'm sure they were all okay, he told Lucia the night before their wedding. A broken bone or two, at worst. Everyone was moving. He hadn't been going fast. It really was an accident. He'd had a couple of drinks, he wasn't drunk. Certainly nowhere near as drunk as the nutty blonde whose car it was.

•

But Patsy, said Lucia, if nobody was hurt, why did he feel so guilty? I bet I heard the story a dozen times. To this day, when I see Jehovah's Witnesses with their briefcases, I think of Bill and his guilt. Working with TV and film crews, I've met a lot of people from the Pasadena area—location scouts, art directors, production assistants like Joey. I always ask if they've ever heard of a hit-and-run with two Jehovah's Witnesses. I've probably asked twenty people over the years, and nothing. Then Joey not only knew about it, she knew you.

•

Our marriage only lasted from 1988 to 1991. I moved up here. He saw Debbie on holidays and for weeks during the summer. Then he lost his job and went through a bad patch and couldn't pay child support. We lost track of him, but a couple of years later, he wrote to say that he'd remarried, and sent some money. He was planning a visit to Debbie when all of a sudden he was diagnosed with a fast-growing cancer in his spleen, and just a couple of weeks later he was dead.

•

You know, said Patsy, I'm still in touch with the husband and father of the victims—Mark Parnham. We've been interviewed in newspapers, on radio and TV about forgiveness, mediated justice, restorative justice. I've watched his son Martin grow up; I've helped with his education. He's in law school as we speak.

Jesus, Lucia said. There's a lot to this, isn't there?

Yes, said Patsy, and wrote on her pad, *A lot to this.*

•

Patsy, said Lucia. If you need something legal, a deposition or some kind of sworn affidavit—

Nothing so formal, at least not yet. But I'm a historian, I like records and documents. If you'd write a short statement . . .

I'll do that. And maybe you should talk to his widow. I have her number. She's since remarried; her new name is Simms. I don't know what Bill told her, if anything. But I bet she got an earful, and more than once. Here, do you have a pencil?

•

Now, Lucia—what if other people want to talk to you? The husband or the son? May I give them your number?

I'll talk to anybody. It's the least I can do.

•

Patsy opened the sliding glass doors to the little deck shaded by oak branches and stepped outside. A body rolling on the hood, the explosion of pamphlets, a mother crouched by her child. A coward's flight. She shivered, hugging herself.

Lucia had been accurate about that heavy old Mercedes; there was always a pause after hitting the gas pedal. The car surged just the way Bill Hogue had described it to his wife. Decades had passed, and that detail had remained indelible in a stranger's mind.

Patsy stood on her deck, facing the stream. Not a murderer. Never killed anybody. Innocent. After twenty years, the truth, like a splinter, had worked its way out. And now she could walk in the light.

She thought something exuberant and silly then: This is the best news of my life. A restoration of at least some buried part of her. Some imp of self.

She had an urge to get on the phone, start dialing, call everyone. Sarah, Margaret, Gloria. She'd really like to call Silver. Silver! Listen to this! Isn't it amazing? Do you think it's true?

She could already hear Silver's low, calm voice. What about you, Patsy? Do you think it's true?

Do you believe in your own innocence?

If not, what will it take to convince you?

Back at her desk, she looked over her notes. The other wife was Ginevra Simms. Area code 773. But what to say? Did your husband ever hit and run?

Patsy dialed. The phone rang and rang before voice mail picked up. A robotic male voice said, Nobody is available right now. Patsy hung up.

Closing her eyes, she pressed the lids with her fingertips, a comfort.

•

Cal's office was in the east wing, next to the library, across from the rooms his daughter and her family occupied. He still spent hours here daily. He read company reports, he corresponded; Patsy mailed stacks of ivory envelopes every week. He called his children. He listened to music on headphones, his beloved Boston Pops.

When she tapped on the open door, he was on the phone. He beckoned her inside, looking at her face. Here's Patsy, he said. And, Audrey, I'd better call you back.

Did something happen, Pats? he said, hanging up. Is everything okay?

She stepped inside. Everything's okay. But when Joey came to lunch yesterday, she had something to tell me.

Bad news?

Not bad, said Patsy. But big.

She sat on the edge of his daybed, and he swiveled around to face her.

Now, Cal, you know the accident, the one I went to prison for?

Of course.

And you remember that I was blacked out when it happened?

Yes, yes.

It turns out that somebody else was in the car, she went on. A man named Bill Hogue. And, Cal, he was driving, not me. I was a passenger. I wasn't driving.

Cal's eyes narrowed. How did this come out?

That's the amazing part, Patsy said, and slowly, careful to describe what a wrap party was and what Lucia Robinson's job entailed, she told him about Joey's visit and the conversation with Lucia. Cal, don't you see? Patsy said. I didn't kill anyone after all.

Cal looked at her with a sad smile. Oh, Patsy, he said quietly. What I'd like to know is why this woman waited so long to come forward. Why now?

She didn't know my last name. Also, Bill Hogue had no idea anybody died. He thought he hadn't stuck around to talk to the cops. He thought his big crime was leaving the scene.

And you believe this?

Why not?

Cal swiveled around to face the window. His office looked out onto the stunning old oak whose great branches were supported by guy wires. Well, it's hearsay at best, he said over his shoulder. It'll never stand up in court. It's unlikely to overturn your conviction.

I haven't even thought about all that, said Patsy. Besides, I pled guilty. It's not like anyone *convicted* me.

Pleading guilty convicts you, said Cal. Being guilty by your own admission constitutes a conviction. You don't need a verdict.

Well, never mind then. She gave a wild little laugh. Though I suppose they could get me for perjury. Wouldn't that be funny—if they sent me back to prison for lying about my own guilt.

She was a little hysterical now. If only he would relent, revel for a moment in the possibility of her innocence.

Instead, he studied her. So what, exactly, do you know about this woman, this wife? What's her name again? Does she work for the city or the movies?

The city, Cal. Besides, what difference does that make?

I'd be very careful. I don't want you taken for a ride.

Why would someone take me for a ride, Cal?

Maybe Joey wants to get into your good graces.

She was never *not* in my good graces.

He shrugged, as if to say that Patsy could be right or wrong about this. Joey might've cooked this up to please you, he said. And got an actress friend to go along with her.

Jesus, Cal, that's downright paranoid.

You only have their word for it.

I know, I know. But it's me, Cal, Miss Historical Method. I'll follow up. Amass evidence. Look up records. The man had a second wife who might know something. Though I don't think anyone could make this up.

You might be surprised.

Lucia will be sending a written statement. She offered to do a deposition.

Make sure that she does.

Here's an idea, Patsy said, standing. How 'bout we don't talk about it anymore and just let it sink in. We don't know what, if anything, this will mean.

Cal stood and caught Patsy with his fingers, pulled her close. What could it mean? he said. After all these many years?

She waited, still as a tree, for him to let go.

•

What did she expect? Cal was always so careful. And so infuriating.

She'd left the east wing by the breezeway door and was walking around the front of the house to avoid running into anyone.

Faced with new and uncomfortable information, Cal often asked unanswerable questions. How often had she advised his children not to take his reflexive doubting personally? Cal has to absorb information at his own speed, she'd say. Audrey moving to Paris. Stan divorcing Katharine. March marrying Forrest. All had been met with the same dry shrug and maddening skepticism.

He resisted change. He had to get used to new ideas. But he was right about one thing. She did need proof from multiple sources.

The Ponderosa was a long, lazy boomerang of a house, its two wings arching off a central living space at a wide angle. Patsy walked along the driveway, past the front door, where a massive stroller—it made her think of a surrey—was parked on the porch alongside a red tricycle. Where the turnaround began curving away from the house, she took broad stepping-stones through a cactus and succulent garden to her deck, where she sat on the steps to watch the fat, foaming little stream crash through the canyon.

So much was accurate. The Hilton, the hedge, the leaping car. The old-timer's bar had to be the SNAFU, her long-gone haunt over by PCC—gone, in fact, by the time she got out of prison.

SNAFU. Situation Normal All Fucked Up.

Did hotel and airline records go back to 1981? The Convention Center must have some kind of log. She should check out Lucia, make sure she existed and held the putative job. Then get up her nerve and try the widow again.

•

You just found this out? yelled Burt. Jesus Christ! You went to prison for this criminal? I'd like to have a little man-to-man chat with the weasel.

Yeah! Patsy said. I wish you could. But he croaked!

Damn! Well, let's hope the miserable sonofabitch had an excruciating, drawn-out death.

Burt! She'd been waiting all day to laugh.

Jesus, said Burt. Man! What a kick in the head! Are you in orbit? Have you told Parnham and son?

Oh god, no. Just you and Cal so far.

Is Cal stoked?

Actually, he asked a lot of questions and isn't convinced. He thinks it may be some kind of story Joey concocted to cozy up to me.

Burt knew Joey Hawthorne; he flirted with and possibly seduced her during his tenure at the Pondo. Patsy never knew, or wanted to know, for sure.

That's a little far-fetched, he said. What's in it for her? Excuse me for saying so, but Joey is hardly a scammer.

I know. Still, it would be nice to find some corroborating evidence, said Patsy. Do you know if airlines keep records? Or hotels?

I assume so, said Burt. But I don't really know.

I should make calls. And talk to the widow. Or hire a detective. Do you know any detectives?

How about that homicide detective who helped get your early release?

Ricky Barrett?

It was his case, said Burt. I bet he'd check things out for free.

•

She wasn't sure where Ricky Barrett was working, but she called his old station in Monterey Park. I'm trying to get a hold of Detective Barrett, she told the dispatcher, who, without another word, connected her to his voice mail.

It's Patsy Sharp, she said. Or Patsy MacLemoore to you. Remember me? I'm calling because there may be a new wrinkle in my case—the accident with the Parnham family. A major wrinkle, actually, that I'd like to talk to you about.

It would be Monday, she thought, before he got back to her. He had the seniority to be a nine-to-fiver now, with weekends off.

Two days to wait, and time already at a standstill. Thank god for student papers, she thought, or she'd be crawling out of her skin. She went back over the last few she'd graded and tempered some superlatives. *Almost* Perfect.

•

Brice called in the early afternoon. I'm meeting Joey at Grounds of Being. Come, and I'll buy you a latte to celebrate.

A small slap of shock. Joey told you? she asked.

Yeah! Unbelievable. To think, after all you went through too. How are you taking it?

I'm still spinning.

So come meet us.

She drove to Pasadena with less of a mind to celebrate than to get out of the house and check Joey's impulse to broadcast the news. What if wife number two told a substantially different tale? What if the whole thing fell apart under scrutiny? Best not trumpet any newfound innocence until the facts were checked.

Grounds of Being was the coffeehouse affiliated with the Pasadena School of Theology. Brice frequented the place for its oversized cookies and student prices. He and Joey had snagged the one cozy corner with armchairs. Around them, seminarians peered, faces glowing, into laptops.

Brice stood to hug her. At almost fifty, he was thicker, redder in face, as if his grouse-hunting, golf-mad, Scotch-swilling ancestors now insisted on their share of his appearance. His hair was dark bronze, with a faint green tint from all his swimming. Some news, he said.

I know, she said. And Joey, Lucia was wonderful . . .

Joey's green eyes brightened. She took such clear joy in being the messenger, it seemed heartless to temper her.

I'm glad Brice knows—a lie, but Patsy didn't want to scold—but I was wondering if you wouldn't tell anyone else until I've had a chance to tell my family. And get used to the idea.

A flicker of shame crossed Joey's face. Which meant she'd already told who knows how many people.

I'd like to keep it close, Patsy said, till I get a grip.

She wouldn't mention the detective.

It does kind of set you up for a major life review, said Brice. What kind of difference will it make? Any idea?

Oh god, who knows? said Patsy. I feel like a creaky old computer processing an enormous problem. With luck, most of it'll be done unconsciously.

Brice went to the counter to order. Patsy gave Joey's thin forearm a fond squeeze. I'm still a little dazed, she said. I can't wrap my mind around the whole thing. But I'll never forget what you did, Joey.

I didn't do anything, said Joey.

You came to me as soon as you could, and you were so excited. So happy for me. That's what I'll never forget.

They watched Brice at the coffee counter, lounging and supervising, making the young male barista smile, blush, and laugh.

Can't help himself, said Joey.

Never could, Patsy said.

Brice could still charm strangers, but he had worn out family and friends. He'd blown or discarded the jobs they'd found for him, he'd stored his things in their garages and attics for decades. In fact, Cal and Patsy had moved some of Brice's boxes and furniture from the Tudor to the Ponderosa. He'd also borrowed money, of course, a lot of it, large sums and small, repaid very little, and had become famous for his sulks and furies at the slightest hint of censure. Neither Cal nor Audrey would lend him another cent; Patsy slipped him a hundred or two when his life got grim, which it did cyclically. But then, she'd signed on for life.

Now, tell me, Patsy said, giving Joey's thin arm another friendly shake. What's with your little house?

The tenants threw some wild party after the eviction, plugged the sinks and tub and let the taps run. Tons of water damage.

What are you going to do?

At first I was just going to sell, but now I'm thinking I'll get a loan, fix it up, and move back. I miss Altadena. And he—Joey stuck a thumb at Brice, now approaching with coffees—has ideas.

I'm sure he does, Patsy said, and hoped Joey could afford them. Brice had insisted she spend forty thousand dollars on antique oak flooring for her kitchen; when she refused, he didn't speak to her for months.

Patsy said, You might have to reel him in at times. Or you'll end up with a fantastic top-of-the-line refrigerator and no walls.

I won't have much money, anyway. It'll be a total scrounge project.

Brice came up then, handing lattes around.

Last Christmas he'd been arrested for vagrancy. He'd been sleeping in his Volvo station wagon and using the facilities at Lacey Park in San Marino for so long, neighbors claimed that he was living there. He charmed his court-assigned social worker into recommending him for a little-known county grant intended for depressed writers—never mind that Brice's first foray into prose was the application essay. He received food stamps, a small housing allowance, and two hundred dollars cash a month. The social worker suggested a room in the Estelle, the single-room occupancy hotel across from the Lyster. But Brice found a tiny rustic cabin in Millard Canyon, on federal land, the very place that Einstein allegedly rented for thinking time.

And how's our gal Cal? Brice asked, settling into the purple wing chair.

He's good, fine, no worries now that he takes that little aspirin, said Patsy. I wish he'd get his hips replaced. He's becoming such a cantankerous stay-at-home bear. Why didn't anybody warn me how much older he'd get than me?

You're just kidding, right? cried Joey, who, like many chronically single people, idolized certain marriages. I saw him yesterday, and he was adorable.

He was just thrilled to see your pretty face, said Patsy.

And what did he say about your news? Joey asked.

Not much, Patsy said. You know Cal. He's a lawyer. He asked questions—Who is this Lucia? Why has this come out now?

I should talk to him, said Joey. I could answer all his questions.

Patsy reached over and caressed Joey's streaked bob. You're very sweet, she said. I'm glad you'll be back on our side of town.

A tinny tune junked up the air. Brice dug out a slim silver lozenge of a phone, leaned away to talk, then stood. Back in three, he whispered.

Joey said, I can't believe Cal wasn't happy for you.

I caught him off guard, said Patsy. And we've got a lot going on at the house. March is there, as you know.

That's why I made Brice call today. I didn't want to chance her answering.

I didn't realize things were that bad between you.

They're not. It's the baby worship. Ava's spit bubble is just so much more important than anything I could ever say.

•

The tiniest flowers were scattered on Patsy's desk: yellow clover blossoms, purple rosemary blooms, crumbs of lavender spikes, miniature bouquets of lantana, all of them bruised, as if released from warm, clenched fists.

Also waiting for her was a voice mail from Ricky Barrett. Patsy MacLemoore! Of course I remember you, he said.

He didn't say she was the one Hallen prof he'd taken a class from *and* arrested. He left his cell phone number and said, Call me whenever you get in.

She closed her office door, dialed, and told him everything.

All right, he said. Let's see here. You know the date of the event?

May fifth, 1981. A Tuesday.

Good. A pause for scribbling. Now, he said, what about this widow? Are you going to talk to her or do you want me to? I might make more headway.

You, then. Please.

You talked to Parnham about this yet?

Not till I'm sure it's legit. I'd hate to stir things up for nothing. Besides, it's not going to make much difference to him.

It'll make some. I have to say, the facts sound pretty compelling. Do you have any reason to think these women aren't telling the truth?

No. But I'm a historian. I always feel better with multiple sources.

How well I know, said Ricky Barrett. If I remember nothing else about your class, I got the source thing. That, and you pretty much killed the Christian deal for me. Jesus was born and he died after eating dinner. And that's all, folks.

Oh dear, said Patsy. I had no idea anyone was actually listening to me.

I can only speak for myself, Ricky said.

•

She dodged dinner, claiming work. Didn't your dad tell you I'm up to my ears right now? she said to March. She graded all evening and was in bed—still grading, only a dozen papers left—when Cal came home from his meeting. He went into his bathroom, brushed his teeth, and emerged in yellow pajamas.

I can feel you thrilling with energy, he said, sliding in beside her.

I'm not the least bit sleepy.

I hope this all pans out for you.

Mmmm. She made a show of reading, lifting a paper closer to her face.

But you know, Cal said. Even if you weren't driving that day, what happened got you to where you needed to be.

Meaning what?

However unjust it may have been, prison got you sober, which probably saved your life.

Prison didn't get me sober.

You know what I mean.

I don't, actually. You honestly think it's okay that I went to prison for two years for something I didn't do, because I got sober there?

Hopefully, my meaning is a little more nuanced.

I hope so. Because I'm hardly in the mood for AA platitudes. If you'd ever been to prison, Cal, you'd never dismiss it so glibly.

I'm not dismissing anything. He took her hand and lightly banged his thigh with it. Two things, he said. First, if you'd kept drinking, you might have wound up incapacitated, dead, or in even deeper trouble, with a longer prison sentence. Second . . .

She had little patience with Cal's old lawyering tic of numbering his points. She tried to remove her hand. He held on.

. . . regardless of what happened back then, the life you've lived is the life you have. And I happen to think it's been a damn fine life and I'm a lucky man to have been a partner to it.

For someone who doesn't believe Joey Hawthorne, she said, you've sure been thinking a lot about it.

Some. More banging of her hand against his thigh. And it's not that I don't believe Joey. I'd just like some rock-solid corroboration.

I know, Cal, she said, now firmly withdrawing her hand from his. Me too. So let's not discuss it till there's something more to say.

I don't want you toyed with, sweetie, he said. Or disappointed.

He patted her leg, then closed his eyes. Within seconds—seconds!—he was snoring softly.

Patsy took her papers and climbed out of bed. Back in her office, she worked on the sofa until she fell asleep.

2 7

In the morning she was the first one up, a coup, and made coffee undisturbed. She took her cup into the chilly garden, huddled in the first sunlight. She needed to talk to someone who could help her think more clearly. An impartial ear. A paid ear would do, if only if she had one.

After Silver, Patsy had managed without any therapy for two years, until her internist referred her to the woman she came to think of as her bland therapist. No matter what subject arose, the bland therapist asked the same question—Does that remind you of anything that happened when you were growing up?—as if all post-homicidal guilt, academic jockeying, marital rough spots, and perimenopausal mood swings could be traced to four people under the age of thirty living together in Stockdale, California, forty-odd years ago.

Patsy curled over her coffee cup.

The bland therapist would want to know: Does this exoneration remind you of anything that happened in your family of origin?

How 'bout nothing? How 'bout not one damn thing?

Except for how she'd felt to blame for the family's disorder, the mother's misery, the rampaging father. If you darn kids would only give me a little peace, her mother would say. If you darn kids could think of someone other than yourselves for a change. Before you darn kids came along, *he* wasn't like this.

Of course, Silver had also had a pet question, one she used infrequently but with exquisite precision. With almost jaunty curiosity she'd say, So tell me, Patsy, why do you think you did that?

Why do you think you took on guilt so readily?

Because the circumstances seemed so obvious—she'd been in her driveway, drunk, in situ with the dead and wounded.

Because guilt was like the check on a table. Somebody had to pick it up.

A quick turn of her head—was that a raindrop?—and Patsy glimpsed her own anger, a boiling turquoise sea.

Enough, she thought, and went back inside.

•

Oh, but Patsy dear, that's amazing news. And no, Cal didn't tell me. But then your guilt or innocence wouldn't make much difference to him. Your past never bothered him one way or the other.

For eight years Audrey had been living with a girlhood friend in a grand old apartment overlooking the Pont Neuf. She worked with the nuns in a children's hospital and went to art exhibitions with a near-religious discipline.

My past didn't bother Cal, said Patsy, because he likes people who are down-and-out. He got me fresh from prison, and you're the one who said he bailed Peggy out of jail the first time he met her.

Cal does like to rescue people, Audrey said. And as I recall, you needed some rescuing back then. If I spoke sharply, you'd jump! Poor thing. Still—Audrey's tone grew firm—you mustn't let Cal get you down just when this big weight has lifted. You must feel so relieved!

I'll feel better after the detective looks into it. Things might not be as cut-and-dried as we think.

They never are. But this could mean a significant shift in your life, Patsy.

I know. Though it'll probably take a while before it all sinks in.

Of course, said Audrey. Years, I would think.

•

March had invited her brothers for brunch, so Patsy took her box of finals and term papers and went to her office at Hallen. She had a key to the building. Nobody was around the department, and the heat was off.

She made herself a cup of hot tea in the lounge and put her feet up on the desk. To her left, out the window, a lone tall woman was jogging around the brick-red clay track followed by a short-legged black dog.

Patsy had come close to leaving Hallen last year. Her friend Margaret, with much search committee wrangling, got her a good offer at

Pitzer. Wes, now Hallen's dean of humanities, countered with an endowed chair, much more money, and a very light teaching load: three courses a year. Pitzer matched the offer but could do nothing about the commute. Wes didn't have to make the case for loyalty—Cal reminded her how few private colleges, so vulnerable to board and alumni opinion, would have rehired a known felon.

Her friendship with Margaret had yet to regain its former footing.

This fall, there was Cambridge, and researching her new book comparing Modernism in England and America and tracing how, after World War I, the death of God seeped through literature.

Or maybe she'd write a different kind of book, a memoir perhaps, along the lines of Lewis's second effort.

Patsy scanned her shelves for his book's red spine. *Hello, Stranger* was exactly as Lewis had described it, part recovery memoir, part biography of his beloved sponsor. The reviews were plentiful and glorious; she'd thought for months of sending him a congratulatory fan note, imagining that it would spark an epistolary friendship. In the end, she'd felt constrained by her promise to contact him only if she'd changed her mind.

Not that he'd been sitting around waiting for her. The jacket flap of the book said *Lewis Fletcher divides his time between Rito, California, and Paris, France.* In an interview she'd found on the Internet, he'd said, It sounds so romantic, I know, but it's a tiny garret studio walk-up.

No mention of living in Paris with a wife, or a wife and child, a wife and cats.

For his sake, Patsy hoped that book sales had upgraded the garret and even changed his luck with women. If they had, she didn't want to know. She preferred to remember his jostling nudge and long-legged pace, the abruptness of his laugh. How urgently they'd talked.

She twisted her hair into a bun on top of her head, but it uncoiled and fell down her back. Two years later, and she still had regrets. They might have at least kissed, and she would have that much more to remember, to sustain her.

She turned back to the thin stack of unmarked papers on her lap and allowed herself a long, deep sigh.

She may not have had a decent night's sleep since Joey's news, but she had never before graded so many papers so quickly. In an hour, she'd finished the last of them. She entered the grades in her computer, set the papers and finals in a box where her students would find them, and left.

Her spring break could now officially begin. She had planned to read the novels and source material for her Modernism seminar and Cambridge lectures. D. H. Lawrence. Woolf. Faulkner and Fitzgerald. But she could hardly swing right into all that after such a manic bout of grading. And extraordinary news.

•

At the Ponderosa, the driveway was clear, the boys had gone. Ava ran up to her as she walked in. Mamie bucked me off. She reared and bucked and reared, and I fell on my vagina.

Ow! said Patsy. She's an evil creature, Mamie. Did you have to go to the hospital?

No, said Ava. Maybe later.

Where's your granddad?

In his office. He's sleeping and sitting up at the same time. Ava grabbed onto Patsy's waist and, facing her, stepped onto Patsy's feet. Take big steps, she ordered.

Patsy, thus encumbered, walked down the hall toward Cal's office. Beckett slithered up alongside them, but Ava nudged him away with her foot—not a kick, so Patsy didn't scold. She tapped on Cal's door.

Hi, sweetie, he said, blinking awake. Who do you have there?

A wild bucking bronco rider.

Cal reached for Ava, who screamed, leaped off Patsy's feet, then ran away.

Patsy came inside and pulled the door closed. I was wondering, Cal, she said, if we could go away for a couple of nights so I can have something of a spring break.

Go away?

Just Palm Springs or Santa Barbara, your choice.

What about— Cal waved his hand toward the kitchen. We can't take off while they're here.

Why not? They're going to Disneyland and SeaWorld. They'll hardly notice.

Maybe you should ask one of your friends, said Cal. I wouldn't feel comfortable leaving the kids.

They'd understand—didn't you tell them my news?

Cal looked at her blankly, cocked his head. News?

About the accident, Cal.

Oh, no, no, no. I thought I'd let you tell them yourself.

•

Cal wouldn't change his mind, and nobody she called could accommodate such a last-minute plan. Between sorting out her house and a job interview, Joey couldn't get away, and Brice was helping her. Sarah had gone to Napa with Henry and the girls. Margaret never returned her call. Patsy didn't feel like going by herself, so she read outside in the morning sun on her deck and took Diotima for long rides. The mountain lilac was in bloom, and she brought back stems of the cool violet flowers to Ava. On the trail, her mind drifted to the past, to the corridors of her childhood home, and to pretty, shabby Pomelo Street, where her yard had been full of crabgrass and plants that bloomed yearly through no help from her: purple sprays of agapanthus, notched-leaf acanthus, and the bush with clumps of red berries the birds loved. Pyracantha. She remembered the shed in the backyard, full of old Yuban cans with rusted screws, the cans nailed in a careful grid to the back of a workbench, the handiwork of the former owner, an old man whose wife had died. He'd shown her the property and wasn't anywhere as old as Cal was now—late sixties, at most—but he'd seemed ancient to her twenty-five years ago.

She'd liked that shed, built of redwood grown black over the years. She'd kept a half-gallon bottle of bourbon there, and a sticky, thick-walled glass.

If she hadn't gone to prison, would she, as Cal believed, have drunk her way to some other tragedy? Who's to say she wouldn't have gotten sober anyway? She always said that she'd joined AA in prison because she needed some proof of remorse to offer Mark Parnham. But history demonstrates that events transpire and narratives are built around them. She may have thought she was getting sober for Mark, or because it was one of the few ways she could feel better about herself, but maybe she really was done with drinking and would've been done anyway, on or around the same date, in or out of prison.

One afternoon she took Ava along on her ride. March favored the boy, and the three-year-old girl, who had her mother's dense curly hair in toffee brown, was growing bossy and insistent. Squirmy at first, Ava fell asleep against Patsy's front as they plodded uphill in the mild spring air.

Patsy kissed Ava's sun-warmed head and wondered lightly if she might have had children after all. Fearing a miasma of regret, she felt her way carefully around the topic. Without the guilt, she might have been more inclined toward kids. Most people reproduced. Even Brice had donated to a sperm bank several times. And Ian, of all people, had three boys. She'd seen him over the years at Sarah's parties. They'd been friendly, but had little to say to each other. He'd married one of his students. In fact, he'd been dating his future wife at the same time he was seeing Patsy—Sarah revealed this recently, thinking Patsy long past caring. But an old anger pinched.

They came to a stream, and Diotima picked her way carefully across. The change in rhythm woke Ava, who grabbed onto the mare's black mane and glanced all around. Make her gallop, she said.

•

Classes started Tuesday, but Monday saw the usual start-of-term meetings at Hallen, departmental in the morning and interdisciplinary that afternoon. In between, Patsy had salty soup with Sarah in the vast, noisy student union. I had something happen over break, Patsy said, and told.

Sarah's pale blue eyes filled with tears. Unbelievable, she said. You must feel so . . . *unburdened*. But, god . . . her voice lowered. That was such an ordeal, what you went through. It changed you so much, Patsy. You were such a free spirit, and so funny before. And so damn much fun. And I know we all lose a certain amount of that anyway, just getting older, getting married, having kids . . . But you used to have this, this *effervescence* that never really came back.

That was the beer, said Patsy. Hi, Georges.

You two! Georges grabbed the back of Patsy's chair. No thanks to you, Patsy, I did get a hold of your friend Lewis and had him send in a letter. We're interviewing next week. He's by far the most qualified applicant we have, though the dean's insisting on diversity. Still, we can keep our fingers crossed.

Georges raised his crossed fingers like a benediction and went off toward the food.

Of course Lewis had applied for the job, Patsy thought. He'd always wanted a tenure-track job in Southern California and had applied to every comp lit position that came open. So far, without exception, the jobs had been awarded to women and/or minorities.

Sarah burst out laughing. Patsy, she said, you're white as a ghost!

•

Dad wants to see you, said March.

Patsy found Cal in the library. His chair had been moved as far back from its usual spot as it could go. He was in it watching a *Gunsmoke* rerun, with Beckett in his arms. What are you doing way back there? she called.

Cal lowered the volume some. March says that I have to sit at least fifteen feet from the screen so this little bugger doesn't get irradiated.

Ahh. Patsy dragged an ottoman over and waggled a finger at Beckett. The baby had March's troubled eyebrows. On-screen, James Arness was walking his horse and searching the ground along a stream. He reached down and picked up a lady's brooch. Music swelled as he gazed up the trail. A commercial came on, and Cal muted.

So we've had some good news, said Cal. The kids' house was open yesterday and there were five bids. Pick of the litter.

They better get home and pack up.

All that's been arranged, said Cal.

Well then, they better start house hunting.

Forrest has to find a job first. Or sell his latest idea.

They just sold a million-dollar home. They could live at the Ritz.

They had no equity, hon. They've been living on a line of credit. They barely broke even.

Which meant, Patsy knew, that they hadn't. She said, You didn't go ahead and tell them they could stay here, did you?

The kids have always come home.

Not as a family of four, with a boat, said Patsy. Why not put them in one of the Glendale units? There are vacancies.

I don't think so. Cal stood Beckett up so he and the baby were face-to-face. We can't have you in one of those rattraps, now can we, little man?

Well then, they have to go into the possum trot. I want my new kitchen back. March has already—

I'm not having the four of them stuffed into that shoebox while you and I rattle around this monstrosity. What's wrong with that picture?

Nothing, Cal. This is our house. And now is a really tough time for me.

Cal reached over and quickly ran his fingers over Patsy's knuckles. I know, my love. I know. But they're in dire straits. I can't just put them out. Can't we give it a try? As a favor to me?

Patsy stood and glanced around the room, its beautiful cedar shelves, the heavy rust velvet drapes and deep reading chairs. Although unmoved by March's plight, she didn't want to seem selfish. I suppose, she said.

Cal nosed his grandson's fuzzy head. You're in, my friend. The missus here says you can stay.

•

If only all my cases were this easy, Ricky Barrett said by way of greeting when she picked up the phone.

You can make that call to Parnham now, he went on. The Hilton had a registration book on-site. Your guy signed in May second for three nights. I'm still waiting for computer records. But I saw his signature. The airlines all have records off-site, but it only took a few days to retrieve data from Continental. There he was, a noon flight into LAX, a 6:40 a.m. flight home to O'Hare.

You're good, said Patsy.

Well, that was kid stuff. That just proved he was here, it didn't establish him as the driver, which was trickier. So then I talked to the merry widow. She assumed I was coming after money. She doesn't have any, and Mr. Hogue didn't leave her any either. I had to tell her that the statute of limitations had run out for any lawsuits. I have no idea if that's true, but it got her talking. She knew the story a little differently. You with me?

Right here, Patsy said, tucking the old rag over her knees.

Well, hang on to your hat. Because it's not only time to call Parnham, but maybe the D.A. too. Because what our Mrs. Simms heard was more of a deathbed confession. Hogue told her flat out that he'd killed a couple people in California—and possibly his passenger too. He told her it was an accident, that he wasn't drunk, he just didn't see anyone. It was getting dark, you and he were yukking it up, and going into your driveway, he gunned it.

A roar in her head as from some distant stadium. A sense of strength fleeing her limbs. So he knew all along, she said.

He knew. And he walked. And you took the rap.

•

She went to her car and in the bright day drove east into Altadena. Her first thought was to update Joey Hawthorne, as she had broken the story and had first rights.

On a cul-de-sac at the very base of the mountains, Joey's small gray Japanese-style house had a flat roof and a grid of square windows. Peering into that grid, Patsy saw bare studs and crumpled canvas tarps in the living room. Nobody answered her knock. Of course, Joey was at work. She'd gotten the job she'd interviewed for, on a feature film with a famous director, at almost twice her usual rate. She was in preproduction now and would go on location—in rural Mississippi, of all places—late in the summer.

Patsy's old Pomelo Street home was only half a mile west. Brice had said that it had sold again for more than a quarter of a million dollars. Altadena, with its big lots, mature trees, and mountains, had become desirable.

The sycamores had been artfully pruned, the house painted a dark olive green with red doors and trim. The buckled concrete driveway was gone, replaced by gravel in slow curves. The whole place looked set-dressed, perfected, and Patsy missed its former white raffishness.

She'd been inside only once since prison; she'd stopped by the open house when she sold it in '92. Otherwise, Cal had an agency that handled the sale, including the cleaning and repairs and the Realtor.

She parked and walked up the new driveway. The oleanders still formed a hedge and were beginning to blossom; they'd been flat-topped and squared and were now so dense, Bill Hogue would never be able to climb through them.

She wondered if guilt had helped kill Bill Hogue. Imagine a tumor in a soft organ and guilt's acid wash absorbed again and again.

From the top of the driveway she surveyed the rangy iceberg roses and tall grasses planted in the new lazy curves. Could she have stayed here all along? Or would the dead still have visited too often, rushing up like pesky neighbors as she left the house, and then loitering on the lawn until she returned.

May I help you?

A young woman in a painted Mexican skirt stood on the porch.

I used to live here. The place looks great.

Oh, thank you. We love it.

She was barefoot, shiny brown hair in a ponytail. A wide silver bracelet.

The driveway is marvelous, Patsy said. I've never seen gravel on an incline like this. Aren't you afraid it'll all wash into the street?

A little will. But it sits on a bed of this absorbent recycled asphalt that holds it in place. Would you like to see inside?

The porch, expanded, was now teak. The entry walls were lichen green, and in the kitchen sat the vast O'Keefe & Merritt range.

Is that my old stove? Oh my god.

We found it in the shed and had it reconditioned. Did you grow up here?

I bought the house when I first moved to town.

Was that before or after the murder?

Patsy turned, mute with shock.

You didn't know? It was part of the full disclosure when we bought the place. A woman and kid were murdered in the yard. Some people won't buy a home if anyone died in it, let alone was murdered. There were six bids, and only three stayed in after full disclosure. We're not superstitious.

Patsy ran her hand on the cool green counter. I like this tile, she said.

I did it myself. I went to Home Depot and took their tiling class, then bought a tile saw. It took a million hours, though.

Gravel crunched underfoot as Patsy walked to her car.

28

In Old Town, Patsy bought a coffee at the counter of an Italian bakery and took it outside to the cobbled patio. It was Thursday, almost three o'clock. She sat at an iron table, the same table where she'd finished the Hull House book. March had been at the Pondo then too; loveless at twenty-seven, she'd been prone to extravagant emotional states. Who could've foreseen in that volatile sad sack today's efficient mother with the copious milk supply and pliable husband?

Patsy?

She looked up into Mark Parnham's gentle eyes. The skin under his chin was looser, his hair a paler brown. He cut a more striking figure in his dark gray suit, this one more Italian, less Rotarian than usual. She stood for a brief hug.

It's good to see you.

And you. Terrific suit. Very dapper.

He looked down at it as if surprised. I'll tell Liz you approve.

His new wife.

How is married life? Patsy asked.

We're just having a darn good time.

Patsy had attended the wedding last year and, at Mark's request, stayed long enough to shake hands with the bride, a plump brunette (another plump brunette) with a formidable bosom, porcelain nails, a ready laugh.

Ricky'll be right here, she said. Why don't you get some coffee?

She pulled her tote bag closer. In its thickets was Lucia Robinson's four-page statement. Patsy had told Mark that new facts had surfaced in their case. Now, seeing him—as ever, he seemed smaller and more fragile than she remembered him—she was worried about his response. She didn't want him to feel bad, and she certainly didn't want any money back. He'd never asked her for a cent and in fact had to be convinced to accept anything. Martin had gone through college and would finish law school without incurring debt. She was still proud of that.

Like his father, Martin Parnham was soft-spoken, unassuming, and, as surprisingly, a talented chorister. When invited, Patsy had attended his school and church recitals, her status there, among grandparents and admiring aunts, that of a distant relation with a blot. She was rigorously ignored, and usually she left with the final chord. On those occasions that Mark intercepted her at the door and brought them together, Martin was cordial. *You remember Patsy? Of course, hi, how are you? Thanks for the card and all.* And at his Pepperdine graduation: *Thanks for sitting through all those speeches!* Which was as close to irony as she'd heard from any Parnham lips.

If Martin had ever despised her or been repulsed or objected to her in any strenuous way, she never knew. Still, for all the times he'd addressed her in writing (*Dear Patsy, Thank you for the check . . .*), he'd never once—and over the years, she'd come to watch for this—greeted her by name. Never said *Patsy* aloud in her presence. Perhaps he couldn't bring himself to, but she tended to think he was holding his own in a way that his father never spotted. She didn't blame Martin, and almost admired how for twenty years now he'd stuck to his guns. She saw it as a secret line he'd drawn, an alliance with the two he'd lost.

Mark returned with his coffee, smiling his serious smile, a lift of his doleful mustache. She'd last seen him a week after his wedding; they'd sat on a blue sofa under klieg lights in some cable television studio in North Hollywood and gazed at each other's faces with fondness (as directed, but not difficult) while the cameras rolled and a commentator talked about the New Healing.

She still wouldn't say they were friends. They were too gentle and polite with each other and had never spent enough time together for ceremony to flag.

Mark pulled out a chair, and Ricky Barrett, big-shouldered and grinning, came out of the café with his coffee. Hands were shaken. Long time, long time, Ricky said to Mark.

A middle-aged woman reading at the next table looked them over frankly before returning to her book.

You start, Patsy, said Ricky. Tell as much as you like, and I'll take over.

She spoke hesitantly, carefully. I have a friend named Joey Hawthorne who works in the movies . . .

Patsy had dreaded describing the accident, was afraid she'd reopen the wound, but now found as she spoke that she need only to allude to it.

So this guy took my keys, and he was driving when we got to my place . . .

Mark listened, his eyes full of movement. Patsy expressed none of her jubilance and was surprised at how quickly she said what she'd come to say.

After talking to the first wife, I asked Ricky to check things out. And I also have this—she reached into her tote bag for Lucia's statement.

Mark scanned the document. He looked up at Patsy. Did you always suspect that you weren't driving? he asked.

Never. Not for a second.

Ricky produced Xeroxes of hotel and plane records, then recounted his conversation with the widow. I talked to her again yesterday, he said. She's agreed to be interviewed under oath.

Mark passed a hand over his eyes, rubbed his forehead. To think you went to prison, Patsy, he said. In that man's place.

He might not have gone, said Patsy. The main reason I did had to do with my priors, and driving without a license.

If we caught him on the run, he'd have done some time, said Ricky. For leaving the scene, criminal negligence.

But the poor fool. He takes my keys to be responsible, and this happens.

I don't feel sorry for him, said Ricky.

The first time I saw you in Malibu, Patsy, Mark said, you told me I had to be angry. I'll say the same thing to you now.

Oh, it's in there. Like I swallowed a crocodile. But mostly, I'm relieved. I finally understand those people who are exonerated after ten or fifteen years in prison. At first when they get out, they're so amazed.

And to think of all you've given us based on false assumptions. We'll really have to come up with some way to—

What's done is done, said Patsy. Besides, Martin is the best investment I've ever made. And Mr. Hogue probably couldn't have done much for you.

Yes, but there was no reason for you—

Actually, there are lots of reasons. I never should have had my car out. I wasn't supposed to be driving at all.

That's a traffic ticket, said Ricky. A fine, court-ordered AA. With priors, ten days in county, of which you'd serve two hours. Not two years in the pen.

I still want to own my part in it, said Patsy. It was my old, unpredictable car, my driveway. And I did pick up that creep.

How do you know he didn't pick *you* up? said Ricky. Everything else he said was a soft soap of the truth—till he was meeting his maker.

And Patsy, what he did's a whole nother order of magnitude, Mark said with enough sharpness to give her a small shock. He left my wife and child to die, and you to take the blame. How Martin and I'll ever square with you—

We're square now, Patsy said. And she didn't regret the money. Giving it away had cost her some degree of self-sufficiency, but that was fair and adequate compensation for her actual role in the debacle, whereas before, when she thought she'd been driving, no amount of prison time or cash would have been sufficient. I mean it, Mark, she said. I don't begrudge a penny.

And then, like that, she wanted to be done. Transfer the blame and close the door.

Ricky offered to get more coffee. No, thanks; no, both Mark and Patsy said, and then they stood, and hugged. Mark, in his new stylishness, walked off into the cool afternoon. Patsy noticed stillness in her chest, a solidity, as if indeed a door had shut. Possibly, and without regret, she would never have to see or talk to Mark Parnham again.

Ricky lifted his coffee cup, swirled the dregs, and drank. He took that well, he said.

He's always taken it well.

How are you taking it?

Up and down, she said. It's hard to know what it means.

It means you had a real bad rap for a long time and now you're out from under it. Ricky hitched his pants and looked up and down the alley. I'll talk to the prosecutor, see what we can do about the conviction. Find out what kind of hoops we got to jump through. I think we've got a good shot at it, though.

One more thing, he said. Don't let that crocodile you swallowed eat you alive. They tell 'em in anger management depression's just anger kept inside.

Just. She smiled to hear Ricky Barrett attempt psychology. I'll keep an eye on it, she said.

•

March routinely cooked dinner, but now, at four-forty, the kitchen was empty and mum. Patsy, her stomach sour from the black coffee, took out bread, peanut butter, jam. Then a commotion of doors, a baby's cry, and in came March with husband, children, and many shopping bags from Whole Foods.

So much traffic on the 2, March said. It took forever, and I have to get these children fed before they completely freak out.

Let me make them a sandwich, Patsy said, lifting the peanut butter so March could see the label. Organic!

Okay, a half one, split in two, March ordered. Just to tide them over.

Patsy started to smile at her imperiousness when March said, Thanks, Patsy. That would help a lot.

The sandwich half, halved, was taken by Forrest, along with the children, into the garden room. March began emptying the bags. Dad gave me his credit card, she said.

Oh, good, said Patsy, who had already guessed as much.

Here, said March. You want a banana with that?

Sure, thank you. Patsy added banana slices to her sandwich, put it on a plate, then helped March put away groceries.

So you've started teaching, Patsy? Or are you still on break?

Tuesday was my first class, Patsy said.

But you're also doing research. Going to libraries and such?

She's asking, Patsy thought, why I'm never home.

Mostly I've been reading for my next class. And today I met with a couple of guys about some old, old business. Patsy straightened boxed cereals in an overhead cupboard. I don't know if your dad said anything yet, but I've had some unusual news.

Nobody's told me anything, said March. Just a sec, she added, turning. Does anyone want some blood orange juice? she yelled to the garden room.

After a chorus of noes, she slung the jug into the fridge. Sorry, go on.

It turns out that I'm actually not guilty of the crime I went to prison for. You know, I was in a blackout, so I never knew what actually happened, but it's come out that I wasn't driving the car when those two people were killed.

Ava ran up and clasped her mother's legs.

March glanced down at her daughter and held up a finger—Time-out!—to Patsy. Ava, honey, did you eat anything? she said.

Daddy ate my sandwich.

Forrest, called March. Why did you eat her sandwich?

I'll make her another real quick, said Patsy.

No, it's okay. Here. March tore open a bag of rice cakes. Take one to Daddy too. Patsy?

No thanks.

So what will you do now? March said. Are you going to sue?

Patsy flattened a bag, then folded it. No, I won't sue.

But this is a big deal. Your whole reputation was ruined, said March. If I were you, I'd definitely sue.

·

Cal was watching the news in the dark, alone. Patsy slid into the chair next to his and waited for him to press the mute button. In the blue glow, the broad planes of his face made her think of granite escarpments.

Is everything okay? he said.

Yes, but I thought I'd bring you up to date. I was just talking to March, and I didn't want you to feel out of the loop.

So loop me in, he said, and leaned toward her as she told him about the meeting with Ricky and Mark.

I could tell you were chewing on something, he said. And of course I had some idea.

Ricky thinks we have enough to get the conviction overturned.

Good, Cal said. I'm glad you followed up on that. His eyes, ink-blue as ever, gazed at her a moment longer. Then he picked up the remote.

I'm sorry, she said. Were you involved in the news?

No, not really.

Are you annoyed because I didn't tell you about this earlier?

I'm not annoyed. If you can get the conviction overturned, I'm glad for you.

But that's not the point, at least not as far as I'm concerned, she said. I don't really care about the conviction.

Okay, said Cal.

God, she said. What's wrong with you Sharps? March just asked if I was going to sue someone. What about everything I went through? Prison, twenty years of guilt and remorse! Doesn't that merit sympathy? How 'bout a little outrage? And aren't you a little bit relieved to find out I didn't kill anyone?

I suppose.

You suppose? You suppose what?

I suppose the fact that you weren't driving mitigates some responsibility.

A sickening fear hit. Cal, do you think I'm still guilty of killing them?

It was your car, he said gently. Your house. Your lower companion. You took that first drink and set the whole thing in motion. As a participant, you have some responsibility for how things played out.

Oh! she said, suddenly seeing things his way. All could be traced to that first drink, that willful abdication of control. She'd known full well that if she drank, all bets were off and anything might ensue: hilarity, oblivion, tragedy. Yet she drank willingly, even knowing she'd be powerless over whatever madness she'd begun. And madness had ensued. So whoever was or wasn't driving at the moment of impact was somewhat immaterial. After all, everyone in the car is guilty in a drive-by shooting. In a bank robbery. In the Weathermen's planting of a bomb. Sharondel at fire camp said she'd no sooner climbed into a car with a john than he stopped for a bottle and held up a 7-Eleven. And she got twice the time he did. For sitting in the car.

A hot tide of guilt, familiar but with a fresh new froth of shame— shame that she'd thought she was free of wrongdoing—spread through her. She imagined standing alongside Bill Hogue before the judge and being sentenced as a team, two hapless drunks whose shenanigans turned fatal.

She'd posited this very idea to Ricky and Mark, but they'd resisted her. Ricky had a soft spot for her, and Mark had forgiven her from the get-go for his own peace of mind. The moral truth, which Cal insisted on, was not so easily sidestepped. She covered her face with her hands as sobs—deep, painful coughs of despair—burst out of her. Cal drew his hand down her back again and again.

I thought I could be free of it, she said, once she could speak. I felt so relieved.

I know, he said. I could see that you did. Come here. He pulled her gently. Come here, my love. My sweetheart.

In standing to enter his embrace, she bumped the table and sent a stack of magazines to the floor. Sorry, sorry, she said, crouching to pick them up.

On her haunches there on the carpet, gathering *New Yorkers* and Stanford alumni magazines as Cal daintily held his knees to one side, another thought arrived, this one in a man's voice, a cowboy's voice: Now just a gol durn minute.

She hadn't been driving. She'd given over her keys when asked—and by all accounts, without a struggle. Bill Hogue was driving because he'd asked to. But he hadn't been familiar with her old, heavy car or the steepness of her driveway. Nor had she anticipated pedestrians in his path—who could have? In many ways, the accident was just that. An accident.

Patsy? said Cal. You okay down there?

Of course she never should have taken the first drink. By the same token, what were the mother and daughter doing out at dusk, the hard-to-see time, the witching hour? What were they doing on private property where they were uninvited, unexpected, unwanted?

She gave the magazines a few sharp bounces to neaten the stack, and stood. Cal reached for her hip. Come on, sweetie, he murmured. Come here.

Cal, she said, no.

He looked up at her, perplexed. Some of his white eyebrows were so long that they looked like tendrils seeking a trellis. My love? he said.

I'm going out, she said.

•

She drove over to the Rose Bowl, where her cell phone had decent reception, and parked alongside the golf course. It was a beautiful, cold evening. White and gray cloud masses slid over each other, tore apart, light breaking through. The wind came in gusts. People were walking and running and skating around the old stadium and greens. She looked like one of them, on the phone before or after a jog.

Burt was home alone, he told her, practicing the banjo.

Cal still thinks I'm guilty, she said.

Oh, he's just afraid that you're going to kick up your heels and run off.

If he's not careful, that could be a self-fulfilling prophecy, said Patsy. I can't stay guilty for his sake.

You've been too haunted for too long as it is. You took the whole thing so damn hard. I always wished you could forgive yourself more than you did.

I know, said Patsy. It's temperament. Some of us take stuff too hard.

And some of us don't take stuff hard enough, Burt said. Which was always Bonnie's complaint about me.

The banjo sounded a twangy flourish.

It amounts to the same thing, said Patsy. Inappropriate response—Freud's definition of neurosis. My last shrink would say it's the result of all that madness in our house growing up. How we dealt with it.

Probably, said Burt. But don't you find as you get older, you say to hell with that psychology and self-help crap and just start doing what you want?

I have no idea what I want, said Patsy.

You will. Especially now. Don't you feel all freed up?

It's only been a couple weeks, Burt. I don't know how to feel freed up.

•

Gloria said, I'd take it easy for a while. Don't make any major decisions. Maybe hit a meeting a day till you're through some of this.

That advice! The last time Patsy went daily to meetings, her higher power was channeled by that other prospective adulteress, Yvette Stevens. Patsy hadn't seen Yvette again until a few months ago, when they ran into each other during intermission at a chamber music concert. Patsy had drawn Yvette aside. You probably saved my marriage, she said.

Me? Gosh. That's funny. How?

Patsy lowered her voice. The last time I saw you, you talked about that curator you liked and how you'd decided to sidestep the insanity. I was so impressed.

Yvette's dark, round eyes began to flash; she ducked her head, her perfect smoke gray pageboy swung over her face. But Patsy, she whispered, we had eighteen months of insanity. Buzz and I separated, the kids chose sides. I left my job. She laughed softly. Oh, Patsy, you must have caught me on a day I was talking a real good line.

•

Night was sinking down to earth, the hillsides west of the Rose Bowl darkening to black. Clouds sealed the sky. Tall mercury-vapor lamps flickered on around the greens. Patsy considered whom to call next. She couldn't reach Audrey from this phone. She thought of phoning Lewis. God, how she'd love to tell him her news, although who knew what he'd make of it. He had found her original story, what?—resonant and powerful?—and therefore might find the new revised version (and the present, revised *her*) somewhat less compelling.

Prison was only romantic or dismissible to those who'd never been.

And if she hadn't gone . . . she probably would've gotten tenure two years earlier, then landed a better job. She might have met a man her own age, perhaps the hyperintelligent, talky Jew she'd promised herself in college. They'd have a small, book-stuffed house in some college town, Palo Alto, say, Poughkeepsie or Middlebury.

Assuming, of course, she'd gotten sober. Cal was right: she couldn't have kept on at the rate she was going. After her second DUI, she knew she'd have to quit, and sooner rather than later. Her drinking had even taken on a certain elegiac tone. She might well have quit right around the same time anyway.

And if she'd gone to Pasadena AA two years earlier, she definitely would've run into Cal and she would've revered him; everybody did back then. *I am powerless over those ink blue eyes.* But without her post-prison abjection coinciding with the mere blip of his widowhood, the chances were they never would've married.

She remembered with a pang the peanut butter sandwich she'd left on her kitchen counter and, starting her car, drove to Pie 'N Burger in Pasadena. In the overlit, too-warm coffee shop, she sat at the counter among CalTech students and lab workers, ordered what she thought of as the Lewis Fletcher Special—a cheeseburger with grilled onions and boysenberry pie à la mode. She ate all but a puddle of melted ice cream.

29

Several dozen brown packing boxes arrived and sat stacked in a solid square mass inside the living room.

A good number of those boxes were labeled KITCHEN.

I don't like it, Cal, she said. But then, you already know that.

It'll be fine, Patsy, you'll see.

She was curious, probably not in a good way, to see how far March, unimpeded, would go.

Unfamiliar canisters of crackers and whole meals appeared on the kitchen counters, along with a baby-food processor, a rice cooker, an expensive espresso machine. The baby's jump seat was hung from a beam in the garden room. Patsy felt twinges—her new kitchen! her new beam!—but did not intervene.

You're waiting in ambush, said Gloria. You're giving her more than enough rope to hang herself. Or martyr you.

Maybe, said Patsy. But it means so much to Cal to have them here, I'm really in no position to deprive him.

Sure you are, said Gloria.

They were driving home with two other AA women from the Women's Institution at Corona on a Thursday night after taking an AA meeting to the maximum-security unit. There, Patsy had told her amended story from the podium for the first time. She told it in order, her drinking and drugging, her prison time, the twenty years of guilt. Then, about a month ago, I got a phone call from a friend, she said, and found out what really happened.

After everyone else on the panel spoke, the inmates could ask questions. A tall woman raised her hand and said, I'm just like you. I didn't hurt nobody, but they put me here anyway.

Mmmm, said Patsy.

Another woman said, So how come you here tonight? Why you come back inside if you never have to be here in the first place?

I'm still a drunk and an ex-con, said Patsy. That part hasn't changed. I still have to carry the message. Which is that alcohol is cunning, baffling, and powerful. It can make you plead guilty even when you're not.

•

So March is living here again, she told Audrey. With her family, and boat, and worldly possessions.

How did that happen?

In pieces. They were visiting, their house sold quickly, and now they're homeless and *here*.

You don't sound happy about it.

I'm not. But we do have all this room, and it seems selfish to refuse them. They're dead broke, it seems. Forrest has to find a job, and he's not the brightest bulb to begin with. Then, his résumé has a three-year hole in it.

But that's not your problem, Patsy. That's their problem. You don't have to put up with them for a minute longer if you don't want to.

But I'd have to stage a *major* battle to get them out.

And you'd win, if that's what you want.

I'm not so sure I would win, said Patsy.

Cal's kids always mattered in ways that she—the third, childless wife—could never hope to eclipse. She'd known her status when she married him. It was the sham of her marriage, really, the don't-look-too-close fine print of their agreement. A healthier, more self-respecting woman—Audrey, for example—would never have signed on.

A soft transatlantic hum filled the silence.

Oh, but nobody really wants to live with their parents, said Audrey. Just write them a great big check. They'll leave.

•

On Easter Sunday, March took her brood and Cal over to Spencer's for dinner. Patsy demurred, citing work. She was reading *Women in Love*, a silly, rant-filled book, although interesting about industrialization and feminism.

She remembered Lewis saying for some reason that the movie didn't hold up.

He'd been short-listed for the Hallen job, with a Korean-American woman and a Mexican-American man. Which meant he didn't stand a chance.

Disgusted by her own lethargy, she went outside, dug up a patch of garden. The soil was black and soft and laced with thick pink worms. She filled a few wheelbarrows full of rotted manure, spread it out, turned it under, then planted peas, cabbage, and chard seeds, although nobody but she and Bob would eat from the garden. For the first time in several weeks, she picked lettuce, pounds of it, washing and packing it in individual gallon-sized plastic bags. She gathered avocados and white grapefruits in a shopping bag.

She drove into Pasadena and left one bag of lettuce on Margaret's porch, another on Sarah and Henry's back stoop. North, in Millard Canyon, Brice's door was locked. She put his sack on the porch table along with another full of grapefruit and avocados.

He'd blown his April cash on a used cashmere coat; she worried he wasn't eating.

She peered in at his one room, which was paneled in wide, rough redwood planks. A wall of books. A small iron bed. A woodstove, a tidy stack of split logs. A big, balding Turkish rug on the floor. Perfection, she thought. Even destitute, Brice insisted on beauty.

Only Joey was home; her family wasn't eating until later. Don't you want to come in, see the progress? she said, and led Patsy through the kitchen. The living room was sheathed in plastic; Joey swept one length aside to show off foil-faced insulation between the studs, stacks of drywall waiting to go up. My stepmother gave me the money for this and the taxes, Joey said. The evil Marlene, believe it or not—I didn't even have to ask. Guess I can't nurse that grudge much longer. Joey dropped the transparent curtain. Which reminds me, Patsy. I've been meaning to ask you something. Has Cal ever said anything about my mom?

They were friends, from the Mojave Club.

Yes, but I'm pretty sure there was something more.

They'd moved back into Joey's kitchen, and stood beside the cooking island. Gosh, said Patsy. Not that I've heard. Do you mean an affair?

For example, said Joey.

With Cal? I doubt it. Not since he got sober and entered the saint-hood. And that's thirty-eight years now. Why? What brought this up?

I saw them kiss, Joey said. That night you pierced my ears. After we took you home, I was wandering around the Bellwood and saw her ar-rive by ambulance. Cal met her and kissed her, and not just a friendly peck either. Nobody else knew she was there, and because I'd had all those beers and Valium, I wasn't so sure what I'd seen. I never got up the nerve to ask my dad about it.

That has to be over twenty years ago, said Patsy.

I know. But last fall I found a lump in my breast—it was only a cyst, completely benign, but because of my mom's history, the doctor wanted to see her medical records and figure out what kind of cancer she had. I had to order them from Norwalk, and they finally came two days ago. And there, a couple pages from the end, it said: *Released to Bellwood Ho-tel.* Her insurance only covered two-week hospitalizations. So she had to check out for a night, and then a new cycle would start.

Wow, Patsy said. To find out after all these years . . .

Not a very romantic explanation, though. Except for the Cal part, maybe.

The kitchen was warm and smelled of fresh paint and old coffee stewing on the machine's warmer.

You never asked him about it? said Patsy.

Me ask Cal if he had a thing with my mom? I don't think so.

Do you want me to ask him?

I don't know. Maybe. I'm sort of afraid to find out. My mom was al-ways so angry, said Joey. I assumed that I irritated her. But maybe she just wanted to be somewhere else. Maybe with Cal she was happy—at least I like thinking that.

Maybe so. Patsy slung an arm around Joey.

They walked out together and stood side by side at the curb. The homes on Joey's street were shingled vacation shacks from the 1920s, their yards filled with cactus, citrus, and old trees. Across the street, one small cottage was being swallowed by blue plumbago, magenta bou-gainvillea.

Patsy imagined it as an office or studio, where she could come every day for solitude and work. With a friend nearby.

Hey, Joey, she said. If any of these places come up for sale, would you let me know?

•

Patsy MacLemoore? Ricky Barrett's good-natured baritone again boomed through the phone. I talked to the prosecutor. Of course, he has a thousand other fish to fry and can't be expected to initiate any action on your behalf. But he was very interested, and he did say if your lawyer filed a motion to vacate the conviction, he'd be receptive to it. Do you have a lawyer?

Not that I know of, said Patsy. I haven't talked to Benny since the late eighties.

Benny Aronowitz? said Ricky. I saw him in court last week.

Do you think I should follow up on this?

I'd say you've got a darn good shot at it, so why not?

•

The Trestle in La Cañada had been remodeled. The burgundy booths were a new, creaky button and tuck; tiny lamps with amber-colored glass shades sat on each table and supplied the only light; waiters dispensed flashlights to those who complained they could not read the menu. Patsy had lured Cal out to dinner on a rainy Thursday night for the monthly steak allowed by his doctor. So many people stopped by their table to say hello to him, she was afraid she'd never get her turn with him. Well well well, look who's here. How you been, Cal? Oh, hello, Patsy. With so many interruptions, it took them an hour to get through their salads. But with their steaks came a lull.

Here's what I think, Patsy said. Let's give March fifty thousand dollars against her inheritance. With fifty thousand dollars, anybody can make a fresh start.

Cal was quarrying out the middle of his blood-rare filet. Without looking up, he said, The money would be gone in six months.

Or less, said Patsy. But we would have done our part.

I don't know why you're so dead set against their being at the house. It's been smooth and fun. You're never home anyway.

I'm scarce because they're here. And March has been very sweet, but I feel outnumbered, Cal. I miss the quiet and need it. I know you love having them . . .

It's more than that, Patsy. All those years Peg was sick, when I was going to ten AA meetings a week and sponsoring thirty men, I was barely thinking about my kids. It was too painful. I let March down especially, right at that age when a girl needs her father.

Patsy eyed him dubiously; Cal was never one to invoke psychologism.

March forgives me, he went on. She believes that I was doing the best I could, but I could've done much better by her and the boys.

Was this also around the time you were seeing Millicent Hawthorne?

Cal grew still. Did Audrey tell you that?

No, Cal, said Patsy. But other people have.

I shouldn't be surprised, he said.

So what did happen between you and Millicent?

Oh, Patsy, that was a long time ago.

Still. I'd like to know.

I always adored Millie. And with Peg so sick for so long . . . Cal set down his utensils, lowered his voice. Millie was my age, and my set. We understood each other.

I can't believe you never told me this, said Patsy.

Very little happened, Cal said. And then she died. All those years, I worried about Peg—her driving, the booze and pills, her liver—and then Millie, this tall, healthy, beautiful athlete in the prime of her life, goes first.

Cal put a hand over his eyes briefly, then picked up his fork and knife.

Patsy let a few moments pass. How come you never told me any of this? she asked again, quietly.

Water under the bridge, Patsy. All a long time ago.

Patsy was silenced by competing urges: to drop the subject, as Cal clearly wanted; to argue that it was only a long time ago *now* and she should have been told about Millicent Hawthorne much earlier; or to introduce herself into the history. What about me? Where do I stand in all of this? How do I fit into the picture? But she was a little afraid of what Cal might say.

All the more reason I owe my kids amends, Cal went on quietly. For years I put my own needs first. The least I can do is help them out now, when they're having a tough time of it.

Except March isn't a little child anymore, said Patsy, relieved to return to that familiar topic. She's an adult with a lazy husband. You're not helping them by giving them a free pass.

Forrest is lazy, said Cal. But whatever else you can say about March, she pulls her weight. She does what's expected of her, and more. She's a marvelous mom. Why should she and the kids suffer for her husband's character defects?

She is a good mother, said Patsy. But she also wants to live above her means, in my house, at my expense.

Cal's eyes narrowed, and he started to speak.

I mean, my emotional expense, Patsy added quickly. Here I am, trying to adjust to a whole new set of facts about my life. I desperately need privacy and refuge, and every time I turn around, there they are.

But the kids have always come home before. Cal seemed genuinely baffled. Stan. And his ex, what's her name? It's always worked out. Anyway, you're going to Cambridge soon enough.

Not till fall! Patsy said, putting down her silverware. And *we're* going to Cambridge, remember? You're coming too.

I've been meaning to talk to you about that, Patsy. I know you want me to come, and I promised to. But I can't. I can't face the plane ride, or being gone so long, or the thought of being holed up in a British flat while you work.

Only a couple hours a day. The rest of the time, we'll sightsee. I've wanted this for years. We have theater tickets.

And you should go. You will go.

I'm not leaving you at the Ponderosa by yourself, she said.

But you see, I won't be alone. The kids . . .

Oh, she said, and kept her voice low. I do see. I see what you and March have been up to all along.

There's no conspiracy, Patsy. There's just the way things worked out.

Patsy made an effort to match his calm. If she grew shrill or angry, he'd revert to his distant, tolerant sponsorial mode. As she steadied herself, an elderly couple appeared at the end of their table. White-haired, frail, in pale clothes, they were the Evanses, who had lived across the street from the Tudor. Their kids had grown up with Cal's, but Patsy had never gotten to know them. Cal, Cal Sharp, they said with a chime of surprise, as if they'd never dreamed of seeing him again.

Barbara! Ed! Cal answered, half rising from the booth to clap their shoulders, clasp their hands.

The names and jobs and whereabouts of all their children were re-
cited in turn, the number of grandchildren totaled and then revised.

Finally, leaning on each other's arm, the Evanses tottered off, two
shrinking old people with the same color hair and clothes, the same
hunch to their shoulders—a matched set.

Cal watched them go with a smile that grew sad. Patsy waited until
silence and a sense of seclusion returned to their booth.

So tell me, Cal. What if March hadn't moved back? she said coolly.
Would you have come to England then?

A quick shake of his head. Stan said he'd move in if need be. Or I
would've made do with Haydee. And Bob, of course. So I had other options, yes.

Patsy pulsed with anger and powerlessness. Yet even as she seethed,
the thought of going to England alone, at this point, was almost a
relief.

·

Cal must have spoken to March because after the dinner at the Trestle,
the family's presence in the house seemed to recede. March wasn't in the
kitchen as often; she moved Beckett's jump seat into their room. In the
afternoons, Patsy saw March and the children up by the barn, feeding
Diotima and Mamie oat grass that had sprouted where hayseeds scattered.
Or March nursed Beckett on a bench while Ava poked around with a stick,
sometimes getting a few good jabs into Mamie before March noticed.

Patsy made herself a cup of tea one afternoon and, since the coast was
clear, drank it in the garden room and looked through the paper. Sun-
flowers now peered in the north-facing windows and clashed with long
canes of pink roses, the Gertrude Jekylls. She couldn't remember when
she'd last sat there.

Forrest came into the kitchen and, seeing her, paused—he too must
have been coached to give her a wide berth—but she put down the paper and greeted him. There's hot water, if you want tea or coffee.

No thanks, he said, and poured himself a glass of milk. After drinking it half down, he came toward her. I don't want to interrupt you, he
said. But I want to say how much we appreciate staying here. I know it's
not easy to have two little kids and us . . .

I don't imagine it's what you want either, she said. I'm sure you'd
rather be in your own place.

He gazed into his milk. Yeah, just I gotta get this thing I'm trying
to do—he half shrugged, half gestured toward the dining room—off
the ground.

•

Benny's office was now in downtown Pasadena, in a pretty stone building where his name was on a bronze plaque sunk into an ivy-covered
wall. Patsy took an elevator to the seventh floor, and in the tiny, three-
chair waiting room she checked in with the receptionist and helped herself to a butterscotch candy. A very good one, sweet and salty.

Benny had gone gray. Never tall, he now stooped, and Patsy, as she
shook his hand, felt as if she towered. He led her into his office overlooking the rooftops of downtown, took her folder of papers.

Ricky Barrett had already filled him in, Benny said. Closing his office door, he sat behind his desk. I find this all very upsetting, he went
on. I keep thinking there was something else I should've done, back
when it happened. Something that would have kept you out of prison.

What else could you have done?

I went back over my notes, he said, and the first time I talked to you
at the sheriff's station, you were pretty drunk and incoherent, but in
retrospect, a couple of things stood out. You kept asking why *you'd* been
arrested. You also repeatedly said, Where's the fucking crutch seller?

The what?

Isn't that our man—didn't Hogue sell medical equipment?

Oh, said Patsy.

I didn't put it together, said Benny. I thought the crutch-seller business was some oblique reference to the victims. It didn't occur to me
that there was another person in the car, let alone a different driver.

It didn't occur to anyone, said Patsy.

Benny picked up a pen and started tapping bullet points on a
scratch pad. I'll put a motion together. I'll need a declaration from the
Simms woman like the one you got from Robinson. Expert opinions
couldn't hurt.

But wouldn't I still be an accessory? Patsy had to ask. A woman I
knew at fire camp was in the car when her john, some guy she'd met
minutes before, robbed a 7-Eleven, and she got more time than he did.

That's different, Benny said. All that means is the guy pled out at
her expense. Not comparable. Yours was all about your driving. Chances

are, if Hogue hadn't left the scene, if he'd told his story and didn't have a record, nobody would have been prosecuted.

So I was prosecuted for what, exactly? Having an accident on a suspended license?

Pretty much, said Benny. They couldn't get you for intoxication, so they took what they could.

The rooftops of Old Pasadena were a study of vent pipes and air-conditioning cowlings, odd hutlike assemblages on tar paper, erected without the least regard for appearance. Off in one corner, she saw the squat, onion-domed turrets of the Bellwood Hotel, now the Bellwood Luxury Condominiums.

Patsy said, Do you think it's worth going through all this rigmarole when I've already served the time?

It depends on how you feel about the public record, said Benny. It's really up to you.

3 0

The quarter was flying by. Her students camped out in the hallway outside her office to discuss their midterm projects, then delivered them in class, one wearing an eye patch as James Joyce, another wrapped in green cellophane to be the light on Gatsby's pier. The job talks by the comp lit finalists were delivered the second week of May: Aimee Song spoke on "Han: Intergenerational Grief, The Postwar Short Story in South Korea"; Fernando Molina on "The Language of Cartoon and Carnival in Asturias's Mulata de tal"; Lewis Fletcher on "Exiled to the Country House: Provincial Life and Suffering in French and Russian Fiction."

Patsy did not attend.

·

They're still there? said Audrey. Haven't you sent them packing? Did you try the big fat check?

Cal wants them here so he won't have to go to Cambridge with me. That's what this is really about.

I'm not surprised, she said. What would Cal do in Cambridge, anyway?

Same thing he does here. Watch TV. Talk to his kids on the phone. Go to British AA. I'm only going to work a couple of hours a day. We'd go out. Besides, he said he'd come. That's why I rented such a big flat.

Do you need him there?

I can't just leave him alone, Audrey. He's almost eighty!

Let March and her dot-com fellow take over for a while. And you, go. Get out, live your life.

I don't know, Patsy said. I'd feel derelict leaving him.

A silence ensued in which Patsy imagined Audrey sitting in her white-painted wood-paneled living room overlooking the Seine, the Pont Neuf, and the pointy tip of Île de la Cité, while nearby, on the gilded-armed Louis Quinze chairs, her housemate's Pomeranians curled like cushions.

Patsy said, By the way, did you know Cal had an affair with Millicent Hawthorne?

A pause. I did know that.

How come you never told me?

Cal asked me not to. The daughter was over there all the time—he didn't want it to go any further. Besides, what difference would it make?

I don't know, said Patsy. But some.

Well, I'm sorry. I was hamstrung. If it's any consolation, I didn't tell Gilles either.

You always said Peggy was his big love.

She was, at first, and he wanted to help her with all her problems. But Millicent was his great friend. He was never so easy and happy as he was with Millicent. They were two of a kind.

So why didn't they just divorce and marry each other?

Audrey sighed. Kids, houses, alimony, inertia, Cal trying to do the right thing. Though who knows what would've happened if Millie had gone to the doctor when she first found the lump instead of waiting three years hoping it would just go away.

•

Bob the boarder had taken to heating frozen pizzas in the possum trot kitchen at odd hours and avoiding mealtimes altogether. Ava sniffed him out and demanded slices; they were discovered one afternoon sharing a pepperoni-and-mushroom pie. March rewarded Bob with a nutrition lecture he described to Patsy as *Das Vegetal*.

She expected another such story when Bob knocked on her home office door, then closed it quietly behind him. I just wanted you to know I gave Cal notice today, he said. I'm leaving June first.

Oh! I'm sorry, she said. But not surprised.

He was renting an apartment in downtown Pasadena with another sober guy. But don't worry, he said. I'll still take Cal to meetings whenever he wants.

She tried to talk Bob into the possum trot. His friend could live there too; it wouldn't cost them much. You wouldn't have to deal with *her*, said Patsy.

Cal suggested that too, Bob said. But I like the idea of living in town, walking to bookstores, the movies, meetings.

Of course, Patsy said. This is sort of the boonies.

I loved living here. You and Cal have been great.

Patsy said, I'm sad to see you go.

Upon reflection, she wasn't sad so much as annoyed that he could pick up and leave, just like that.

•

Sarah said, You just have to find March a house. You find her a house she wants, slip her the down payment, she'll be out of your hair in a second.

Patsy wasn't sure she had a down payment to slip anyone, and for one seditious moment she wished she'd kept more of her own money over the years. But if March asked him for a house, Cal might have a hard time refusing her. He had a hard time refusing her anything else.

And another thing, Sarah went on. Comp lit offered that job to the Korean woman, but apparently she's had a better offer from Michigan.

•

On two successive Sundays, Patsy drove up to Altadena looking at FOR SALE signs. She took Brice along for company and opinions.

They toured homes that echoed the aesthetics Patsy recalled from March's trim, modern Sunnyvale home. Then, because they were close by, Brice showed her a tiny hermit's cabin across the stream from his place. And because they liked the snapshot in the newspaper, they looked at a small, thick-walled adobe overlooking the arroyo.

The next Sunday, Patsy wanted to look at the adobe a second time. In a sunny spot on the property, she flung open her arms. This is where I'd put the orchard.

Brice, sunglasses sagging at the neck of his T-shirt, hands lightly on his hips, glanced all around at the trees, the fence, the back patio. His assessing gaze landed on her. So what's really on your mind here, Pats, he asked. You leaving the old guy, or what?

His directness drew her up short. Didn't he know that this vague, unfocused home search was the closest she could come to addressing that question?

The next open house they visited was a clean three-bedroom mid-century home with a glittering pool. The wood floors needed to be sanded, and ivy had taken over too much of the backyard, but the price was about half of what the same place would cost in La Cañada Flintridge. Patsy took a flyer.

She found Cal reading the Sunday paper in his office. Why hello, darling. She kissed his dry cheek.

She sat on the edge of his daybed, the flyer in hand. I've been thinking, Cal, about how we live and how we can keep going, you and I.

A wave of amusement passed through his eyes. And what have you come up with, Patsy?

I used to think we could stay here and just scale back. But as long as we have all this square footage, the house will keep filling up. And it's so much upkeep and expense, so much more than we need. Neither one of us rides much to speak of. Nobody swims. Aren't you ready for a change?

I haven't given it any thought, said Cal.

I have. And I think we should move to a smaller place. A condo, even. We could sell this place and buy two smaller ones. One for us, one for the kids to use whenever they need to.

Oh, Patsy. Even the idea of moving makes me want to take a nap.

I know, Cal, she said. But the Ponderosa is too much for me. I need more privacy and control in my own home.

With large, quavering hands, Cal shut his laptop.

You know, Patsy, I don't mind old age half as much as I thought I would, he said. I used to be afraid of it when I was younger, but I'm not now, because here it is, I'm old. The only bad part is I get fatigued so easily. Walking to the mailbox fatigues me, people arguing on television . . .

Yes, but Cal, I'm—

He held up a hand. That said, I don't want to be reinvigorated. I don't want a whole new life or a smaller one—and certainly not a lonelier one. I like life going on around me. I'm happy with a grandkid on my lap and a heap of brown rice on my plate. Things don't taste as good as they used to, anyway. As for your energy, that beautiful drive of yours to go here and move there, Patsy, it's wasted on me. I want to sit in the sun on our patio and hear the baby chirp in the kitchen. I don't want to hole up in some condo and wait for the end. And I don't want to strag-gle all over the world for the sake of straggling all over the world. I've seen the sun in Kensington Gardens, and the sun here is just as good.

You're not that old, Cal. A lot of people travel at your age. And move. Everyone at some point starts to scale back and simplify.

Because they need to. But we don't need to. We can afford to stay here. And there's plenty of privacy right on this property. Cal leaned forward and covered Patsy's hands with his. Nobody bothers you in your office. But if you want your own refuge, why not redo the pool house or the possum trot, or build that little studio down by the stream you used to talk about.

I don't want to hide on my own property, Cal. I want a life with my husband. Meals with him. Trips with him. Him alone.

I love you, Patsy, and admire you, but you've got to stop thinking I can keep up with you. Especially not with this newfound energy of yours. I hear Audrey wants you in Paris. Go! And go to Cambridge for as long as you like. Send me postcards. Send me e-mails with attach-ments. I know how to open them now, thanks to Forrest. I want to stay here and growl at my grandkids and eat that sour yogurt goop March makes with prunes.

I think you're saying something, said Patsy, but I'm not completely sure what. Something to let me off the hook.

There is no hook.

Meaning what?

It's caught up with us, Pats. You're a great girl, and you gave me the best years of your life, but you're too damn young to grow old with.

Tears fell from her eyes, landing in fat drops on her jeans.

You hum, Patsy, he said. It makes me nervous. I can't keep up with you, and I don't want to. I have no desire to hop the pond to live some-place cold and strange that's thousands of miles from my kids. I like it right here.

I know that, Cal. I'm not talking about Cambridge. I'm talking about our life together here and in the future. Now and when I come back.

We can talk about that, Patsy. But not if you're going to hound me about watching television at night or falling asleep too early. That's what I do. I'm old. And the kids will come and go as they need to. This is still their home. That doesn't change.

Patsy sobbed, and caught herself. It was so nice when we had the house to ourselves. Didn't you like it with just you and me, and Bob?

I like it better now, said Cal.

She wiped furiously at her face with the heel of her hand. I don't see why March and Forrest can't live someplace else, she said. Someplace they can afford. Look. I found this in Altadena. Pool, big trees. For a song, Cal. She tried handing him the flyer.

He shook his head. No, he said. I won't have them in Altadena.

There's nothing wrong with it, Cal. That's how young families live when they're just starting out. I'm sure they'd rather have their own home, and this is a really good one.

His jaw was resolute, his lips turned down. He looked like a turtle with an alert, shiny eye.

She balled up and tossed the flyer into the wastepaper basket. Do you want a divorce, Cal? she asked. Is that what you're saying here?

His face darkened. He gave a small, regretful shake of his head. Let's just have one conversation at a time, Patsy, he said. Can we do that? Because this one's already worn me out.

•

She made her way out of the house and was surprised it was still light outside, as if she'd been in a movie or dark church for hours. In fact, it was only midafternoon, three or a little after. She went to her car and, for a moment, sat behind the steering wheel trying to catch her breath. Her hands shook as she put the keys into the ignition.

She had no destination and drove down to Foothill Boulevard, then into Hahamongna Park, bumping over potholes until pulling into one of the more remote picnic spaces in a large oak grove.

She wept somewhat noisily and self-consciously, but only for a minute, then stared dully out at the white boulders bordering the site and a thick wooden picnic table on which blue jays hopped, pecking at crumbs. Through the trees, the water glinted in Devils Gate Reservoir.

He hadn't said, What the hell are you talking about? *Divorce?*

He hadn't said, No, Patsy, I don't want a divorce.

A terrible noise came out of her mouth, and the jays flew off in a blue flash.

Hopelessness washed through her, flooding her with an icy heat, hollowing her out, making the beautiful world—the backlit little oak leaves, the rain-scrubbed granite boulders, the water glinting through leaves—look as false as a small painted backdrop fluttering over the void.

She'd been pushing him, forcing his hand, but she never imagined this, that he would prefer for her to leave. And March to stay.

She blamed Audrey and Sarah for egging her on, when she knew Cal better than they did.

Although she could stay, he'd said so. She'd just have to stop complaining. Accept March. And let Cal be old, as old as he liked.

That was better than being turned out on her own.

She couldn't even remember what bothered her so much about March and Forrest, what was so irritating. As for Cambridge—at this point she'd be perfectly happy not to go.

One jay returned to the picnic table. The pain in her chest eased.

God knows, little Ava could use a champion.

Patsy whimpered and wept in a brief spasm.

The sun had warmed the car, and she let the heat build up. Exhausted, cried out, almost dozing, she was afraid to move lest the terrible prospect of banishment return.

Her cell phone rang, a deep gurgle in her purse. She dug it out.

It's me, said Brice. I was on my way home from the store and I saw an open house on Concha Street, up by the park. You'll see the sign. If you hurry, I'll wait.

Oh, Brice, she said. March doesn't—

This isn't for her, he said. It's got your name all over it. Patsy MacLemoore! Patsy MacLemoore!

At the sound of her name, she sat up, rolled down her window, unplastered a fat strand of hair glued to her cheek. Cool air flowed into the car. Where are you, again? she said. Where is Concha Street?

3 1

The days turned foggy and cold again in the mornings. June gloom in late May. The marine layer turned yellowish by afternoon; those who didn't understand the distinction called it smog.

Students again clogged the hall outside her office, this time waiting to talk about their term papers. Georges waded through them to stick his head in. After stringing us along for weeks, he said, our Mr. Molina has decided to take the job at Santa Cruz. And now we can't get a hold of Fletcher. Is he already in Paris? Do you have his number there?

I don't know where he is, said Patsy. And I don't have his number. But if you really need it, I can dig it up for you.

That's okay, Georges said. I probably have it somewhere.

·

Benny left a message saying that a courier had dropped off something of interest to her and he'd be in all afternoon if she wanted to stop by. He hadn't sounded pleased. Then again, he hadn't sounded dire. She'd either been exonerated or not. They couldn't haul her back to prison for filing a declaration.

In Benny's waiting room, she went right for the candy bowl, so no matter what happened, she'd have a mouthful of that salty butterscotch.

Benny ushered her down the inner hallway and handed her a manila envelope. She undid a short string, pulled out a typed document.

No wordsmith, our judge, Benny said.

She barely glanced at the headings and went directly to the text itself:

Defendant's unopposed motion to vacate her 1981 conviction for vehicular manslaughter is before the court . . . Mr. William

Hogue, rather than defendant, was driving . . . Hogue effectively and repeatedly confessed to driving the car at the time of
the accident . . .

Defendant . . . did not remember that she was not driving
her car . . . In the absence of opposition . . . the court hereby va-
cates Defendant's conviction and sentence.

Benny refused a check. It's the least I can do, he said.

On her way out, she helped herself to a big handful of those marigold-
yellow candies and crammed them into her purse. They were really, she
thought, exceptionally delicious. She'd slip one to Ava.

At the Ponderosa, she set out to find Cal, to show him the court
document. Partway into the east wing, she turned around. She already
knew what he would say. You took that first drink. It was your car. Your
lower companion.

In the two months since they'd had that conversation, he had never
asked if she'd sought out an attorney or pursued exoneration. Nor had
he mentioned the accident or her involvement in it.

A bedroom door opened, and Ava in a pink Cinderella costume
grabbed onto her waist and stepped onto her feet. To the barn, she said.
Big steps.

•

A woman named Charlotte Ebberts phoned later that evening, when
Patsy was about to shower. Remember me? I wrote a story about you
and Mark Parnham for the *Times* back in 1983. I was going through this
week's court filings and found your exoneration. Of course I've got to
write about it! What a story! Are you too busy celebrating? Or do you
have time for a few questions?

Patsy could already see the columns of words, the fuzzy photo. The
prospect of public vindication was as sharp and pleasing as the snap of
a flag.

But then came Silver's low, reasonable voice. When are *you* going to
vindicate yourself? When does Patsy vindicate Patsy?

And if the story ran, there would be the calls and comments—and
the piece itself. God knows, she'd read enough articles about her crime
and punishment over the years. To a one they'd been awkwardly writ-

ten, with niggling inaccuracies: she was not born in Altadena; Mark Parnham's son had been younger, not older, than his deceased sister; Ricky Barrett's last name had two *t*'s.

Before, for newspaper stories, radio interviews, cable TV, and countless AA pitches, she'd overridden shyness, qualms, and embarrassment. She did so because Gloria said that sharing her experience transformed the tragedy into a redemptive, cautionary tale, and because Gilles, in his high-handed twenty-year-old superior manner, told her she should keep no secrets, and because Cal too insisted that her story helped others.

She hoped she had helped. That would be some recompense. To provide a false tale that helped others was not such a bad thing. Look at literature. Or for that matter, religion.

Patsy? You still there?

I am. But Charlotte, I don't have time to answer your questions. I'm on my way out the door.

Speaking of lies.

What if I called you later? Or tomorrow morning? The woman's voice rose with enthusiasm. Would that work for you?

I'll be blunt, Patsy said. I appreciate your interest, but this time, Charlotte, I'm not going public.

•

On the way home from her last class, with a small sheaf of term papers—only twelve of them—Patsy drove into Pasadena to return a pair of khakis she'd bought for Cal in the wrong size. Before getting on the freeway for home, she stopped for gas at a Shell station, and while her tank filled, she went around back to the restroom.

Turning on the light also activated a noisy little fan. The concrete floor by the sink was littered with wadded brown towels overflowing from the trash, but the place wasn't otherwise filthy, just hard-used and basic—like jail. She used the toilet, then flushed. Unlike jail, the toilet flushed easily. She rinsed her hands, balanced her own wadded towel atop the pile, and grasped the doorknob to leave. The little center button popped out, but the knob spun freely.

Around and around it went. Nothing engaged. The little metal tongue or stub—what was the thing called that went into the doorjamb?—did not retract. She twisted and depressed the lock button and turned the knob. The button popped back out, but the stub-tongue thing did not retract.

Jesus Christ, she said, shaking it.

The door was steel, painted blue, and battered, the bangs and scratches rusted. She pounded it so hard the heavy door rattled in its jamb. But the restroom was around the back of the station, and two-thirty in the afternoon was a slow time. Though sooner or later somebody would come. Or the cashier would wonder why her car was sitting in the self-service bay, hose in, driver gone.

She leaned against the sink, facing the door. She tried the knob again. Banged. Waited. Banged again.

Luckily, she had her purse and cell phone. She called directory assistance and asked for the Shell station on Fair Oaks. The operator connected her.

Hello? said a man.

I'm locked in your bathroom, she said. The doorknob doesn't work.

Do you have the key? he said.

No, I just walked in.

Someone took off with one of the keys, so we're down to the spare. If you've got that one, we have a problem.

I don't have a key, she said.

I'll be right there, said the man.

She waited, standing by the door, but off to the side. At any moment she'd hear his voice, the knob would rock and be steadied, a key inserted. If it didn't work, at least her rescue was begun.

A minute passed. Another minute.

The porcelain sink had rust stains under the spigot. Where the dispenser leaked, a puddle of pink soap was rimmed in soft gray grease. She looked at herself in the mirror. You. You'll be out in a minute.

She banged on the door.

She had to call directory assistance again to get reconnected. The same man answered. I am still in your restroom, she said.

I went back there with the key, and nobody was there. You must be at another Shell station. This is the one on Fair Oaks at Glenarm.

Oh, said Patsy, and I'm at the one at Walnut. Sorry about that.

That's *North* Fair Oaks, said the man.

Do you have the number?

Not offhand. No.

This time the directory assistance operator was a man. I show no listing for a Shell station on North Fair Oaks, he said, or on Walnut in Pasadena.

But I'm here, locked in the bathroom, at that Shell station.

I'm sorry, ma'am. Sometimes service stations are listed under another name, like So-and-so's Shell.

Is there any way you could check that?

I've done what I can. Do you want me to connect you with the police?

No! said Patsy. Police seemed excessive. But thank you, she added.

Patsy went back to banging on the door. Hello? Hello? she called. Pausing to listen, she heard only the clattery fan.

She went through directory assistance again and had them reconnect her to the other Shell station, as the man there might know the owner's name of this one, but he had stopped taking her calls. She speed-dialed the Pondo. Cal or even March might remember the name of this service station, but the voice mail picked up—her own cheerful voice. She phoned Cal's cell phone, which rang and rang. Oh, Cal, she whispered aloud, pick up! But he'd probably silenced it for an AA meeting and forgot to turn the ringer back on. She tried him twice more before leaving a message. It's just me, she said. If you get this, call my cell.

She closed her eyes, breathed in the smell of urine and disinfectant, the must of wet paper towels. She wished for more air. There was no window. Just the noisy fan and weak, shivering light. Her heart was pounding. She was beginning to hyperventilate. But this was not prison. This was finite—and funny. To be locked in a gas station bathroom for what, six minutes? By tonight it would be an amusing story. A comedy of errors. *I'm sorry, ma'am, I show no listing for a Shell station on North Fair Oaks or Walnut.*

She gave the door a sustained loud pounding and heard herself whimper. She tried Cal's cell phone again.

She started scrolling through the phone book on her cell phone for someone else. Brice in the B's.

Hey, Pats, he said. What's up?

Don't laugh, she said, and realized she herself was on the verge of tears. But I'm locked in a gas station bathroom and can't get anybody's attention. The doorknob has no torque.

No torque? A pause. Did you say no torque?

Whatever! I can't get out. Where are you?

Burbank, looking at refrigerators for Joey, but I'll come spring you.

Burbank was at least twenty minutes away. Patsy said, Or just tell me the name of the Shell station on Walnut and Fair Oaks.

It's an Armenian name, said Brice.

That's a big help.

Look, I'm on my way, he said. I'll call from the car, keep in radio contact.

I hope I'm out long before you get here, she said.

She put her cell phone back in her purse and banged some more on the door. I'm just locked in a goddamn bathroom, she said, but tears ran down her face. What's more, she couldn't seem to catch her breath. Darkness gathered at the corners of her eyes.

There was no lid on the toilet, so she sat sideways on the seat. Beside her, under the sink, in an intestinal curl, the pipe fed into the wall, with lime encrusting each joint. Two feet to the left, the implacable, battered blue door.

Standing, she took the knob in her fingers and, listening like a safe-cracker, turned it a fraction of an inch first to the right, then to the left. Was that the faintest click, like a bone shifting deep in the ear? Holding her breath, she gently, tentatively twisted it again to the right, and yes, there was a little grab, the resistance of a lightly coiled spring. Slowly, with the least possible pressure, she kept turning, as far as it would go. A nudge then, and the door opened. She stepped out into the bright, hot sunlight.

EPILOGUE

Summer 2001

Dinner at the Ponderosa mostly consisted of the children demanding food, rejecting it, and insisting on something else, with March hopping up to humor each swerve in appetite. Green beans were spurned for applesauce that in turn was ignored for broken-up clumps of garden burger. Beckett screeched steadily when he was strapped in his highchair, and why shouldn't he, when his sister sat with queenly self-possession on the adult's lap of her choice, usually Patsy's.

Tonight's meal was short, fifteen minutes, with Forrest packing Beckett and Ava off to their bath as soon as sufficient nutrients had been ingested.

Relax, March, I'll put on the water, Patsy said, and cleaned up, loading the dishwasher, wiping down those stone counters. Brice had shown her how to sand and smooth out the chip, and she could find it only if she ran her hand along the edge, a subtle declivity. She lingered with Cal and March over mint tea until the children reappeared wet-haired in their pajamas to kiss their grandparents and spirit their mother off to read bedtime stories.

Patsy watched the news with Cal in the library until his eyelids fluttered down and he began to breathe with a soft snore. A light was on in the kids' room, so she poked her head in and waved good night before leaving by the front door.

•

Brice had been right about the house on Concha Street, a roomy two-bedroom Spanish on a deep half acre very close to the mountains: it was the house for her. The front yard was sunny; the backyard had once been a formal garden, but the trees had grown up and the shade allowed only

ivy, ferns, and leggy camellias. A small, ramshackle barn was tucked up
in the far corner of the lot, so she could have Diotima. And Mamie to
keep Diotima company.

Patsy pulled up to the garage door and parked, then took the path
up to the barn to feed them. The day had been hot, but now the air was
perfect and abuzz. Under the deodars and redwoods, the ground was
soft with needles. A few doors over, in the park, there was a softball
game, so the night sky above had the cool purple glow from banks of
mercury-vapor lights. Cheers rose at intervals, and once, the crack of
the bat.

The move here was easy. She'd encountered no resistance. Cal and his
kids seemed chastened by her decision, but no one begrudged her the
house or questioned her decision, and why should they, when for the
moment, they too were getting what they wanted?

Patsy still dreamed about the Ponderosa. In her dreams she would
go back to find corridors she'd never seen, rooms she'd forgotten existed,
all of them dusty and neglected, screens rusting, blinds sagging, paint
bubbling off the walls. She found odd items like the vacuum cleaner
Brice gave her at the Lyster, one of Stan's tennis trophies, a plastic booze
bottle with some dried brown residue. To wake up in her new room
with the powder-white plastered walls and mountain view was a relief.

Outside the small two-stall barn, she ran the hose in the corral's wa-
tering trough and gazed up at the black hump of mountain, the light-
bleached sky and faint stars overhead.

She was getting used to living in a neighborhood, this neighborhood,
again—weekend noise in the park; people stopping their cars in the middle of the street to talk with no way to go around them; the too-loud
party three blocks over that the sheriff didn't shut down till midnight.

But she suffered no remorse. She'd attached herself to the house and
recalled it was hers with jolts of pleasure. Like a mother with an infant,
she had eyes for no other dwelling; the grand ones were too grand, the
tidy ones too tidy. This one, just right.

Still, on Saturday evenings, if she hadn't made plans, a small buzz of
fear could start, a sense of being disregarded or overlooked, of having
exiled herself to an out-of-the-way corner of the world.

Joey said she was getting used to living alone, that she must manage
loneliness as a chronic condition, like flyaway hair.

One Saturday night, at the last minute, she'd prevailed on Joey; another time she'd run down to Sarah's. But then she was antsy sitting on Joey's deck, in Sarah's ballroom. Antsy and disappointed in herself. In fact, she missed the feeling she was fleeing, that unpleasant fizz of desperation. It interested her.

She stepped inside the barn, which was lit by a single incandescent bulb, and opened the grain bin to the dense, sweet smell of molasses on the corn. She gave each horse a partial scoop and then a half flake of hay, which was so dry and dusty Patsy sneezed breaking it apart.

She stood in the doorway listening to the low molar rumble of the horses chewing, the whisk of hay as they pulled at it. Stepping outside, she checked the street to see if Brice and Joey had arrived. Now that they lived less than a mile away from one another, they were at each other's houses a couple times a week. They fixed meals together, or on nights like tonight, when she ate at Cal's, Patsy might meet them later for a movie or an ice-cream run.

Tonight Joey was bringing one of her director's films to watch. Patsy had the best television set. For a housewarming present, Cal had bought her a new flat screen TV, a top-of-the-line model Forrest recommended.

Another cheer went up in the park. Diotima made a soft, wet snorting sound.

This was a lovely moment of time. Being in her new home. Spending time with old friends. But it would pass. Was passing. Joey was going on location to rural Mississippi next week, and in a month, Patsy would fly to England.

She had thought about canceling or shortening her trip; she would miss her new home, be eager to get back. But then, Lewis would be at Hallen.

He had written to her when he had accepted the offer, in that same gray ink.

Dear Patsy,

Common decency compels me to violate our no-contact agreement to tell you personally that I took the job. As you know, I've been looking for a tenure-track position for years. I can't turn down the only one I've ever been offered.

*I will do anything to make my presence on campus easy for you—
everything short of turning down the job. (If you are truly, violently
against my coming, I suppose I would consider even that.)*

*As long as I'm writing—Burt told me your astounding news. I can't
imagine how you must feel, how vindicated and relieved. Although I'm
sure it's more complex and far-reaching than that.*

Yours as ever, Lewis

P.S. As far as I'm concerned, our old agreement still holds.

Burt had told Patsy what Lewis's reaction was to her news. He'd spit
out a whole mouthful of mineral water and started yelling, Un-fucking-
believable! Then his eyes had filled with tears.

Burt had no doubt kept him up to date since.

She had written back to Lewis, thanking him for his concern and
congratulating him on getting the job and, belatedly, for his book.

We will manage, I'm sure.

*So you know, I will be in England through October. This was
arranged last Christmas and has no bearing on your coming to campus.*

Still, with England, she was buying time.

She had been in the new house only six weeks. No time at all.

Three, even six months were probably not enough to get where she
needed to go. She would not be rushed. She had lectures to give, research to do. A book to write. A new life to navigate and know. That
low-grade whirr of fear.

Up here, near the top of her property, she could see down to the
street on either side of the house, and she saw Brice's clattery Volvo pull
up to the curb. He and Joey got out. Brice took something out of the
backseat. A plastic bag—ice cream, she guessed; there was a new gelato
place between Joey's house and hers, and they all had trouble resist-
ing it.

Earlier today Joey had mentioned over the phone that tomorrow was
the twenty-first anniversary of her mother's death.

My parents were so miserable together, Joey said. At least my dad
had his crack at happiness with Marlene.

Oh, but Joey, Patsy said, I think Cal might have really loved your
mother.

I hope so, Joey said. I hope she felt loved when she died. It's still hard to imagine her as an adulterer. Or Cal—even though I saw them with my own eyes! Cal always seemed so *good*. Although owning your own hotel probably made assignations easy.

Remembering this, Patsy smiled as, down below, Joey and Brice crossed the street.

Joey's mom had been gone twenty-one years. An adulthood. An adulthood since that day Patsy had helped Brice babysit Joey. And—regrettably—pierced her ears.

How in love they'd been with Brice! Both of them.

Patsy smiled again to see Brice's easy, lanky strides, the bag of gelato swinging by his knee. Twenty-one years ago she'd been sure she couldn't live without him.

Fortunately, she hadn't had to.

Joey and Brice started up the path to her front door, and Patsy lost sight of them. Latching the barn, she went down to the house to let them in.

Acknowledgments

For their friendship, readings, and expertise, I would like to thank Mona Simpson, Carol Blake, Maxine Groffsky, Lily Tuck, Mary Corey; my agents, Scott Moyers and Sarah Chalfant; Martha Ronk, Dennis Phillips, Thaisa Frank, Laurie Winer, Lynn Dumenil, Holly Hall, Claire Nelson, Claudia Parducci, Andy Pearlman, Shelby Rector, Gordon Smith, Tracy Sullivan; the whole crew at FSG and my editor, Sarah Crichton.

I am grateful to Beverly Strohm, for her experience, strength and hope: *We do not regret the past nor wish to shut the door on it.*

A NOTE ABOUT THE AUTHOR

Michelle Huneven has an M.F.A. from the Iowa Writer's Workshop. She has received a General Electric Younger Writers Award and a Whiting Writers' Award. Her two previous novels are *Round Rock* and *Jamesland*. She lives with her husband in Altadena, California.